Praise for Diana Rowland

"*Mark of the Demon* is a nifty combination of police procedural and urban fantasy. Not too many detectives summon demons in their basement for the fun of it, but Kara Gillian is not your average law enforcement officer. In the course of Rowland's first book, Kara learns a lot about demons, her past, and above all, herself."

—CHARLAINE HARRIS, *New York Times* bestselling author of *From Dead to Worse*

"Rowland spins a tale that is riveting, suspenseful, and deliciously sexy. With a unique take on demons, and with one of the most terrifying serial killers ever, *Mark of the Demon* will keep you up late at night turning pages."

—JENNA BLACK, author of *Speak of the Devil*

"*Mark of the Demon* is a fascinating mixture of a hard-boiled police procedural and gritty, yet other-worldly, urban fantasy. Diana Rowland's professional background as both a street cop and forensic assistant not only shows through but gives the book a realism sadly lacking in all too many urban fantasy 'crime' novels."

—L. E. MODESITT, JR., author of *The Saga of Recluce*

"A well-woven supernatural procedural that keeps the pages turning, hooking you on both the characters and the crime."

—LAURA ANNE GILMAN, author of *Free Fall*

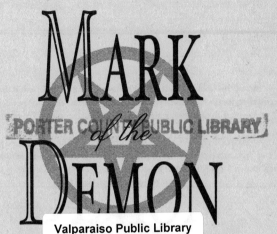

MARK of the DEMON

DIANA ROWLAND

BANTAM BOOKS
NEW YORK

MARK OF THE DEMON is a work of fiction. Names, characters, places, and incidents either are the product of the author's imagination or are used fictitiously. Any resemblance to actual persons, living or dead, events, or locales is entirely coincidental.

A Bantam Books Mass Market Original

Copyright © 2009 by Diana Rowland

Published in the United States by Bantam Books, an imprint of The Random House Publishing Group, a division of Random House, Inc., New York.

BANTAM BOOKS and the rooster colophon are registered trademarks of Random House, Inc.

ISBN 978-0-553-59235-1

Cover design: Jamie S. Warren
Cover illustration: Juliana Kolesova

Printed in the United States of America

www.bantamdell.com

468975

For Jack and Anna, my two favorite Demons

Acknowledgments

Since this is my first published novel, I feel I should thank everyone who helped me get this far. On the other hand, my publisher might get a bit testy about having to add an extra twenty pages just for the acknowledgments, so I'm going to have to cut it a bit short and hit the highlights.

Therefore, thanks go to:

My mother, Sue Rowland, for encouraging a love of science fiction, fantasy, and all things weird.

My sister, Sherry Rowland, for tolerating the weird little brat who shared her house, and for continuing to tolerate the weird, middle-aged broad who shares her life.

Kat Johnson, for introducing me to the demons. *Dak'nikahl lahn. Tah agahl lahn.*

Laura Joh Rowland, Andrew Fox, Fritz Ziegler, Marion Moore, Gwen Moore, Mark McCandless, and the rest of my writing group for suffering through the early drafts.

Kent Brewster, for being everything that *is* Kent Brewster.

Daniel Abraham, for helping me through several varieties of angst over the years, for continuing to believe in me despite my angst, and—most importantly—for telling me what was wrong with this book.

The entire St. Tammany Parish Sheriff's Office. You Rock.

Dr. Peter R. Galvan, and the rest of the St. Tammany Parish Coroner's Office. Y'all made death *fun*!

Dr. Michael DeFatta, for answering heaping scads of questions related to forensic pathology—far more than any one man should ever have to answer. Lots of questions. Seriously. Lots.

Lindsay Ribar, for pulling my manuscript out of the slush pile, for falling in love with it, and for being a completely awesome chick!

My agent, Matt Bialer, for agreeing with Lindsay, for being an absolute rock of support, and for finding my book a wonderful home.

My incredible copy editor, Kathy Lord, for taming my wild use of commas and the word "just," and for keeping track of demons, victims, and phases of the moon far better than I was able to!

My editor's assistant, David Pomerico, for patiently answering my many stupid questions.

And finally, my editor, Anne Groell, for not letting me get away with any degree of authorial laziness, for devoting incredible amounts of time and effort and patience, and for guiding me and goading me into making this book a thousand times better than I could have ever imagined.

MARK
of the
DEMON

I COULD HEAR THE INTRUDER BREAKING INTO MY HOUSE.

Unfortunately, it was in the same instant that the demon appeared before me.

The sound of shattering glass upstairs disrupted my focus for only a fraction of a second, but it was enough for the arcane portal to shift from my control and leap away from me like an untethered water hose. I made a frantic grasp at the portal, cold sweat breaking out under my arms as I struggled to wrench the power back into place. My heart slammed in my chest as I fought the uncontrolled energy, seizing each strand to bind and anchor it. My technique was raw and inelegant, but I didn't give a crap. I was only interested in surviving, not in how pretty it looked.

It felt like an eternity, but it was merely several frenzied seconds before I had the wildly fluctuating potencies settled and calmed. I cautiously loosened my hold as I took several deep, ragged breaths, struggling to slow the mad galloping of my pulse. That had been *far* too close for my peace of mind. If that loss of focus had come just a few seconds earlier, I most likely would have been ripped apart—either by the maelstrom of the arcane portal I'd opened in the basement of my house or by the claws of the demon I'd just summoned through that portal.

I exhaled a shuddering breath, finally releasing my hold on the portal as I looked with no small amount of triumph at the massive demon on one knee before me, his head lowered and his wings tucked along his back. He had remained utterly still throughout my battle with the portal, and I silently thanked whatever powers existed that I had already sealed the terms with him before losing control. I could feel a grin spread across my face. I'd done it. I had summoned a *reyza,* the highest of the twelve levels of demons.

I was officially a full-fledged summoner.

The sharp *crack* of more glass breaking spoiled my reverie. My grin shifted to a scowl. *A burglar. Just great.* If I went upstairs to deal with the idiot, I would have to abandon my ulterior motive for summoning the demon. And summoning a *reyza* was worth more than a few wordly possessions. Besides, my wordly possessions weren't worth very much.

But the demon snapped his head up at the sound. "Someone intrudes on your demesne," he growled, deep voice resonating powerfully through the basement. Before I could take a breath to give a response or command, the demon bounded up the heavy wooden stairs of my basement, bursting through the door that exited into the main hallway of my house.

"Son of a bitch!" I swiftly anchored the potency that I hadn't yet grounded. *Well, so much for that plan.* My legs shook as I staggered up the stairs after the demon, and I snarled at the fatigue that slowed me down. I was used to feeling somewhat drained after a summoning, but this was more than I'd expected.

I heard a panicked shriek coming from the front of my house and I took off in that direction, forcing my wobbly legs to move. *Okay, I managed to summon him. Now can I control him?* The shriek of terror abruptly spiraled upward as I lurched down the hall.

"Kehlirik! No harm!" I shouted, commanding the demon with my voice even as I exerted mental pressure on the arcane bindings.

I rounded the corner to the living room, panting for breath and grateful that my house was "cozy" instead of palatial. I wasn't sure if I could have made it much farther without falling on my face. I made a quick mental note: *Get more rest before summoning a twelfth-level demon!*

The demon snarled and turned to me, holding a rail-thin, gibbering man by the collar and looking insanely incongruous against the muted sage-green walls and cherry-wood furniture in my living room. One wingtip brushed the computer on my desk, and I resisted the urge to grab that wing and yank him away. Probably *not* a good idea when I still wasn't certain if the demon would abide by my will.

"You should let me slay him, summoner," the demon said in a deep voice that sounded like rolling boulders. He held his captive dangling above the floor with no apparent effort and no strain showing in his heavily muscled body. He towered over me, his head topping mine by several feet, with leathery wings the color of burnished copper extending several more feet beyond that. In a house with eight-foot ceilings, the demon would have been forced to crouch awkwardly and tuck in his wings in order to fit. Fortunately for him, my Acadian-style house had the traditional fifteen-foot ceilings designed for the subtropical climate of south Louisiana, where high ceilings helped keep houses cool.

I took a deep, steadying breath. The demon wasn't resisting my control. One less thing to sweat right now. "No, Kehlirik," I said carefully. "Our justice works differently in this sphere. But I thank you for your aid." The demon's captive had ceased his shrieking, at least, now reduced to whimpering moans. I rubbed the sudden gooseflesh on my arms, still horribly unnerved at how close I'd come to disaster. *Just a few seconds earlier . . .* I threw off a shudder and forced my attention back to the present.

A throbbing growl came from the demon's throat. "He is a thief. Worthless. He has no honor." He crouched and dropped the man to the floor, then pinned the intruder down with one foot. He tucked his wings behind him, clasping wickedly clawed hands together in front of him. A thick, sinuous tail curled around his legs, tip twitching in indication of his mood, and a dark and spicy scent surrounded him, foreign and wild. Crouched, his head was level with mine, and I was relieved that I could stop craning my neck to speak to him. This was only the second *reyza* I had ever seen, and I was still shocked at how *large* they were.

"It is . . . different here," I said, even though I heartily agreed with the demon's assessment of his captive. "I'm going to have enough trouble explaining away his talk of winged monsters."

"If I slay him, he cannot speak of winged monsters," Kehlirik replied, with undeniable logic. Then his broad nostrils flared as he snorted, "Not that I am a monster."

I had to smile. "No, *reyza*. You are no monster." Though the demon was monstrous in appearance—flat nose set in a bestial face, a wide mouth accented with curved fangs, and a thick ridge crest that swept back over his head and down his spine—I knew far too well that he was anything but a monster. "But it would be more difficult to explain a dead body," I continued. "Murder is a serious offense here."

He bared his teeth, lips curling back from the wicked fangs. "No body would be found, summoner. But I will respect your desire." He inclined his head to me, then spread his wings, somehow managing not to knock any of my pictures off the shelves. I looked at him in uninhibited delight. I'd spent almost ten years studying and training, carefully guided by my mentor and aunt through the summoning rituals of each level of demon, gradually working my way up to working solo. A solo summoning of a *reyza* was considered "graduation," and here I was with one in my living room.

I crouched to get a look at the wide-eyed man beneath Kehlirik's foot, unconsciously echoing the demon's posture. Pale and skinny with scraggly hair that stood out from his head, the intruder was probably in his early to mid thirties, though I knew that my estimate could be off by about a decade. Heavy drug use tended to age a person, and I could easily peg him as a meth or possibly crack user. He also had the distinct sour odor of someone who hadn't paid close attention to hygiene for quite some time, and I found myself shifting slightly closer to the *reyza*, whose scent was far more appealing.

"Wow, did you ever pick the *wrong* house tonight," I said. Then I had to laugh as a realization hit me. "Wait. I bet you're the one who broke into those two houses up the highway last week. Am I right?"

The man whimpered and shook his head, his eyes wild. "No! No, not me! I . . . I thought this was my buddy's house—"

Kehlirik snarled down at the man, causing him to yelp in terror again. "I'm not stupid," I informed my intruder. "Don't insult me again."

The man began to shake with sobs. "OhGodohGod, p-please don't let it eat me! I'll never do it again, I swear. I just needed enough to buy a rock. Oh, God!"

I shifted my regard to the demon. Kehlirik rumbled low in his throat, returning my gaze with eyes full of intelligence and cunning. I was ridiculously tempted to screw with my burglar and ask the demon if he was hungry, but I wasn't *completely* sure that Kehlirik would realize I was kidding. I was fairly positive that demons had no taste for human flesh, but it was probably best to not test the issue. There were plenty of unknowns when it came to demons.

I stood, shaking a slight cramp out of my leg. I really couldn't allow the demon to kill him. The guy was a drug addict and probably had a rap sheet a mile long, but I doubted that any of his offenses were of the capital variety—most likely nothing more than theft to support his habit. Besides, I was supposed to be one of the good guys.

Oh, well. There was no doubt that he was going to babble about what he saw. I would just have to trust that no one would believe any ravings he might have about winged monsters.

Besides, it was his own damn fault that he'd picked *my* house to break into, on a night that I'd summoned a demon.

A deliciously wicked compromise occurred to me. "*Reyza*, I do not wish this one slain, but perhaps you could do me a service."

The demon's eyes glowed a ruddy orange in the dim light of my living room. "Name your desire, summoner."

With effort, I kept my face composed. "I would have

him punished for his intrusion, yet he must be returned to me *physically* unharmed."

The demon inclined his head gravely, but I was fairly sure I could see amusement in his eyes. "It will be done, summoner."

I barely had time to step out of the demon's way before he snatched up the pathetic man and bounded out the front door. I followed, pausing just long enough to grab my cell phone and handcuffs off my desk. I exited onto my porch just in time to see Kehlirik leap into the air with my erstwhile intruder firmly grasped in clawed hands.

I let out a snicker and sat on the front step. I listened as the panicked screams faded into the night sky, then dialed the number for the St. Long Parish Sheriff's Office.

"Hi, this is Detective Kara Gillian with the PD," I said when the dispatcher answered. "Could you please send a patrol unit to my home address? I have a ten-fifteen on a 62R here." A 10-15 was an arrest, and a 62R was a burglary. Though I worked for the Beaulac Police Department, I lived outside the city limits, which meant that if something criminal happened at my house, it was sheriff's office jurisdiction.

"A 62R . . . Kara, someone broke into your house? Way out there?"

I recognized the woman's voice as a dispatcher who'd previously worked with the PD. Slightly pudgy with harshly dyed red hair, but I couldn't remember the woman's name to save my life. "Yeah, but all he managed to do was break a window by the door."

The dispatcher laughed. "Bad choice of houses!"

You have no idea, I thought. "No kidding," I said instead. "Good thing the noise woke me up."

"All right, I'll get a unit out there."

I set the phone down and clasped my hands lightly around my knees, looking up at the moon that shone full through the barest sheen of clouds. A languid breeze twined through the dark trees, rustling needles and bringing a deep, rich scent of earth and pine to me. I hugged myself against the slight chill, listening to the faint buzz of a mosquito and the song of a nearby cricket. A satisfied peace stole through me, an almost-Pavlovian response to my environment. I'd lived in this house my entire life—with the exception of one terrible month after my father was killed by a drunk driver. I was eleven and had been placed in foster care until my aunt Tessa could return from Japan to take over as my legal guardian. My mother had passed away three years before that, from ovarian cancer that had gone undetected until it was far too late, and there were no other relatives—or even close friends—to take me in, a fact that had not pleased my aunt at the time, especially since the one time she'd met me before I'd been in diapers. But she'd done what she could to lessen the upheaval for me, despite her reluctance to take on the enormous responsibility of raising a preteen kid. She'd moved into this house with me instead of yanking me out of the only home I'd ever known, knowing that in time I would find more comfort than grief here.

I was nearly thirty now and finally beginning to realize just how important that comfort was to me. I loved it out here, far from town and other houses. I lived on a seldom-traveled highway, my driveway was long and winding, and the nearest neighbor was well over a mile away.

It was the perfect house for someone who required privacy.

And it wasn't until I was fifteen that I'd learned my aunt's ulterior motive for the decision to raise me in this house. My aunt Tessa was a summoner of demons, and the basement of this house was an ideal place for a summoning chamber.

A few minutes later, the demon swooped down to land neatly in front of me, dangling his ashen-faced prisoner by one ankle. "I believe he is suitably cowed."

Too bad I couldn't give this treatment to all my arrestees. *We'd probably have fewer repeat offenders,* I thought as I handcuffed the unresisting man. I left him whimpering softly on the porch with his hands cuffed behind his back, then returned my attention to the demon. "My thanks again, Kehlirik."

The demon slowly sank into a crouch. "Summoner, this was the first time you called a *reyza* unaided, yes?"

I gave a wary nod. Had I screwed something up?

He snorted, flaring his nostrils. "I did not think that you called me for the sole purpose of thwarting an intrusion. Had you another desire for this summoning?"

I rubbed the back of my neck. "I . . . had been hoping to learn how to reverse a portal without having to close and reopen." *That* was why it was worth the effort to summon the higher-level demons. With the proper negotiation of terms, they could be persuaded to share a measure of their knowledge and skills.

The demon ticked his claws against his leg, a thoughtful expression on his monstrous face. "And you were forced to anchor and close when I left your control to apprehend your intruder. Forgive me. I should have waited to know your wishes first."

"No, it's all right," I said, more than a little shocked by the apology. "Trust me, I'm very pleased that you caught the guy, especially before he did any real harm."

"Still, I should have waited to know your will first." He

gave me a small bow, moonlight glinting off the curved horns on his head. "When next you summon me, I will school you in the technique to allay my shame in failing you."

I controlled my expression, with effort. I knew that matters of honor were deathly serious among the demonkind, but this was my first experience at being owed a debt of honor. "You have not failed me," I said, carefully choosing my words and trying not to show my glee, "but I would be honored to learn this and would consider any debt between us null."

Kehlirik abruptly went still, hissing softly.

I took a cautious step back. "Is something wrong?" Crap. What had I done now?

The demon gave a low growl. "Something touches the arcane in this sphere."

I started to relax, then frowned. "What do you mean? Another summoning?" There weren't many other summoners in the region. In fact, I didn't know of any in all of southeast Louisiana except for my aunt, though I figured New Orleans probably boasted a couple. Of course, people who made a practice of summoning demons didn't usually hang signs on their door advertising the fact, and summoning itself was not exactly a common skill. You had to have someone mentor you in the art for several years, plus you had to be willing to shed some blood now and then.

I'd been mentored by my aunt Tessa, of course. By the time I hit my teenage years, I realized that there was more to the world—and my aunt—than met the eye. The day after I received my driver's license, my aunt "introduced" me to my first demon, who confirmed her suspicion that I had the ability to be a summoner. After beginning my training, I discovered that here, *finally*, was something I excelled at. The rituals, the forms—all felt as natural as breathing.

Training under my aunt had not always gone smoothly, but I'd never regretted starting down that path to become a summoner.

Maybe Tessa had summoned tonight as well? The spheres were in excellent alignment for the higher-level summonings, and with the moon at full it couldn't get much better.

The demon settled his wings, as if uneasy. "I cannot tell, but it has a taint to it."

"What sort of taint?"

Kehlirik growled again, a deep, throbbing sound that made the hair on my arms stand on end, even as used to demons as I was. "Blood and death." His eyes narrowed. "More I cannot determine. I am not versed in such. You would need to call another to learn more."

Crap. There was no way to summon again tonight. Two summonings in one night was far too draining and dangerous. I glanced up at the moon again. It would still be full enough tomorrow. That would work.

Kehlirik gave a heavy snort. "A vehicle approaches this place. Do you require more service of me?"

"No," I said, after a brief hesitation. "My thanks again, *reyza*. Your help has been invaluable this night." My original reason for summoning the demon had been blown, but it had been more than made up for by his promise to school me in the more-advanced forms. I would definitely summon him again on the next full moon.

Kehlirik folded his wings in close and bowed his head before me. I took a deep breath, finding my focus, then lifted my arms and began to speak the words of dismissal as I pulled potency to me. A sharp wind rose from nowhere, sending dust into my face and bringing with it an acrid, sulfurous smell that burned my nose. I squinted against the wind at the massive form of the demon, carefully holding my focus as I finished the chant. Kehlirik rose up with a bellow, spreading his wings and throwing his head back. A blinding sliver of light formed behind him, and in the span between one heartbeat and the next he disappeared, with a sharp *crack* like a breaking glacier. The light dissipated and faded, spinning off sparklets that danced briefly in my peripheral vision before disappearing.

The wind died instantly and I dragged my hands through my shoulder-length mud-brown hair, finger-combing it as best I could. Just in time too; I could see headlights coming up my long driveway and hear the crunch of tires on gravel. My legs wobbled and I sat heavily on my front step again, taking deep breaths to get rid of the black spots that briefly pirouetted through my vision. Dismissals were nearly as draining as summonings, though nowhere near as dangerous.

The sheriff's unit stopped just a few feet from my front porch and out stepped Justin Sanchez—a short and skinny deputy with uneven teeth and dark hair that looked unkempt no matter how short he cut it. He sported a scraggly mustache that looked like a balding caterpillar beneath a nose that had a slight bend to the right. He'd been with the PD before he transferred to the sheriff's office and had been one of my teammates back when I first became a cop, teaching me early on that size wasn't everything in a fight. More importantly, he taught me how to snap my gum—an annoying trick I used to harass my aunt until she threatened to cease teaching me if she ever saw gum in my mouth again.

He gave me a grin. "Looks like this moron picked the wrong house, huh?"

I batted my eyelashes and put on an innocent expression. "Why, Officer, I'm jest a helpless li'l gal. I was skeert to death!"

He laughed. "Yeah, right. For some reason I feel sorry for this guy."

If you only knew.

"By the way, nice jammies," he said with a sly smile.

I hurriedly crossed my arms over my chest. The "jammies" were just the silk shirt and pants that I wore to summon, but it hadn't occurred to me to throw on different clothes. Or even a bra. Not that I was so well-endowed that it was instantly obvious, but Justin was a cop and a guy. And it was chilly out. He had noticed.

And while I knew he was just teasing me and giving me shit, I never knew quite how to respond when guys joked with me in a quasi-sexual way. My aunt Tessa was not the most sociable of people, and I'd been forced to figure out the complexities of social skills on my own—with varying degrees of success. That was one of the reasons I loved being a cop: There was a built-in sense of brotherhood that satisfied a long-buried desire to somehow *belong.*

That was also why I loved being a summoner—there were *rules* when dealing with demons. Dealing with humans was never simple or straightforward.

Justin didn't seem to notice my angst—he just snickered at my reaction, then settled down to the business of taking my statement and the report of the burglary. He took a few obligatory pictures of the damage to the window by the front door but didn't bother going inside. Damn good thing, since the door to the basement was still ajar. That would have been a tough one to explain—the chalked circle, the carefully placed candles, the tinge of incense. I kept my smile fixed on my face while I gave myself a mental head-smack. I had no desire to be dubbed a "Satanist" by people who had zero clue about demons and the arcane. Even though there was no such creature as "Satan" or "Lucifer" or a "Prince of Darkness"—at least not among the creatures I dealt with—that fact wouldn't help me explain away my penchant for summoning the other-planar creatures that were known as demons.

Finally Justin had all the information he needed and had my perp stuffed into the back of his car. He scowled as he closed the door. "Dopehead. He's totally zoned out." He glanced back at me as he climbed into the driver's seat. "Hey, I think you cut yourself on some of the glass."

I followed his gaze to my left forearm, where a thin trickle of blood was snaking its way down to my hand. I quickly swiped at the blood with the hem of my shirt. It wasn't the first time I'd stained the shirt with blood. "Yeah, looks like I brushed against something. It doesn't look too bad though." I knew it wasn't a serious cut. The knife I'd used was razor-sharp, and I'd become skilled at making the requisite slice no deeper than it needed to be. It was always worth that small pain to feel the sense of utter satisfaction after a successful summoning, to know that, as long as I didn't screw up anything in the ritual, I would be able to control a demon. Even if I couldn't control anything else in my life, I knew I had that.

"Well, be thankful that you're not working tonight. Apparently the night watchman at the wastewater plant found a body."

I leaned against his car. "Unless the guy was killed with a bad check, I doubt I'll be involved." That was one nice thing about working mostly white-collar crimes: I very seldom got called out in the middle of the night for an investigation.

Okay, that was the *only* nice thing. Everything else about

it bored the living crap out of me. For two years I'd busted my ass as a detective in Property Crimes, and three weeks ago I'd finally been rewarded with a transfer to the Violent Crimes Division. However, I had yet to have a case assigned to me, and since there were still plenty of check-fraud and identity-theft cases, I'd continued to work those while I learned the ropes of homicide investigations.

But I could live with that. The feeling of accomplishment at the promotion had been damn near as sweet as a successful summoning. Here I was with *thirty* looming on the horizon, and I could actually say that I was finally getting somewhere in my life. I had a solid career and something resembling a future, despite my best efforts to fuck up my life when I'd been young and stupid.

"Girl," Justin corrected as he pulled on his seat belt. "Not a guy. Cut all to shit, from what I heard, with a big mark on her chest."

Goose bumps sprang up on my arms. "You mean, cut as in torture? Is the mark on her chest a symbol?"

Justin snorted. "Now, why you gonna go thinking like that? It's probably some crack whore who got on the wrong side of her dealer."

"Or it could be the Symbol Man—"

"Yeah, yeah, you're as bad as the rookie officer who called it in," he chided with a teasing smile. "He was squalling that he had a 'Symbol Man murder!' Don't you be overreacting and jumping to conclusions too. I mean, it's been three years since the last body was found. And the methodology is different too. All the other bodies were found in remote areas, pretty decomposed. This one's a fresh dump, in a place with a security guard, which would guarantee that the body would be found quickly." He lifted his radio and keyed up, advising the dispatcher that he was clear of the scene with one arrest. "If anything, it might be a copy-cat," he said, after replacing the mic in its holder. "He killed twelve people, then stopped. Why start up again after three years?"

"Thirteen," I corrected, an odd excitement and unease running through me. "There were thirteen bodies found. I read through the case files just a couple of weeks ago. And maybe he stopped because he got sick, or was in jail." *Or maybe he was just waiting for the right time to come around again?* A sliver of sick fear wormed its way down my spine at the thought. I didn't want this particular theory of mine to be right.

The phase of the moon was only one factor when summoning a demon. The spheres containing this world and the demon world moved in patterns much like the orbits of planets, and summonings could be performed only when the spheres overlapped. The greater the overlap, or convergence, the easier it was to perform the more-complex summonings. The convergence had been so small for the past few years that it had been damn near impossible to summon anything higher than eighth level.

But now the convergence was nearly as high as it could possibly be and would remain so for at least another month.

If those murders were part of some sort of summoning, that would explain why he'd stopped. And why he would start again now. I rubbed at my arms, unsettled.

"Whatever. Guess we'll find out eventually," he said, glancing back to see if his arrestee was still zoned out. "All right, lemme get this dumb-ass to the jail. You just go on back to your nice comfy bed, and don't worry your little head about any more mean ol' bad guys coming in."

I pushed my unease aside and gave him the laugh he was expecting. "I feel *so* safe."

"Protect and serve and all that shit," he said, giving me a mock salute, then he rolled up his window and drove back down my winding driveway.

My smile died as soon as he was out of sight. I returned to the porch, mincing over the gravel in my bare feet as quickly as possible, then snatched up my cell phone and scrolled through my stored numbers.

"Turnham here," my captain answered crisply on the first ring. I breathed a mental sigh of relief that I hadn't woken him up. I'd taken a chance in assuming that, if there was any suspicion at all that this was a Symbol Man case, he'd be on the scene.

"Captain, it's Kara Gillian. I heard you might have a Symbol Man case at the wastewater plant?" I was trying to keep my voice level and calm and professional, but I had a feeling that my eagerness leaked through.

"How the hell did you hear that? Do you keep your radio on twenty-four/seven?"

I couldn't help but smile. There were plenty of cops who lived and breathed police work and who *did* keep their police radio on at all times. In fact, I'd been one of them when I was first hired, listening obsessively to every call and keeping mental tabs on what was going on in the world outside my house. I loved being a cop, and it had been like a deep breath of fresh air for me to be a part of something special after more than a decade of what was often bitter loneliness. It had taken nearly a year for me to finally accept that I could, in fact, occasionally turn my radio off and still be just as much of a cop. "No, sir," I said. "I had a 62R at my house, and Deputy Sanchez clued me in when he picked up my perp."

"Ah. Well, that's all right, then." He sounded mollified.

"And I'm glad to hear you nailed the guy. I take it you want to be in on this case?"

"Well, sir, if you don't think I'd be in the way. It's just that I probably have the most familiarity with the case files right now, and I think I could help." I held my breath as I waited for his response. Most likely he'd tell me to meet up with the lead detective in the morning to fill him in. But what I really wanted was to see the body.

"If you don't have a problem coming out to the scene at this hour, that's fine with me. You have something to contribute, and it would be good experience for you," he said, to my relief.

"I'll be there in twenty minutes," I promised. I raced back inside to change as soon as I hung up, suddenly deeply grateful to my drug-addicted intruder for choosing tonight to break into my house.

SO, WHAT ARE THE CHANCES THAT IT'S THE SYMBOL MAN AGAIN?
The question dominated my rattling thoughts. The tower-
ing pines that crowded the road created an ominous illusion of a dark tunnel as I sped down the deserted highway.
*Just because a body was found with similar injuries doesn't
mean it's the same killer,* I reminded myself. And I wasn't
sure if I'd be relieved or disappointed if it turned out to be
something else. Obviously I didn't want more people to die,
but at the same time I'd been burning with curiosity about
the Symbol Man and his victims for nearly three years, and
the desire to *know* was nearly smothering.

The creaky Ford Taurus shimmied annoyingly as I
crested a low hill. I could see the lights of Beaulac in front
of me, the moonlight reflecting off Lake Pearl beyond the
city. It was breathtakingly beautiful, but I wasn't in the
frame of mind to appreciate the view. Perhaps it was merely
coincidence that he would start up again now. Just sheer
happenstance that the three-year break would coincide so
perfectly with the alignment of the two spheres. *Anything*

is possible, I tried to convince myself, but the feeling in the pit of my gut wasn't buying it.

St. Long Parish was mostly rural but still within reasonable driving distance to New Orleans—which was why I liked living there so much. A small, quiet parish with the city of Beaulac as its hub, it boasted only a few murders a year and not much other crime except for the usual mix of drug abuse and burglaries. And those rare murders were most often the result of disagreements that had been fueled by alcohol and testosterone.

Lake Pearl had been formed centuries earlier from a convergence of several bayous, and the city of Beaulac had sprung up on its shore, developing a comfortable industry catering to sportsmen and weekend vacationers. Though Beaulac was a city only by the strictest definition, for a few years it had gained unfortunate notoriety because of a serial killer who'd become known as the Symbol Man.

I smacked the dashboard of the Taurus in a futile effort to stop one of the more annoying rattles. Even if this victim bore the same symbol, I had to accept the chance that the killer could be a copycat. I grimaced and whacked the dashboard again, muttering something rude as the radio knob flew off and bounced under the seat.

Even if it's a copycat, it would still have to be someone who knows the details about the symbol. Pictures or specific descriptions had never been officially released, but I knew that information had a way of leaking out. It only took one officer to talk about it after hours in a bar to make it common knowledge. But Captain Turnham would rain hot death on anyone who spread confidential information about this case. He was an absolute stickler for protocols, which made me even more appreciative of his approval to come to the crime scene.

I made the turn onto the gravel road that led to the water-treatment plant. Surrounding the plant was a wooden fence emblazoned with a large red sign that proclaimed: *City of Beaulac Wastewater Reclamation Facilities.* A white metal building housed the main offices of the facility, and behind that were a number of large vatlike structures that I assumed had something to do with the actual treatment of the water. I gave a low whistle when I saw how many police vehicles were already there. Parked just outside the wooden fence were five marked units, a half dozen unmarked cars, plus a crime-scene van for good measure. I searched for a spot close by, then finally gave up and parked out on the road. I needed the exercise anyway.

I climbed out of my car, shoving my keys into the pocket of my jeans and tucking my *Beaulac PD* T-shirt in. I grabbed my notebook, made sure I had a pen that worked, then took a deep breath to quell my sudden nervousness. I'd been working my ass off for so long to get to this point that it felt almost surreal to actually be here, on my first homicide investigation. *And then to have it be a possible Symbol Man case . . .* Doubly surreal.

I adjusted the badge holder around my neck as I walked up to the scene. I'd harbored a burning curiosity about the Symbol Man murders ever since I was a street cop on the scene of one of his body dumps. I'd seen the body only from a distance, but even from a dozen feet away I could see the faint scattering of light in my *othersight* and feel the resonance that would be noticed only by someone who was attuned to the arcane. It had shocked and baffled me, and I'd been left with an uncomfortable certainty that the murders had something to do with the demon realm. What little I'd been able to sense of the arcane resonance felt familiar, and I'd waited with morbid eagerness for another body to turn up, determined to make any excuse necessary to get close enough to feel that resonance again.

And then it stopped. No more bodies were found, and in the last three years I'd even begun to doubt what I'd seen and felt from that victim. I'd been promoted to detective a year after the last murder, assigned to Property Crimes, and now—finally—I was a Homicide detective. I could hardly believe that, in just a few minutes, I might have some answers.

What I would—or could—do with those answers was another matter entirely.

The officer by the crime-scene tape gave me a sour look as he thrust a clipboard at me. I didn't recognize him, which meant that he'd probably been hired within the last two years—after I became a detective.

"Is it really the same symbol?" I asked as I took the clipboard from him and signed the crime-scene entry log.

"Beats me," he said, a scowl drawing his mouth down. "I didn't get a chance to look at the body too close. The suits don't want us road cops looking around the scene." I could see he was deeply affronted that he'd been prevented from contaminating a major crime scene. Poor baby.

I kept a neutral smile fixed on my face. Yeah, I was a "suit," but I'd paid my dues as a patrol cop for five years before becoming a detective. "Bummer," I said simply as I handed the clipboard back and ducked under the tape. No point in trying to educate him about preservation of evidence at a crime scene. He didn't seem the sort to be willing to hear what I had to say.

It was easy enough to figure out where the body was. Halogen lamps had been set up to illuminate an area between two enormous vats. White metal staircases led up the sides of each vat, but positioned almost directly between the stairs lay a small lump surrounded by stained concrete. As I skirted the area I could see an outflung arm, dark-blond hair, and a body covered with what I thought might be some sort of net or sheer patterned fabric. I wanted to go check out the body so badly it hurt, to see if there were arcane traces, but I held myself back with a discipline born of a decade of summoning demons. This was *not* my scene, and I was here only because of my captain's benevolence. I wasn't about to risk getting kicked off before I had the chance to soak in as much experience as possible.

I did stretch out mentally to try to see and feel with my othersight, but I was almost fifty feet away from the body and I sure as shit wasn't sensitive enough to feel anything from that far away, even if the arcane residue had been fresh and strong.

A petite crime-scene tech wearing dark-blue fatigue pants and a PD T-shirt came around the curve of the tank on the left, a sour look on her face as she wound up a long measuring tape.

Her expression cleared when she saw me. "Hey, chick!" she said brightly, giving me a wide smile. "Whatcha doing out here? I thought you were still in Property Crimes."

I returned the smile. Crime Scene Technician Jill Faciane was not only an exceedingly cool person but she also knew what she was doing and wouldn't screw the scene up or allow it to be screwed up. Jill had come over from New Orleans a couple of years after Katrina, bringing a wealth of experience and a sharp wit as well. A slender woman with short red hair and an elfin face, she had a determined set to her jaw, a quick smile, and keen blue eyes that were quick to notice details of scenes that escaped most others. She was also smart and sarcastic, which meant that she and I got along great.

"I was assigned to Violent Crimes three weeks ago," I said. "And, since I'm pretty familiar with the Symbol Man cases, the captain gave me permission to come out and help."

"Yeah, this is some insane shit! Here, make yourself useful," she said, as she handed me one end of the measuring tape. "I have a bunch of measurements left, and those useless lugs over there," she jerked her head toward a knot of people by the main building, "are too *important* to help get the scene processed."

I held the end of the tape obediently. "They're detectives. Come on, you don't expect them to actually *work*, do you?"

"Ha!" she snapped, as she manhandled me to stand with the end of the tape near a pipe sticking out of the ground. "You're a detective, and *you* work."

"I know." I gave a tragic sigh. "I think it's holding me back too."

She snickered, then trotted off to a point near the body, made a notation on her pad, and returned to me. "My God, you'd think the media could have come up with something more exciting than 'Symbol Man.'"

"Well, it was a long time ago. In fact, it was right about the time I became a cop, seven years ago. And it was *the* big news for a while."

"Stand by the fence," she ordered, making more notes. "Well, this is seriously nasty stuff. And what's the deal with the thing on her chest?"

I moved to the fence, holding my end of the measuring tape as if I'd been born to do it. "You mean the symbol? I don't know what it is"—and that bugged the crap out of me as well—"but all the victims had that same symbol somewhere on their bodies, burned or carved into the flesh.

Thirteen murders in four years, all linked together by that symbol. Then suddenly it just . . . stopped." I shrugged and spread my hands, causing the measuring tape to flutter and earning myself a reproving scowl from Jill.

"Almost done," she said, peering down at her notes. "Lemme get the distance to the gate. Have you seen a bunch of his victims?"

"Nope," I replied, relocating to the gate. "By the time I became a detective, he'd stopped and it was a cold case, shoved to the bottom of the stack." I slid a glance to the body, then looked back to Jill. "Didn't help that his victims were homeless or drug addicts."

Jill grimaced, rolling the tape up as she walked back to me. "So not much pressure to solve the cases."

She'd pegged it. "Not much," I said. "Once upon a time there was a semblance of a task force assigned to the case, but it was a lackluster effort." I shrugged. "Without a lot of public outcry about the murders, local and federal agencies were less inclined to spend a lot of time or money on them. You know how it is."

Her brow creased in annoyance. "Oh, yeah, do I." She took the tape from me and shoved it into one of the side pockets of her fatigue pants. "So how do you know so much about the cases?"

"Got lucky, I guess. I'm brand-spanking-new in Violent Crimes—haven't even been assigned my first case yet—so I figured I'd see what I could learn from reading old case files. Since the Symbol Man cases are still unsolved, I decided to start with them." I didn't mention my own long-standing desire to get my hands on those files. Until I was transferred to Violent Crimes, I'd had no way to justify the request, and, with the convergence approaching, I'd already made up my mind that I was going to find a way to get to those files by any means necessary. Fortunately, my transfer had come through in time and I'd been spared the need to break into the file room. "And since I had some spare time—"

"You *what*?" Jill chortled. "Y'all get spare time? Oh, man, I so need to transfer!"

"We can trade," I replied. "How hard can your job be? Take some pictures, measure some stuff, maybe throw some fingerprint dust around." Her eyes widened in mock outrage, and I laughed. "Anyway, Captain Turnham handed me a large box full of files, pictures, and notes and said, 'Knock yourself out. Don't let any of your other cases suffer.'"

"So you *do* have spare time!" she crowed.

"Nah. I just have no personal life." I gave a helpless shrug. "Some people date. I bone up on local serial killers."

"Dear God almighty," she groaned. "You *so* need to get laid." Her gaze shifted to a point behind me. "Well, here comes Crawford," she said, before I could form a retort to her evaluation of my life.

Not that I had any idea of how to respond—especially since she was frustratingly correct. But there really wasn't anything I could do about it. I had too many secrets to get intimate with just anyone, and I sure as hell couldn't risk anyone finding out about the summoning chamber in my basement. I'd simply accepted that a dearth of companionship was one of the prices I paid to be a summoner of demons.

In my entire life I'd had only two boyfriends, and neither relationship had lasted longer than a few months—each man ending it with the complaint that I was too private and wouldn't "open up." I'd fabricated lies and excuses for why I was always busy on the full moon or why he couldn't stay the night at my place, but the constant deception had been tiring. It was the same reason why I'd never had any sleepovers when I was a kid and why I'd had so few friends—none of them close—in high school. *There are worse things to endure,* I told myself, not for the first time. *Being a summoner is worth it.*

I shoved aside the doubt that always accompanied that thought and glanced back at the man coming toward us. Jill kept her expression neutral, but I knew that she didn't care much for Detective Cory Crawford. He was another transplant from the south shore, though he was from Jefferson Parish instead of the city. Jefferson Parish was just west of New Orleans and had almost as much crime as the city. He'd been with the Jefferson Parish Sheriff's Office for almost fifteen years and working Homicide for over ten of those years, which meant that he had the most experience of anyone at Beaulac PD except for the captain.

And he made sure everyone knew it.

"Prepare to be *astounded* by his brilliance," Jill said in a low voice before Crawford reached us, and I had to bite my tongue to keep from laughing.

Cory Crawford was a stoutly built man, not quite gone to fat though obviously battling a growing midsection. He had gray hair that he stubbornly dyed a dull brown, a neatly trimmed mustache that was dyed to match, and brown eyes that were so close to the color of his hair that many suspected he had specifically matched the two. In stark contrast to the all-consuming brown of his coloring, Crawford preferred to wear highly colorful ties, especially favoring the mildly psychedelic Jerry Garcia brand. A faint scent of wintergreen and tobacco clung to him, and I was exceedingly grateful that we were on a crime scene so I wouldn't have to be subjected to the sight of him spitting tobacco juice onto the ground or into an empty bottle.

Detective Crawford gave a bare nod to Jill and a slight glower to me. "I hear you're the resident expert on the Symbol Man cases."

I dragged my eyes up from the wild red and blue pattern of his tie. "Expert? I've read the file on the old cases. That's about it."

Crawford's expression soured still further. "And that apparently makes you more of an expert than anyone else here. Or so our captain has stated."

It obviously pained him to admit that he wasn't the sole fount of all knowledge. But the detective who'd been the lead on the cases before was retired and long gone, living in North Carolina. And the two other detectives who'd worked with him had both gone to work for other agencies. I knew I was pretty much the only one in the department who was up to speed on the cases, but I sure as hell hadn't expected the captain to champion me to such a degree. "Er . . . I guess I am." I ran my fingers through my hair, somewhat discomfited. *No pressure. Yeesh.* "So who recognized the symbol?"

"No one has *recognized* it," Crawford corrected me gruffly. "This is not yet deemed a Symbol Man case. But Captain Turnham told me to let you take a look at it."

Holy crap, but that had to have hacked him off. "All right. Let me take a look at it, then," I said, feigning casualness. I wasn't about to let him know just how badly I wanted to do this.

Crawford's lips tightened, then he shot a look to Jill. "Are you finished processing enough for her to go look at the body?"

Jill nodded, maintaining an outward appearance of serene calm. "Yes, of course."

Crawford spun and marched off toward the body. Jill

and I exchanged a glance that we both knew meant *What a dick,* and then we followed him, trying not to laugh.

All thoughts of laughter died away as I got my first close look at the damage that had been done to the young woman. I sucked my breath in as my stomach clenched. "Holy shit."

A muscle in Crawford's jaw twitched. "I've never seen anything like this, Kara. It turns my stomach, and you know that I can handle a lot."

There was nothing covering the body. What I had thought to be netting was actually the woman's flesh. Precise parallel cuts had been made along the woman's arms, legs, torso—a slice every half inch from the neck down, so perfectly placed that I could have used the cuts as a ruler. The only deviation in the meticulous spacing of the slices was the symbol that was centered between her breasts, carved into the flesh.

I breathed shallowly as I took in the hundreds and hundreds of thin cuts. None of them was deeper than a quarter inch, but I knew that I was looking at days of torture. It was almost a relief to drag my gaze up to examine the ligature marks at her throat—deep grooves in the flesh of her neck, with her face mottled and red above it. At least the ligature had meant an end to her agony, even if it had also meant an end to her life.

She was probably praying for an end by then.

I struggled to remain impassive and clinical as I looked over the precisely mutilated body, but it took every ounce of my self-control. I swallowed, throat achingly dry, and crouched to get a better look. This was not a brutal hacking. This was almost elegant and artistic, even as it was thoroughly horrific. *All these cuts . . . This was all done while she was alive.* And this matched the other victims.

Even decomposed, there had been evidence of significant torture on those bodies.

I took a shuddering breath and steadied myself to look more deeply. More important than the strangulation and the mutilation were the features I could see that others couldn't. I let my vision shift into othersight, breath catching in a mixture of relief and revulsion as the flickers of arcane light appeared. They were faded, but I could definitely see traces of arcane energies scattered on the body.

Just like the body I'd seen three years ago.

And now I could feel the arcane resonance—a hum of power, like a bass speaker a room away. Keeping my hand a couple of inches from actually touching the body, I spread my fingers over the symbol carved into her chest, opening myself further to that resonance. I knew that it probably looked weird as shit to anyone watching me, but I wanted to soak up as much sensation from this arcane resonance as possible.

I pulled my hand away and glanced up at Jill and Crawford, relieved to see that they were looking at the area surrounding the body and had apparently missed my faith-healer impression. Regardless, it would have been worth it. Whoever had killed this woman had been working deeply in the arcane at the same time. Was this the arcane touch that Kehlirik had felt? He'd said it had the taint of blood and death, and there was certainly plenty of that here.

I shifted my awareness back to normal sight. I could still feel the resonance, but at least now it didn't feel as if my teeth were going to vibrate out of my head. "If it's not the Symbol Man, then it's one hell of a copycat," I said for Jill's and Crawford's benefit, but I knew this wasn't a copycat. *Not with the symbol and the arcane traces* and *the timing that coincides so perfectly with the convergence of the two spheres. That's just way too much coincidence.*

"Looks like we're going to be busy for a while," Crawford said as I stood. "Oh, by the way, the captain said he wanted to see you when you got here."

I nodded. "Is he on the scene?"

Crawford snorted. "As if. No, he's conferring with the chief and some of the other brass."

I scanned the area beyond the tape for the distinctive silhouette of the head of the detective division. Captain Turnham seldom went inside the crime-scene tape unless his presence was vitally needed. He despised being subpoenaed simply because his name had been on a crime-scene sign-in sheet and also despised seeing extraneous people on a crime scene, refusing to be one of that number. *I guess he doesn't consider me extraneous,* I realized, allowing myself a brief flush of satisfaction at the thought.

Taller than most of the others on the scene by nearly a head, the captain was easy to pick out. As expected, he was standing just beyond the perimeter of the crime-scene tape. With him were Boudreaux, Pellini, and Wetzer—the three Violent Crimes detectives other than Crawford. *And how are they going to handle hearing my input in this case? Will they even take me seriously?* Pretty doubtful, considering that lot. There'd been a few times when my white-collar crime cases had intersected with an armed robbery or a homicide, and they'd made it quite clear that I didn't know dick about what they did and that any opinions I had were unwelcome and unnecessary. Crawford had a huge capacity for being an ass, but at least he was fairly good at his job and was usually willing to listen to input.

I left Crawford and Jill by the body and headed toward

Captain Turnham. He stepped away from the other detectives as I approached, full attention focusing on me. A tall, thin black man with arms and legs that seemed too long for his body, he'd been a police officer in New Orleans for fifteen years before moving out to "the boonies." He'd been with the Beaulac PD for almost ten years now. He seemed humorless and dour to those who didn't know him, but the people who worked with and for him knew that he was merely relentlessly dedicated and overly meticulous. Even now, at three a.m., he was wearing a crisp white dress shirt and khaki pants with creases sharp enough to slice bread, while every other detective on the scene was in jeans and PD T-shirts.

"Morning, Gillian." Captain Turnham looked down at me over his wire-frame glasses.

"Morning, Captain," I said with a small nod. "Thanks for letting me come out on this."

His lips twitched into something vaguely resembling a smile. "I'm going to give this one to you, since right now you know the most about the Symbol Man cases."

I stared at him for several heartbeats, certain that I'd misheard him. "You want me to work with Crawford and the others on this?"

He shook his head. "No. I want you to take this case."

I was suddenly insanely grateful that Crawford had remained by the body. I didn't even want to think what his reaction would be to this. "Sir, you do remember that I have *no* experience with working homicides?"

"And you never will unless you work one," he replied with calm logic.

"Well, yes, but—"

He held up his hand to cut me off. "Gillian, you'll be fine. You've proven yourself with your white-collar crime cases, which is why your transfer to Violent Crimes was approved. And it's not like you're going to be on your own with this. Crawford and Boudreaux can help point you in the right direction, and I plan on pushing the chief about forming a task force."

"Yes, sir." *Holy shit. He really is throwing me a Symbol Man case!* I gave him my best effort at a confident smile, trying to avoid looking either cocky or nervous. I'd heard that Captain Turnham liked to throw new detectives into the deep end. I just hadn't expected to be forced to swim so quickly.

"You're a good detective," he continued. "You'll do just fine." Then in the next breath he said, "But don't relax too much. It's in our jurisdiction, which means if we do get a task force, I'm going to make sure you're the lead."

Are you fucking serious? I thought. "I appreciate the opportunity," I said instead, keeping my voice even and calm. It was a damn good thing that he couldn't hear the racing of my pulse. *Holy shit! I'm the fucking lead on a Symbol Man case!*

Captain Turnham nodded toward the other detectives. "Tell Crawford to get you caught up. I need to go talk to the chief."

"Sure thing, Captain." Oh, yeah, this would be interesting.

Crawford and Jill walked up to me as soon as the captain left. "So, what's his take on it?" Crawford asked.

I turned to him, making an extra effort to maintain a cool and professional demeanor, even though I wanted to jump up and down in excitement or do something else that would have been completely inappropriate on a murder scene. "Well, he thinks it looks enough like a Symbol Man case to treat it as such."

He shrugged and nodded. "Okay, makes sense. I'll need you to fill me in on details as soon as you can."

"Yeah. About that."

He looked at me expectantly.

"Captain Turnham said that the case is mine," I added in a rush.

His eyes widened in shock. "Are you fucking kidding me?"

Yeah, he wasn't one to hide his emotions. "Actually, no, I'm *not* fucking kidding you." I kept my tone cordial but firm. "He said I need the experience, and since I have the most knowledge of the Symbol Man cases—"

"You read through the case files a couple of weeks ago," he exclaimed, face reddening. "That doesn't make you a fucking expert!"

I blinked, briefly shocked by the force of his reaction. Then I recovered and narrowed my eyes. Screw *cordial*. I leaned forward, lowering my voice and drawing on my experience in dealing with demons to keep from losing my careful composure. "It's not my fucking fault, Crawford," I said, nearly snarling. "I didn't ask for it, and if it bugs you that fucking much, then take it up with the fucking captain!"

He looked at me for several heartbeats, expression stony. "The security guard who found the body is ninety if he's a day and is waiting to be interviewed at the front office," he finally snapped. "You have no other witnesses. Have fun." With that, he turned and stalked off.

I watched him go, clenching my hands to keep them from trembling.

"Okay, he's a dick," Jill said quietly from beside me.

"Yep," I replied, seething. *Sure, Captain. They're just bending over backward to help me out.*

Jill gave me a rueful smile. "You'll be fine," she continued. "If a moron like Crawford can be a reasonably competent Homicide detective, you should kick ass at this shit."

I let out a weak laugh. "Thanks. Actually, I'm pretty excited." I'd never in a million years imagined that the case would be handed to me, but now that the initial shock was starting to wear off, I wasn't about to let anyone take it away. Three years ago I'd been just a road cop, working the perimeter of a body dump like this one, not knowing if I'd ever have a chance to dig into why there were arcane traces on that body. I'd even begun to doubt what I'd seen and wonder if it had been a fluke.

But now I knew. The Symbol Man was doing some sort of arcane work and, like it or not—ready or not—I really was the best person for the job.

Jill laughed. "I know that look. You're hooked in now."

"Yeah. I am," I said with a grin. "I'm gonna get this fucker."

"Good deal. You tell me if you need anything. Don't be proud."

"I will. I won't."

Jill gave me a thumbs-up, then walked off to speak to the coroner's office personnel. I leaned against the metal building of the main office, watching as the body was carefully gathered up into a black plastic body bag.

I would definitely summon tomorrow night. There were a number of demons who could probably help me. Perhaps Rysehl? He was just a fourth-level demon, a *luhrek*, resembling a cross between a goat and a dog with the hindquarters of a lion. He was also a much weaker demon than Kehlirik, which meant that he would be considerably easier to summon. But Rysehl was usually a very cooperative creature and a good resource for esoteric information, despite being merely a *luhrek*. I could think of several questions to ask him about the kinds of arcane activities that could leave those types of traces on a body.

I pushed off the building. *Screw Crawford*, I thought. *I am the best detective for this case, and I'm gonna prove it.*

THE DEAD BOLT ON THE FRONT DOOR SLID HOME WITH a soft *click*, the last step in my preparations for the summoning.

I'd nearly changed my mind about going through with it. After leaving the wastewater plant, I'd gone to the station for several hours to do preliminary legwork and write up my initial report, but by early afternoon I could hardly keep my eyes open—not that surprising once I realized I was operating on zero sleep.

I'd finally given up on coherent thought and headed home to grab a nap, staying awake on the drive home only by keeping the window open and singing along loudly to bad country music. By the time I'd crawled into my bed, I was seriously doubting my ability to summon again, even a minor demon. But six hours of sleeping like the dead did wonders for my energy level, and by midnight I felt ready to go.

I wandered through my house, the usual excitement twining with the usual nerves as I made certain that the house was secure. All of the various mundane tasks were complete. I'd closed the gate at the end of my driveway, checked and secured all the windows—which included nailing several boards over the broken window—then locked all the doors, double-checking everything compulsively. I'd learned the hard way last night that a locked door wouldn't do much to keep an intruder out, so for tonight I'd added just a tweak of power around my house.

Arcane work could be pretty tiring, which was why I seldom did much outside of summonings. But, after last night's near disaster, I had to grudgingly admit that I needed to expend the energy. I wasn't exactly highly skilled at crafting arcane wardings, which meant that it took me nearly an hour to pull together a small protection that would cause anyone approaching the house to experience feelings ranging from mild fear to terror—an arcane version of a subsonic frequency, and hopefully just enough to make a person think twice about trying to get inside.

The house was still spotless from top to bottom from the deep scouring I'd given it before my summoning of the *reyza*. I wasn't in the regular habit of keeping my house in pristine condition, but the messes and piles of clutter could harbor unwelcome pockets of energy, or so my aunt Tessa always said—though I suspected that was probably just a way for her to get me to clean the place up at least once a month. It was tough to motivate myself to tame the clutter, since I didn't exactly encourage visitors. I kept it *clean*—after all, this was the South, and I'd be neck deep in bugs if I didn't—but my dirty laundry usually ended up on the floor, and my bed got made only once a week when I changed the sheets.

I owned just over ten acres out here, and most of it remained woods. My house was smack in the middle of the property, with only about a hundred-foot radius around the structure cleared of thick forest and underbrush, though there were still plenty of trees around the house to shade it beautifully all year long. The house itself was a single-story Acadian with a steeply pitched roof, high ceilings, and a broad porch that extended across the entire front. The high ceilings also made it hard as shit to heat in the winter, but I had long ago accepted that electric blankets were made for just that reason. Besides, in south Louisiana it didn't get all *that* cold. The house was close to one hundred years old, with walls and ceilings that had been made with precise tongue-and-groove construction. The exterior was supposed to be a dusky blue, but it was also unfortunately in dire need of a new paint job and had a rather mottled appearance where the white of the old paint showed through.

But the best feature of the house was its elevation. It sat on enough of a hill that I was able to have a basement, though not so high up that it could be seen above the surrounding trees from the highway. Houses with basements were practically nonexistent in this region, and the large basement of this house was absolutely perfect for the kind of arcane activities that my aunt and I dealt in. Aunt Tessa had converted the attic in her own house into a summoning chamber, but she frequently moaned that it wasn't as good as a basement. It was a lot harder to make an attic noiseproof and lightproof, and the earth that surrounded a basement helped soak up excess arcane resonance. Plus, the heat in any attic in the South was damn near unbearable in the summer.

I returned to the foyer, compulsively checking everything again and quietly pleased with how nice it looked. *I could have people over every now and then,* the thought intruded. *Maybe a crawfish boil in the backyard for people from work?* It really was a lovely little house, and there was a part of me that wanted to show it off. I had dim child-hood memories of my parents throwing parties and hav-ing people over—before my mother got sick. But neither of them had dealt with the arcane, I reminded myself. They'd had no reason to be secretive and private.

I had plenty of reason. *I'd have to scrub the shit out of the basement to make sure there was no evidence of a sum-moning diagram.* I grimaced. *And hide all my implements.* Would anyone come, anyway? I had plenty of casual friends from work, but Jill was probably the only one I felt any real "friendship" toward, and I could count on zero hands the times we'd hung out together outside of work. *Baby steps, Kara,* I chided myself. *Make some friends, then worry about throwing a party.*

I scowled and pulled my focus back to the task at hand. I could worry about my social life some other time. I checked one more time that the curtains completely cov-ered the windows, then headed to the hallway door that led to the basement. I paused in front of it, taking a deep breath and rolling my head on my neck to work the tension out. I was *good* at this, I reminded myself. This was going to be a very low-level summoning, and I'd performed plenty of them successfully. I'd worked my ass off for the past de-cade to learn everything I could about summoning demons. I knew the chants, the bindings, the names. I'd studied rituals dating back centuries, when it was first discovered that there were people who were genetically gifted with the ability to open a portal between this world and another—a world of creatures that came to be known as demons. Last year I'd even taken leave from work and scraped together the money to spend two months in Japan, studying under the summoner who had been my aunt's mentor—a waste of time and money, I later decided. The convergence had been too weak to summon anything really interesting, and Tessa's mentor—a wisp of a man who looked old enough to have been around for the first summoning—was a rude, condescending asshole.

I slipped off my bathrobe, folded it neatly, and set it against the wall in the hallway, despite my usual habit of dropping clothing wherever I happened to be. For the thousandth time I reminded myself that I needed to put a hook on the door for just this reason. I opened the basement door and walked naked down the stairs, skin prickling with goose bumps at the slight chill that lingered in the air despite the fire I'd lit earlier. It was spring closing in on summer, but the basement held the cold fiercely at times. I pulled the waiting clothing off the hook at the bottom of the stairs—drawstring pants and a loose shirt made from a gray buttery-soft silk. I'd never bought into the whole flowing-silken-robes thing—far better to be free from distractions, able to move about.

I stepped off the stairs, bare feet chilling against the concrete of the floor. The basement was huge—almost the same square footage as the main floor of my house. There was a fireplace in the south wall that tended to get a lot of use, since the basement stayed cool in the summer and became downright frigid in the winter. A couple of years ago, I'd converted the third of the basement that contained the fireplace into a mini-office, carpeted in a plush deep-red shag that only barely avoided looking like it belonged in a bordello. A heavy oak table and a comfortable wingback chair that I'd scored at an estate sale completed the ensemble. The other two-thirds of the basement floor was smooth concrete, unmarked except for the intricate and large circular diagram I had laboriously chalked out earlier.

I rubbed my arms as I scanned the room. The only light came from the fireplace and a few low candles placed around the circle, but it was enough. It wasn't as if I would need light to read anything. There wouldn't be time to read if things went wrong.

I'd already put my materials out, the implements I would need set in precise alignment outside the complex diagram. I was reusing the diagram I'd created for my summoning of Kehlirik, with the changes needed for the different-level demon that I would be calling. A diagram for a twelfth-level demon was a large and complicated construction that usually took me a good three hours to complete. The changes needed to summon the *luhrek* Rysehl had taken only twenty minutes.

Placing myself so that the fire was at my back, I moved to the edge of the diagram, careful not to touch it with my feet or clothing.

I took a deep breath, allowing myself to bask briefly in the rich and warm contentment that I found in summoning. I was in *control* during a summoning ritual. If something went wrong, I had no one but myself to blame. I knew what the consequences were, and even though they could be dire and extreme—especially if a demon's honor was somehow impugned—the end reward of having a demon at your service was worth the risk and occasional pain. Performing the rituals and dealing with the demons was headier than any drug—something I knew from brash experience, unfortunately.

But this summoning tonight was a straightforward one. Not even a tenth as difficult as the one from last night. I knew better than to be cocky—I bore a few scars from summonings that had not gone well—but I was quite familiar with Rysehl, and I knew what to expect from him.

Taking a deep, calming breath, I lifted my arms and began, my voice echoing off the wood-paneled walls as I spoke the words. Working carefully, I began by laying the shields on the room itself, then progressed to setting the wards on the diagram.

I kept my arms up as I chanted, finishing the wards, then starting in on the bindings, setting them carefully so that I could trigger them with the merest thought. Those could *not* fail. Demons were bound until suitable terms could be reached—an agreement on an offering in return for the demon's service. Once terms were set, a demon's honor wouldn't allow it to break the agreement, but until that time the bindings kept me safe from claws and teeth and arcane perils. This was especially important when summoning the higher-level demons—the *reyza* and *syraza* and *zhurn*—where you had to be utterly certain that the terms were set before releasing the bindings. The higher demons did not like being summoned. In fact, some utterly despised it, submitting only after intense and protracted battle with the bindings that the summoner had in place.

Finally I lowered my arms and assessed. The first phase—the protections—was finished. I could see in my peripheral othersight the bindings and wards that wove throughout the room.

That was the easy part.

Now to summon the demon.

I took a deep breath and began to chant. There was no turning back now.

A wind rose from nowhere, swirling about my legs and teasing my hair. The fire jumped and popped in the fireplace but I continued to chant steadily, holding my concentration.

The diagram began to glow more brilliantly, until the light from the floor rivaled the fireplace.

The wind grew cold and swirled angrily around the room, whipping the words from my lips and flinging them into the forming portal. The light from the chalk patterns gleamed fiendishly, near blinding in its incandescence. The wind shrieked as I raised my voice, nearly shouting the words, never stopping or pausing. If I stopped, the portal would consume me, sucking me into a nether region of neither death nor life. The wind swirled into a screeching crescendo, then hovered there.

I spoke the demon's name.

"Rysehl."

The instant the name left my mouth, the wind and the light vanished, as if they had never been. The name of the demon leaped out harshly into the sudden silence as my eyes burned with the afterimage of the glowing diagram. The fire still cast its light, but after the brilliance of before, I felt as if I was staring into pitch blackness.

I invoked the bindings quickly, then lowered my arms. I cautiously tested the protections, letting out my breath in satisfaction as I sensed a presence within the circle. My vision slowly cleared as I held the bindings carefully, ready and waiting for the demon to test me, to try to escape me. Rysehl never put up more than token resistance, and I already had the offering for it ready and waiting—a six-pack of Barq's root beer. The lower demons seemed to enjoy being summoned—like kids on an adventure—and their taste in offerings ran to simple items that they found unusual and interesting. Offerings for higher demons were never simple. The razor-thin scars on my forearm were a testament to that.

I blinked furiously, peering into the circle, trying to pick out the small canine figure of the demon.

I heard a low growl and I tightened my grip on the bindings reflexively, bracing myself for a tussle with the scrappy little demon.

The growl repeated, resonating throughout the room, and was far different than any sound I'd ever heard come from *any* level of demon.

"Who . . . dares . . ."

I nearly jumped out of my skin as a stab of shock and confusion speared through me. That was *not* the voice of a *luhrek*. This was a voice filled with power. A voice filled with menace. A voice that promised pain and suffering and a lingering death.

My heart began to slam in my chest as I looked upon the crouched figure in the center of the dark diagram. This obviously wasn't Rysehl. I'd screwed something up, and somehow a higher-level demon had come through. *I don't understand! I thought I did everything right!* My thoughts whirled in a brief burst of panicked chaos before I was able to force myself into enough focus to be able to think. *The bindings. Those are still in place and intact.* A sliver of calm returned. *I'm fine. It's going to be fine.* It would take me only a moment to send this creature back, and I could figure out later what the fuck had gone wrong. I just had to finish the binding, close and ground the potency, then reopen the portal. I scowled blackly. If that damn burglar hadn't come last night, I'd have known how to reverse the portal without going through all this bullshit.

"I am Kara Gillian," I stated clearly as I rewove the potencies, naming myself as part of the binding process. I had no intention of completing terms and releasing the bindings, but the forms still had to be followed. "I have summoned you to serve me—"

The laughter stopped me—a cold sound that cut through my words and sent a chill up my spine.

"Serve you?" The voice flowed from the crouched figure, serene and vicious. "I will rend the flesh from your bones and scatter your blood to the wind."

Oh. Shit.

I frantically gathered power to me. Screw the forms. I wanted that portal open *now*. This was feeling worse and worse, and I had no desire to find out what kind of patterns my innards could make on the floor. I gabbled out the chant for a dismissal.

In one fluid, graceful motion, the demon stood, and the light from the fire illuminated him fully.

I stared, slack-jawed, my words dying away. I had seen many startling things as a summoner, but not this. Never this. I hurriedly checked for signs that it was some sort of illusion or glamour, but there were none. There were twelve levels of demon that could be summoned. This was most certainly *not* any one of them.

He was beautiful. Angelic. White-blond hair hung in a satin-smooth fall down the length of his back. His skin glowed in the firelight, so perfect as to be ethereal. He was well muscled and tall, and the insanely incongruous thought came to me that he was probably about the same height as Captain Turnham. But this . . . being . . . wore nothing as mundane as a dress shirt and khakis. A shimmering white silk shirt hung on broad shoulders that tapered down to a narrow waist. Leather breeches the color of fresh cream fit snugly to well-muscled legs. He had the body of an Adonis.

And he looked human.

Only his crystal-blue eyes told me that this was a creature of deadly and terrifying power. Eyes that were deep and ancient, full of a dominance and strength that belied the angelic beauty of his face.

This . . . is no ordinary demon. Oh, shit, Kara. What the fuck have you done?

His lips curled into a smile as those eyes traveled over me, weighing and measuring me.

I swallowed hard and drew breath to restart the chant for the dismissal. I still held the bindings firm. I still had a chance.

I could feel pressure against the bindings as I choked the words out, could feel him probing, testing, but they still held. My shredded confidence steadied. I could hold this creature. He finished his lengthy appraisal of me, then looked around the room, slowly turning, still not moving from the center of the chalked diagram. Finally he returned his gaze to me.

"Ah." He smiled. "This will prove interesting."

I felt the bindings tremble, and then, before I could react, they snapped like threads.

I gasped in horror as the bindings unraveled and dissipated. How could he have broken them so easily? I abandoned the dismissal chant as I struggled to gather up the shreds of power. The wardings were my only hope. I threw all the potency I could seize into the diagram, seeing the runes flare into life.

His laughter mocked me as he brushed the wardings aside like old cobwebs, shattering the runes. Then he stepped out of the diagram and locked his eyes on mine as raw potency exuded from him in a smothering wave. "I am so glad you have brought me here." His voice was calm and melodious, but in his eyes I could see a black fury.

My breath froze in my chest as I began to back away. Terror warred with barely controlled panic despite all of my training and preparation. I knew how much the higher-level demons despised being summoned, yet somehow I had fucked up and pulled this creature through—a creature that was undeniably far beyond the level of a *reyza*. I was about to die. And badly.

The flight reflex took over and I turned and bolted for the stairs.

And came up against a blank wall.

I stared in horror at the place where the stairs were supposed to be, then whirled back to face him. "Let me go!" My voice shook, but I didn't care. I was far beyond any need to appear strong.

He laughed—a beautiful, musical sound that only increased my terror. "I do not hold you." He took another step forward, his angelic features and rage-filled eyes catching the firelight. "I do not hold you at all."

My stomach clenched. All of the bindings, the wardings, the protections were gone—useless. Even my police training would do me no good against this creature. I could feel the wood paneling of the illusory wall at my back, and I fought to control the urge that screamed at me to turn and claw a way out.

"Then where are the stairs?" I demanded, hating the note of hysteria in my voice.

He shrugged eloquently as he stepped closer. "I am responsible for careless architecture? I think not."

He stepped to within a pace of me as I tried to press back into the wall. He reached out to touch my face, and I jerked away from his hand. A snarl curved his mouth, and then, before I could move, he seized me, holding my face in both hands, pinning me firmly though not hurting me. *Yet,* I thought wildly. *It's going to start hurting really soon.*

He gazed down at me for at least a dozen heartbeats, eyes locked on mine as if searching through my essence— eyes that promised death and pain and vengeance. I could feel the rage that he held in check, could feel myself trembling violently in his hold, but I couldn't look away, didn't want to look away.

Then suddenly the fury in his eyes faded. "I see," he murmured, so softly I never would have heard it if he hadn't been inches away from me.

I gasped for breath as my heart hammered so loudly I knew he could hear it. "Let me go . . . please."

He was silent for several more heartbeats, his eyes still holding mine. Then he smiled—a dazzling sight—and gave a small laugh. "But . . . you do not want me to let you go." He bent and brushed my lips lightly with his.

My heart jumped in a combination of confusion and shock. What the fuck? Surely he was toying with me. He would destroy me, but first he would humiliate me. . . .

"No. Don't do this," I breathed. "Just kill me quickly. Get it over with."

He continued to cradle my face, then trailed the fingers of one hand lightly down my throat before slowly withdrawing them. He tilted his head slightly, eyes on mine. "So eager to die," he murmured, then laughed low in his throat, shaking his head. He no longer looked enraged. Instead, he looked amused and . . . delighted? I blinked, terror shifting into bafflement.

He lifted a hand and I flinched, expecting a flare of pain, but instead he merely reached out to stroke my hair, sliding his hand to the back of my neck. My confusion increased tenfold. Was this just a prelude to some sort of complex torment?

"Look," I said, working hard to keep my voice from quavering. "I'm very sorry I summoned you. I didn't mean to. It was a mistake. Please, let me go, and I'll dismiss you and send you back."

He gave no indication that he heard me and trailed his other hand over my cheek and down my throat. The unmistakable caress slid slowly over the buttons of my shirt and over the swell of my breast until his hand came to rest lightly on my hip.

I stiffened and sucked my breath in through my teeth, dark memory suddenly crowding in. Another time I'd been pressed up against a wall, an unwanted touch fumbling over my body . . .

His eyes caught mine and a sudden shiver raced through me. I could feel the slow and gentle movement of his hand on my hip and along my side. Not so unpleasant. Not unwanted. No reason for me not to want it, to enjoy it.

I blinked. There'd been a reason. Hadn't there?

He smiled down at me, his hand still moving in a slow caress. A tingle of warmth simmered through my body. It had been a while since anyone had touched me like that. A *long* while. And I hadn't realized just how much I'd missed it until this moment.

He pulled me closer with the hand cradling the back of my neck, then bent and kissed me—lightly at first, then gradually with more depth and insistence.

Oh . . . wow. I'd *never* been kissed like this before. His lips moved sensuously against mine as I briefly struggled to keep from responding to the kiss. But I didn't struggle for long. My lips parted and I groaned softly as his tongue whispered sweetly against mine. Damn, but he was good at this. My hands reached up automatically to circle his neck, and I quickly jerked them back down. But his skin was warm and smooth, and the feel of him pressed against me made thoughts of resistance difficult. *But this is no human,* I reminded myself as I fought to gather my scattered wits. He was a damn good kisser, but other than that I didn't know a thing about him. I didn't even know what he was, except that he sure as shit wasn't Rysehl.

I broke the kiss with a rough gasp. "Please. Stop." I was no prude, but this felt wrong and dangerous and a thousand other things.

He slipped a hand around to the small of my back, caressing lightly as he looked down at me, ice-blue eyes echoing the faint smile on his lips. I let out a small moan at the feel of his hand. Maybe I was being silly. He obviously wasn't going to kill me. It didn't matter who or what he was. Would it really be so wrong to enjoy a little bit of comfort and pleasure? I deserved it. I needed it.

He lowered his head down to mine again, teasing my mouth open and quickly deepening the kiss. I groaned against the heat of his mouth as he pulled me close against him. I could feel the strength of his form, the smooth muscle of his chest and legs, and I could feel the hardness that pressed into the curve of my belly. Warmth surged through me as I felt the power of the arms that held me. His mouth was hot and sweet, and in the kiss was all the power and strength and dominance that I had seen in his eyes.

His hand slid up to gently fondle my breast, his fingers lightly circling my hard nipple through the thin silk of my shirt. I put my hands on his arms to try to push his hand from my breast, but the muscle beneath the silk of the shirt was hard as iron and soft as velvet. I moaned softly and slid my hands up higher, holding on to his shoulders. The lustrous fall of his hair tumbled over me, and the pleasant, musky smell of him filled my senses.

He broke the kiss gently and nuzzled my throat as I tipped my head back, gasping, trying to gather my scattered wits. He released me slowly, and I clutched at the wall to support my wobbly legs. Smiling, he stepped back and turned away.

I stared at him, confusion and wariness mingling with a healthy dose of horniness. He walked to the fireplace, then turned back to me, looking at me expectantly.

What the fuck just happened? I took a deep breath, feeling as if I needed more oxygen so that I could wake up. "Are—" My voice cracked. I took another deep breath and tried again. "Are you going to kill me?"

Amusement lit those crystal-blue eyes. "Do you wish me to?"

"No!" I replied quickly. I cautiously pushed off the wall and took a wavering step forward. "No, I'd really rather you didn't."

His shoulders lifted in an elegant shrug. "Then I will not." He held his hand out to me. I blinked stupidly at the proffered hand, then looked back up to his beautiful face.

"Come to me, Kara," he said, voice rich and inviting.

"Why?" I asked, still wary. "What are you going to do?" With him across the room from me, it was easier to think clearly.

He laughed, still holding his hand out to me. "I would like to kiss you again."

"Why?" I asked again, not moving. It wasn't a stupid question. I was no raving beauty. I was the one who'd had a grand total of two boyfriends in my entire life, neither of whom had lasted for more than three months.

A look of surprise flickered across his face, then was

gone. "Because I enjoyed it," he responded simply. "Did you not enjoy it as well?"

I slowly walked toward him, brow furrowed. I stopped in front of him but didn't take the proffered hand. "I did enjoy it. But . . . I don't understand."

He lowered his hand and tilted his head, regarding me. "Must you?"

I opened my mouth to respond, then closed it. A few minutes ago I'd been absolutely certain that I was going to die a hideously painful death. Now this unspeakably powerful and gorgeous creature wanted to kiss me, and I was going to argue the point?

He gave me a dazzling smile and held his hand out again. Damn, but he was seriously hot. Was he so beautiful because he wasn't human? His gaze met mine, his eyes displaying a power and passion that sent another wave of warmth rushing through me.

I looked away quickly, swallowing hard to regain control of my body. The sudden burn of anger in my belly helped, now that I had an idea of what was happening. "Well . . . yeah," I said tightly. "I'm funny that way." I didn't know what he was, but I knew that he was seriously fucking powerful, and I was suddenly afraid of something other than a painful death.

"I . . . would be dishonored," I said, heart pounding, "if I could not resist an unwanted act because my willingness to resist had been taken from me."

He was silent for over a dozen heartbeats, while I kept my gaze fixed on the table in front of the fireplace. I hadn't wanted to phrase it as an accusation, but I wanted to be sure that my meaning was understood. Cold sweat prickled my lower back as I waited for his reaction.

"You may look at me, Kara Gillian," he said finally, voice

low but still somehow managing to fill the basement with throbbing intensity. "I give you my word I will not dishonor you again."

I wanted to sag in relief but instead cautiously slid my gaze back to him. He stood with his hands clasped behind him, regarding me with those ancient and power-filled eyes. "I will not dishonor you," he repeated. "But I would give you what you crave." Once again he held out his hand.

My throat tightened as I looked at his hand. He knew. Whatever he was, he knew how bitterly lonely I was, how much I just wanted to be *touched*.

I flushed and looked away, embarrassed and dismayed that he'd so clearly seen this weakness in me. "I'm fine," I insisted, voice a bit louder than it probably needed to be.

"You are a summoner of demons. You are isolated among your own kind because of your power. I have seen it a thousand times over. There is no shame in that."

I scowled, still not looking at him. He stepped closer to me and laid a hand alongside my face. "I dishonored you by seeking to compel you for the sake of my own pleasure. I would atone for that if you would allow me."

I turned my head and met his eyes again. "Atone how?" I said with asperity. "By sleeping with me anyway?"

His thumb stroked my cheek. "By giving you what you will not find elsewhere. Comfort without secrets, without hiding. Release from the fear that has locked you away from seeking out companionship. You have been hurt, but you are safe with me, Kara Gillian," he said, potent voice oddly gentle. "I give you my word that I will not hurt you or compel you."

For a brief instant I wanted to laugh. How crazy was it that the "safest" way for me to get laid would be with an insanely powerful arcane creature that I'd summoned by

mistake? *But he's offering me more than just "getting laid."*
He understands. Where else am I ever going to find that?

I slid my hand into his grasp. He pulled me close and I
went without resisting, feeling somehow relieved.

"So beautiful," he murmured as he bent to kiss me
again.

Who does he think he's kidding? The thought flashed
through my mind with a distant ache, and I almost pulled
away. Dark memory flared again—the horrible month after
my father's death, no longer suppressed beneath the compulsion of this arcane creature. I shivered in his arms, suddenly gripped in the hideous recall of the times I'd been
pushed against the wall by the seventeen-year-old son of
my foster parents. The whimpering horror as he'd thrust
his hands beneath my shirt and into my pants, groping
roughly and stealing from me the idea that a man's touch
could bring comfort and pleasure.

The clumsy and awkward attentions of my boyfriends
had done little to dispel that. But this . . . this was different.
His hands were warm and strong on my back, and the kiss
was gentle and deep and hot all at the same time. His touch
eased me, silently coaxing me to calm and granting me en-
ticing glimpses of what an attentive and skilled lover could
give. I relaxed into him, feeling the warm rush of pleasure
once again as I moaned softly into the kiss. It was *real* this
time and a thousand times better.

He broke the kiss, pulling away only far enough to slip
his shirt off and cast it aside. He looked down at me, and
after a brief hesitation I unbuttoned my own shirt and let it
slide from my shoulders. He smiled, gaze traveling over my
body as an oddly shy gratification swirled through me. His
hand came up to my breast, fingers lightly encircling my
nipple, and I shivered as I felt it harden against his touch.

He slowly slipped his hand down to the waist of my silk pants, a line of gooseflesh springing up on my skin, following the trail of his fingers. His mouth found mine again and I leaned into the kiss with a low groan, unresisting.

He pulled me down to the thick carpet in front of the fireplace, still kissing me. His hair tumbled over me and I twined a hand in the silken mass, silently relishing the exquisite texture of it. His arms encircled me, holding me close as he shifted his hips into mine. I shuddered and threw my head back, grinding against him. I'd never felt anything like this—never had anyone shown this much passion, this much desire for *me*. He was showing me a world I'd given up on, giving me back what had been stolen from me.

He shifted, placing me on my back, gently parting my knees and moving between them. He kissed me deeply, his mouth strong and sensuous, then his lips moved down to kiss my throat. His tongue caressed gently over my neck, gliding further down to eventually circle my erect nipple.

I made a sound of pleasure as he caught the nipple between his lips, then between his teeth. He bit lightly and teasingly and I twined both hands into his hair, arching up into his mouth. His hand came up to fondle my other nipple, then he slowly kissed his way down my belly, fingers still lightly squeezing the captured nipple.

I sucked my breath through my teeth, shivering at the wealth of sensations. His lips traveled over the laces of my pants, tugging, then he went lower and pressed his mouth against me, biting lightly as he rolled my nipple between his fingers. I cried out, gripping his head in my hands and pressing my hips upward.

He lifted his head to look at me, one hand toying with the laces of my pants. "Do you wish to leave these on?"

I smiled down at him, silently marveling at the smooth

muscle, the perfection of his body. I didn't know what he was, but at this point it didn't matter. He'd dishonored me by his initial compulsion of me and was repaying that small debt of honor by giving me the solace and release that an attentive partner could give. The irony wasn't lost on me that the end result was awfully similar, but the crucial difference was that this way the choice was mine to make.

I laughed. "No, I do not."

He tugged my pants down and off in one smooth motion, then pulled away from me just long enough to slide his own boots and breeches off, eyes flashing in what I almost thought was triumph. He returned to cover me, his deep eyes holding mine for just a moment. Then, with a sound that bordered on a growl, he slid into me. I threw my head back as he filled me, giving a shuddering moan as the heat rose between us. I rocked my hips up to his, meeting his steady thrusts.

He kissed me hungrily as he drove into me, groaning against my lips. I returned the kiss eagerly as I clung tightly to him, nails digging as my climax built. His muscles were like malleable iron beneath my hands, rippling with each driving thrust.

My climax exploded, shocking me with its depth and duration—stronger than anything I'd ever experienced before. I cried out and clutched at him as he let out a guttural snarl, emptying into me, grinding his hips into mine. I continued to lift my hips to his as he released. Finally he slowed, then stopped, his breathing deep and heavy.

He rolled to the side and wrapped his arms around me. I sighed and pillowed my head against him.

"I don't even know who you are," I said after a moment, looking up at him.

He stroked a finger down the line of my jaw, expression unreadable. "Your call was not for me."

I shook my head. "No. I was trying to call a *luhrek*. Rysehl."

A strange smile quirked his lips, then he kissed me lightly and stood. Baffled, I sat up and stared at him as he dressed.

"Wait," I said, finding my voice. "Please. Who *are* you? I mean, I was trying to call Rysehl, but you obviously aren't Rysehl, and I didn't mean to call . . . whoever you are. So, what . . . er, who are you?" I realized I was babbling, and I clamped my mouth shut.

His eyes met mine, and once again the power in them took my breath away. "I am Rhyzkahl," he said, giving me an enigmatic smile. "And, Kara Gillian, you may call me whenever you need me."

Then he was gone.

4

I STARED AT MY REFLECTION IN THE MIRROR. I WAS
not a beautiful woman. I knew that. I was by no means un-
attractive and I did my best to keep my figure in shape, but
I was usually referred to as "cute," sometimes "pretty," occasionally "quite appealing," but almost never "beautiful,"
unless it was someone who wanted something from me. I
had boring-brown hair that refused to take any sort of curl,
dark gray eyes that refused to be hazel or blue-gray or even
sparkling, legs that were about three inches shorter than I
would have liked for them to be, and an insistent little layer
of pudge at the top of my jeans. Not *beautiful*.

So why had it happened? Why was I still alive? I was too
realistic to think that my charm and beauty and sexuality
had swayed a creature of that much power from rending
me to shreds or keeping me for a plaything to be tormented
at his leisure. And why *seduce* me?

Reality had crashed in on me seconds after he vanished
from my basement summoning chamber, and I'd wallowed
in a full-blown freak-out for nearly an hour, indulging in

plenty of self-loathing and heaping servings of crippling doubt. I'd finally gone to bed, but sleep had been elusive.

Two enormous issues kept battling with each other in my head over which was worth stressing out about more. First was the matter of *what the fuck went wrong?* It had been a simple summoning. A fucking fourth-level summoning! And Rysehl was a demon that I'd summoned dozens of times before. After I'd calmed somewhat, I walked around the diagram, obsessively checking every sigil and rune that I'd sketched out, looking for any deviation, any smudge or change that could have altered the portal, and finding nothing to explain what had happened.

But this creature had said his name was Rhyzkahl. Had I mispronounced "Rysehl"? Somehow garbled the word? I cast my mind back over the summoning, the ritual, over and over until it was all little more than a jumbled blur. *I thought I said it right. The names are close, but not that close.*

I felt as if someone had pulled the floor out from under me. *I thought I knew what I was doing. I thought I was good at this.* I shuddered and scrubbed at my face, struggling to push away the aching doubt.

But forcing myself to stop thinking about the summoning only shifted my thoughts to the other elephant looming in the room. *Oh, fucking shit,* I silently wailed, *why the fuck did I fuck him?*

I couldn't even give myself the "easy" out and blame it on his compulsion of me. I knew that he was capable of doing so, since I'd managed to figure it out and call him on it. *But then he gave me his word. . . .* And a demon's word was inviolate. No, I'd just been incredibly needy and pathetic.

I grimaced and turned on the water, cupping it in my hands and splashing it onto my face. I scrubbed away the grit in my eyes, keeping the water deliberately cold to try to shock myself back to a reality I could understand and accept.

I sighed and reached for the towel. Nope, still the same haggard and confused face staring back at me in the mirror. I'd already taken a hot shower, with water as close to scalding as my water heater would give me, seeking to sear the memory of the night away.

But you don't want to forget, I accused myself. *You enjoyed it.*

I sighed and straightened. And that was the truth. That had been some seriously incredible sex. No doubt. Best. Sex. Ever.

Which circled my thoughts back to: *Why me?* Why seduce me? Was sex that hard to come by in the other spheres? That made no sense. He wanted something from me. An alliance? A summoner of his own? It was possible, I supposed. I'd heard of summoners who allied with particular demons, though such alliances were unpredictable and fraught with danger.

I had to assume that Rhyzkahl was some sort of demon that I'd never heard of before. My portal had opened into the demon realm—I felt reasonably confident of that. The demons I knew were creatures of arcane power, inhabitants of one of the many other planes of existence and one of the few that was accessible from this plane with the proper forms and rituals.

There were twelve varieties, or levels, of demons that could be summoned, or so I had been taught. When I had first begun my training as a summoner, I started with simple summonings of *zrila*—first-level demons not much larger than a cat, though with reptilian bodies and six legs. Limited intelligence and easily controlled. Ten years later I had progressed to the twelfth level: *reyza*. And not once during that time had I seen or heard of anything like Rhyzkahl. He was obviously a creature of great power—that much was clear by how easily he'd shattered the bindings and wardings. But I had no idea what he was or what his place was in the hierarchy of the demons.

My mind kept going back to what he'd said to me. *Call me whenever you need me.* Call him? Summon him? Who was he to say such a thing? And how was I supposed to do that when I didn't know how I'd done it in the first place?

I walked out to the living room and fired up my computer, then pulled up a search engine. It was a long shot, but I'd struck gold with the Internet before. There were no formal organizations or cabals of summoners that I knew of, but there were a few message boards—the type that catered to the "paranormal nutjob" faction—that were sometimes used to exchange information between arcane practitioners. A good 99.9 percent of the posts were incredibly fantastical piles of bullshit, from people who claimed to be "masters" of arcane power. But every now and then a nugget of promising information could be unearthed from someone who actually knew what the hell they were talking about.

No such luck this time, though. I ran searches with every possible spelling variation of *Rhyzkahl,* but the only hit I came up with was with *Rhizko*—which turned out to be the user name for a pudgy and pasty online gamer of indeterminate gender.

I leaned back in the chair and rubbed my eyes. "Shit." The two hours of fitful tossing that had preceded my alarm going off had not done much for my energy level or mental sharpness. "Shit," I said again for good measure, then stood. It was barely seven a.m., and the autopsy on the victim from the wastewater plant wasn't until noon. I had time to seek answers from a far more reliable source.

I pulled on jeans and a T-shirt from a Miami–Dade PD training seminar, shoved my hair up into a ponytail, and jabbed some mascara at my eyelashes as a pitiful concession to makeup. After the autopsy I would come back and change into something decent. It was sorely tempting to just bury myself in work, push all of this crap to the back of my mind. That was the way I usually dealt with stress in my life.

But I already knew that this was one problem I wouldn't be able to put aside until later. I needed to *know,* and since the Internet had failed me, the next best hope was that my aunt would have some useful information in the library at her house.

Now I just had to figure out how to explain to my aunt how I'd screwed up such a simple summoning.

AUNT TESSA'S HOUSE was on the lakefront, a century-old two-story with gleaming white paint and lovely blue gingerbread molding adorning the porch. Most of the equally lovely old houses in this area had been restored and were now tourist attractions. Many offered tours. My aunt's was not one of them.

There was a cheerful *Welcome!* sign on the door—a standing joke, since my aunt encouraged visitors about as much as I did. I avoided people by living in the middle of nowhere, and my aunt did so by maintaining carefully crafted wards and protections that were set around her house. Unless a person was invited or had significant need to be there, most who came to Tessa's house remembered something more pressing that needed to be done or decided that the visit could be put off until another day.

I once asked her why she bothered with the welcome sign at all. She replied that she didn't want people to think her too odd or standoffish, so having a welcome sign on the door would mollify people's attitudes toward her.

I had learned long ago that the best way to deal with that type of rationalization from my aunt was to just nod and change the subject.

I could feel the faint prickle of the wards as I entered her house, a sensation like passing through an invisible beaded curtain. I wiped my feet automatically, though I doubted that my shoes were dirty. But Aunt Tessa kept her house clean enough to be a showplace, even if she never allowed anyone inside except me. She'd restored the house by herself right after I started with the PD, and it still looked just as perfect as the day she'd finished—gleaming hardwood floors, elegant flowered wallpaper, and exquisite crown molding—all immaculate and flawless.

"Aunt Tessa?" I called.

"Front room, sweets!"

I stepped around the corner to see my aunt ensconced with a book upon an antique love seat. Sitting lotus-style. How a woman in her late forties could be limber enough to sit like that was beyond me, but Aunt Tessa was remarkable in numerous ways beyond her flexibility.

To most in the community, Tessa Pazhel was the mildly eccentric and extremely unpredictable woman who ran the natural-food store downtown. Tessa dressed the part, too, wearing brightly colored skirts and clashing shirts in eye-searing tones one day and then muted khakis and combat boots the next. Wild kinky blond hair sprang out from Tessa's head, the polar opposite of my painfully straight brown hair. Tessa was whippet-thin, while I had to fight tooth and nail for every ounce of fat loss. The only feature we had in common was our gray eyes.

I was the spitting image of my mother—Tessa's sister. At least that's what I'd been told and shown in pictures. My own memories of my mother were dim at best.

Today my aunt was dressed in a mid-calf-length blue velvet dress, with heavy silver chains draped around her waist and black suede boots on her feet. She lifted her eyes from her book and peered at me as I sat in the chair next to her.

"Well, you're alive," she said without preamble, setting her book aside. "Which means that if you summoned Kehlirik it didn't go too horrendously wrong." She leaned forward, eyes narrowing as she looked into my face. "But you sure don't look very happy about a successful summoning."

"The summoning of Kehlirik went fine," I said. "I've officially completed my training and am now a full summoner." I paused. It would be so easy to just leave it at that. But then I wouldn't get any answers. "I . . . uh, tried to summon again last night, and . . . well, things didn't go quite the way I'd planned."

The angles in her face seemed to sharpen. "That right there is a very bad thing. When there's any deviation from the plan in a summoning, someone usually ends up in bad shape." She arched an eyebrow. "So, what happened? You tried to summon a higher-level demon again and couldn't hold it? You dismissed it? It didn't come all the way through?" She shook her head. "Two big summonings in a row is pretty dicey."

I groaned. "Aunt Tessa, I don't know what went wrong. I wasn't trying anything ambitious at all. I was trying to summon a lower demon, Rysehl. Easy. And I *called* Rysehl, but that wasn't what came through."

Tessa went very still, and when she spoke, her voice had lost all trace of its usual gaiety. "Kara, what came through?"

Shit. How was I going to explain to my aunt that not only had I somehow screwed up the summoning but then I'd gone and had *sex* with the creature?

Tessa reached out and grabbed my hand, bony fingers painfully tight on mine. "Your silence is unnerving me, kiddo. Spill it."

I winced. "I called Rysehl—I'm sure I did! But it wasn't Rysehl. I'm still not sure what he was, but he said his name was Rhyzkahl."

My aunt was silent, and when I looked up at her I was shocked to see a stricken expression on her face. "Aunt Tessa? What is it?"

She swallowed visibly, throat bobbing in what would have otherwise been a comic manner. "Rhyzkahl." She let out a ragged breath. "Yet here you are still, and in what appears to be one piece."

I tried to give a diffident shrug. I didn't *have* to tell her about the sex part, did I? "Yeah, well, I mean, I, uh . . . just remembered what you taught me about dismissals." I avoided looking directly at my aunt. *I am such a damn chickenshit.* "So, um . . . what is he?"

"You . . . dismissed him," Tessa stated, voice flat with disbelief.

"I'm still here, right?" I tried to keep my voice steady and blasé.

My aunt remained silent, and after several seconds I risked a peek at her face. Tessa crossed her arms over her chest and glowered at me.

"Young woman," she said in a voice that was cold enough to destroy the entire citrus crop of Florida, "you are going to tell me exactly what happened last night."

I took a nervous breath. "Not until you tell me who or what Rhyzkahl is."

I steeled myself for a verbal flaying, but instead Tessa just sighed and nodded. "Yes, you need to know that. I'm sorry I didn't already teach you that, but, by the spheres! I'd no idea you'd be insane enough to call one of his ilk."

"I didn't do it on purpose! Who *is* he?" I looked at my aunt warily. "Is he some kind of creature that can take human form?"

Tessa shook her head. "No, nothing so simple as that. Library. Now." She unwound her legs and was out of the room before I could stand. By the time I walked down the hall and into her library, Aunt Tessa was already sitting cross-legged on the floor with a stack of books piled about her.

I set my bag down on a pile of papers on the table. There was no point in looking for a clear space. In fact, I had always thought that *library* was an inappropriate term for the room. Describing a room as a library gave one the impression that it was fairly ordered, with books on shelves and arranged in some logical manner or system. But order and logic did not apply anywhere here.

True, there were shelves on the walls, all of which were filled with books or papers of various types, but the books were shoved onto the shelves in a completely haphazard manner, often without any attempt to keep the spine out to make it easier to look for a specific title. There was no free wall space; absolutely every inch, from floor to ceiling, all the way to the molding around the door, was bookshelves.

A broad wooden table dominated the center of the room, with two worn leather-upholstered chairs beside it. Books, scrolls, and papers tumbled over one another on the table and chairs, with more piles of books in scattered locations on the floor throughout the room.

And from the center of the ceiling hung an enormous, luxurious crystal chandelier—utterly out of place and looking far more suited to the ballroom of an ocean liner.

I'd once had the temerity to throw my aunt's own words back at her and point out that the chaos in the library could attract unwanted energy and interfere with her summonings. I'd been rewarded with the crisp response that just because I didn't *understand* her organizational system didn't mean it didn't exist. Hell, for all I knew she really did have some sort of methodology, but in ten years I had yet to fathom it.

Tessa scratched the side of her nose, then motioned me over. "Are you *sure* it called itself Rhyzkahl?"

I moved over to my aunt and knelt beside her. "Umm, yeah. Pretty darn sure." More than sure. Those words were seared into my memory, along with the memory of him lying beside me, his hand resting on my hip, his lips on my skin. The sight of him standing and pulling his shirt on, muscles rippling more pleasingly than any male model—

I abruptly realized that my aunt was peering at me, eyebrows drawn together. I summoned an innocent look and worked on controlling the flush.

Tessa gave me a measuring look, then pointed to a picture in the tome before her. "That's Rysehl." The picture showed a wingless creature that looked like a goat/dog/lion, with an elongated reptilian face and small stubby horns that curved up and forward from the sides of its head. A spiky ridge crest rose from the middle of its forehead, extending down to the nape of its neck. In the picture the demon crouched, head tilted to one side as if listening for something. I knew this demon, knew the face. This *was* Rysehl, a fourth-level demon. The one I'd intended to summon.

I shook my head. "Definitely not what came through last night."

Tessa shrugged and turned to a page that was marked with a black feather. "All right, then, how about this one? This is Rhial." I didn't recognize this particular demon, but I could see instantly that it was a *mehnta*, a ninth-level demon—which was obviously not the one I had encountered. *Mehnta* looked like human females—albeit winged human females with clawed hands and feet and dozens of snake-things coming out of their mouths. Most assuredly not Rhyzkahl.

"No." I was starting to get annoyed. I knew what demons looked like. The differences between the lower- and higher-level demons were unmistakable. The higher the level, the bigger and more intelligent they were. Seventh and up were winged, with the twelfth-level *reyza* nearly half again as tall as a normal human. The faces of *reyza* were still bestial, with mouths full of deadly sharp teeth and long extended fangs, but not as much so as those of lowers. The higher demons' bodies were far closer to a human's, too, though with more muscle and power than any human could ever hope to attain. "It wasn't a *zrila, savik, ilius, luhrek, nyssor, faas, kehza, graa, mehnta, zhurn, syraza,* or *reyza*." I rattled the names off quickly.

"Thank you for that lesson in demonology," my aunt replied dryly.

I sighed. "Aunt Tessa, I thought you recognized the name Rhyzkahl. What is he?"

Tessa ignored me and flipped to another section of the tome. "This one is Rhykezial."

This picture didn't show a creature that I had any familiarity with at all. It looked more like a painful cross between a squid and a spider, and I figured it was one of the multitudes of creatures that could not be summoned between the planes. Or perhaps something from another plane entirely. There were a multitude of planes, but the demon realm was the only one that ever intersected with this world, as far as I knew.

I let my breath out gustily. This was starting to feel like looking at a lineup. "No, Aunt Tessa. Can't you just tell me what Rhyzkahl is?"

Tessa closed the tome with a soft *thud*. "I just don't want to believe that you summoned that one. To be honest, I find it very *hard to believe* that you summoned that one." She gave me a sidelong look. "Especially since you're still here and still you."

I could feel the flush starting to rise again. "I'm here and I'm me. And I told you. I *didn't* summon him."

Tessa stood, pressing her lips together as she moved to a bookshelf by the door. She hummed to herself—a tuneless, discordant thing—tapping her finger on her chin while she scanned the shelves. Finally she made a small noise of triumph and pulled a thin volume off the top shelf, turning and dropping it in front of me.

I blinked. "Aunt Tessa, that's a comic book."

Tessa sniffed. "It's a graphic novel."

I managed to hold back the eye roll. "Okay, it's a *graphic novel*. I thought you were going to show me Rhyzkahl."

"Well, these creatures don't exactly want to sit still for portraits. But this artist managed to make one of his characters look almost exactly like Rhyzkahl. Or what

Rhyzkahl is presumed to look like." She leaned over, then flipped quickly to the middle of the volume. "Here." She stabbed her finger at a panel.

I exhaled in a rush. It was *him,* or as close as a human artist could capture. The same build, the same hair, and the artist had even managed to capture a trace of the power in his eyes.

"He's seen him," I murmured, eyes on the drawing. It depicted Rhyzkahl standing on the top of a battlement with a *reyza* to his left. A smirk curved his lips as he looked down at a man dressed in medieval-style garb kneeling before him. "He doesn't call him Rhyzkahl in this, but he's seen him." I scanned the rest of the page, seeking other depictions.

Tessa muttered something under her breath that sounded suspiciously foul and vulgar. "And so have you, it seems." She reached in front of me and slammed the graphic novel shut, then snatched it from my hands as she straightened, turned, and shoved it back into its space on the shelf. She spun and stabbed a finger at me. "How? How did you survive?"

I lifted my chin mulishly. "You haven't told me what he is yet!"

Tessa rubbed at her temples, grimacing. "I'll tell you, but then you need to tell me what you did during your ritual that allowed Rhyzkahl to come through."

"I don't know what I did!" I wanted to stand and pace, but there was no possible way to do that in this room. "It was a summoning of Rysehl, for fuck's sake! I made a fourth-level diagram! I called his name!"

"Well, you must have done something!" she snapped. "I doubt Rhyzkahl just decided to drop in for tea!"

"I don't know! That's why I fucking came here—to try

to find out!" I had my hands clenched to keep them from shaking, but the quiver in my lower lip betrayed how unsettled I was.

Tessa exhaled. "I'm sorry," she said. "I'm just worried about you."

I nodded, throat tight. "Sorry I yelled."

Tessa rubbed her eyes, then shook her head, as if she'd lost an internal argument. "Rhyzkahl . . . is not a regular demon, not a creature that can be summoned by the usual means. Or at least not by the means that we employ for summonings of any of the twelve levels of demon." She toyed with the chains around her waist. "I know I've mentioned them to you briefly, but I can understand why you wouldn't ever think that one had come through." She sighed and spread her hands. "Rhyzkahl is a lord. One of the Demonic Lords."

I stared at her. "Wait. I thought they were like demigods."

"They are. They are incredibly powerful and refuse to be bound or subservient. This is why they are so dangerous."

I swallowed harshly. "All of them?"

Tessa locked her gaze on me. "All of them." She lowered her head, eyes still on me. "Rhyzkahl is ancient and has one of the largest followings of any of the lords. He is ambitious, and devious, and takes matters of honor very seriously. Even if he could be summoned, he would *never* submit to any manner of terms and would destroy any summoner who dared to bring him through."

I struggled to parse this new information. I didn't doubt my aunt's knowledge, but Tessa's description of Rhyzkahl didn't match my own experience of him. Or did it? *He was certainly terrifying when he first came through. I thought I was going to be destroyed.* I'd felt the menace of him in that first rush of terror, when he'd scattered the bindings like dust. Perhaps it was true. *So why* didn't *he destroy me?* I asked myself for perhaps the thousandth time.

I mentally replayed Tessa's words, then abruptly snapped my gaze up to my aunt. I wasn't a slightly experienced homicide investigator for nothing. Aunt Tessa was keeping something back. "How would you know that the drawing resembled him?" I demanded. Then I pointed at Tessa. "You've seen him too!"

To my surprise, Tessa went pale and sank to sit on the floor. "Powers of all, yes. I have. I was a stupid teenager. And the only reason I'm still here is because he . . . was otherwise occupied."

Something in my aunt's tone told me more than any words could. I knew enough about demons that if my aunt—my powerful, experienced-summoner aunt—was this shaken by a memory that had to be over thirty years old, it had to have been bad.

I leaned forward and placed a hand solicitously on her knee. "I'm sorry, Aunt Tessa. Are you all right? Do you need me to get you anything?"

"Oh, for the love of all the spheres. I'm not about to fall over." She rolled her eyes, color returning to her face, then stood, brushing imaginary dust off her skirt. She looked up at the graphic novel on the shelf. "I don't know how you survived, but I can only be intensely thankful that he chose to spare you."

My throat felt tight. I knew what a Demonic Lord was, but it had simply never occurred to me that I might have called one, even inadvertently. The other-planar creatures known to me as demons had a strict hierarchy, with each level of demon jockeying for position and power within their respective levels. At the highest, above the twelve levels, were the lords—potent creatures who could wield devastating power and who utilized the powers and skills of the demons who served them. I hadn't thought that they could even *be* summoned, which was why I had so little knowledge of them.

"You've always told me that the demons are neither good nor evil," I stated, watching my aunt.

Tessa shook her head. "Don't try to fling my own words into my face. I didn't say he was evil. I said he was devious," she said, shoving books back onto the shelves in utter defiance of details such as available space and the laws of physics. "Remember, good and evil are human terms that merely refer to the application of human morals. Demons are absolutely and utterly self-serving, and at the same time they are completely honor-driven. Which is a good thing, because without that driving sense of honor, nothing would ever get done in the demon realm. Everything is tied to honor and status." She gave me a piercing look. "And a summoning is *enormously* offensive to a lord. Any demonic creature who did *not* take revenge against such an offense would be seen as weak and would lose huge amounts of status. Offend a demon—or a lord—at your own peril."

I stayed silent. Tessa would never believe that Rhyzkahl had just let me go. *Is that what happened? Did he just let me go? I guess he did, since I'm here and alive, but how could it be so simple?*

Tessa sighed. "Go. You can tell me later exactly what happened, since you're obviously not ready to tell me now." She adjusted the chains at her waist, shaking her head. "You're alive. That's what matters the most." She leaned in as I stood up and gave me a quick kiss on the cheek, then took me by the elbow and steered me toward the door. "I'll talk to you more later." And with that she pushed me out of the library and shut the door.

I looked back at the white door, relief warring with confusion. At least now I knew what Rhyzkahl was. But I had a feeling I was happier not knowing.

Work. Now I can bury my stress under work, I told myself as I drove to the parish morgue. My visit with Tessa had done little to soothe my worries. Fortunately I had an autopsy to attend, which I hoped would distract me from obsessing over the events of the previous night. Maybe once I had my mind wrapped around the case instead of around my visitor, I'd feel sane again.

If an autopsy couldn't stop me from thinking about sex with a demon, nothing could.

I STEPPED INTO the outer office of the morgue, automatically wrinkling my nose as the distinctive odor of the place struck me—intense even a room away from the cutting room. Though this was my first homicide, I'd attended a number of autopsies. Captain Turnham liked his detectives to be familiar with all of the various procedures for all types of investigations, no matter what the detective's permanent assignment was. Much bitching and moaning usually resulted, though never in the captain's hearing. Personally, I thought autopsies were utterly fascinating and had never complained about being sent to one, even when my cases were stacked up.

Dr. Jonathan Lanza, the forensic pathologist for the St. Long Parish Coroner's Office, glanced up from his desk as I entered. "Morning, Kara. You can leave the door open."

I couldn't help but smile. The smell was obviously a bit much for him as well. It didn't have the stench of decomposition, as one normally would expect in a morgue, but that was due to Dr. Lanza's morgue tech, Carl, a self-proclaimed OCD cleaning fanatic. So instead of the vague odor of rotted flesh and formalin, it had the often-overpowering aroma of Pine-Sol and bleach and any other industrial-strength cleaner Carl could dig up. Doc often said that he was prepared for the day when he came into the morgue to find that Carl had died from some toxic combination of cleaning supplies.

"Morning, Doc," I said as I propped the outer door open with a rock that seemed to be just for that purpose. "Is this the only one you have today?"

He shook his head. "Nah, I have a probable overdose in the cooler, but I'll do him this afternoon." He made a sour face. "I was actually on vacation this week. First real vacation I've taken since I started working here." Then he gave a shrug. "But I'm glad they called me to ask if I was willing to come back in town for this. Otherwise it would have been sent to New Orleans, and that office is pretty overloaded."

I understood completely. Even years after Katrina, the city and its surroundings were still getting everything put back in place. And some things would never be the same again.

"I took a look at your girl when I came in," he continued. "It sure does look like another Symbol Man victim, doesn't it?"

Unease rippled through me. "Sure does, Doc. Not too many people know the details of the symbol. I just can't see it being a copycat."

I watched as he began writing the case numbers on stickers and affixing them to empty vials and plastic containers. "So when are you going to join the twenty-first century and get a printer to do that for you?" I asked, laughing.

He made a rude noise. "I'll be glad to just get into the twentieth." The morgue for the parish reflected the shockingly low budget that the office worked with. The space to perform the autopsies was loaned from an area hospital, which meant that maintenance issues were seldom addressed.

A couple of decades ago the walls probably had been white, but now they were a sickly beige mottled with stains and spots of dubious origin. When I'd first started attending autopsies, one of the morgue techs had warned me to wear gloves whenever I came into the autopsy room, since blood got everywhere and even leaning against a wall could be an exercise in contamination. After the first time I saw an autopsy and watched the bone dust scatter through the room during the skull-cutting portion, I'd taken the advice to heart and worn shoe covers and gloves every time I came in.

"Well, let's get to it," Doc said, standing and donning a blue plastic smock and disposable apron. Dr. Lanza was a slender man, about my height, with dark hair and eyes and a friendly smile beneath a distinctly Grecian nose. He was also incredibly experienced, having spent several years working for the coroner's office in Las Vegas, as well as a few years in Houston. I wasn't sure how the little podunk parish of St. Long had managed to snag someone with his credentials, but, like most everyone else, I wasn't about to complain.

The room where the autopsies were performed looked like something out of a B movie from the forties. A metal table was flush against a long metal sink, with the body of the victim already laid out on the table, cleaned and ready for Doc to begin. The cutting board and the array of nightmare-inducing implements were set out neatly on the counter next to the sink—scalpel, scissors, a long knife, and other devices that I knew had friendly names like "skull-crackers."

I stepped in and took a closer look at my victim—easier now, after she'd been cleaned up. Easier to see the damage that had been done to her, the torture she'd had to endure. With the blood and dirt washed off, I could see her features, see that she'd most likely never been accused of being beautiful, or probably even pretty. She had a hooked nose and weak chin and eyebrows that had never known the sting of waxing. Her eyes were a flat brown, but death could dull even the brightest of eyes. Her body was skinny in the legs and flabby in the midsection. I automatically glanced at the woman's torso, looking for stretch marks or other outer signs that she'd had children, but it was impossible to tell amid the many parallel cuts. Doc would be able to tell with more certainty later on, after examining the cervix. *Which would be worse,* I wondered, *for her to have had children and left them motherless, or to have no one to wonder what had happened to her, no close kin to care?*

Carl snapped pictures of the body, starting with overall shots, then focusing in more closely on face and hands. The pictures of the injuries took a while, but I knew how important it was that all of this was documented thoroughly, and I didn't mind waiting. Finally he unslung the camera and set it aside, then retrieved a syringe from the table by the sink. He glanced at me with a questioning look and the barest flicker of amusement in his eyes. "Ready to give it a try?"

He did this to me every time. It was the only evidence of a sense of humor I'd ever seen in the placid tech. "No way," I replied, shuddering.

He twitched his shoulders in a shrug, then moved to the body and plunged the needle into the side of one eye. I cringed and stepped back as he slowly drew the vitreous fluid out, filling the syringe. Even though I knew that vitreous was very useful when running toxicology tests on the victims, it still gave me a shiver to see a needle stuck into an eye, and Carl loved to tease me about my squeamishness.

I turned away and looked at Doc. "Do you have an ID on her yet?" It was the office of the Coroner that was responsible for making identification and then the subsequent notification of next of kin, though of course law enforcement always worked hand in hand with them.

A pained expression crossed Doc's face. "Not yet. We'll take dentals and make a DNA card for comparison in case anyone comes forward, but Jill said that her prints didn't come up with anything. If this is anything like the other Symbol Man cases, it's going to be hard as shit to ID the victim." He sighed. "And his previous victims were usually too decomposed to get prints from. We were lucky on this one, except for the fact that she'd never been arrested and wasn't in the system."

I echoed his sigh. "No missing-persons reports match her so far. She probably wasn't somebody who was missed."

"Just like the others," said Doc. "What was it, twelve? Thirteen?"

"Thirteen. The skulls were sent to a forensic anthropologist at Tulane, who did facial reconstructions on all of them. IDs were made on four, so I guess it was worth the effort." I'd spent several fruitless hours poring over the photographs of those clay faces, trying to see if there was any possible link between the victims, other than their social status.

My gaze traveled over the precise design of cuts in the woman's skin. "All these cuts—could she have bled out from this?"

Doc took a gloved finger and probed one of the cuts. "Doubtful. None of them is very deep, but they would have hurt like shit." He motioned toward the ligature marks on her neck. "We'll probably find that the cause of death is strangulation. She's got a ton of petechial hemorrhaging." He pulled the lower lids of the woman's eyes down to show the pinprick spots of blood inside the lid and in the eyes— a clear sign of strangulation. I could see similar pinprick marks all throughout the woman's face and neck. I could also see the faintest prickles of arcane energy but so faded and fleeting that, if I hadn't already known it was there, I would have likely missed sensing it.

"Go ahead and roll her," Doc said to Carl. The morgue tech moved to the opposite side of the table and grabbed the woman's wrist and hip, rolling her onto her side with a practiced yank so that Doc could examine her back. "Well . . . that's interesting," he said with a frown.

I peered at her back, trying to see what he deemed interesting. All I could see were more of the precise cuts amid the dark red lividity. I glanced at him to see if he was going to elaborate.

"There are injuries consistent with a fall." He palpated the back of her head and then moved his hands down to her hips, taking hold of her pelvis and shifting it in a gruesome and unnatural manner. "From a considerable height, too, I'd say. Ten, maybe twenty feet or so. Looks like she landed mostly on her back and left side. Her pelvis is shattered. The back of her skull is a mess, and so is her shoulder." He picked up Carl's camera and snapped a series of pictures, while the morgue tech silently held the body on her side. Then Doc motioned for Carl to roll her back to a supine position.

"Was she still alive?" I asked. "Could that be the cause of death?"

He shook his head. "There's some abrading of the skin, but there's no bruising or swelling, so it was after she was already dead."

I thought of the vats at the wastewater plant. Could the killer have carried the body up those stairs, hoping to dump her up there? Perhaps he'd dropped her? That could explain why this body had been so much easier to find. If he'd left her atop one of the vats, it might have been much longer before she was found.

Doc continued his perusal of her injuries. "Some of these cuts are healed or healing."

I didn't like the sound of that. "How healed? I mean, how long was he doing this shit to her?"

"A few days. Maybe a week." He pointed to a section of her lower legs that was scabbed over. "I don't think more than a week."

Shit. "That's a long time to be tortured."

"And I have a bad feeling that we're going to be seeing more of this," he said, picking up his scalpel and beginning the Y incision. "I guess our boy is back in action after his little holiday."

I grimaced in agreement as I backed a few feet away

from the metal table—far enough to avoid accidental blood spatters but close enough to still be able to see if anything interesting or unusual was found. It was obvious that Dr. Lanza had performed several thousand autopsies. He had the torso Y-incisioned and filleted back in about half a minute. But once he got into the body, he was meticulous and thorough, cataloging trauma and irregularities with precision.

For some reason I felt incredibly comfortable around Doc. He was one of the few people around whom I didn't feel ever so slightly inadequate. Maybe it was the way he talked to me like an equal, even though he had light-years more education, training, and experience. Or maybe it was because he was so incredibly patient when answering my questions about trauma and the human body, even when I knew the questions were stupid. He never acted as if the questions were silly, even when I could see as well as sense the other detectives rolling their eyes. He always gave me a patient and thorough explanation and then would tie the answer in to some aspect of whatever case I was working on.

"So, Kara," Doc said as he removed the lungs. "How'd you get lucky enough to get into Homicide *and* snag this case as primary?"

I shrugged. "The captain says I've busted my ass enough in property crimes, and handling a big case like this will be good experience for me."

He glanced up at me, a lung in his hand. "Well, that's a pretty big vote of confidence."

I smiled wryly. "Now I just have to make sure I don't fuck it up."

He *tsk*ed at me and placed the lung on the cutting board, slowly slicing through it and looking for defects. "You have a team, you have your supervisors, you have your coworkers, and you even have me." He grinned and gestured grandly at himself with the bloody knife. "The only way you could really fuck it up would be if you got in over your head and didn't ask for help." He sliced a sample of the tissue off and dropped it into a tub of formalin.

"Careful, I may end up bugging the shit out of you," I teased. "Of course, I also have a sneaking suspicion that they figure it's not that risky to have me working it, since the Symbol Man victims are usually 'nobodies.' "

An annoyed expression crossed his face. "Much as I would love to argue with you, I think you might have a point, serial killer or no," he said. "No one gives a shit about this woman. She hasn't been reported missing, and she's apparently never been arrested. She's possibly mentally ill and probably has been homeless or living out of shelters for years." He took up a pair of large scissors and began to cut out the heart. "The serial killer in Baton Rouge got a ton of reaction because the victims were young women from nice families. The serial killer in St. Charles got about a tenth of the attention, because the victims were homeless men who led 'high-risk lifestyles.' " He shrugged. "The response to this killer has always been a bit below par, in my opinion. But that's just my take on it."

"Yeah, well, I give a shit."

He glanced up at me and smiled. "I know, Kara. That's why you're going to do great."

I could feel a blush rising, and I ducked my head as Doc returned to his examination of the woman's interior.

A tapping on the observation window drew my attention, but I couldn't see who was standing on the opposite side. The other room was darkened to make it easier for observers who didn't want to get too close to the smell and gore to view the autopsy. Doc apparently knew who it was. He lifted a blood-covered gloved hand and motioned the person in.

The door to the autopsy room opened, and a man dressed in a dark-blue suit with a bland yellow-and-blue-striped tie entered. Brown hair that held just the barest touch of red in it was cut short but still had enough length to show that it would probably be wavy if ever grown long. Green eyes flecked with gold that were almost too pretty for a man were set in a rugged face that was *not* pretty but still managed to be handsome. He had an athletic build and was taller than I was by about a head, which I figured made him about six feet tall. And he was a Fed. I could almost smell it on him.

He gave me a brief, almost dismissive glance, then turned his attention to Doc. "Good morning, Dr. Lanza. I'm sorry I'm late. I hope I haven't missed too much?"

I kept my expression controlled, trying not to show my annoyance at the way he'd dismissed me. Okay, so I didn't look very detectively at the moment, wearing jeans and a T-shirt with my hair in a ponytail, but I'd learned the hard way about wearing nice clothing into an autopsy. Had a task force been formed already? Was this one of the Feds assigned to the case? It would have been nice if someone could have given me a heads-up.

"How ya doin', Agent Kristoff?" Doc said. "Have you two met? This is Detective Kara Gillian. She's the lead on this case for the Beaulac PD."

Agent Kristoff returned his attention to me again, eyes narrowing in another appraisal—one I obviously failed the second time around as well, since he merely gave a tight shake of his head. "No, not yet. Special Agent Ryan Kristoff, FBI." He extended his hand and, when I returned the gesture, he shook my hand for the absolute minimum length of time necessary for politeness, then dropped it and returned to ignoring me—even going so far as to step around me and approach the body.

Doc caught my eye and gave a barely perceptible shrug. I just sighed. And to think I'd been looking forward to having the help of the FBI.

"Dr. Lanza," Agent Kristoff said, hands clasped behind his back as he leaned over and peered into the already dissected torso, "does the symbol on this victim match what was found on the previous Symbol Man victims?"

Doc gave Agent Kristoff a slightly puzzled smile, which delighted me, since I knew the expression was a total act. "I can't say, Agent Kristoff. I haven't reviewed the old case files to be able to make a comparison." He paused. "Detective Gillian's the resident expert on the Symbol Man."

At that moment I *loved* Doc.

Kristoff's eyes slid back to me. "You know the case?" he asked, the trace of disbelief so slight that I wasn't sure if it was even there. Maybe I was being overly sensitive.

"I do. I'm sorry, but are you on the task force?" I asked, keeping my tone ingenuous.

The skin around his eyes tightened fractionally. "Yes, I was assigned this morning. I just drove over from New Orleans."

I put on a friendly smile, forcing my face into the position. "Ah, I see. I'll have to get you up to speed, then."

"I've read the files," he said flatly. "I was only hoping that Dr. Lanza had some recollection of the markings from when the previous Symbol Man was working this area."

Dr. Lanza shook his head. "Sorry to disappoint you. The only Symbol Man victim I posted was three years ago, right after I first came over here. We had a hard time finding the symbol at first, and even when we did it was tough to make it out. I just trusted the detectives when they said that it matched the others."

I folded my arms across my chest. "I'm sorry, Agent Kristoff, but you keep saying 'the previous Symbol Man.' What makes you think this isn't the work of the same person?"

His expression shifted to something between a glower and a smirk. "I'm not willing to jump to the immediate conclusion that this is the same person. That line of thinking would limit the investigation far too much, and I don't think that would be a wise thing to do so early on."

Holy shit, how I wished I could smack the smug right off his face! But through sheer force of will I managed to merely give a shrug and a nod. "I suppose I can see that point of view. But, in my opinion, it's a waste of time and resources to be looking for other options when so much of the data and evidence points to it being the same person. Sure," I hurried to continue when he opened his mouth to speak, "I can understand that we need to keep other options open, but I prefer to keep them on the back burner at the moment, unless some compelling evidence comes up to give us more of an idea that it's a different individual." I tilted my head and smiled. "I'm pretty familiar with the case and the symbol and all of his methodology." *And the arcane traces,* I added silently. "So I figure that if this guy *is* a copycat, he's a damn good one. Which means that he'll most likely follow the same methodology as in the previous murders. Which means that focusing on that methodology would be a good thing." I found myself masking a grin. Had I really just said all that?

I could see a muscle in his jaw twitch. He opened his

mouth to reply, but Doc spoke, interrupting the brittle tableau.

"She was strangled repeatedly."

Agent Kristoff and I both turned to Doc. I stepped over to the table. "Repeatedly?" I asked, peering down at the neck muscles that had been peeled back.

"See the bruising?" he said, pointing to clots of blood within the muscle with the tip of his scalpel. "It's in several lines across these strap muscles. She died of ligature strangulation, but it was tightened and loosened several times."

"More torture," I murmured. "Poor thing." I wanted to add, *Just like his other victims,* for Agent Kristoff's benefit, but managed to resist.

Doc grimaced. "Yeah, she didn't die easy, that's for sure."

I glanced at Agent Kristoff. He was watching me again, those too-pretty eyes fixed on me and an unreadable expression on his face. He shifted his gaze back to the body when he saw my attention, not speaking.

I felt another flare of annoyance. Was he looking down on me because I expressed sympathy for the victim? I'd run into that a time or two among other police officers—disdain for people who'd lived the sort of lifestyle that made them easy prey.

Well, if he's that sort, he won't last long on my task force, I decided. Not that I was sure I even had the power to remove people, but it made me feel better to think it.

We stepped back as Carl snapped pictures of each layer of muscle, showing the depth and position of the bruising. Then Dr. Lanza took a pair of scissors and removed the throat. I watched him as he palpated the trachea.

"Hyoid bone's fractured. Definitely a strangulation."

This wasn't a surprise, since the markings had been so livid on the girl's neck, plus there'd been so much hemorrhaging in her eyes and face. But it was still hard hearing it actually said out loud. It was almost as if it could be denied, as if the obscene cruelty had not occurred if it was not voiced.

"So that was the cause of death?" I asked.

Doc nodded and set the section of throat aside. "That's what I'm going to put in my report. I mean, she's suffered a ton of other trauma, but as hideous as it all is, none of it's life-threatening. She was tortured for probably close to a week, then killed slowly."

"Fucker," Agent Kristoff muttered. I glanced at him, then back to the body. Finally something we could agree on.

"But I think she was bled too," Doc continued.

A cold knot formed in my gut. "What do you mean?"

Doc lifted her arm and pointed to a notch cut in the crook of her elbow. "The vein is nicked there, and there are similar cuts in the other elbow and in her ankles." My sick horror grew as Doc pointed out the notches in the veins. I'd missed those deeper cuts among all the other shallow ones. Had those been on the other victims? After a couple of weeks of decomposition, there'd be no way to tell with all of the other trauma.

"So she might have died of blood loss?" Agent Kristoff asked.

Doc shook his head. "No. She died of the strangulation, but she could have lost up to a liter of blood and still been alive when he decided to finish her off with the ligature."

I suppressed a shudder, with effort. This was very unwelcome news. Especially with the arcane traces on the body and the timing of this new murder. Bloodletting and death magic were an ugly combination that could lead to all sorts of unpleasant possibilities.

Dr. Lanza stepped back and motioned to Carl to take

over and sew the body up. He peeled off his bloody gloves, then stripped off the apron and plastic smock and tossed both into a wastebasket with a red plastic liner. "I'm just glad that this one was so fresh. I'd say that she'd been dead only a few hours when she was found. Rigor was beginning to recede and lividity wasn't fixed."

"Can you give a closer estimate of time of death?" Agent Kristoff asked as I pulled my gloves and shoe covers off and dropped them into the same biohazard container.

"Nope," Doc said flatly as he picked up his clipboard and started to make notes. "Time of death is pretty inexact and depends on too many different factors, despite what you see on TV. Unless the death is witnessed, all the other factors are merely sufficient to give a range of time. Skin slippage—when the body decomposes enough that the outer layer of skin starts to slough off—is usually around three days, but that can be hastened or slowed by humidity, temperature, etcetera. Rigor mortis can come and go anywhere from three to thirty-six hours, depending on the person's physical condition and what they were doing right before they died. Lividity—the settling of blood in the body—is a good indicator, but even that gives us a pretty broad range of time."

I resisted the urge to smirk. I'd been through this with Doc before. People were always trying to pin him down about time of death, but he maintained that if he was the one who had to get on the stand and testify to it, he wasn't going to just guesstimate. Especially since, most of the time, it really didn't make a difference.

"Very well, then," Agent Kristoff said, extending his hand to Doc. "I appreciate you allowing me in to view this autopsy, Dr. Lanza. I'll be heading back to the office now."

Dr. Lanza shook his hand. "Glad to have you."

Agent Kristoff gave me a slight nod, then brushed past me and exited.

Doc glanced at me. "Don't sweat it, Kara. Maybe his mind's on something else."

"Yeah, sure," I said with a scowl, unconvinced. *Or maybe a pair of pretty eyes is wasted on a total prick.*

I KEPT MY PROMISE TO MYSELF AND WENT HOME TO change clothes as soon as I finished at the morgue. This time I made a point of dressing as if I actually had a clue about being a detective, pulling on black twill pants and a tailored blue shirt, belting on my Glock 9mm and badge, and telling myself that this was *not* because I might see the obnoxious Special Agent Kristoff again. I was just trying to look professional. *Yeah, right,* a tiny voice in my head mocked me. But I also took the time to brush my hair out and apply proper makeup. *Just trying to look professional.*

It was late afternoon when I made it back to the station, and there were two news vans in the parking lot when I arrived—media from New Orleans, which surprised me. Someone had probably tipped them off that the Symbol Man might be back in action. I could see the chief of police, Eddie Morse, standing in front of the station, cleverly positioned so that the *Beaulac Police* sign with the picture of the badge was just over his right shoulder as he spoke to the reporters. Chief Morse was slightly above average height, with perfectly styled gray hair and barely an ounce of spare fat visible. He had an angular face that looked as if it had been carved from stone and never smoothed out, yet its "tight" look had many people whispering that he'd had some work done. Set in this chiseled face were blue eyes that were always scanning, as if trying to find the best person in the room to be seen with. He proclaimed himself to be a model of physical fitness and often stated that he wished to be an inspiration for the men and women who served below him. He ran, lifted weights, bicycled, and ate a clean, healthful diet. He looked like he was in his forties, even though he was probably into his sixties. He was never sick and credited his healthy lifestyle for the fact that he'd had no need to see a doctor in over a decade. He claimed to be unaffected by the heat, even going so far as to work out in long pants and long-sleeved shirts.

He was roundly despised.

I made a face as I drove past. I was all for being in good shape—especially as a police officer—but no one liked to have it shoved down their throat.

I parked on the far side of the lot, well away from the little news conference out front. I had no doubts as to the subject matter. The only interesting thing that had happened in the parish for the last month was the murder, and since I was supposedly leading the investigation, I didn't want to risk being called to speak on camera. I was a little surprised that the chief was even allowing himself to be interviewed; he usually preferred to let the Public Information Officer handle press conferences. He definitely wasn't a media whore like most of the public figures around here. Then again, he was appointed, not elected, so he didn't have to be. But I supposed a possible Symbol Man murder was interesting enough that he felt obliged to make a statement. I walked quickly and quietly to the back door, managing to duck in before anyone outside spotted me. I'd been on camera once before, after a large check-fraud operation was shut down, and had managed to give a fantastic impression of a babbling idiot. I had no desire to repeat the experience.

". . . waiting on autopsy results before we are willing to connect this murder with the Symbol Man murders." I heard the chief's voice as the door closed, and I continued down the wood-paneled hall and on to my closet-size office. Other than his fitness fanaticism, the chief didn't seem like a bad sort, though I had shockingly little personal experience from which to form any real opinion of him. He was appointed chief of police by the mayor nearly a decade ago, causing more than a few bruised feelings among the upper echelon of the Beaulac PD at the time. Eddie Morse was not a local boy. A former deputy chief of a small town in north Louisiana, he had moved to Beaulac only about a year before his appointment. After the previous chief died of a heart attack, the higher-ranking officers at the Beaulac PD were all jockeying for the position, only to have it yanked away and handed to a total stranger, and there were many who felt that the job should have gone to someone with more-intimate knowledge of the area.

Personally, I didn't think that background mattered at all as long as the chief knew how to be a chief, and in the past decade he'd managed to avoid any major scandals—which was a minor miracle in Louisiana. The only beef I had with him was that he rarely, if ever, associated with any of the patrol officers or nonranking detectives. But, of course, that was a two-edged sword. There were many times when it was nice to go unnoticed.

I could see Detectives Boudreaux and Pellini down the hall by the coffee machine. Their backs were to me, and I paused. *Should I make the diplomatic move and ask them for advice?* Not that I was all that sure their advice would be worth a crap, but some things were necessary for the sake of diplomacy and making an effort to fit in. I made a sour face. I knew I needed to make some sort of overture to them, since they sure as hell weren't going to come to me and offer up their assistance.

". . . nothing but bullshit cases," I heard Pellini moan in his distinctive nasal baritone. "I shouldn't have to work this domestic violence crap. They shoulda been assigned to Gillian, y'know, since she's a chick."

"No shit," Boudreaux answered. "I can't believe the captain gave the murder to her. What a crock of shit." I couldn't see his face, but I could hear the scowl in his voice. "She's gotta be fucking the captain. Betcha that's how she scored the transfer too."

Pellini sniggered, but I didn't bother waiting to hear his response. *Fuck diplomacy,* I thought, as I strode up to them.

"Hi, guys!" I chirped as I reached for a coffee cup. "Whoo boy, do I ever need a hit of java right now." I gave them both an extra-cheerful grin as I poured the coffee. "All that work fucking the captain in order to get all the good cases is wearing me right the fuck out!" I saluted the two with my coffee cup as they stared at me. "Y'all should try it some-time!" Then I leaned forward and lowered my voice. "But you two should probably practice on each other first so's ya don't embarrass yourselves. I mean, I know it's been ages since either of you has fucked anything other than your hand."

With that I turned and sauntered back down the hall. I could have sworn I heard a bark of laughter come out of Crawford's office, although when I passed by, his back was to the door and he appeared engrossed in a report on his

computer. But Wetzer appeared in the doorway of his office, and to my shock he laughed and lifted his hand in a
high-five salute.

"Dude, that was fucking *awesome*!" he exclaimed.

I grinned and returned the high five. As I ducked into
my office, I heard Wetzer as he called down the hall to
Pellini and Boudreaux: "Duuuudes, she fuckin' *owned* your
asses!"

I laughed as I shut the door behind me. The insinuations
concerning my sexual activities were more annoying than
offensive. I'd grown used to that sort of thing a long time
ago and had accepted that I couldn't talk to anyone of the
male persuasion without being suspected of rampant lust.
However, it was a seriously cool feeling to realize that I'd
just scored points with others in the department for giving the two dickheads a smackdown for stirring up that
bullshit. *I'm one of them now. I just proved that I can hold
my own.*

I squeezed past my desk and plunked down into my chair.
My office was only about the size of the walk-in closet in
my bedroom, but it was mine. The walls were plain white,
which I kept meaning to decorate with pictures or posters,
but somehow I never managed to get around to it. I had a
desk, a chair, a filing cabinet, and barely enough room for
one extra chair. I didn't mind having a small office. That
just meant I didn't have to share.

I spent the next several hours typing up my notes and
running more checks on missing persons, placating the
twinges of hunger with the cereal bars I kept stashed in my
desk for when I worked late. A few possibilities emerged
among the missing persons, and those I set aside. They were
probably long shots, but I'd get with Dr. Lanza later to see
if we could compare dental records, if they were available.

DNA comparison would be used only if we were reasonably certain that we'd found a match, since it was expensive and took *forever.*

I leaned my head back and closed my eyes. Agent Kristoff's remarks about not limiting avenues of investigation came back to me, and I frowned. Was I doing just that by clinging to my deep-seated conviction that this was the Symbol Man again? What if I really was being narrow-minded? It *was* possible—albeit remotely—that this could be a different killer, one who was also versed in the arcane. Perhaps the symbol on this victim had been a coincidence. No one—including several experts in the arcane whom I'd consulted—had ever figured out just what the symbol was supposed to represent.

I mulled over the possibilities, eyes still closed. And that Agent Kristoff—was he always such a prick? Maybe he was just having a bad day. *But he does have some nice eyes. . . .* My thoughts drifted to another set of eyes—crystal blue, full of power, ancient and potent . . .

He stood behind me, potency surrounding me and arms loosely clasped around my body as I looked out over a stone battlement into a lushly forested canyon. Above were tumbled cliffs split by a shimmering waterfall that plunged to mist-filled depths. I could see creatures in flight—at first I thought them to be birds but then realized they were reyza and syraza, wheeling and diving in some sort of complex aerial sparring match. I looked to my right to see a reyza crouched upon the stone wall and beside him a man wearing what looked like some sort of medieval guardsman uniform, with a sword at his waist. The man didn't seem to have any fear of the reyza. In fact, they seemed to be deep in conversation. I looked down, oddly unsurprised to see myself dressed in a black silk shirt and leather breeches, with a sword strapped to my side.

He lowered his head to nuzzle the side of my neck and I smiled, leaning back into him and holding his arms tighter around me. "All yours, dearest," he murmured. "Call me to you, and I will give it all to you."

"All of what? This?"

His hands slid over my breasts, teasing, caressing. I dropped my head back against him and gave a languorous sigh. "This world. Your world. All worlds," he breathed. "Call me to you."

"But you never gave me your number," I said. "You have a cell phone, right? Isn't that it ringing . . . ?"

I jerked awake, still hearing the insistent trilling. I blinked several times, trying to clear away the lingering shards of the dream, finally realizing that the trilling came from my pager, not from a cell phone that a Demonic Lord was carrying.

I fumbled for the pager, wincing as a sharp crick in my neck made its presence known. I jammed the button to silence the pager and tossed it on my desk. *Teach me to fall asleep at work.* I smiled wryly as I finger-combed my hair back from my face. Small wonder that I'd fallen asleep, and small wonder that I'd had a crazy dream that threw me into the comic book my aunt had given me. Maybe something about getting only two hours of sleep in the past two nights?

I picked up the pager and tried to get my eyes to focus. *Why the hell did they page me instead of just calling me here?* I glanced up at the clock, blinked, then looked frantically at the time on the pager.

"Holy crap," I murmured, shocked. I hadn't just fallen asleep. It was five in the morning! No wonder my neck had a crick in it. I'd been damn near unconscious!

Then my eyes focused on the actual message on the pager. My throat tightened as the meaning penetrated. Another victim. That made two victims in three days. The Symbol Man was definitely back.

THE BODY HAD been found at Leelan Park—only a couple of miles from downtown Beaulac on the east end of the lake. The park was one of the pride and joys of the city, built within the last decade through the combined efforts of residents, local businesses, and the estate of the previous mayor of Beaulac, the late Price Leelan. There were sports fields, basketball and tennis courts, and a sprawling playground with nearly every conceivable climbing or swinging activity represented. A boat launch was in constant use on nice days, and on weekends when the weather was pleasant the park was packed with people.

At five a.m., I could hold on to the hope that the body hadn't been found by a kid.

The park was large, but it wasn't hard to figure out where to go. About half a dozen police vehicles were clustered on the end farthest from the lake, near the baseball fields. I parked my little Taurus in the first free spot I could find, did a quick makeup check-and-fix in the rearview mirror, then grabbed my notebook and exited my car. I scanned the area quickly, subtly relieved that I didn't see any sign of Kristoff. At least I'd fallen asleep sitting up, so I wasn't too wrinkled. I really needed to keep a change of clothes in my office, or at least in my car. I *felt* like I'd slept in my clothes, and I had a sneaking suspicion that I smelled like it too.

I could see Pellini and Boudreaux leaning up against one of the unmarked vehicles. They didn't look very pleased at being up at this hour, nor did they seem eager to provide their help. Not that I gave a fuck about their help, but I did enjoy a bit of perverse pleasure that they'd been dragged out of bed. Pellini puffed on a cigarette, face drawn in a scowl as he took note of my presence, while Boudreaux remained deeply engrossed in the sports section of the newspaper. I quickly ceased to worry about my appearance. Pellini had quit battling the fat on his midsection many years ago, which meant that his gut had reached the point where it flopped over the top of his belt. He was sporting a Beaulac PD T-shirt that was so worn it looked more like *e ulac P,* and to add to the insult to onlookers, anytime he lifted his cigarette to his mouth the shirt rode up enough to display a couple of inches of pale and hairy stomach fat. Boudreaux didn't have a weight problem, but his shirt was so wrinkled I suspected it had been balled up at the bottom of his laundry basket for weeks. And I didn't want to know whether it was the "clean" or the "dirty" basket.

I knew they'd seen me, but neither felt it necessary to acknowledge my presence with any form of greeting. *No help from that quarter. Fine with me.* As least I knew it going in so that I wouldn't have to worry about being disappointed by them.

There was enough of a chill in the air that I was regretting leaving my jacket in my office. The sun was well above the horizon, but the western sky still stubbornly held on to the dark-purple hues of dawn. Yellow crime-scene tape fluttered sluggishly in the morning breeze, blocking off the entrance to one of the baseball fields. I walked up to the tape, dew scattering off the grass and soaking my shoes.

The officer manning the crime-scene log was one of my old teammates from when I'd been on the road. Scott Glassman was a self-described "good ol' boy" from the sticks, with a bit of pudge beginning to show in his midsection and with no desire to ever move over to the detective bureau. Scott was more than content to remain a street cop for the rest of his life. And I had to privately agree that the street was the best place for him. He had a good manner with people, knew *everyone,* and would go quietly nuts if he had to endure the slower pace and the paperwork required in the bureau. He kept his uniform pressed, his head shaved, and his nose clean. I fully expected him to eventually retire with thirty years of service, still a street cop.

Scott sketched a wave to me as I approached. "Another victim for ya, darlin'. Doesn't look good." Then he frowned, brows drawing together in concern. "And neither do you. Whatcha been up to?"

"I've had a couple of rough nights," I said as I signed the scene log. "Not much sleep."

He laughed. "You? You lead such a normal, boring life. What, didja finally drag a man home?"

I blinked at him in brief shock as I wondered how he could possibly *know,* then realized that he was just teasing me. But it was too late. Scott began to laugh even harder. "Oh, my God! You did!"

"I did *not!*" I struggled to control the guilty-as-charged expression on my face. "C'mon, Scott. You know me. I have No Life. Where's this body?"

Scott sobered. "Looks like your guy struck again. Same signs of torture, same marks, same symbol. Crime Scene's just finishing their pics now." He gestured toward a figure on the ground just past the pitcher's mound. I could see Jill crouching near the body, snapping pictures.

"Who found the body?" I asked, eyes on Jill and the latest victim.

"Some guy out walking his dog. A preacher."

Jill stood and walked over to us, giving a shudder as she

approached. "Ugh. I'm really disliking this Symbol Man," she said, rubbing her arms. "That was seriously nasty." Then she gave me a smile. "Heya, darlin'. Nice way to wake up, eh?"

"Heya, chick. That's why I love this job. I don't need to waste money on alarm clocks."

Jill laughed, then peered into my face. "You look . . . different. Are you okay?"

I shrugged with a casualness I didn't feel. "I've been busy. Not much sleep. Working, you know."

Jill shook her head. "No, that's not it. You look different. I can't explain it." She gave a wicked grin, blue eyes flashing. "Did you finally get laid?"

"Oh, come *on*! Why is everyone saying I look like I got laid?" I glowered at Jill and Scott.

Jill smiled and shrugged. "Dunno, darlin'. Maybe it's the 'freshly fucked' hair thing you have going on."

I laughed and shoved my hand through my hair in a futile attempt to make it lie flat. "No, that's called falling-asleep-at-desk."

She set her hands on her hips and glared at me. "You are so incredibly pathetic. Would it kill you to ease up on the work and go out and have fun?"

"Why, yes, I *am* pathetic," I said, with a grin that I didn't quite feel. *Yeah, I'm pathetic enough to have a one-night stand with a demon. Pathetic and desperate. I'm even having weird-ass dreams about him at my desk.* "And I can't exactly slack off on work when it's my first crack at a homicide investigation," I reminded her.

"Okay. I'll let you slide for now." Then she leveled a sharp look at me. "But as soon as this case is wrapped up, I am going to drag your pathetic ass out drinking."

A warm flush filled me, as if I'd downed a slug of hot

to carry the body over here. He doesn't look like h
ghs all that much."

"Yeah. Skinny little fuck," she agreed. "Probably a home-
s crackhead."

"Maybe this one will actually have a criminal record, so
stand a chance of identifying him."

"I'll take prints when the coroner gets here and run
em as soon as I get back to the office."

I smiled, grateful. "You rock."

Jill laughed. "Yes, I do."

A whistle caught my attention, and I looked up to see my
captain standing on the other side of the crime-scene tape,
motioning me over. Jill made a rude noise beside me.

"God forbid he should actually enter a crime scene," she
said with a roll of her eyes.

I suppressed a groan. I respected his reasons for not
entering scenes. I really did. But, unfortunately, Captain
Turnham still wanted to know what was going on beyond
he tape, and he had developed a rather aggravating habit
f whistling to his detectives and motioning them over ev-
y few minutes so he could find out what they'd come up
ith.

Not even six in the morning and he was already show-
d, shaved, and dressed in clothes that held more starch
n I had ever worn in my entire life. "Morning, Gillian,"
said when I reached him. "What do you have?"

Morning, Captain. It fits the pattern of all the others.
load of torture—burned in a zillion little lines." I shud-
d. "It'd look really cool if it wasn't so nasty."

ymbol on the body?"

ight above the pubic bone. And cause of death is prob-
going to be ligature strangulation."

nodded, face impassive. "I pulled Boudreaux an

---

brandy on a cold day. "Deal," I said, smiling. "Now show
me what we have."

Jill made a face and headed back toward the body. I followed, mentally bracing myself for what I would see.

I had seen bodies. Natural deaths, suicides, homicides,
motor-vehicle accidents. Enough years in police work and
you get to see more than your share of death. No matter
how many times I'd seen the horror of what one human
could do to another, I was always shocked at the result.
But this was worse than anything I'd ever seen. Even worse
than the woman from three nights ago. *Victim number two,
or maybe number fifteen—however you want to count it. And
the killer's already stepping it up.* Usually it was months between bodies being found. Now it was days.

It was a male victim this time, with a stick-thin frame
that spoke of some sort of drug addiction, perhaps in his
twenties though it was difficult to be sure. He had dark
greasy hair and a scraggly beard and mustache that looked
like they hadn't been trimmed in months, and for a bizarre
instant I thought that he was my intruder from the other
night, until I remembered that he'd had stubble, not a full
beard.

But the pattern of injuries drew my attention quickly. The
Symbol Man had changed his technique from the previous
victim. Instead of perfect and precise lines carved into the
flesh by blade, this victim had been *burned* in the same sort
of pattern. All I could think was that the killer had merely
turned the blade over and heated it, using the thin edge to
lay hundreds of agonizing brands up and down the victim's
body. *A thousand times more painful,* I thought. There were
even perfect patternings of burns seared onto his genitals.
I'd seen similar signs of this sort of ritual torture in the

pictures of previous victims, but it was far different to see for myself.

I shivered at the mere thought of how agonizing it had to be for this victim. *It's a wonder he didn't die of shock. And how long did all this take? How long was he tormented before being finished off?* And a disturbing realization: *The Symbol Man had this guy and the other girl at the same time. He just finished with her sooner.*

Now that I knew to look for it, I could see that this man had the same deep cuts at his elbows and ankles as the other victim, and the symbol was there as well, burned perfectly into the skin just above his pubic area. A pattern that was oddly beautiful and at the same time disturbing, the symbol was an intricate writhing of circular forms that hinted of teeth and claws, twisting in on itself and defying identification. It looked vaguely Celtic but with shades of Egyptian or perhaps Oriental flavor. My frustration coiled more tightly. Damn, but I wished I knew what that was! This same symbol was on every victim, though not always in the same place. I just *knew* it was something arcane. I'd shown pictures to Aunt Tessa and had spent countless days poring through every book and scroll in my aunt's library, but while Tessa agreed with my conviction that the symbol was arcane, nowhere could we find what it meant or to what it could possibly refer.

I took note of the deep ligature marks on his throat, red and purple flesh squeezing up between the deep grooves, as well as the petechial hemorrhaging that indicated strangulation, just like on the other body. And this victim had the arcane smudges too. I frowned and crouched. The body flickered with sigils barely visible to my othersight. Just traces, like smeared fingerprints, but they would be there

only if the murderer was using the deaths as a ritual.

It *had* to be a summoning. Everything fit, esp way the timing of the three-year break fit with t gence of the spheres. But why use blood magic magic for a summoning, unless it was for a de couldn't be bargained with? One with whom terms could not be set? But what demon could b all of this trouble and mayhem? None of it made a to me.

I clenched my jaw in frustration. If I could just fig some way for my aunt to see these smudges, surely w able to decipher them—or at least more so than I wa to do on my own. Unfortunately, there wasn't even en left of the arcane traces and sigils to sketch. I scrubbe hand over my face and sighed. I really needed my au actually look at the body.

Too bad I had no idea how to manage that. I was aware of Jill shifting behind me, but I continued on the traces and smudges, gathering as much in from them as I could. They were fading even as them. Beyond frustrating.

I finally stood, knees creaking after being fo crouch for so long. "All right, I guess we can ca ner." I turned and walked back the way I'd co sume the rest of the area has been swept?"

"Nothing," Jill replied. "I mean, the usual c and trash, but nothing else. It's a ball field, ton of footprints all over. But no tire tracks on the field itself."

I looked around at the field and its plac ence to the road and driveways. "It would

Pellini from their other cases for the day to canvass for witnesses, but I'm working on getting you some permanent help."

"I met Agent Kristoff yesterday during the autopsy on the other victim." Some sourness must have crept into my tone, because my captain gave a dry laugh.

"He didn't light your fire?"

"He barely spoke to me."

"You know how some of those Feds are. He isn't even officially assigned yet. He called me after the body was found at the wastewater plant and asked for the file."

"Well, that's strange," I said, frowning. Hadn't Kristoff said that he'd been assigned to a task force?

The captain gave a half shrug. "Actually, not really. He's on another task force that focuses on ritual murders and cult things. He's probably evaluating the case to see if it falls under their sort of thing."

"Oh, jeez." I groaned. "Is he the kind who's going to insist that it's satanic rituals?"

Captain Turnham's mouth twitched slightly. "I'm well aware of how you feel about that."

"Sorry, Captain, it's just that it gets a little old having the 'satanic' label slapped onto everything—especially when the people don't have a fucking clue about satanism. It's almost as bad as when they start screaming about witchcraft."

He lifted an eyebrow at me. "Your aunt's been ranting again?"

"Yeesh, you should hear her whenever she gets wind of that sort of thing. She's considered an expert on the occult and paranormal, you know."

"Oh, yes, I know." He tilted his head. "It still amazes me

that she never gets hassled for that. This is the Bible Belt, after all."

I shrugged. "Everyone just thinks of her as a harmless eccentric."

He nodded, absently polishing his glasses on his sleeve. "So, did Crime Scene find anything that we can work with?"

"Not yet." I paused, then decided to take a chance. "Look, Captain, I know this is going to sound insane, but is there any way I can bring my aunt out here to take a look at the body?"

His brows lifted. "Are you kidding? Look, I know she's an expert on the occult, but the chief would lose his mind if I brought a civilian in to look at a corpse." He paused. "But I'll let you show her some pictures, see if maybe you can get that symbol identified."

I'd done that right after I got the old Symbol Man file, but of course I wasn't about to tell him that.

"So, is there going to be a task force? I'm thinking it would be pretty nice," I said. *Even with Mr. Personality,* I added silently. *Boudreaux and Pellini aren't exactly falling over each other to help me out.*

A grimace flickered across his face. "I agree with you, Gillian. I think that there's sufficient reason to form one, and I'm still pushing the issue. But the chief isn't ready to announce that these bodies are Symbol Man victims. Bad press, you know?" He spread his hands.

I looked back at the pitiful lump on the ground. "Yeah, well, if either of these victims had been the daughter or son of an upstanding member of society, we'd have had FBI, CIA, NSA, FAA, you name it, crawling all over this place."

"He's picking his victims well. People no one gives a shit about."

"No. He's wrong," I said, eyes narrowing. "Because I give a shit about them."

"And that's why you're the lead on these cases. Because you're a stubborn, obnoxious, tenacious bitch." His dark eyes flashed in rarely shown humor and something that might have been approval.

I laughed. "Aw, Captain, I didn't know you cared."

"Don't let it get out. I have a reputation to maintain." He lifted his chin toward the bleachers, where a man sat with an imposing Rottweiler on a leash. "That's Reverend David Thomas over there. He's the one who found the body."

"Thanks, Captain. I'll let you know what I find out." I turned and headed to the bleachers.

The man looked up as I approached, and my first thought was that he didn't look at all like a preacher. He was dressed in utilitarian gray sweats and worn sneakers. Then I realized that I was looking for a clerical collar but that this was a preacher, not a priest. His hair was salt-and-pepper and his face was weathered, though not heavily lined. He looked to be well on the far side of middle age, probably late fifties, perhaps early sixties, though he also looked like he was in pretty good condition, which made it hard to tell. I had known out-of-shape forty-year-olds who looked older than fit and trim octogenarians.

The dog gave a low growl as I got close. I slowed, and the preacher put his hand on the dog's collar. Light-blue eyes lifted to mine. "I'm sorry," he said, brows furrowed. "He's usually very friendly."

He smells the demon on me was my automatic thought. Then I realized that didn't make sense. It had been two days since I'd accidentally summoned Rhyzkahl, and I'd certainly bathed since then. I couldn't see how his scent or *feel* would still linger on me. "That's all right," I said, keeping a distance of about ten feet. It wouldn't be the first time that a dog owner had insisted a dog was perfectly safe right before it attacked. "I can stand right over here, if you could just answer a few questions for me?"

He nodded, then gave the collar a slight jerk as the dog growled again. "Easy, Butch," he said to the dog, then he looked back up at me. "Ask away, ma'am."

I asked the usual identification questions, quickly jotting the info down in my notebook, and was surprised to find that he was actually in his early seventies. He was the preacher at a nondenominational church in town—one with which I was familiar, though certainly not as an attendee. It was a popular church—so much so that the church hired off-duty officers to help with traffic control on Sundays. I'd worked that particular detail a couple of times when I was in desperate need of extra income.

"Can you tell me what happened?" I asked.

"I was out walking Butch this morning. I go out every morning at about five a.m., unless it's raining." His mouth twitched into a smile. "Fortunately it does that enough in Louisiana that I get a break every now and then."

I echoed the smile and waited for him to continue.

"Butch started acting really strange, pulling on the leash and barking. Then he finally pulled right away from me and ran over to the ball field." Reverend Thomas grimaced. "He was going crazy, and so I had to go get him and pull him back. I saw it was a . . . body, so as soon as I could drag Butch away, I tied him up here and called 911." He patted his pocket. "Thank God I always carry my cell phone."

"Did you see anyone else in the park while you were walking?"

"No, I'm usually by myself this early in the morning. I don't worry about it too much, since Butch looks fairly intimidating." He gave me an apologetic smile as the Rottweiler continued to emit a low, unnerving growl in my direction. "I really am sorry. He looks fierce, but he's normally incredibly placid and friendly. I guess he's unnerved by the body."

"But you don't seem to be," I pointed out.

He met my eyes. "I was a POW in Vietnam. Unfortunately, I've seen quite a bit of what one human can do to another."

I exhaled. "I see." I made a note to myself to check his military record. "Do you always walk in this park?"

Reverend Thomas shook his head. "Not always. I mix it up a bit, among this one and the lakefront and some of the parks south of here. Depends on how far I feel like driving. But this one's closest to my house, so I usually end up here at least three days a week."

"Do you think you would notice anything unusual? Any vehicles?"

"I think I would notice," he said. "But, unfortunately, I'm fairly positive that I saw no vehicles other than mine this morning." He gave me another apologetic smile. "However, I think I can be of help with identifying him." He gave a nod toward the body, an expression of pain crossing his features.

"You know him?" That would be a hell of a break.

"I . . . think so. I would have to take a closer look to be sure, but I think it's a young man who was in a rehab program I used to work with." He sighed and scrubbed at his face. "It's so disheartening when these young people get caught up in drugs. It's like they're drowning, but by the time they realize that they're in the riptide, it's too late for them."

I nodded in full agreement. "I know. I've watched people completely destroy themselves. It used to be crack, but lately it's meth." I closed my notebook. "Would you be willing to come take another look at this victim, to see if you know him?"

He hesitated. "Yes . . . yes, of course," he said after a few seconds. He bent and made certain that the leash was well secured to the bleachers, then stood. The dog gave a soft whine and the preacher patted his head. "I'll be right back, Butchie," he said, then followed me as I turned and walked back toward the crime scene.

The coroner's office personnel were just finishing placing the body in the body bag as we approached. The reverend leaned over the bag and then gave a heavy sigh. "Yes, that's him."

"Do you know his name?"

"Mark Janson. He used to live with his mother, but she died a couple of years ago of various health problems, and after that he just went downhill. He'd always had issues, but she managed to keep him vaguely in line. Without her guidance, he fell apart."

I wrote the info in my notebook. "Reverend Thomas, you've been a huge help. I'll be in touch if I have any more questions."

"I appreciate everything that you and the other officers are doing." His smile was warm and sincere. "Please don't hesitate to call or come by the church."

"You can count on that," I assured him as I shook his hand. I could see why his church was so popular. Too bad his dog hated me.

7

I MADE A QUICK DETOUR HOME AFTER LEAVING THE SCENE
to grab a shower and change of clothes, then raced back to
the station to get started on putting my notes in order. It
was nearly mid-morning by the time I made it back, and
I circled the tiny lot reserved for detectives and patrol several times, looking for a space, before finally giving up and
parking on the street.

The broad glass doors at the front of the station swung
in at a touch, revealing a spacious lobby with the Beaulac
PD emblem worked into the tile of the floor. A scattering
of people sat on chairs, probably waiting for copies of police reports or for appointments with detectives. I avoided
eye contact with any of them and went straight to the door
that led to the offices, swiping my ID card and heading on
through as soon as the lock clicked open.

I hardly ever entered through the front door, but I
couldn't see the point of walking all the way around the
building to get to the back entrance that patrol officers and
detectives often used. However, using the front entrance

meant that I passed right by all the offices for administration and the higher-ups. Normally that was no big deal, but to my surprise I heard my name called out just as I passed by Chief Morse's office.

I blinked and took a step backward, peering around the door frame in case I'd misheard. It was by no means common for the chief to call random passersby into his office. In fact, he hardly ever associated with the troops, and I didn't think he even knew my name.

I was wrong. Chief Eddie Morse stood in the foyer of his office, in front of his secretary's desk, a manila folder in his hand and a slight frown on his face as he looked at me. As usual, he was dressed impeccably, white shirt starched within an inch of its life and tucked perfectly into place, dress slacks immaculately pressed, tie in a tight double Windsor. Not a single steel-gray hair on his head was out of place. "Detective Gillian," he repeated. "Do you have a minute?" It was asked in a tone that said that he didn't give a shit if I had a minute or not but that I'd better make a minute.

I resisted the urge to gulp nervously and merely nodded. "Yes, sir."

He jerked his head toward his office, then headed that way, clearly expecting me to follow.

I obliged and followed him, taking in the surroundings in a quick glance as he moved to the far side of the broad oak desk. The office was neat and perfectly styled, much like his person. Dark-blue carpet matched the colors in the Beaulac PD seal, which had been painted on the wall behind his desk. Books were arranged by height. Certificates and plaques on the wall were ordered in perfect harmony with one another. One shelf was devoted to trophies, and the brief glance that I was able to make told me that they were either for athletic events or firearms competitions.

The chief motioned me to sit with the folder in his hand. So I sat, trying to not appear uncertain, even though I definitely felt that way. Chief Morse never called nonranking detectives or patrol officers in. Even if someone was in serious trouble, the chief preferred to have his immediate underlings take care of ugly tasks like discipline or firings.

He leaned back in his chair while I remained sitting stiffly upright. He flipped open the folder, looked at the contents for a second, then made a "hmmf" noise and looked over at me.

"You're working these murders," he said.

It didn't sound like a question at all, but I gave a small nod. "Yes, sir."

His frown deepened, though I couldn't tell if it was a frown of displeasure or of thought. This was the first time I'd spent more than five seconds in the man's presence, so I didn't have much experience to draw on.

"I read your initial report on the first case," he said, voice clipped. "Same symbol on this latest one as well?"

"Yes, sir."

"You've read up on the previous cases?"

"Yes, sir." I resisted the urge to fidget.

"So you're the resident expert." There was still no clue from his tone as to where he was going with this. He hadn't phrased it as a question, but he was looking at me as if expecting a response.

I hesitated briefly before answering. I didn't want to appear cocky, but I probably did know more about the case than anyone else in the department. "I don't know if *expert* is the right word, sir," I finally said, "but I have a strong familiarity with the case."

Chief Morse set the folder down, expression still unreadable. "Captain Turnham says that you asked for the Symbol Man files not long ago."

"Yes, sir. I was transferred to Violent Crimes just a few weeks ago, so I figured I'd take a look at some old case files to start getting a feel for it all."

His lips pressed together and he leaned forward, resting his forearms on the desk and lightly clasping his hands together. "Why the Symbol Man cases?"

"Well, sir," I said, as I tried to gather my thoughts into something coherent, "it's not often that any detective gets the chance to work this kind of case, or even see the details of the case. I've been a detective for only a couple of years—in Property Crimes—and I thought that by reviewing the files I could learn something about homicide investigations. And that's pretty much the biggest unsolved case we have, and . . . Well, I've been interested in the case for quite some time."

His eyes were intent on me, as if expecting me to say more. "I see. So you're just trying to be a better detective?"

I couldn't read his tone at all. Very frustrating. "Well, yes, sir. I mean, I really enjoy police work and intend to make a career of it." I could feel myself getting flustered despite my best efforts at control. "I'm sorry, sir, but have I done something wrong?"

"I saw you out on the scene at the wastewater plant, Detective Gillian," he said, ignoring my question. "You seem to be pretty meticulous and organized."

He'd obviously never seen the inside of my kitchen cabinets. "I do my best, sir."

"What were you doing to the body?"

"Er, what?"

He scowled. "You were squatting by the body and waving your hand over it." He made a horizontal waving motion with his own hand. "What was that all about? Did you touch the body?"

Shit. He'd seen me trying to feel the arcane resonance. "No, sir, I didn't touch the body," I said, thinking furiously. "I, uh, was trying to see some of the cuts better, and there was some glare from the halogens."

He leaned back in his chair. "Glare. Uh-huh. And Tessa Pazhel is your aunt?"

I just nodded, not wanting to say anything that could make me look like more of an idiot. Glare? That was the best excuse I could come up with?

"She has a rep for being a weird little bird," he said, "but I'm sure you know that."

I couldn't help but bristle at the slight. "Sir, my aunt is—"

He lifted his hand, cutting me off. "I know, I know. I'm out of line maligning your family. I shouldn't have said that. But I want to make it very clear, Detective Gillian," his sharp blue eyes stayed on mine, "that I want these murders to stop, I want the bad guy to go to jail, and I don't want any bizarre shenanigans on scenes. It's not enough just to solve a case. We have to be able to take it to court as well. You weren't wearing gloves, and it looked like you touched the body."

"Yes, sir." What more could I say? He was right. "I didn't mean to get so close to the body. I'll be more careful, sir."

He looked steadily at me for what seemed like several minutes, though I knew it was probably only a few seconds. I willed calm, maintaining my demeanor as he regarded me only by utilizing my training as a summoner.

Finally he waved a hand at me. "You're dismissed, Detective. Just keep in mind what I said."

I stood. "Yes, sir. I will." I turned quickly and exited. The secretary glanced up as I passed, giving me a small wink and smile that managed to drag my morale back to normal levels. She'd probably overheard quite a few ass-chewings over the years, and I felt a bit better after the silent reassurance.

Returning to my office, I shut the door and sat heavily at my desk. *I deserved that,* I had to admit. At least he hadn't pulled me off the cases. I forced myself to take some comfort in that—not easy after being rebuked by the chief. But apparently he still had faith that I could handle it. I just had to be more careful. The last thing I needed was for people to think I was as strange as my aunt. It was besides the point that I *was* as strange as my aunt, but that didn't mean I wanted people to think it. *Who are you kidding,* I thought wryly. *They probably already do.*

I finally exhaled heavily and spread my hands on the top of my desk. *I can* handle *it. I'll solve these cases, using every fucking trick in or out of the book.* So what if no one had been able to solve the Symbol Man murders the last time he was doing his killing. None of them could see the arcane. That gave me an advantage.

Now I just had to use it.

Leaning back to reach my filing cabinet, I yanked open the middle drawer, then riffled quickly through the files until I came to the thick folder containing the pictures from all the previous murders—Series One, as I was beginning to mentally refer to them. I flipped through the pics quickly. All those bodies had been dumped in places that were traveled infrequently, which meant that they were often not found for days or weeks. The body at the wastewater plant had been found quickly, but the fracture injuries made me think that he'd meant to place the body up on the vat, or somewhere else less visible.

But the victim at the ball field was *meant* to be found quickly. So why the change?

I worked my way through the pictures, taking note of something else. The Series One victims had been killed in a variety of ways, except for the last two—who'd been strangled. They'd all shown evidence of prolonged torture, but the main feature that had tied those murders together was the symbol. Always the same symbol, though not always in the same place on the body. Sometimes not even in an immediately visible location. Both victims from my cases—Series Two—had been strangled. So, why the change? *Could it be a copycat?*

It doesn't matter, I finally decided. *It's still a murder investigation.*

But there was one more striking similarity between Series One and Series Two. Every single victim was the type of person who had no one to miss them. Homeless, prostitute, drug addict, mentally ill. Sometimes all of the above. Black, white, Hispanic, Asian—all were represented. And the victims were chosen carefully—of that I was sure. These were not random snatches off the street. The killer studied them, followed them, and made certain they were alone and would not be missed for some time.

I sat back in my chair, drumming my pen on my chin. How did he take them? Tox screens on the victims had never come up with anything more than traces of "street" drugs, which was to be expected with the types of victims he chose. But if he was holding them for several days before killing them, then any drug he used to subdue them would probably have time to clear from their bodies, though I'd need to check with Doc for specifics. Did he gain their trust? Was there a connection? The investigator on the original case hadn't found any link between the victims, but I had no idea how deeply he'd dug either. Somehow, the Symbol Man snatched his victims without anyone seeing it happen, then transported them to a secure location where they were heinously tortured for several days and then ritually killed, sometimes suffering for up to a week before finally being put to death. And always the arcane smudges left behind on the body, as well as that unidentified symbol.

But why? What was he doing arcanely? There were a number of things that involved death and blood, but unfortunately—or fortunately—Aunt Tessa wasn't an expert in any of them, other than the basic knowledge of Things That Are Bad.

I picked up the picture of the girl found at the treatment plant and scrutinized the parallel cuts and the symbol carved onto her chest. *That shit had to hurt like crazy.* And the knife had to be insanely sharp, judging by the precision in the cuts.

I sighed and pulled out the pictures from the very first body, seven years ago. This one was a young black male in his mid-twenties who'd hit three of the four factors: homeless, prostitute, and drug addict. I flipped through the pictures quickly until I found one of the symbols. It had been meticulously burned into the inside of his left upper thigh, just below the scrotum.

I replaced that file, then grabbed up the next: a white male in his sixties, homeless, no family, mentally ill. His symbol had been seared directly onto his genitals. *More torture. Not just a brand, but one that was meant to cause incredible pain as well.*

But why should that surprise me? It didn't tell me anything new about the killer. But maybe it told me something about the symbol itself. If it was an arcane marking, then maybe the pain involved in its placing was important. Somehow generating more potency?

I replaced the files, then pulled out the one on the victim I'd actually seen when I was a road cop. But I didn't need to look at the pictures. I remembered vividly where that symbol had been. In fact, at first the detectives hadn't believed it to be the same killer, because no symbol had been found on the body. It wasn't until the pathologist removed the tongue and trachea during the autopsy that it was found— seared onto the base of her tongue.

I jumped at the knock on my door and bit my tongue against the yelp. "Come in," I called, then had to work to control my expression when Cory Crawford opened the door. His flat brown eyes flicked over the files and pictures scattered around my desk, then he looked at me, a sour expression curling his mouth.

"Dr. Lanza called to say he has court in the morning, so he's not cutting your latest until tomorrow afternoon."

"Okay," I replied, guarded. "Thanks for the heads-up."

Cory's gaze swept my office again. "You making any headway?"

"It's . . . a lot to go through. I'm trying to find a link between the victims now."

He gave a stiff nod, opened his mouth to say something, closed it, then shook his head. "Kara, I was a dick the other night. You're going to do just fine. Sorry."

I let my breath out. "It's cool."

He nodded again, then closed the door. I could hear his footsteps fading down the hall as I leaned back in the chair, feeling as if a bit of the weight on me had been lifted. *Yes, all better now. Now you only have to stress about the chief thinking you're an inadequate nutjob, Agent Kristoff thinking you're incompetent, your one-night stand with a demon . . .*

oh, yeah, and a serial killer still on the loose. I made a face and sat up again, pulling the scene pictures to me and wishing for the millionth time that there was some way to photograph those arcane smudges.

I can't photograph them, I thought with a growing realization, *but maybe I can sneak Aunt Tessa in to look at them.* If Doc wasn't going to cut until tomorrow afternoon, that would give me the time to do it.

I chewed my lip as I mulled over the utter stupidity of such an idea. "Ah, screw it," I muttered, grabbing my bag. "It's only my career."

BREAKING INTO THE MORGUE WAS PAINFULLY EASY. THE coroner's office suffered from a lack of funding more than any other agency, mostly due to the fact that people didn't like to think about death and thus didn't want to fund it any more than absolutely necessary.

"I've done my share of crazy things in my day, kiddo," Aunt Tessa remarked dryly as she watched me work the lock, "but I don't believe I've ever broken into a morgue in the middle of the night."

"Yes, this would normally be far too tame for you," I replied as I slipped the edge of my folding knife into the doorjamb, noting with wry amusement that the jamb was already scored a dozen times over, probably from people who worked for the coroner's office. The door clicked open and I stepped inside, wrinkling my nose at the ever-present odors—the combination of cleaner and decomposition and bleach, each struggling to overpower the others.

I quickly flicked on my key-chain LED flashlight, then

stepped inside and pulled Aunt Tessa in, closing the door behind her.

"Needs incense," I heard her mutter from behind me.

I swung the tiny flashlight in an arc, blue light reflecting eerily off the metal table and stained walls. "Let's just hope no one gets brought in while we're doing our little bit of breaking and entering."

The cooler was locked, but I knew that the key was oh-so-cleverly hidden in a drawer right next to it. A wave of cold dead air rolled out as I swung the door open, and once again I pulled my aunt inside, this time propping the door slightly ajar with an office chair. I panned my flashlight around the cooler, relieved to find that there was only one stretcher with a body bag atop it. I checked the tag on the outside of the bag to be sure. Yep, this was my victim, Mark Janson.

The bag was secured with a plastic zip tie, which I sliced through with my knife. I quickly tugged on latex gloves, then unzipped the bag, exhaling as the sight of the young man struck an emotional chord once again. Then I grimaced. The arcane smudges had faded drastically, as I'd feared.

"There's not much left of them, Aunt Tessa. Can you see anything?"

Tessa leaned over the bag, slowly scanning the body, nose wrinkling at the faint odor of sweat and blood and death. "I see what you're talking about." She frowned. "Turn your flashlight off, please."

I switched the flashlight off, suppressing a shudder at the near-absolute blackness inside the cooler, broken only by the faint illumination sneaking past the propped-open door. But I could see why my aunt wanted less light. The smudges were far more visible to othersight in the dark.

"There's not much to see," Tessa said, "but it's definitely a male who left these."

"The profiles that were done all indicated a white male in his thirties—"

"Lives alone, parents divorced, yeah yeah yeah," my aunt cut in with a laugh. "Isn't it funny how every profile is darn near the same?"

"No shit! But I was going to add that I also got the impression of a male."

"Hmm . . . But that doesn't mean he's the killer."

"Sure, but that's some pretty damning evidence." I shrugged. "I mean, if any of this were admissible in court."

Tessa made a low noise in her throat. "They."

It took a second for my aunt's comment to register. "Wait, there's more than one?"

"Yep. At least, there are two different sources on this body." She sighed. "But I can't really tell anything about the second one. Can't even tell gender or species."

"Species?" I said, startled. The dark shape of my aunt's head turned toward me.

"Yes, dearie. Not necessarily human."

I groaned. "Aw, crap. So this guy could be teaming up with a demon?"

"You weren't listening," she chided. "I said I couldn't tell. It could still be a human, it could be a demon. It could be a squid person from Mars."

I snorted softly and smiled. "Of course, Auntie Dearest."

"Oh, please," she groaned. "Enough of that. Now gimme some light, Darling Niece."

I flicked the flashlight on again, only to have Tessa pluck it from my fingers and shine it directly on the symbol on the man's lower abdomen. She stared at it, mumbling softly under her breath, then finally sighed and shook her head. "I can't figure that thing out at all." She handed the light back to me. "We'll have to ask one of the demonic ilk for advice on that one. I wish we knew how you muffed up the Rysehl summoning."

My jaw tightened. "I didn't muff it up."

She winced. "Sorry, that came out harsher than I meant. But something went wrong, and I'd be a lot happier if I knew what it was." She smiled and patted my cheek. "Don't worry, sweetie, we'll figure it out."

I zipped up the bag, then pulled a fresh zip tie out of my pocket and resealed the bag. "Fine. Whatever. Let's go."

We left the cooler and I relocked it, but Tessa paused before following me out of the morgue. "I'm not your enemy here, Kara. I know I've screwed up in the past, but I'm really trying here."

My shoulders slumped. I was being a jerk and letting my own stress spill onto her. "You haven't screwed up."

She shook her head. "You and I both know that's not true. That month while I dithered in Japan and left you in that awful foster home—"

"You made that right," I cut in, voice a bit rough. I looked at her, seeing the guilt on her face again. "Aunt Tessa, that's in the past. You . . . did the right thing. You made it right," I repeated.

She exhaled, nodded. "Well, I should have made sure you had more friends in high school. Made you get out more—"

"Okay, are we just going to stand here and flail around in guilt all night long?" I gave her a mock glare. "Because if that's really your plan, I'd like to do it someplace that doesn't stink so damn much."

She laughed and gave me a quick, bony hug. "Impudent little bitch. I don't know why I bother with you at all."

"I don't either, but you're fucking stuck with me." I gave her a squeeze, then released her. "Come on, let's get out of here."

THE NEXT SEVERAL DAYS WERE SPENT DOING THE MOST exciting police work I ever thought I would be involved with.

Not.

I sighed and popped another VHS tape into the VCR and settled back onto my bed, hitting the play button on the remote. They never showed this stuff on TV, the endless hours of searching through surveillance video on the mere hope that *maybe possibly hopefully* some glimpse of something that *might occasionally* point the investigator to a lead could be found. The day after breaking into the morgue with Tessa, I'd gone to every business and convenience store and gas station within a mile of either crime scene and collected surveillance videos for the times between sundown and a few hours after the bodies were discovered.

Then I'd brought the box of videotapes home, settled in, and watched. And watched. Watched until my eyes crossed, searching for anything that could help, any consistencies between the time frames surrounding the two murders. Hoping to see someone walk into one of the gas stations wearing a T-shirt that proclaimed, *I AM THE SYMBOL MAN!*

I scrubbed at my eyes. I'd been at this for nearly a week. I'd seen seventeen instances of shoplifting, four instances of employee theft, nine drug deals, twenty-one gas drive-offs, and one instance of a couple having sex by the beer cooler, but nothing at all that leaped out as being relevant to the murders.

I finally turned off the TV and flopped back onto my pillows, looking up at the shifting shadows cast by the waning moon filtering through the trees. I hated to think that these murders were unsolvable. This killer *had* to have slipped up somewhere, left some clue. Or maybe he had, and I was just missing it? With zero leads, I knew that I wouldn't be allowed to keep working this case exclusively forever. I was spinning my wheels chasing down nebulous possibilities, while others were picking up the slack with my other cases—the assaults and robberies that continued despite the Symbol Man. Beaulac's police force wasn't large enough to have detectives dedicated solely to homicides, and I knew that there was resentment simmering among other detectives about the shift in caseload. Boudreaux and Pellini had made it crystal clear that they weren't content with the fact that I'd snagged a primo case.

I sighed and pushed the pillow into a more comfortable position. Of course, I still had the arcane angle to pursue. But I'd feel a lot more comfortable performing another summoning if I had even the slightest idea of what had gone wrong with the Rysehl summoning. "I screwed up," I said aloud, hating the sound of it. It still felt terribly jarring. I wasn't an anal perfectionist, and I'd certainly made mistakes in summonings in the past, but I'd always known *what* the mistake was. What if I summoned again and accidentally pulled another powerful creature through—one who was perfectly fine with killing me in spectacular fashion instead of merely fucking my brains out?

I smiled wryly. Yeah, I'd definitely gotten off light, though the question of *why* Rhyzkahl had chosen to seduce me instead of kill me would probably haunt me for the rest of my life.

And I've angsted over my choice to sleep with him long enough, I decided firmly. Yeah, so I had no love life. Okay, so I'd had the equivalent of a one-night stand. It was over and in the past, and at least the sex had been pretty damn worth it.

With that small aspect of my psyche dealt with, I punched my pillow into a more comfortable position and settled in to sleep.

I WOKE TO a soft sound—a scrape of a shoe on the floor, or the brush of clothing against a piece of furniture. I was instantly wide awake but I didn't move, kept my breathing as regular as possible, though I could feel my heart slamming in my chest. *My gun is in the nightstand drawer,* I reminded myself, breathing shallowly and listening for a repetition of the sound that had woken me.

Nothing. Just the sounds of the night, the muted rush of the air conditioner, a faraway car passing on the highway. I waited and listened, counting silently to fifty before reaching out slowly and pulling the drawer open. My disquiet eased tremendously as soon as my hand curled around the rough butt of the gun, and I flicked on the bedside light with one hand while pointing the gun at the foot of the bed.

Rhyzkahl stood at the foot of my bed, still as carved marble and emanating the power and strength that I remembered so vividly from that night a week ago. The ivory fall of his hair rippled in an unfelt wind, and his beautiful eyes bored into mine. He wore robes of pale silk, and a sensuous smile curved his lips.

I stared at him in shock as a frisson of sudden terror coursed through me. *He's here. How is he here?* My thoughts careened wildly as I kept the gun pointed at him. *It's not even a full moon. How the fuck can he be here?*

He finally spoke.

"You have not called me."

I blinked, disoriented for a heartbeat as I remembered vague snatches from the dream I'd had at my desk. "Wh-what? Call you? What are you talking about?"

He moved for the first time, shifting with inhuman grace to sit on the bed beside me. "You have not called me." His smile turned dazzling.

I looked at the gun in my hand, then slowly lowered it. It wouldn't do me any good against a Demonic Lord anyway. *Shit. I have a* Demonic Lord *in my bedroom!* "You said that already." I swept a glance throughout the room in a vain hope that I would see something that could explain his presence here. "How can you be here? What the fuck is going on?"

He reached out and stroked my cheek with the back of his hand. "I wished to see you," he said. "You interest me."

"So, what—you just popped over to this sphere to look me up?" My voice was a bit shriller than I would have liked, but I figured I was entitled to a small amount of freak-out after waking up to a Demonic Lord in my bedroom.

He laughed, a sound like crystal in water. It delighted me and at the same time sent shivers through me. "Not so simple as that." His fingers lingered on my chin, brushing my lips ever so lightly. "I am not truly here. I am merely touching your dreams."

"My . . . dreams." I couldn't decide if that was reassuring or not.

"It is not an easy feat, even for one such as myself."

I regarded him with narrowed eyes, initial shock and terror giving way to confusion and distrust. "So why are you doing it?"

He tilted his head, a smile playing on his angelic face. "You are not pleased to see me again? You did not enjoy our . . . tryst?"

I had to privately admit that there was a small portion of me that *was* pleased to see him again. Even knowing what he was now, I couldn't deny that he was awfully damn good to look at, and I sure as shit couldn't deny that our "tryst" had been awfully damn nice. "You didn't answer my question," I said instead.

He gave a slight nod. "As I said: You interest me. I have not encountered another like you in centuries. And the brief time we had together was . . . enjoyable." Without warning, he slid his hand to the back of my neck and leaned in to kiss me. I didn't stiffen or resist—I was too surprised to do either, and by the time it occurred to me that I should make some sort of reaction, he had deepened it into a sensuous kiss that promised pleasure and heat and pulse-throbbing passion. After a moment, he released me and pulled back, regarding me with a smile.

"Well, damn," I breathed shakily. It was sorely tempting to grab him and pull him back for more, but the memory of Tessa's warning about his nature stayed me. *Why is he doing this? There's just no way he's this smitten with me.* "I, uh . . . am flattered to know I have that sort of effect on you." I took a steadying breath. "But please don't do that again."

He lifted a silky eyebrow. "You have regrets?"

"I . . . don't know," I said honestly, relaxing a bit now that I knew he wasn't *really* in the room with me. I grimaced and pushed my hair back from my face. "The thing is, I don't usually do that sort of thing. I mean, the casual-sex thing." I met his eyes. "And if not for the fact that you gave me your word, I'd be worrying that you had somehow compelled me."

His expression hardened ever so briefly. "I did not break my word. The choice you made was your own."

I nodded. "I know, and I'm glad that you let me make that choice."

He stood and folded his arms across his chest, looking down at me. "I wish for you to trust me."

"I don't even *know* you," I said with a touch of asperity. "And you're a Demonic Lord. Why do you care if I trust you?"

"Why do you deliberately avoid and evade companionship?" he countered. "We shared a potent pleasure, you and I. I gave you my word that I would not harm you or compel you. You ache for something that I would gladly give you. Why do you deny yourself?"

He was getting way too close to psychoanalysis territory for my liking. I scowled. "It's not just about the sex, y'know."

"You desire a partner—one with whom you can share your hopes, dreams, desires, and fears. Someone with whom you can face the trials of existence and make plans for the future."

I stared at him in surprise. *Wow.* He got it.

"I cannot be that person for you," he continued before I could speak. "But would you deny yourself the single course placed before you simply because you cannot have the entire banquet?"

He sure did know how to present a convincing argument. But doubt still nagged at me. "Okay, well . . . I'm gonna run with your metaphor here and say that if I have nothing but dessert I'm going to be too sick to enjoy a banquet if it ever comes my way."

He laughed and sat beside me on the bed again. "You are as clever as you are strong. It is no wonder I desire more of you." He reached a hand toward me and then paused, not yet touching me. His eyes met mine. "May I?"

That simple request sent an erotic rush through me that nearly knocked me over. *He's unspeakably powerful, yet he respects my boundaries. . . . Or at least he can put on a good show of it,* my inner cynic pointed out.

"What do you want to do?" I asked, somewhat breathlessly.

"Touch you. That's all. May I?"

"Yes." I managed to choke the word out, pulse suddenly throbbing.

He reached to my breast and caressed lightly through my nightshirt, circling the nipple casually. Heat flooded me, and I had absolutely no fear that it was due to any compulsion from him. This was 100 percent my own reaction.

A smile lit his blue eyes, then he took hold of my nipple and squeezed lightly, releasing it at my intake of breath and returning to a slow and incredibly sensuous caress.

"This is really all a dream?" I said with a shaky grin.

His laugh was crystalline beauty, sharp and bright. "Truly, it is."

"But . . . I'm not just dreaming about you being here. I

mean, you came into my dream, like, um . . . a telepathy sort of thing, right?" The inexorable movement of his hand was making it tough for me to think.

He inclined his head slightly. "That is a reasonable analogy."

I took an unsteady breath. "Look, even though this isn't . . . um . . . real, I'm not sure I want to sleep with you again."

"I respect that," he said gravely. "Yet I would still freely give you pleasure if you would accept it."

Just a dream. Safe. I swallowed, pulse galloping in an incredible combination of anticipation and apprehension. "Why? I mean, don't get me wrong . . . but what are you getting out of this?"

He was silent for several heartbeats, a brief expression of sadness skimming across his face almost too quickly for me to register it. But when he lifted his eyes back to mine, there was only the deep and potent power in them. "I enjoy your company. I wish for you to trust me."

Is he lonely? I wondered suddenly. Did Demonic Lords experience feelings of isolation? *Okay, that's just crazy.* But he was watching me intently, and I found myself giving him a nod of permission.

He placed his hand in the center of my chest and gently pushed me to my back. He kept me pinned down lightly, and I knew he could feel the mad pounding of my heart beneath his hand. He slid his hand between my legs and began to slowly caress me. "There is much pleasure I can give you," he said, voice like silk. "You are safe with me." He slid a finger inside me, slowly working me with an expert touch. I dropped my head back, breathing unsteadily.

"*Daaaamn.*" There was no denying that he was good at this. He'd probably had centuries of experience. I groaned and clenched my hands in the sheets. "Holy shit . . . do you do this often?" I said with an unsteady laugh.

He didn't answer, merely smiled and continued to work his fingers. He kept his other hand between my breasts, giving me just the lightest suggestion of being held down, without making me feel trapped or threatened. My climax began to build and I moaned, squeezing my eyes closed, insanely aroused. He expertly toyed with me, bringing me repeatedly to the point of climax, then slowing and allowing it to retreat until I was nearly screaming in frustration.

He brought me to the peak again when I was near mindless from wanting it, then abruptly stopped, fingers stilling within me as I throbbed and pulsed in need.

"This is not the only gift I could grant you." His voice was soft but intense.

I let out a low whimper. I could feel the orgasm, see it just barely out of reach. All he had to do was flick his fingers *that* way.

I took a ragged breath. "Please . . . What do you want from me?"

"Call me, Kara." He moved his hand, skillfully bringing me to my climax, working me perfectly as I cried out and arched my back in release, keeping me at the peak longer than I could have ever imagined possible.

I gasped unevenly as he finally slowed and gently withdrew his fingers. I opened my eyes and focused on him, with effort. He was watching me carefully, an unreadable expression quickly shifting to a brilliant smile as he met my eyes. He straightened. "Call me to you. I can give you so much more."

———

THE ALARM CLOCK shrilled, sending me fighting through the tangled sheets in shock. It took nearly half a minute of the familiar sound penetrating through the fog that filled my brain before I realized that Rhyzkahl was no longer in the room. I slammed my hand down on the alarm clock to silence it, still feeling the shimmering echoes of the orgasm. Light filtered through the blinds, but I fumbled the nightstand light on as well and looked carefully around the room.

He was most assuredly not there anymore. And a continued inspection of the room confirmed that my gun was still in its usual spot in my nightstand.

"That was . . . unexpected," I murmured, frowning. So he could touch my dreams? I threw off the covers and stood, feeling a ridiculous urge to run through the house and turn each and every light on, unable to shake the lingering sense of disquiet. I didn't feel tired, so whatever he'd done hadn't robbed me of any sleep. In fact, I felt quite rested.

I worried my lower lip as I padded barefoot to the kitchen. *But he can come to my dreams. That's . . . fucked up.* Even *with* a mind-scrambling orgasm. Or maybe because of it. I hadn't expected to ever encounter him again, and yet he'd sought out my dreams just to . . . to what? Just to please me?

I put on a pot of Café du Monde coffee with chicory, allowing my thoughts to ramble unchecked as it brewed. *Call him. He wants me to call him.* He'd said that several times. But what the heck was that supposed to mean? Did he want me to summon him again? He was out of his demon mind if he thought I was going to attempt a summoning of a Demonic Lord—especially after somehow fucking up a fourth-level summoning.

I groaned. I wasn't at all willing to risk summoning him,

but here I'd had a powerful arcane Demonic Lord in my dream and I'd completely missed my chance. *I could have asked him about the traces and the symbol!*

I sighed and poured my coffee, adding significant amounts of creamer and sugar to dull the bite of the chicory. *I wonder if Rhyzkahl would really tell me what I want to know if I called him.* Though it would probably help if I knew what this "call" entailed. *He said "call," not "summon,"* I mused. What was the difference?

I took my mug out to the back porch and sat on the wooden swing. The view was limited to a small wooden shed and the woods that surrounded my house, but it was quiet and serene and usually allowed me to forget about the outside world. I didn't maintain anything resembling a lawn around the house, and this time of year, wildflowers sprang up in chaotic arrangements anywhere there was enough sunlight. A mockingbird sang lustily from somewhere nearby, and I tucked my feet underneath me while I curled my hands around the mug, warming my hands against the morning chill and trying to settle my nerves.

"Right, settle your nerves by slugging down some double-strength coffee," I muttered to myself. But coffee was one of my comfort foods, and next I'd go after the chocolate and the potato chips.

The memory of Rhyzkahl's visit was vivid, unlike a dream, which would have faded to haziness by now. Had he merely touched my dreams? I had to admit, there was no physical evidence on my body or in the room, which would have been there had he been present in the flesh.

Just a dream. Just a strange and erotic and unsettling dream visit from a Demonic Lord with whom I had a one-night stand. Nothing at all to get worked up about.

I scowled and finished my coffee, then showered and

dressed. And on the way to the office stopped and bought a half dozen chocolate doughnuts.

I SPENT THE morning in my office on the Internet, running queries on absolutely everything I could think of, from demons, to symbology, to blood magic and anything else that popped into my head. By lunchtime, I'd come up with a ridiculous amount of useless information—most of it inaccurate—and had eaten all of the doughnuts.

I groaned and leaned back in my chair, feeling slightly ill from the massive quantity of sugar and fat slogging through my bloodstream and frustrated and uneasy about my lack of progress on the case.

Oh, yeah, and my dream visitor who sure as hell didn't feel like a dream. That was just one more piece of fun to throw into the mix.

A dull headache began to pound behind my eyeballs. I sighed and rubbed at my temples, then on a whim leaned forward, pulled up a search engine, and typed in the name of the comic book that my aunt had shown me.

"Hot damn," I breathed. It was apparently a fairly popular graphic novel, with a pretty comprehensive website devoted to it—ordering information, history and storyline, and even quite a few sample graphics.

Including pictures of Rhyzkahl.

Okay, it probably wasn't actually him, but how the hell had this guy managed to draw something so damn close? I hit the print button on my computer as I continued to scrutinize the pictures. I hadn't examined the comic very closely at my aunt's house, so I took the opportunity now.

It was him. The more I looked at it, the more certain I became. The white-blond hair, the Adonis-like build, the enigmatic smile, and the crystal-blue ancient eyes—holy shit, the eyes! Somehow this artist had seen or met Rhyzkahl before.

I clicked through the site, looking for information about the artist, but it was surprisingly bare. That was odd. You'd think that an artist would want to promote himself. Or herself. There was only a name: Greg Cerise.

But even if there wasn't much artist information on the site, there was a page all about how to order and where to order from. To my surprise, the address for mail order was a local P.O. box.

"So how did this artist encounter him?" I murmured to myself as I did another search on the artist. On a whim I pulled up LexisNexis.

I narrowed my eyes at the information on the screen. Now, wasn't that some shit? Not only was there actually a person named Greg Cerise, but—surprise, surprise—he lived in Beaulac.

A thrill of excitement ran through me. I could go talk to him, find out what he knew about Rhyzkahl—get a viewpoint other than my aunt's. And I could even justify going while on duty, since I knew that the murders were connected somehow to the arcane, right?

Okay, so that was a stretch. The guy drew pictures of my demon lover. That hardly qualified as a connection. I suppressed my insistent twinge of guilt and tried to ignore the voice that reminded me that the chief had recently chewed me out for acting like a nutjob. *Yeah, well, the chief has no idea that the Symbol Man is working in the arcane.*

I allowed myself a smug smile as I quickly printed out the address information. *Being a nutjob might prove to be a job requirement.*

THE HOUSE DIDN'T LOOK LIKE MUCH, JUST A SINGLE-STORY brick thing with unadorned windows and lackluster landscaping. The lawn had been mowed in the past few days and there was no trash in the yard, but it had a kept-up-just-enough look that made me suspect Mr. Cerise rented the place. A dark-blue Toyota Corolla with two flat tires was parked in the driveway, and a quick peek inside revealed what looked like a gym bag in the back seat, a pile of papers that looked like they might contain drawings, and several crumpled bags from various fast-food establishments. I jotted down the license number in my notebook on the off chance I might need it later, then made my way up the cracked walkway.

"He's not there during the day," I heard from behind me before I could ring the bell.

I turned to see a woman standing at the edge of a driveway on the opposite side of the street. She was easily well into her eighties, dressed in bright yellow velour sweatpants and jacket, with her silver hair pulled back into a bun so tight that I decided the woman probably had twice as many wrinkles as were immediately evident.

"He's usually gone all day," she said, glancing up and down the street before crossing, chin up and a fixed smile on her face. I could see the woman's eyes flick busily over me, from my clothing to my badge and gun, all the way down to my shoes.

I could peg this one. The ultimate in nosy neighbor. As a detective, I usually loved this sort. As a person, this was why I had a house twenty minutes away from civilization.

I gave the woman a bright smile. "I appreciate the information. I'm Detective Kara Gillian with the PD. Do you know where he works?"

The woman wrinkled her nose. "A pleasure to meet you, Miss Gillian. I'm Nora Dailey. And Mr. Cerise doesn't work."

I didn't miss that Ms. Dailey had deliberately left the "Detective" off my address, but it wasn't worth making a fuss over right now. "He doesn't work? So where is he during the day?"

"Oh, he hangs out with all sorts of unsavory characters down at that church, that outreach center," she said primly.

That was a new one. I didn't usually hear about unsavory characters and churches in the same breath. Well, except from my aunt. "I'm sorry, I'm not sure I understand. What does he do at the center?"

Ms. Dailey rolled her eyes. "Oh, heavens, he sits at that place and doodles in a notebook, sometimes talking and joking with those drug addicts." She made a disgusted noise. "If he's not careful, he's going to end up just like them!"

Yeah, wouldn't want anyone to actually reach out to those

people. I knew the center she was talking about. A couple of years ago, several of the local churches had cooperated to create a community outreach center that I had to grudgingly admit was proving to be pretty effective. Though I was about as far from a churchgoer as one could be, even I had occasionally steered people who were having trouble coping toward the place. It had also become the "in" thing to be involved with for local politicians, and just about anyone of any importance was on the board of directors in some capacity.

But now I was intrigued about Mr. Cerise. "I'm sorry, I don't understand," I said, being deliberately obtuse. "He does drugs with them?"

Her eyes widened. "Well, it's possible! It's not just that outreach center either. He wanders in bad sections of town, hangs out in the park, gives money to bums . . ." She gave a not-so-delicate shudder. "Plus, he dresses like a hippie, and with that long hair of his . . ." She gave a sniff. "I've called his landlady several times about him, but all she says is that he pays his rent on time and doesn't cause any problems." She made a face. "I don't know why she won't listen to me."

"Did she ever live here?" I had a suspicion as to why the landlady didn't pay much heed to Ms. Dailey.

The woman nodded. "Oh, yes, for several years. Then she got married and moved to the other end of the parish. She put the place up for rent, and he moved in near the beginning of this year."

No wonder she doesn't listen to you. She's dealt with you in person, I thought, controlling my urge to snicker.

"Is Mr. Cerise in trouble?" Ms. Dailey continued, her expression eager and hopeful, very obviously wanting it to be true so she could have proof that all her suspicions were correct.

"Oh, no!" I said with wide-eyed disingenuousness. "I'm just here to talk to him about his volunteer work with crippled children," I lied smoothly.

Her smile turned rigid and forced. Ms. Dailey's disappointment was obviously crushing, but she put on a brave face. "Ah. I see. How nice."

"Is Mr. Cerise a bad neighbor?"

Ms. Dailey wagged her head. "Oh, he just worries me to death." Now she was changing her act to Concerned Neighbor. "He comes in and out at such strange hours." Then she leaned close and lowered her voice. "But at least he isn't *black*," she said, giving me a knowing nod. "I was worried when Dana told me she was renting the place out, and I even asked her to make sure she didn't rent it to any of the wrong sort."

I somehow managed to keep my face immobile. "Well, don't you worry about anything, ma'am, and I appreciate the information about where to find him."

Ms. Dailey gave a sniff, then spun and marched back across to her house, bright yellow velour swishing with each step.

I watched her go, feeling ever so slightly soiled, then returned to my car. If I were that landlady, I think I'd have been tempted to rent to the "wrong" person just to annoy Ms. Nora Dailey.

MOST OF THE churches that had sponsored the outreach center were in the middle of town, a lovely area with clean streets and flowering trees and a pleasant view of the lake.

The outreach center was nowhere near there, since the nice people who diligently attended worship didn't care to have the tourist section of town marred by such a thing and didn't want to have to actually *see* any of the people who used the center. As a result, the outreach center was located several miles away, on the outskirts of town, well away from the lake and any possible contact with tourists.

Trash lingered a bit longer in the streets here, the sidewalk was cracked, and the few trees were scraggly, pathetic things that did little to improve the looks of the area. The stores were a far cry from the dainty antiques shops and upscale clothing stores that could be found in midtown. Instead, there were scatterings of secondhand-clothing stores, pawnshops, and the occasional bail bondsman. A diner of questionable cleanliness did a fairly steady business across the street from the center.

The building that housed the outreach center was unremarkable—a two-story white structure made of cinder blocks and aluminum. The sign above the double glass doors in the front was peeling and leaning at a dubious angle, but the glass was spotless, and there was no trash out front.

I pushed in through the doors and walked down a short hallway, entering what looked like a common room. I saw the eyes of everyone inside flick to me and then quickly away as soon as they marked me as a cop. There were about half a dozen people in the room, watching TV, flipping through magazines, or quietly playing board games. There was an unoccupied pool table in the corner and an unused computer on a scarred metal desk against the wall. Faded inspirational posters were scattered on the walls, some with "artistic" additions and commentary that had likely been done by the people who were meant to be inspired. I scanned the room, vaguely recognizing a couple of faces from encounters on the street, then realized with chagrin that I had no idea what Greg Cerise even looked like. Well, I knew that he dressed like a hippie and had long hair. Unfortunately, that didn't narrow it down too much in this crowd.

"Detective Gillian?"

I turned at the sound of my name, then smiled as I saw the preacher from last week in the park approaching. This time he was dressed in attire that made it far easier for me to believe he was a clergyman—dark pants, oxford-style shirt, modest-size crucifix on a chain around his neck. "Reverend Thomas," I said with a smile. "It's good to see you again. I didn't think I'd run into you over here."

He smiled, weathered face crinkling around his eyes. "My church is heavily involved in this center. I like to come by here and help out when I'm not too busy." His expression turned more serious. "So what brings you down here? Do you have any more information about Mark?"

I shook my head. "No, I'm sorry. I'm still working on that. Actually, right now I'm looking for a man named Greg Cerise. I was told he sometimes comes down here. Do you know him?"

A flicker of what might have been surprise crossed Reverend Thomas's face, so quickly that I didn't have time to fully identify it. "Yes," he said, with the barest of hesitations. "Yes, he's here. He's not in any sort of trouble, is he?"

What was it with thinking this guy was in trouble? "No, I just wanted to talk to him about some of his artwork."

Relief suffused his features. "Oh, whew." He gave an apologetic grin. "Sorry. I like Greg. I really do, and I think he's incredibly talented. I just worry about him sometimes."

"Why is that?"

He spread his hands. "I can't really put my finger on it. He's a nice guy, but he seems very lonely. He's not a 'loner,' though," he said, making quote marks with his fingers. "He gets along with everyone, and I think he's really made a difference to some of these folk. He's a terrific artist, and he draws a lot of the people here, but . . ." He smiled. "It's hard to explain, but it's as if he draws the reality of what they *could* be. It's for this comic book he puts out. But when the people see the drawings he does of them, it . . . it makes a difference."

Now I was intrigued. "How so?"

"I think it makes them see what they have the potential to be and motivates them to achieve it."

"That's fascinating. Is he here?"

Reverend Thomas nodded. "He's upstairs, in the office all the way at the end of the hall on the left. Just go through the meeting hall and you'll see the stairs in front of you. Greg tends to spend the mornings out here with the people or down at the park and then works up in the office in the afternoons. He rents it from us." He gave a small laugh. "We've told him he could have the space for free, but he insists on paying for it. He says he can't get as much work done at home, because there's always something else that needs to be done, and this way he doesn't see the laundry and the dirty dishes." He gestured in the direction of the meeting hall. "You can go on up. He doesn't mind interruptions."

"Thanks, Reverend. And I'll let you know as soon as I find anything out about Mark."

He gave me a warm smile and took my hand, squeezing it gently. "I appreciate everything you're doing. Let me know if you need anything from me."

I returned the squeeze, then turned and headed through the doors to the meeting hall and up the stairs.

Even though the carpet was stained and worn, the place was kept as clean as it was possible to keep an old building. There were no inspirational posters upstairs. The walls and doors were bare up here, except for one. It wasn't hard to figure out which office was Greg's; it was obviously the one with pencil sketches and fragments of scenes pasted haphazardly all over it. I took a moment to peruse the drawings, narrowing my eyes in satisfaction as I saw rough sketches that closely resembled several different levels of demon.

I tapped politely at the door.

No answer. I leaned my head toward the door. I thought I could hear someone in there moving around. I knocked again, a little harder.

Still nothing. I grimaced. I didn't want to make a big scene and pound on the door, but I also didn't want to walk away empty-handed. I sighed and gave a normal police knock.

The door was yanked open so suddenly that I took a defensive step back, then recovered and took stock of the man in the doorway. Above-average height, wearing worn jeans and a dark T-shirt, with light-blue eyes and a slender, unmuscled build. He was older than I'd expected, with gray scattered throughout his shoulder-length light-brown hair and lines adding texture to his face. Probably about my aunt's age, I decided, and with an open almost-smile on his face that made him seem incredibly likable even before I'd spoken word one with him. A smell of cigarette smoke clung to him, and I could see a scattering of ash on the front of his shirt.

The almost-smile split into a true smile and he laughed. "I'm so sorry," he said. "I was listening to music on my iPod and was caught up in a little project, and then I heard the knocking on the door so I leaped up, thinking it was some kind of emergency, and then instead it's a gorgeous woman, and I'm sitting here wondering what kind of lottery I won!" His grin was beyond infectious, and I found myself grinning as well.

"No lottery," I replied. "Sorry. Actually, I'm with the police." I handed him my business card. "I'm Detective Kara Gillian. I was wondering if you might have a few minutes to talk to me?"

The grin vanished, replaced by a wide-eyed-little-boy expression of awe. "Oh, wow, police! Has something happened?"

Was he really this innocent or was he one hell of an actor? "No. To be honest, this isn't really a police matter. I'm hoping you can help me out with something." This would get weird and uncomfortable if he'd never actually met Rhyzkahl. What little rep I had would go south pretty damn quick. "You're Greg Cerise, the artist for the *Shattered Realm* comic, right?"

The smile returned, shy pride, but now with a touch of wariness. "Yeah, that's my best work. What do you need to know?"

I shifted my notebook in my hand and gave a mild grimace. "This may take a moment to explain. Do you mind if I come in so we can talk?"

"Oh! Sure. I'm so sorry. Come on in!" He stepped back and gestured me in. He was like a puppy, all eager to please. A thick odor of nicotine surrounded me as I stepped into the office, which was so small I thought I could probably touch both walls at the same time by extending my arms. There was a small desk with a portable drawing table set upon it, with a work in progress of what looked like a mermaid fleeing a sea creature. An ashtray overflowing with butts perched precariously on the arm of a chair, and the walls had the faint yellowish stain of nicotine. Every wall was covered with more sketches and drawings, a few in color but the majority in either pencil or pen and ink. There was also nothing arcane in the room, I noted. No traces or resonance, which would be there if anything related to the arcane had ever been done in that room.

"Have a seat!" Greg said before I had a chance to examine any of the drawings on the wall closely. He picked up a stack of notebooks from a chair and dumped them onto the floor. I sat carefully as he perched on the edge of his work chair and looked at me expectantly.

I took a deep breath. This was where it was going to get weird. "Okay, this is going to sound kind of . . . out there," I began. I pulled out the picture that I'd printed from the website. "Who is this?" I pointed to the drawing of the character that so resembled Rhyzkahl.

Greg went still, looking down at the drawing. I watched him closely as his animated face shuttered and withdrew, color fading in it like a dress left in a store window for too long. He gave the casual shrug that I was expecting. "It's just a drawing. I mean, all my stuff is fictional." He looked up at me, an expression of puzzlement on his face, but after seeing the true animation of before, I could see how this expression was a pale copy of his true emotions. He shrugged again, one shoulder twitching up on command. "It's no one. Why?"

I touched the image lightly with my forefinger. "I don't

think this is no one." I looked up at him with a small smile. "I think this is someone you met once."

He swallowed visibly but gave another shrug. Each time he performed the gesture it became more and more twitchy and awkward, as if descending down a slope of unbelievability. Could he really be this ingenuous? If not, he was a fucking good actor.

"You can't really be serious," he said, shaking his head in a quick vibration. "It's no one. Just something I thought of."

I leaned forward, lowering my voice to make him work to hear me. "No, it's not just something you thought of. I need to know when and where you met him."

He paled completely this time, color draining away. "I . . . don't know what—"

"Yes. You do," I said softly. "You know his name. You've seen him."

A bead of sweat formed on his forehead, and I watched in morbid fascination as it began to make its way down the side of his face.

"You don't know," he said, voice cracking. "You don't know what you're talking about." He looked at me with fear in his eyes, and I suddenly realized that it was not the usual fear that the public has for the police but a fear that I was something more. *Well, I am*, I thought.

I turned the piece of paper around so that he could see the drawing fully. "His name is Rhyzkahl, isn't it?"

He let out a strangled moan and rose from the chair. I stood as well, not certain if he was about to bolt.

"How . . . Oh, dear God, how do you know that?" He looked at me with terror forming in his eyes.

I let out a breath, relieved. I'd been a little worried that perhaps I was making myself look like a total idiot with this insistence that this was Rhyzkahl. With Tessa's help, of course. Tessa had led me on many other wild chases that had proved embarrassing and fruitless. It was strangely refreshing to find that this one might actually pan out.

But right now Greg Cerise was terrified of me. Well, maybe he could stay terrified of me, at least a little. I drew myself up. "Because I've called him to me."

To my shock and dismay, he laughed and relaxed. "Oh, right. *You* called Rhyzkahl. You? Who are you?"

I blinked. "I'm a summoner."

He sat down again, this time leaning all the way back in his chair and looking up at me. "Okay, I can *maybe* buy that. Maybe." He shook his head. "But there's no way that you called Rhyzkahl."

I scowled and sat, feeling myself losing ground quickly in this questioning. "Then how do I know that you know him?"

He shrugged, a true gesture this time. "A picture? Someone told you?" He leaned forward. "So, if you're a summoner, who's your mentor?"

I suppressed a sigh. I'd definitely blown this interview. "How do you know about mentors? You're a summoner, too, aren't you?" I said, struggling to regain control of the conversation.

He laughed. "Hell, no. That's not my path." He reached over to the table, shook a cigarette out of a pack, and stuck it in his mouth. He tilted the pack toward me, offering, then lit the cigarette when I shook my head. "I've just been around some who are."

I tilted my head. "Oh? Who?"

He gave me a smile that was back to being nice. "What was your name again?"

I didn't bother to hold back the sigh this time. "Kara Gillian."

He laughed. "Oh, man. I wasn't paying attention when you introduced yourself at my door. I don't usually pay attention to names. I mean, not on purpose. But I'm kinda ADD, and names tend to slide right by me. Two seconds after someone introduces themself I have to ask their name again." He grinned at me. "Is Tessa your aunt?"

Oh, jeez. "Yeah," I said, resisting the desire to slouch. "Tessa Pazhel is my aunt."

He nodded. "All right, then. I believe that you can summon." He took a long drag off the cigarette and shook his head. "But trying to say that you summoned Rhyzkahl?" He rolled his eyes. "That's a stretch to believe for anyone with any clue."

I was quickly going from liking the guy to finding him intensely aggravating. I leaned back in the chair, away from the smoke, and folded my arms over my chest. "And why is that?" My voice was calm, but there was certainly challenge in it.

Greg looked at me, pausing with the cigarette halfway to his mouth. "Because you can't just *summon* Rhyzkahl. Not and survive. He's a Demonic Lord." He snorted in a way that reminded me way too much of my aunt. "So either you're a completely clueless summoner—and those don't stay alive very long—or," he pointed at me with the cigarette, "you're fucking with me and trying to get me to say something." He took a drag off the cigarette and then leaned forward and stubbed it out on the arm of the chair. "You don't need to fuck with me." He gave me a smile that was back to being normal and friendly. "Just tell me what you need to know."

I put on a sweet smile. "I would very much like to know how you know what Rhyzkahl looks like."

Greg sighed and scrubbed his face with his hands. "Your aunt knows. I mean, we were there together."

I frowned. "You two are friends?" Tessa had never mentioned him.

He spread his hands, regret tingeing his expression. "We were friends when we were young and even dated awhile when we were teenagers. But even the best of friendships grow apart. We went our separate ways a long time ago. I don't get out all that much. I like what I do, and I don't like people all that much."

I couldn't help but smile. "Yeah, I can understand that."

The corners of his eyes crinkled. "You probably do. You get to see the worst that humanity has to offer. That's one of the things I like about a small town. Fewer people to avoid." He grinned. "I went to New York for a few years, trying to do the whole artist-in-New-York thing, but I couldn't take the whole big-city attitude and could barely afford to live. Then, this past December, I found an investor for the comic, so I moved back down here in January. And sales have been picking up every month."

"That's terrific," I said, since I knew that was expected. But that wasn't what I was interested in. "Can you tell me how you saw Rhyzkahl?"

He pulled another cigarette out of the pack but didn't light it. "It was almost thirty years ago. Tessa and I had both just turned seventeen." He grimaced. "My father was a summoner." He slowly tapped the cigarette against the pack. "Tess and I used to spend a lot of time together. Even when we were little, you know, back in the days when kids actually went outside and played instead of the crap now where they sit inside and play video games—"

"Or read comic books?" I couldn't keep myself from interjecting.

Greg gave a small bark of laughter. "Oh, no, they had comics back then, and we read plenty of 'em. But then we'd go outside and pretend that we were those superheroes and bad guys." He smiled, a reminiscing look on his face. "We had long complex stories . . ." He shook his head. "Then when we got older we moved on to other interests. Anyway. My father was a summoner, as was Tessa's mother."

I couldn't completely keep my face still as that bit of information sent a shock through me. Fortunately, Greg wasn't looking at me and didn't seem to notice my reaction. *My grandmother?*

Greg let out a heavy breath. "My father was pretty well skilled. He had no problems calling the minor demons and even called high-level demons fairly regularly." Greg's expression grew brooding. "Then my mother became ill. Cancer. I took her to the doctor, but . . ." He shook his head as if to dislodge an unpleasant memory. "My father decided that he needed the level of . . . assistance that could be gained only from a Demonic Lord." He crumpled the cigarette in his hand, watching the flakes of tobacco drift to the floor. "My mother and Tess's mother, Gracie, were the best of friends, and so Gracie assisted my father in his plan to summon a lord. There were a total of six summoners there—my father, Gracie, a husband and wife from here in town, and then two solo summoners from New Orleans. And, of course, my mother, though not in the circle itself. They all wanted this chance to perform such a major summoning."

I tried to breathe silently, not wanting to do or say anything that could distract from the tale.

"I knew that my father was planning this summoning.

He'd decided he would try to summon Szerain, a minor lord who supposedly was more open to this sort of assistance with the proper callings and terms. I . . . didn't agree with my father's decision. I told him so, several times." Old pain flickered in his eyes. "I knew when they were going to attempt the summoning and I didn't want to be alone, so I asked Tess over. Tess and I . . . well, we used to go down to the basement to fuck." His mouth quirked in a boyish smile, while I tried not to show my surprise at the frank admission. Then shame flickered briefly across his face. "I didn't tell her why I wanted her to come over. Just let her assume . . . Anyway, that night we were going at it hot and heavy when we heard people coming down the stairs, so we hid and watched."

He took a dragging breath. "I have no idea what went wrong—whether it was the way the call went out or the way it was received out in the other sphere. Tessa told me later that she believes that when one summons a lord, there are different forms and protections and terms that have to be used." He shrugged. "I'm not a summoner, so I didn't really know what she was talking about."

I swallowed and said nothing.

"Anyway, the circle made the call to Szerain," he continued after a moment, "and something came through. Only it wasn't Szerain."

"Rhyzkahl," I murmured, forgetting my desire to stay silent.

Greg nodded. "They invoked the bindings, but . . ." He shuddered. "They didn't realize what they'd done. Didn't realize at first that it wasn't Szerain—that they'd summoned a lord who was *not* amenable to such things." He rubbed his arms. "They didn't realize how dangerous and powerful he is. He's so . . ."

"Beautiful."

He looked up at me. "You *have* seen him."

I just nodded.

"Damn," he breathed. "Someday I want to hear how *that* happened."

"Finish your story, please?" I urged.

He ran his fingers through his hair. "He was . . . angry, God almighty, so angry. I could feel it, like a smothering blanket. The bindings that they had were useless. Rhyzkahl scattered them and . . ." He paled, his hands beginning to shake.

I leaned forward. "What happened?"

Greg clenched his hands together. "I don't remember everything. But what I do remember is that he knew that Tess and I were there. I don't know why he didn't destroy us like the others, but he knew we were there."

"How do you know?"

He looked up at me. "Because he said so. Pointed right at us while his hands were still—" His voice faltered. "His hands were still covered with my mother's blood." He gave a low moan and dropped his head into his hands. "My father asked him to remove her cancer. And he did. God almighty, he did. Every bit of it. Ripped it all from her. It's been almost thirty years and I still remember that. My father lying dead at his feet, and my mother . . ." He shook his head, unwilling or unable to say anything more.

I was silent for a moment, then risked touching his knee. "Was everyone else killed?"

Greg took in a heaving breath. "Yeah. It was a slaughter. A fucking slaughter. As soon as Rhyzkahl finished and left, Tess grabbed my hand and dragged me out of there." He scrubbed at his face. "She kept her head, I'll give her that. I was totally hysterical, nearly catatonic. She got me away and to a safe place, then she went back and dumped every can of gasoline we had down the stairs and started a fire. Covered it all up." He sighed, and I could see him pushing the memories back down. "Her mother had been killed, too, but she held it in until it was all over."

Suddenly so much about my aunt made sense. *What a hideous burden to hold for all those years.* I felt an odd twinge of guilt for some of the unkind things I'd thought about Tessa. And there was a small part of me that wanted to deny, to refuse to believe that it could have been the same Rhyzkahl, the same Demonic Lord that had killed all those people, but deep down I knew that it was true, knew that he was capable of wreaking that sort of vengeance to satisfy his honor. I'd felt that same rage coming from him, that same capacity for slaughter, before he inexplicably changed his mind and decided to seduce me instead.

"I'd always heard that it was a heater explosion during a cocktail party," I said.

Greg shrugged, color beginning to return to his face. "There wasn't much of an investigation. I mean, back then they didn't have CSI. And the fire was so hot that there wasn't much left anyway. They just went in and found bone fragments and teeth and didn't think much more of it except that it was terribly tragic. I mean, this is a small town." He laughed weakly. "Which is kinda funny when you think about how many damn summoners were living around here."

I nodded, but it made perfect sense to me. There were areas of arcane power here that tended to draw in people with the ability to take advantage of them, which was one of the reasons that New Orleans was such a hotbed of the "supernatural."

I closed my notebook. "I appreciate you telling me all of this, Greg," I said, standing.

He stood as well. "You've seen him. And you're alive. How?"

I shrugged, an unconscious imitation of him. "I wish I knew."

I STOOD AT THE DOOR TO MY AUNT'S HOUSE, STARING at the blue-and-white wood with the stenciled flowers at the edges and the way-too-cheerful *Welcome!* sign on the door, working up the nerve to knock and face her. Okay, facing my aunt wasn't the big deal, but telling her just what had happened in my summoning was. *She's going to freak. Totally fucking freak.* I sighed and knocked. It was past time that I talked to her about it. I'd been finding every possible reason to put it off in the last few days, and now two weeks had passed since the summoning.

My aunt pulled the door open a split second later. "Took you long enough to knock," she said with a questioning smile. "I was starting to wonder if you'd fallen asleep on my doorstep."

I stepped inside, automatically wiping my feet. Today my aunt was wearing a full Japanese kimono with an expertly tied obi—with her frizzy blond hair in two ponytails that stuck out from the sides of her head. Shockingly, it worked on her.

"If you knew I was out there, why didn't you open the door?"

"You were obviously deep in thought about something. And I hate it when people interrupt me when I'm deep in thought, so I figured I'd let you finish first." She smiled brightly, then closed the door with a shove of her sandaled foot. "Okeydokey, sweetums. What's cookin' in that head of yours?" She eyed me shrewdly, and I was reminded yet again that, despite my aunt's eccentricities and mannerisms, she was smart and perceptive and more than a little dangerous, though not to me. So far. She might yet kill me after hearing what I had to say.

"I need to talk to you about my summoning. I mean, about what happened in my summoning."

As if a switch had been thrown, Tessa was all seriousness. "Yes, it's about time we had that talk, but I knew there was no point in doing so until you were ready." She took my arm in a gentle but inexorable grasp and led me into the kitchen, pushing me onto a wrought-iron stool and then setting a cup of steaming tea in front of me as if it had been conjured. *Don't be silly, she can't conjure. She just saw you on the step and got it ready.*

Tessa sat on the stool on the other side of the counter and folded her arms in front of her.

I took a sip of the tea. Sweetened just the way I liked it, just the right temperature, and not one of those hideous fruity teas that Tessa usually favored. *She's worried about me,* I realized. Knowing now what I did about the death of my grandmother, I found myself understanding—or, at least, willing to accept—a bit more about my aunt's manner. Tessa had been seventeen and her sister, Ellyn—my mother—had been nineteen when Gracie Pazhel and the other summoners were killed. Michael Pazhel had dealt with his grief over the loss of his wife by examining the bottom of a bottle of Jack Daniel's. About a year later, Ellyn escaped by marrying my father, Marcus Gillian, leaving Tessa to figure out her own way in life.

I'd never really thought about it before, but Tessa had probably felt terribly abandoned by her older sister. Add to that the stress of finding her way as a new summoner, and Tessa had basically decided not to give a rat's ass what other people thought of her. Under "normal" circumstances, her mother would have become her mentor and trained her as a summoner. Instead, Tessa had been forced to go to Japan, to a summoner there who'd been willing to take on a student.

I took another sip of my tea, stalling. *No wonder she and my mother barely spoke. And no wonder she resented the fact that, before she was even thirty, she got saddled with raising a preteen kid and had to put her own life on hold.* Those first few years together had been unpleasant in a variety of ways. Tessa hadn't tried very hard to hide her displeasure at being forced to completely change her life to care for a niece she'd met only once before. And I'd responded like any preteen would to the enormous loss of everything I'd known—by developing discipline and attitude problems and being an overall pain in the ass. In fact, if it wasn't for the fact that I had the ability to summon, I think we'd have each given up on the other. Through the summoning of demons, we'd found a common ground—and just in time too. I was barely into high school and I'd already gone considerably beyond "experimentation" with a variety of drugs. As soon as Tessa confirmed that I had the potential to become a summoner, she—finally—laid down the law, telling me that I could become an arcane practitioner, too, but I had to clean up my life first and prove that I was worth teaching.

And I did. It took a couple of years, but this time she took an active interest in me and helped me kick the drugs and get my life back on track.

"Okay," I began, setting the cup down, "so here's the thing. I *know* I called Rysehl. I've gone over it in my head a thousand times, and I just know that's the name I said."

Tessa was silent for a breath, then gave a reluctant nod. "There *have* been other instances of someone else coming through during a call."

I hesitated, wanting badly to ask about the summoning that Greg had described. *No, I need to figure this one out first. Then I can ask.*

"So, I called, and this other . . . demon came through. I mean, I thought it was a demon, and so I invoked the usual bindings and protections." I spread my hands on the flecked black granite of the counter, not looking at my aunt. "He just laughed, and said that 'this would prove interesting.' Then he broke the bindings." I shook my head. "No, that doesn't even describe it. He just swept them aside like they weren't even there."

"Yes," my aunt said. "Those sort of bindings are completely useless against his sort."

I fiddled with a fingernail. "I tried to escape—I mean, just run away, but he made it seem like the stairs weren't there anymore."

"An easy enough illusion for him."

"Yeah, and I even knew it was an illusion, but that still didn't help me."

Tessa exhaled gustily. "A Demonic Lord would be too strong for simple denial to work."

"And so then he . . . um, came up to me, and . . ." I took

a deep breath. "Okay, so I figured that I was totally screwed, y'know? I mean, I didn't know who or what he was, but I knew he was bad, and powerful, so at first I figured it was just going to get really ugly and he'd throw me to his minions or something, but then he totally changed and got all sexy and I was—"

"Kara!" My aunt's voice was a verbal slap. "Just *tell* me what happened."

I groaned and dropped my head to the counter with a *thunk*. "I fucked him. Or, rather, he fucked me. Okay, we fucked each other. Fuck."

My aunt was silent, and after a moment I dared to lift my head slightly and peer up at her through my bangs. Tessa was looking off into space, chewing her bottom lip.

"What did he say?" Tessa said after a moment.

"When—before, during, or after?"

Tessa gave a bark of laughter. "I can only imagine what was said during. 'Oh, baby, yes yes yes!' or something to that effect."

I smiled ruefully. "Not quite, but I suppose it's not that important."

"So what did he say *afterward,* you impudent girl?"

I sat up again. "He said that he knew that my call had not been for him."

Tessa's frown deepened. "And then what?"

"Then he got dressed and said, 'Kara Gillian, you may call me whenever you need me.' And then he was gone."

Tessa stood and took her cup to the sink and ran water in it, standing with her back to me. "I don't know, sweetling. That sounds very . . . odd."

I watched my aunt wash the cup. I could see her hands shaking as she dried it and set it in the drainer, and I realized with an abrupt shock that Tessa was deeply upset. That was why she was facing away, so that I wouldn't see it.

"Yeah, it's kinda freaky," I said casually, giving my aunt time to recover. "I thought I was dead meat, then he seemed to change his mind. But it doesn't make any difference now. I mean, well, obviously I'm not going to summon him again." *But he can come to my dreams. . . .*

Tessa turned, gripping the towel. "No, silly girl, you don't get it. You don't need to summon him now. You can just call him to you."

I blinked at Tessa, dream visit forgotten. "Okay, yeah, I understand that, but . . ." I paused, then shook my head. "Okay, maybe I don't understand. I can call him without doing a formal summoning ritual?" Is that what he was talking about? What was the big deal about that?

Tessa dried her hands briskly. "That's what he said. Call him. Just call him, with intent. Saying his name like normal isn't going to do it, which is a damn good thing, the way you've been throwing it around." There was a touch of asperity in her voice, which was a curious relief. She was getting back to her regular self. "But he's set some sort of connection to you now. I've heard of these things before, but only in the ancient literature." She busied herself with hanging the towel back on its rack for a few seconds. "The only problem is, if you call him, you still don't have any control over him. All that does is let him through." She turned and gave me a look of deathly seriousness. "He'd be here in this sphere without restraint, without terms, without any bonds of honor controlling his actions. Don't you even *think* of calling him, Kara."

"I'm *not*!" I held up my hands. "Do you think I'm a moron?"

Tessa frowned at me. "Gimme a break, Kara. Of course I don't. I just want to be sure you understand the danger."

"I'm not going to call him," I repeated with a sigh.

Tessa gave a short nod. "Good to hear, because the last thing this place needs is an unrestrained Rhyzkahl seeking to expand his power base. That would be worse than a Rhyzkahl summoned and controlled by an unscrupulous summoner."

I frowned. "Wait. So he *can* be summoned—and controlled?"

Tessa plopped back onto the stool. "It's possible, I suppose. But the amount of power and preparation needed would be incredible."

An icky feeling began to form in the back of my head. But now wasn't the time to tease it out and examine it. Instead, I picked up my cup and took it to the sink.

"Hey, do you think I could borrow that graphic novel that you showed me the other day?" I said as I washed and dried the cup. "I'm curious to see what kind of story it is." And I wanted to see more of what this Greg person was like.

Tessa smiled, obviously relieved by the change in subject. "Sure thing, sweetling. I'll go get them."

Them? I didn't have too much time to think on that, because in about ten seconds Tessa was back, with a stack of what looked like a dozen volumes.

"All right, this is the entire series, and please do take care of them because these are in good condition. That means don't crack the spine, don't spill anything on them, and don't read them in the bathtub!"

I took the stack of comics from my aunt, resisting the urge to scowl. So much for my bathtub reading plans. "I'll be careful. I promise."

My aunt gave me a brisk nod. "You'll love them."

I sure hoped so, because I had a nagging feeling that these were somehow important. "I'll let you know, Aunt Tessa. Okay, gotta go!" I said, hefting the stack of graphic novels and heading toward the door.

It wasn't until I got to my car that I took a look at the cover of the one on top. *The Shattered Realm Saga, Vol. 1—Visits and Dreams.* And that's when I realized that I'd neglected to tell my aunt about the dream visit. I turned around to go back inside, then stopped at a trill from my pager. Shifting the books in my hand, I pulled the pager off my belt clip and read the message with a rising feeling of dread. Another body. A woman, found in an alley behind the outlet shopping center.

Telling my aunt about the dream visit was going to have to wait.

ANOTHER VICTIM. I DUG MY FINGERS INTO THE CUSHIONING on the steering wheel as I drove, the sick feeling increasing. That made three murders in less than two weeks. They'd never been this close together before. *He's building up to something, and it's going to be soon.* Why take the risk otherwise? The previous murders had been at the rate of one every two to three months, not more than one a week.

But with three in two weeks, the heat was definitely going to rise on this shit.

I wonder if I'll be allowed to stay on the case? A small pang of dismay went through me at the thought of being removed, but I knew that with three murders it was pretty likely, considering my inexperience. I'd understand, though I sure as hell wouldn't be happy about it. *Think positive; maybe they'll form a task force now.* I suddenly realized that my feelings on that were mixed. It would be terrific to get more manpower and more resources, but how the hell was I going to explain the arcane aspects of the case without looking like a complete nutjob? Plus, would I have to work with Agent Obnoxious?

I sighed. I was being stupid. I needed all the help I could get. And I also had to accept that there was a very real chance I'd get pulled off the case completely so it could be handled by someone with more experience. Which was pretty much anybody in Investigations.

I pulled up to the mouth of the alley that ran behind the stores, joining the throng of other police vehicles. The area where the body had been found was known as the outlet mall, but that was a poor description for what it was now. Ten years ago it *had* been an outlet mall, but it had lasted as such for less than a year, the victim of a very poor layout, a lousy location, and greedy local politicians. In its second year, the stores had begun to pull out in desperate acts of self-preservation. Eventually it was a run-down strip of empty storefronts, interrupted occasionally by a struggling entrepreneur who had been lured in by the low rent. Unfortunately, even the folks who tried to tough it out ended up going out of business, since the rest of the mall was so trashy no one wanted to go there to shop, simply out of fear for the safety of themselves and their vehicles.

I walked past the other cars, taking stock of the vicinity before getting to the actual scene. About half a dozen battered yellow Dumpsters were spaced along the alley, each surrounded by scattered trash that had missed its mark. I didn't think that the Dumpsters had been emptied in several months, and the aroma of old garbage clung to the area like mildew in a shower. There was enough room to drive a car down the alley, but not many people would be willing to risk their cars passing over all of the debris back here.

I also knew I wouldn't be looking through any surveillance video of this scene. Even though there were a few cameras left on the corners of buildings in places where people couldn't get to them and steal them, there hadn't been film in them in many years.

I looked ahead and saw my captain talking to three men by the crime-scene tape that had been stretched across a section of the alley. My steps slowed. I'd been right; I was finally getting some help. *Be careful what you wish for, right?* I thought with a grimace. *But hopefully this means I'll be staying on the case.* After all, I'd been paged to report to the scene. That had to be a good sign.

Special Agent Kristoff, aka Obnoxious, was one of the men speaking to Captain Turnham. Another of the men was much shorter than Kristoff, and when he turned I bit back a groan. Detective James Harris was with the St. Long Parish Sheriff's Office, a supercilious man who was very full of his own importance and thus difficult to get along with. A couple of inches shorter than me, he had a thick build with a paunch that stretched his dress shirts to their limits and a fleshy, ruddy face that tended to get even redder whenever he was annoyed. Unfortunately, he was fairly good at his job, had experience with ritual and cult murders, and was no doubt more than eager to get on a task force for this sort of case.

I didn't recognize the third man—though judging by his suit and his haircut, I figured him for a Fed as well. He looked like he was barely eighteen, with short blond hair and a healthy tan that made him look more like a surfer. I knew he had to be older to be an agent, but I did have to wonder just how long he'd been with the bureau.

"Oh, yay, now *everybody* gets to think I'm a nutjob," I muttered, resisting the urge to go back to my car and do a quick makeup check. Since I'd visited Tessa on my way to work, I was at least dressed like a detective today, in a red tailored shirt with dark-blue dress slacks and matching jacket. I'd even remembered to accessorize, which in my world meant that I'd stuck little pearl stud earrings into the holes in my earlobes.

Captain Turnham gave me a nod as I approached. "Gentlemen, this is Detective Kara Gillian. She's been the primary on these cases. And," he said with a quick glance at me, "as I said before, I intend to keep her on as the detective in charge."

I struggled to keep the professional smile on my face. My captain had been serious about having a rookie detective on the lead! Unbelievable. And I had the distinct impression that there'd been some discussion about this already. Kristoff wore a stony expression, while Harris was actively frowning, face red. The only one who looked at me with a smile was Surfer Boy.

"Gillian, this is Agent Zachary Garner," Captain Turnham said, indicating the blond agent. "I believe you've already met Agent Ryan Kristoff, and I'm sure you know Detective Harris, with the sheriff's office."

I shook their hands in turn, but my attention was already on the body that I could see beyond the tape. I smiled and murmured something appropriate, then turned away and ducked under the tape, distantly realizing though not caring that the three had followed me. The arcane energy practically crackled on this one, and it nearly took my breath away.

I stopped several feet from the body, and when Agent Kristoff continued forward, I threw up my arm to stop him, only realizing that I'd done so afterward. I looked up at him and gave a grimace of apology. "Sorry . . . uh, just thought that there was something on the ground there."

He frowned and peered down at the ground, taking off

his sunglasses to do so. *Damn, he has pretty eyes,* I thought again, then gave myself a mental slap to get my focus back.

Cautiously stepping forward, I watched the arcane flickers crawl and twine about the body. *This is freshly dumped,* I realized. *This is what the shit looks like unfaded.* I let out a sound of frustration. There was absolutely no way that I'd be able to get my aunt here, not with the Feds present.

"Are you all right, Detective Gillian?" Agent Kristoff asked.

I realized I was standing with one foot off the ground. I quickly put it down, avoiding a strand of energy that had wiggled off the body and was already beginning to fade. "I'm fine. There's just evidence here that I don't want to lose."

Kristoff narrowed his eyes and replaced his sunglasses on his face. Harris cleared his throat and stuck his thumbs behind his belt. "We realize that, darlin'. That's why our crime scene people and yours are going to cover every inch of this area and process the body as well."

I forgot to hide the scowl as I looked at Harris, obscurely pleased that he was short enough for me to look down at him. "Can I at least have a few minutes to look before your folks come swooping in to save the day?" *Darlin'? It's "Detective," asshole,* I wanted to add.

Harris's face reddened again. *Crap, there goes your Tact and Diplomacy merit badge again, Kara.*

"Detective Gillian," Kristoff said, voice unbearably cool and even, "our greatest desire is to work together with local law enforcement in order to accomplish the apprehension and conviction of the perpetrator of this series of criminal acts."

I blinked. Then I gave him a bright smile. "Cool! Thanks,

darlin'!" I smacked him lightly on the arm and turned back toward the body. "I'll just be a minute, then."

I heard someone stifle a laugh behind me. I knew it couldn't have come from Kristoff or Harris, so I figured it had to be Garner. Could Feds even laugh? I'd always thought that the ability had been burned out of them in their training.

I ignored them and crouched about a foot from the body. Even as I watched, the strands were dissipating. Another twenty minutes and they would be just smudges. Definitely a fresh dump. And, unfortunately, not too difficult to believe that it could be dumped here unseen. "Who found the body?" I asked no one in particular, not taking my eyes off the arcane leavings.

"Anonymous call," Garner answered. "No luck tracing it."

He wanted us to find this body quickly. But why? I couldn't wrap my mind around any answer that made sense. I could accept that the body at the treatment plant had been found quickly by accident, but the one at the ball field had been in plain sight. And now this one—with the phone call to make sure that we found it quickly. I was missing some key connection, some compelling reason for the change in method.

I leaned closer, looking at the ground beside the body. A single strand of arcane energy was twisting, and I realized with a shock that it was forming and unforming a rune. Excited, I hurriedly pulled my notebook out and sketched the rune, shielding the page from the eyes of the others as best I could. As soon as I was done with that one, I focused on another, sketching it as well. I forgot about the men clustered behind me as I slowly crabbed my way around the body, sketching runes as I saw them. Finally, when all the runes had faded away, I stood and closed my notebook.

Kristoff had taken his sunglasses off again, a frown creasing his forehead as he eyed me. Harris stood with his arms crossed and a dark scowl on his face. *Crap, they think I'm totally crazy.* Now I had to hope that the chief wouldn't hear about this.

Kristoff's eyes slid away from me and went to the body on the ground. I followed his gaze and realized with a guilty start that I had yet to actually look at the body.

She was nude, with dark hair that had been permed a few too many times. Bile rose in my throat as I looked at the girl's eyes. At first glance I merely thought that the girl had died with her eyes wide open, but then I realized with a sick jolt that the eyelids had been cut away. Like the others, she had the deep ligature marks in her throat from strangulation, and she also had the hundreds of precise slices on her limbs and torso, just like the first girl. I looked for and found the nicks in the veins at her elbows, but when I looked to see if her ankle veins had been cut as well, I had another jolt: the girl's achilles tendons had been cut.

No chance to get away. Had she tried to escape? Had she fought back?

"Jesus," Agent Garner breathed. "He cut her eyelids off."

I glanced up at him and nodded, then went back to examining the body. I couldn't see the symbol, but I knew it was there. This was my guy. I *knew* it.

Kristoff frowned. "I don't see that trademark symbol on her."

"It's there," I replied.

Harris spoke up, tugging at his tie. "This could be a copycat. The details of the symbol have never been released to the public, correct?"

I turned to look at him. "You're right, it hasn't, but just because you don't see it right here doesn't mean it's not on her somewhere. A couple of times the pathologist has been the one to find it. Plus, the other two *did* have it."

Harris pursed his lips sourly. "These murders have never been so close together, either, or so easily found. It would make sense that these newer ones might be a copycat."

I shook my head. "No, there are—" I stopped. How the hell was I going to explain the arcane smudges? "There are other details that are similar."

"What other details?" Harris challenged. "We've read all your reports."

Crap. I hadn't expected them to be up to speed so quickly. "All my reports? How?"

Agent Garner spoke up with a smile. "Your captain forwarded everything to us after the body was found at the park. We were actually going over the details for getting the task force organized when this call came out, so we headed right on over here."

Okay, he was definitely a newbie. He hadn't learned how to be a dick yet. "Ah, well, there are still some things in my notes, you know. I didn't realize my captain had spoken to y'all." I turned and glared at my captain, but he was too far away to feel my gaze.

"What were you sketching, Detective Gillian?" It was Agent Kristoff again, watching me with a carefulness that was close to unnerving.

I gave him a bright, ingenuous smile. "Oh, you know. Doodling to get my thoughts in line." Okay, so they were going to think I was crazy *and* incompetent. This was just great. "Look, guys, how about we meet up back at the station and go over all of this?" I really did want the resources of the task force. I just didn't want them to think I was nuts.

"That's acceptable," Harris huffed, glancing at his watch.

"We'll meet you back there in one hour." It wasn't a question.

I plastered an accommodating smile onto my face. "One hour works for me."

"And bring *all* of your notes," Harris said.

"Oh, absolutely, guys. I'm eager to get y'all's take on this stuff." I even meant it. Sort of. But I realized that I was going to have to be careful to keep Harris from walking all over me.

Just like keeping a demon in check.

Harris and Garner turned to walk back to the cars. I began to follow them but stopped when Kristoff put his hand on my arm.

I frowned and looked down at his hand on my arm, then back up at him. "Is there a problem?" I asked, tone icy, refraining from saying something equally nice like, *Get your fucking hand off my arm, asshole.*

He didn't release my arm. Instead, he glanced to see that the others were still walking away, then leaned in closer to me. "You saw something on the ground. What was it?"

I clenched my jaw and pulled my arm away from him. "I didn't see anything. I was just making notes."

His expression darkened. "Detective Gillian, we do not need to be withholding information from each other. If you saw something, you need to share it with me."

And have you order a commitment hearing? Fat chance, darlin'. "If I had information that would benefit you in the slightest, I promise I would be sure to pass it on."

He made a noise of frustration in the back of his throat, then jammed his sunglasses on and stalked away. I watched him walk off. *He's going to put an eye out if he keeps this shit up,* I thought, then followed after him and returned to my car.

I WAS FEELING ornery, so I took my time getting my notes together, deliberately making the others wait a few extra minutes. I was also dawdling because I'd begged and pleaded and wheedled and promised Saints tickets to Dr. Lanza, and he'd relented and told me that he would go ahead and perform the autopsy on the latest victim that afternoon.

"I'll let you know the instant I find it, Kara," he told me after I'd reminded him for the sixth time that I really needed to know where he finally found the symbol.

That he would find it I didn't doubt. But I wanted that info quickly, to prove to the Feds and Harris that I had a fucking clue.

Now you just have to prove to them that you aren't fucking crazy, I reminded myself, as I entered the room and plopped my notes onto the table. The others glanced up at me, then returned to their perusal of the photos spread before them. Each murder from both series had been separated into a section of the table, with the photos of the facial reconstructions or IDs at the top and the crime scene photos distributed below.

I cleared my throat, and they all looked back up at me with a variety of expressions: Kristoff frowning, Harris glowering, and Garner smiling.

"The, uh, old bodies were all too decomposed to make any sort of ID," I began, gesturing to the pictures of the clay faces, "so the previous investigators had a forensic anthropologist work up some reconstructions, just to get a starting point."

"Any luck?" Agent Garner asked.

"Four IDs were made, confirmed with DNA," I said.

"Not bad."

"I don't know how much time y'all have had to read through the case files," I said as I began to sort through my notes. "One thing I did want to point out is that the symbol is not always in an obvious location." I resisted the urge to look pointedly at Harris.

Kristoff nodded, frown still on his rugged face. "The one where it's on the tongue is particularly gruesome," he said, as if he were describing an ice cream flavor.

"Yeah, and they're also all premortem injuries," I continued. "In fact, the injuries on each of these victims show that they were inflicted over a period of several days, sometimes up to a week."

"All of the victims died of ligature strangulation?" Garner asked.

I shook my head. "The first eleven victims were killed in a variety of ways—stabbing, shooting, drowning, you name it. Victims twelve and thirteen from before the three-year break were strangled with a ligature, as were these last three. On the first two of these latest deaths, the pathologist said that there was indication that the ligature had been tightened and released several times, judging by the bruising pattern on the strap muscles. He's performing the autopsy on this latest one today, and he said he'd call with his findings."

Kristoff leaned back and crossed his arms. "Repeated strangulation. More torture."

I nodded and sat down. "None of these victims died nicely or quickly. It's as if he wanted them to be in as much agony as possible."

"Or as much fear as possible," he said quietly.

I looked at him. "Or both." We locked eyes for a moment and then I broke first, pulling my gaze away and clearing my throat. "Anyway, the previous detective wasn't able to find a link between the victims, other than the fact that they're all the type who aren't missed." I grimaced. "But I'm not sure how hard he tried."

"You haven't found a link either," Harris interjected, and I couldn't tell if it was a question or a challenge.

"No," I replied as evenly as I could. "But I've had the case for only two weeks."

"I'm sure you're doing your best," he replied, and once again I wasn't sure if he was being understanding or condescending.

I decided not to take issue with it. The rest of the meeting was uneventful and, to my relief, actually worthwhile. The agents had the potential to be patronizing and annoying, but they also had significant training and access to greater resources than did my dinky little department. Even Harris had some useful input, once he stopped being obnoxious and belittling.

This is cool, I thought, even though I didn't hold out a lot of hope for success in a mundane route. But, then again, with the murders coming so quickly now, maybe he would slip up and make a mistake. *If we have that time.* I rubbed my temples. I couldn't shake the growing certainty that he was preparing for something big.

"Detective Gillian?" Agent Kristoff's voice broke through my train of thought. I sighed and looked up at him. To my surprise, I saw that the others had already left. I'd been so absorbed that I hadn't even noticed. "You know this murderer better than any of us," he continued. "Do you think this increase in murders is going to continue?"

I blinked, somewhat surprised at the admission that I could possibly have insight into the killer's mind-set. I ran my fingers through my hair. "I . . ." I grimaced. "I think he's gearing up to something. Something big."

"Such as?"

"I'm . . . not sure," I said, truthfully enough. I had my suspicions, but I sure as hell couldn't voice them.

He leaned toward me across the table, green-gold eyes on mine. "But you have suspicions?"

Jeez, could he read my mind? "Well, yeah," I said, doing my best to not squirm uncomfortably. "But they're all pretty nebulous, y'know?"

He leaned back and gave me what looked suspiciously like a friendly smile. "Well, why don't you air them out? Sometimes these kinds of brainstorming sessions can really open up some new avenues of thinking."

That was Fed-speak for, *Tell me everything you know.*

Like hell, darlin', I thought. But maybe I could air out a few allusions. "Well, I think he's . . . um, attempting to do something arcane. Or what he thinks would be arcane."

He gave a grave nod. "So, some sort of death magic? A ritual of some sort?"

I watched him carefully. "Yeah. Something along those lines."

"Perhaps some way to gain some sort of influence or power?"

I could feel my eyes narrowing, and I had to force my face to relax. "Sure. Why make the effort otherwise? It has to be worth doing all of the torture and murder."

He nodded again. "Perhaps to summon some kind of arcane creature." He flicked a glance at me. "I mean, he could be operating under the belief that he could do that sort of thing."

"Right." This was getting strange. "An arcane creature

that would require a great deal of death magic to hold and control."

"Maybe some sort of demon?" He tilted his head and shrugged.

An odd buzz of excitement ran through me. "Yes. That makes a lot of sense. I think he's . . . I mean, I think *he* thinks he's going to try to summon a demon." I watched him closely for his reaction. To my surprise, he didn't flinch or twitch.

"I'm inclined to agree," he said instead.

"You do?"

"Yes. He could be planning to summon a demon." He tapped his chin thoughtfully.

I blinked at him, thoughts churning until I remembered what my captain had said about Agent Kristoff being involved in a ritual-murder task force. *Okay, so this line of thinking isn't totally bizarre to him,* I thought, oddly relieved. *He's probably thinking a demon-from-hell kind of demon, but at least he's open to the general idea.* "Right. He . . . um, believes that he's gathering power, using the torture and the prolonged deaths, and especially the blood. I think he's going to try to summon a—" I stopped. I'd been about to say, "higher demon," but I suddenly knew that wasn't right. Even an unwilling *reyza* wouldn't explain the need for murders, the gathering of that much potency. A chill crept through me. "He's planning to summon a lord," I breathed. "A Demonic Lord. That makes perfect sense. This has been going on for almost a decade, and that's probably how long a preparation for that kind of summoning would take if the summoner wanted to avoid being ripped to shreds. . . ." I trailed off and looked up at Agent Kristoff. Had I really just said all that? Out loud? *Shit.* "I mean, that's what he thinks. I think. I mean, you know, that he thinks he can call up a Demonic Lord." *Shit.*

"That makes sense," he said, voice intense and quiet. I stared at him in shock, but for the life of me I couldn't see anything in his expression or demeanor that indicated he was toying with me or teasing me.

"Excuse me?"

His eyes were steady on mine. "You were sketching runes, weren't you? By the body."

My throat felt oddly dry. "Are you really an agent?"

"Could I see your sketches, please? I wasn't able to see them very well at the scene."

I just stared at him. "No, really. Who are you?"

His mouth twitched. "I'm really an agent. I swear. I just have . . . well, my grandmother always called it 'othersight.' It's not very strong, but it's helped me out on a few cases. And that's why I tend to get assigned to anything that they think might be 'satanic' or the like." He rolled his eyes and I smiled, surprised and pleased.

I hesitated several more heartbeats, then opened my notebook to the page with my sketches and pushed it over to him. He examined them carefully, chewing his bottom lip in a fashion that was very un-Fedlike. After several moments he looked up at me. "I think your othersight is a lot stronger than mine," he said, without a hint of rancor or jealousy.

I shrugged. *Don't relax too much,* I reminded myself. *Just because he understands you doesn't mean he won't screw you over later.*

"So, what are these runes? I don't recognize them," he said with a touch of chagrin in his voice.

"I don't know," I said honestly. "I'm going to have to ask someone who knows more than I do."

He gave me a crisp nod. "I'd appreciate it if you could let me know as soon as you learn anything." He handed my notebook back to me. "And thank you for trusting me," he said as I took the notebook back. His smile was genuine as far as I could tell.

I gave him a careful smile in return. "Just don't make me regret it."

MY CELL PHONE rang as I was walking out to my car, with Dr. Lanza's name on the caller ID. "Hiya, Doc," I said as I answered the phone. "Where'd ya find it? You did find it, right?"

"Kara," Doc said, voice strangely rough, "I've been a forensic pathologist for almost fifteen years, I've done over five thousand autopsies, but I've never ever seen anything like this."

"What are you talking about?"

"I found the symbol."

"Okay. Where was it?"

Silence.

"Doc?" I prompted. "Where was it?"

"Jesus, Kara. You're not going to believe this, and I have absolutely no explanation for how the symbol got there. I mean, there are no entry wounds to explain it. . . . I suppose it's *possible*, but—"

"Doc! Where the hell did you find it?"

"It was . . . on the inside of her uterus, Kara. Just, for the love of God, please don't ask me to explain how it got there."

After I hung up, I sat in my car and stared at the phone. If I'd ever wanted physical confirmation that these murders were arcane in nature, I'd just gotten it. Could a demon have placed that symbol? Tessa had said that there were two sources of the traces. Could the killer be summoning and using a demon to help? Once again, I was way out of my depth.

Explain that one, Harris.

I WENT HOME AND SCANNED THE SKETCHES OF THE RUNES and sigils into my computer and emailed the scans to my aunt, but Tessa had no familiarity with any of them, to my disappointment. *I need some expert advice. I need to summon a demon.* A sliver of unease ran through me at the thought, which in turn angered me. I couldn't be afraid to summon. I couldn't just *stop* being a summoner. It was too important to everything that I was now.

The door to the basement beckoned to me, but I found myself hesitating. I still didn't know how the last summoning had gone so badly awry. That one had been as close to a disaster as any summoner could get—and still survive. *And I survived that only because . . . why? I got lucky?* The question continued to plague me despite every effort to push it aside. I was more than willing to give myself a compliment or two, but I knew that I was no drop-dead beauty with the looks and charm to stop a Demonic Lord in his tracks.

I was stalling. If I was going to summon, tonight would be a decent night to do so. There was no moon, which lent a certain stability to the proceedings, though potency was low. It was easiest to summon during a full moon, especially for higher-level demons, but I had no intention of getting crazy with this. *Maybe I could summon Kehlirik again?* He owed me a favor, which meant that it would be fairly safe to summon him. And surely a *reyza* would be able to identify those runes.

I considered it for several minutes, but finally, reluctantly, discarded the idea. It was true that I wouldn't have to expend as much energy for protections and bindings, but the mere act of summoning a twelfth-level demon would take more potency than would be available during the dark of the moon. I'd have to wait until the next full moon to summon Kehlirik.

Tonight I would make do with just a very low second- or third-level demon, hopefully one who could give me some clue about what was going on with these bodies and translate the runes and sigils for me. A very small and simple summoning.

In fact, it might be best that I'm doing this while the moon isn't full, I decided. With luck, the lack of potency would prevent anything unexpected from happening again. *Though it would be a lot easier to prevent something from happening if I knew just how the hell it had happened in the first place!*

Before I could change my mind or chicken out, I marched over to the basement door and yanked it open.

Cold, stale air pillowed out of the door, and I realized with a guilty start that this was the first time I'd opened the door to the basement since that night with Rhyzkahl. The awareness sent a deep spear of chagrin through me. I couldn't afford to be weak like that. I couldn't lose my focus. And I certainly couldn't be afraid. Not and be a successful summoner. Summoners had to be cautious, wary, and vigilant, but fear caused you to lose focus. The time for fear was afterward, when you could learn from it.

I flicked the lights on with the switch at the top of the stairs. With fluorescent lighting, the basement hardly looked like an arcane summoning chamber. My annoyance with myself grew as I looked around, seeing the implements still left out from last time—the candles on the floor, the knife on the carpet, the chalk and the oil near the smeared diagram.

"You suck," I scolded myself, but I could still do this. It was early—barely seven p.m.—which gave me plenty of time to do the necessary cleaning and preparing.

It didn't take me long to get into the rhythm of the cleaning. I wasn't usually a neat and tidy sort, but, when my mind was scattered, it was one way that I could get my thoughts gathered.

My house was ready well before midnight, the chamber cleaned and my garments hanging on the hook at the bottom of the stairs. I took a shower, then wrapped my fuzzy bathrobe around me as I walked to the front door to check the lock and pull the curtains closed.

I nearly jumped out of my skin when a knock sounded on the door just as I was turning the lock. I scowled, taking a breath to settle myself as I stood there with my hand on the lock. Who the hell would be coming by at this hour? No one ever came to visit, which was fine with me. I was too far from the road for it to be someone with an emergency.

Shit. I hadn't placed any arcane protections around the house yet. I'd planned to save those for last, since they were such a pain in the ass. I stood quietly for a moment, waiting to see if the person would leave, but that hope was dashed when the knock came again, hard and heavy. Like a police knock. *Shitfuckdamn.*

I peered through the peephole, shocked to see Agent Kristoff standing outside my door. I frowned, trying to see if anyone was with him. I couldn't see anyone else, but the peephole didn't exactly give the best view of the porch.

I tugged my robe closer about me, snugged the belt tight, then unlocked the door and pulled it open about three inches. He was wearing a long-sleeved black oxford-style shirt and khaki dress pants—a really good look for him, I thought in an incredibly private part of my mind. The porch light did interesting things to his facial features as well. He had a fairly rugged face, like a man who wasn't afraid to work outdoors and get his hands dirty, but the overhead lighting made him look positively craggy. I couldn't help but mentally compare his face with the unearthly and perfect beauty of Rhyzkahl, and that same incredibly private part of my mind wasn't sure which I found more appealing.

I gave myself a mental slap to get back to the here and now. "Agent Kristoff. Are you lost?"

"No, Detective Gillian," he said. "I was wondering if you had a few minutes so that we could discuss some of the aspects of the case that we were, ah . . . unable to go into at the station?"

I stared at him. "Now?"

He gave a half shrug. "Well, yes. I'm sorry. I know it's late, but there aren't too many opportunities that I'm going to have to speak to you without the others around."

Well, that was most likely the truth. I grimaced and glanced up at the sky out of habit. *No, you're not going to see a full moon, silly. You're doing a full-dark summoning.* I looked back at him. "Your timing is kinda awkward."

He blinked, then his mouth twitched. "Oh, I'm sorry. I

didn't realize you might have company. I didn't see another car in your driveway."

I groaned. Yep, that's exactly what it looked like, answering the door in my bathrobe and not wanting to let him in. "Oh, good grief, no! There's no one else here." I ran a hand through my still-damp hair. "No, I was just . . . uh . . . getting ready to do something."

He gave an apologetic smile. "Sorry. I hope I wasn't being insulting just now."

"No." I suppressed the sigh. "Heck, if you knew me any better, you'd know that it's pretty damn rare for me to have *any* company here."

"Now that's just a damn shame," he said, still smiling.

Was he *flirting* with me? "No, I mean, any company, not just male company. Though I don't have any of that either. Crap! I mean . . . Crap." I pulled the door all the way open. "Just come in," I growled, turning away and stalking down the hall to the kitchen before I could humiliate myself any further, if that was even possible. Why didn't I just tell him straight out that I hadn't had a boyfriend in three years? And that I hadn't gotten laid in—

I winced as I scooped coffee into the coffeemaker. No, I'd gotten laid just a couple of weeks ago. Though technically I could still claim that I hadn't had a *man* in a while.

I dumped the water into the top of the machine and jammed the start button, then turned back to him. He stood in the doorway of the kitchen, leaning against the jamb with his hands in his pockets, watching me with an amused yet puzzled expression on his face.

"I'm sorry," he said. "I didn't mean to bring up a sore subject."

I shook my head. "No. It's not like that." I tugged the belt a little tighter. "I just don't like people coming out here. I don't really like having visitors." I realized after the words left my mouth how rude that had sounded.

But he didn't seem to be at all fazed. His gaze traveled around the kitchen, taking in the spotless white tile, the yellow flowers painted near the ceiling, the matching towels, the copper trivets hung on the wall. "Well, you keep a nice neat house, even if you aren't expecting company."

I crossed my arms. "Sorry to burst your bubble, but this isn't how this place usually looks."

"Oh?" He arched an eyebrow at me. "So you *were* expecting visitors tonight?"

I hesitated. He obviously had knowledge of the arcane, and he seemed to be accepting of the concept of "demon summoning," but that didn't mean he knew about the kind of demons I dealt with and the kind of summonings that I performed. Summoners—my kind—weren't exactly a dime a dozen. I'd never asked any of the demonic ilk, but I didn't think there were more than a hundred or so in the entire world. Supposedly there'd been more a few centuries ago, but as the world had changed and evolved, knowledge of the arcane had gradually faded.

Best to play it safe. "No visitors," I said. "I just try to make a point of cleaning up at least once a month. You caught me on a good day."

"Ah," he said. "I thought that maybe . . ." He trailed off, looking oddly discomfited.

"Maybe what?"

He shrugged. "Well, you seemed to be pretty familiar with the concept of demons, and Demonic Lords. I thought that you might be, well . . ." He gave a self-conscious laugh. "I thought that maybe you were a summoner."

Holy shit. He does know! "Umm." Oh, what the hell. "Okay, I am," I said, before I could change my mind. "I'm a summoner. And . . . I was going to try to summon to-night."

His face lit up and he pushed off the doorway. "Seriously? You are? You're a summoner? Of demons? That's too cool!" Then he grimaced deeply, shaking his head. "Shit. I can't believe I just said that. Sorry. I sound like a teenager."

I blinked, then grinned. "No, it's okay. I'm pretty surprised you even know about summoners."

He smiled ruefully. "I can understand that. It's not a very common skill, or so I've heard. But with the kind of work I do and the cases I've seen, I've learned a bit about it." Then his smile turned boyish. "And of course my grandmother used to tell me stories."

"Was she a summoner?"

"No. At least, I don't think so. I have a private theory that one of her parents was, and that's where she got some of her ability to sense the arcane. But however she got it, by the time the ability trickled down to me it was pretty well watered down." He shrugged, not seeming to be at all upset by the admission. "So you're really going to summon a demon tonight?"

It was my turn to shrug. I busied myself with pouring coffee and setting out mugs. "I was thinking about it. I was going to see if I could get those runes identified. Cream and sugar?"

"One Equal, if you have it. I thought you could summon only on full moons."

I handed him his mug. He knew more than I'd given him credit for. "Traditionally, yes. And the reason is that there's just more arcane energy available. But if the convergence is high—as it is right now—summoning on the dark is possible if you're only trying to hold a minor creature. And even though it's not as potent, there's more stability."

He held his mug in both hands. "That's what you're going to summon? A minor demon?" He was trying to be calm and cool, but I could see the tightening of his hands on the mug and hear the edge of excitement in his voice.

"Yes . . . but I don't think I'm going to now."

His disappointment was palpable. "Oh. Why not?"

I couldn't help but smile. He was being so very un-Fedlike—a radical departure from his demeanor when we first met. "Summonings require a great deal of preparation, even for a minor demon. And a lot of that preparation is mental."

He winced. "And I've totally blown that out of the water. I'm very sorry. Now I understand why you discourage visitors."

"It's all right," I said as I sat down at the table. "I can still summon tomorrow night. I had a . . . strange experience during my last summoning, so I'd rather not take any chances this time."

He sat down opposite me. "What happened?"

I propped my chin on my hand and regarded him. "Is this Special Agent Kristoff asking?"

He laughed. "No. No, this is Ryan asking."

Damn, but he did have some really nice eyes. And he was a lot cuter when he wasn't being all FBI-ish. "I was attempting a summoning of a fairly 'popular' demon. He's a lower demon, he's summoned quite often, rarely if ever causes any trouble, and is pretty easy to bring through."

"And he decided to act up this time?" he asked.

"Nope. He didn't come through at all. Something else came through. Something incredibly powerful and a thousand times more dangerous. He destroyed my bindings and protections with a gesture." I rubbed my arms, still chilled at the memory of that moment of terror. "And I still don't know why he came through instead of Rysehl."

He was quiet for a moment, brow slightly furrowed. "But you're still alive," he said finally. "How did you defeat him?"

I leaned back in the chair, rubbing my eyes. "I didn't. It's complicated, but he left without . . . um, harming me." I certainly couldn't say *without touching me*.

He ran a finger around the top of his mug, watching me. "What was it?"

"A Demonic Lord."

His eyes narrowed. "I thought you said that they couldn't be summoned."

"Well, normally they can't. And I didn't summon him. He came through instead of the demon I *did* summon. And I don't know how or why." I made a face. "The 'not knowing' kinda bugs me."

His gaze seemed to sharpen on me. "I think you should do it."

I cocked an eyebrow at him. "You're not the one who will get the chance to look at the pretty patterns your blood makes on the stone when it goes wrong."

"Will you put it off again tomorrow?" His tone was challenging. "Knowing what those runes say could be vital to solving this case."

I scowled, stung. "You think I don't know that? I know we need to identify those runes, and I know that asking a demon is probably the best way to go about it. But I'm going to do it when I'm prepared, physically and mentally, and right now you're *not* helping."

He sighed and rubbed the bridge of his nose. "I'm sorry. You're right. It's not my place to tell you to do something that's so dangerous. I wouldn't ask a fellow agent to run after an armed man into a blind alley with no weapons or backup. And asking you to summon when you're not prepared is no different. I guess it's just the excitement of being so close to a summoning." He hesitated. "Look, I don't quite know how the protocols for these things work, but, er, is there any way I could be present for a summoning?" He looked at me hopefully.

"No." My reply was flat, firm, and fast.

He gave a short laugh. "Okay, well, since you've had time to think about it and all . . ."

I shook my head. "Agent Kristoff—"

"Ryan, please."

I took a deep breath. "Ryan, it's not that I want to keep evidence or information from you. But it's just too dangerous. And I have enough uncertainty right now with the botched summoning. The last thing I need is to have you—or anyone—as a distraction in the room. I've also never attempted to keep protections on myself and another person. The only times that I've summoned with another person in the room, the other person was a summoner and didn't need me to provide protection."

"It was worth a try," he said with a smile. "You don't get anywhere if you don't try."

I returned the smile. "I know what you mean."

My hallway clock chimed midnight, and he cocked his head. "It is true that summonings have to be done by midnight?"

"No," I said, "not at all. But it helps if they're completed before sunrise, because everything gets a bit unstable when the potencies shift from lunar to solar. There are some rare summoners who work in the daytime, and they always try to finish before sunset. Same principle."

Ryan grinned. "I feel like I should be taking notes. This is great stuff to know."

I shrugged. "But that's one of the reasons summoners

aren't generally all-powerful people with demons at their beck and call. It's fucking hard to summon a demon, and then it's tough to keep control of a demon for more than a few hours. Especially higher-level demons. They don't like being summoned in the first place." It was certainly possible to keep a demon for longer than a few hours, but that was another skill I had yet to master.

He leaned back in the chair. "So how did you get into law enforcement?"

I curled my fingers around my mug. "My mom died of cancer when I was eight and my dad was killed by a drunk driver when I was eleven, so my aunt came to live with me." Best not to mention the fact that my aunt was a summoner. Let Ryan figure that out on his own. "I turned into something of a wild child—acting out and all that stuff—but somehow I managed to graduate from high school with an adequate GPA." I didn't know him well enough to tell him how I'd nearly destroyed my life with drugs and how finding out I could summon demons brought me back from that edge.

"Anyway," I continued, "when it came time for me to go off to college, my aunt sat me down and had a serious talk with me about how in this day and age education was a priority. I got my act together and went off and got a degree—art history." I rolled my eyes. "Talk about a pointless degree. I found out that there aren't too many jobs that use art history degrees, and after I whined for about three months about not being able to get a decent job, my aunt got fed up, threatened to kick me out, and told me to go apply to the Beaulac Police Department, since they were accepting applications." I smiled. "Best thing she ever did for me. So at the ripe age of twenty-two, I became a street cop, though I think my aunt had something safe like 'dispatcher' in mind when she told me to go apply."

"She sounds pretty no-nonsense."

I let out a bark of laughter. "She doesn't take shit from anyone, that's for sure. I worked as a street cop for five years, then transferred over to Investigations. I've been a detective for two now."

"Are there enough homicides here to keep you busy?"

"Well, before the Symbol Man, there really weren't that many at all. We'd get three or four in a *bad* year. But we're small enough that we don't have detectives who work homicides exclusively. Actually, this is my first homicide case." I fought the urge to squirm in embarrassment. "I worked in Property Crimes before this."

"So you became a cop about the same time the Symbol Man started up?"

I nodded. "The first body was found the day after I got out of the police academy. Of course, as a rookie, I couldn't get anywhere near it." I swirled the dregs of coffee in my mug. "He was dumping the bodies in remote locations back then, too, so they were usually pretty decomposed by the time they were found. But I got the chance to be on the scene of a body dump about three years ago when I was still a street cop. The body had been there for only about two weeks, and I saw what I just *knew* were arcane traces." I looked up at him. "And I've been fascinated with the case ever since."

His expression grew serious. "And you think he's gearing up for a major summoning." He frowned and leaned forward. "Didn't you say something about him possibly preparing to summon a lord?"

"Yeah. It would make sense."

He was silent for a moment. "That's pretty bizarre."

I looked at him quizzically. "What is?"

"Well," he said, voice oddly smooth, "the murders started happening more frequently right about the time that a lord came to visit you."

I stared at him. The pleasant feeling I'd been having about his company began to fade rapidly. My throat felt dry. "No, a lord did not *come to visit* me. He came through without being called."

"Still, it seems like a strange coincidence." His expression was calm, his eyes steady on me.

"Yeah, it is," I retorted. "A coincidence. I have no explanation for it. But Rhyzkahl is not the only Demonic Lord in the other plane," I added, tone icy.

He looked at me levelly, and I got the distinct impression that this was 100 percent Special Agent Kristoff speaking to me now. "I'm just thinking that it's pretty amazing that you're a summoner, and it seems clear that the killer is either a summoner or someone else with strong ties to the arcane. Add that to the fact that the murders started right after you became a cop . . ."

I stood, a slow and hot anger building. "Are you accusing me?"

He remained perfectly calm, no doubt all that fed training in action. "Should I? Don't you think those are strong coincidences?"

I took three deep, careful breaths, using every speck of control I had developed through my work as a summoner to not fly into a rage or burst into tears. Either was equally possible right now. "I think that you have no idea what you are talking about." I was pleased to find that my voice was level and calm, even though I was raging inside. "The chances of having two people working the arcane in one area? Well, if you had the slightest damn clue about how the arcane works, you might know that this area happens to lie on a focal point of arcane power, and thus it's very possible there are quite a few people in the area with arcane connections. And even though summoning is not a common skill, I promise you, I am not the only summoner in the world." I took another breath, trying not to shake. "For that matter, have you considered that the reason I'm assigned to this case is the same reason you're assigned to this case? Because we both have sensitivities to the arcane?"

He looked at me, then gave a slight shrug. "Of course. I don't know what I was thinking."

"You were thinking that I was a suspect," I said flatly.

"Can you blame me?" he said, getting to his feet. "Can't you see the coincidence?"

"Yes, I can, and it really *is* a fucking coincidence. And I *can* blame you. You don't know me. I've been incredibly forthright with you, considering what and who I am. If I was the killer, why the fuck would I tell you that I thought the killer was a summoner and then tell you that I was a summoner too? You came to my house in the middle of the night completely uninvited, I answered all your questions, and then you accused me of being the Symbol Man. So, yes, I can certainly blame you. If this is your style of investigation, I don't need your help. And you need to leave."

His eyes narrowed. "Just remember, you don't have the authority to kick me off the case. The FBI works with you, not under you."

"I have the authority to tell you to get the fuck out of my house, Agent Kristoff!" I said, anger definitely showing in my voice and volume.

"Yes, you certainly do, Detective Gillian," he replied,

drawling out my title in insulting fashion. "Since I am here as a guest. This time." And with that he turned and stalked out of the kitchen and down the hall. A few seconds later I heard the front door open and close heavily, just short of a slam.

I LEANED BACK AGAINST THE SINK, HEART HAMMERING
as I heard the sound of his car engine revving and then
gravel crunching. What the *fuck* just happened? In less than
a minute, the conversation had gone from being pleasant
and friendly to a shouting match full of accusations. And I
had a sick feeling that I knew what "this time" insinuated.
If he truly considered me to be a suspect, the next time he
visited would be with a search warrant.

You were an idiot to trust him! I berated myself. Had any
of his manner toward me been real? Or had the whole thing
been some kind of game to get me to reveal what I knew?

I groaned and scrubbed at my face with both hands. I'd
actually been starting to kind of like him. The nice him—
Ryan. What a mess.

So much for summoning. If there was even the slightest
chance that he would return with a search warrant—and I
knew all too well that, if he was determined, he would find
enough probable cause to get one—I needed to get moving on some serious cleanup and hiding of my implements.

There was no way I'd be able to explain away the summoning chamber. I'd be labeled a "satanist" for sure, probably lose my job, and definitely ruin what little standing I had in the community.

Muttering expletives under my breath, I went to the door to lock and secure it, peeking out first to make sure that he had really left. I changed out of my robe and into sweats, then hurried down into the basement. There were hiding places that I was fairly confident would pass a mundane search, but there was a chance that Agent Kristoff might be able to see any little arcane "touches" I put out.

It took me nearly three hours to clean up the basement and remove all evidence of arcane activity, scrubbing down the concrete floor to erase any traces of diagrams and hiding away my implements. It took me another hour to gather together the potencies to lay a few false trails and place some small protections—all the time certain that the knock on the door would be coming at any minute. Of course, it did occur to me that, if he never came back with a warrant, this whole fiasco had been a good exercise in concealment and use of potency. And, I had to admit to myself, one that I probably should have done a while back.

I stepped back and surveyed the room. To any mundane eye, it looked just like a basement library—a comfortable little quiet study, with smooth concrete floor and wood-paneled walls. To the arcanely trained eye, there was far more to see, but most of it was false trails and muddled signs. *Yep, I definitely need to have a quicker method for hiding and cleaning up.* In fact, I realized guiltily, I really needed to make it a habit to clean up and hide my implements after every summoning, just to be on the safe side. I'd become far too lazy and complacent. A drawback to having hardly any visitors.

The sun was just beginning to poke through the curtains in the foyer as I emerged from the basement, but at least I was ready for him to come with a search warrant now. I sighed heavily and flopped onto the couch in the living room. The clock on the mantel read five a.m. He probably wouldn't be able to get a judge to sign a warrant before eight a.m., unless he wanted to go wake one up. And then it would take at least an hour to get a team together. Enough time for a nap, I decided, eyes already closing. I curled up on the couch, tugging an afghan throw over me. Screw him. I was ready.

"You are entertaining men in your house? Should I be jealous?"

I opened my eyes, blinking in the sunlight shining onto the couch. Someone stood in front of the window, and all I could see was the silhouette of someone tall. "Huh?" I squinted and shaded my eyes. "Ryan?"

The figure laughed, and I went cold. Not Ryan. He stepped forward and now I could see the heavy fall of white-blond hair, the angelic features, the exquisite beauty. He was dressed in shirt and breeches, much like the first time I encountered him, except that this time the breeches were black leather and the shirt was a shimmering green that seemed to catch the light and toss it back into the air. Trepidation stabbed through me as I sat up. "Rhyzkahl. This is another dream, right?"

He smiled brilliantly. "Can you not tell?" He stepped closer and then dropped fluidly to one knee, reaching and stroking the back of his fingers across my cheek, sending a hot thrill of sensation through me. "Do I feel like a dream?"

My breath shuddered in my chest. "You . . . you felt real the last time, but that was only a dream."

His eyes flashed in amusement. "Was it? Perhaps that was real and everything after has been a dream." He leaned into me, breathing against my neck. "The line blurs, does it not?"

I pulled back. "Don't fuck with me like that," I said. "I didn't summon you, so this must be a dream. You're not really here."

"Does it matter if I am here or not?" His voice was soft and silky. "You still can find pleasure from my touch."

"Pleasure isn't everything."

He sat back slowly, regarding me. "An existence without pleasure would be difficult to bear."

I found myself smiling. "True enough. Perhaps I should have said that sexual pleasure isn't everything."

He inclined his head in acknowledgment of my point. "There are infinite pleasures in this existence." He stroked a finger along my jawline. "I would share many such experiences with you, if you would allow me."

I took a careful breath. "If I call you to me."

"Yes. There is little that can be done in this dream state."

But I knew now what such a call entailed. I struggled to change the subject quickly, before he could press me further. "Actually, there is something you might be able to help me with."

One perfect eyebrow arched silkily. "Go on."

I felt suddenly giddy. "I was going to do a summoning tonight—of a low-level demon. But since that didn't work out, maybe you could share a measure of your knowledge with me?"

He laughed. "I have much knowledge, my darling Kara. What could you possibly desire to know?"

"I saw some runes today on a body, and I was wondering if you could tell me what they are." I watched him carefully.

He sat gracefully on the floor, with one knee up and an arm draped across it. "I am intrigued, dear one. Tell me more."

I leaned forward. "They were on the body of a young woman. She'd been tortured and murdered, and I could see arcane traces that had been left behind."

Rhyzkahl *tsk*ed softly, shaking his head. "Such a pity."

I looked at him sharply, oddly jarred by the tone of his response. His expression showed the proper sympathy, but his voice had been utterly devoid of it. "Yes. It is," I said after several heartbeats. "She suffered an agonizing death, and I'm trying to find out who did it. So would you please look at these runes for me?"

His blue eyes glittered. "Of course, dear one. Run and get them for me."

I leaped to my feet and ran for my notebook before I even realized I was moving. I seized my notebook off the table, though the thought occurred to me that I might not be able to read if this was really a dream. And would I be able to remember what he told me? This was getting complicated.

I returned to him and quickly flipped the notebook open to the pages with my drawings, then handed it to him. He stood, looking down at the notebook, running his fingers lightly over the paper. I watched, breathless, as he lifted his hand, pulling a rune from the page in a pattern of writhing crimson light, setting it to spin slowly above his palm. He no longer looked amused or complacent. He regarded the rotating rune with narrowed eyes, silent.

After what seemed like an eternity, I cautiously cleared my throat. "Lord Rhyzkahl, can you tell me what they are?"

"I can," he said, voice suddenly dark and dangerous, all trace of laughter gone. I drew back from him, unaware at first that I had done so.

"They are sigils of control, of binding," he continued.

"So, um, her killer used the runes to control her?"

He bared his teeth and I could feel his forming anger. "No. These are for control of another." He flicked his hand and the rune shattered, fragments of light spinning off and dissipating like scattered droplets of blood.

My throat felt as dry as the Sahara. "Who?" I dared to ask.

He snarled, a wave of fury flowing from him that sent me backing to the wall. His aura swelled, choking me with its potency—an anger even more deep and horrifying than when he'd come through my portal. I slid down the wall, curling in on myself, mewling in terror as the consuming aura of rage and anger smothered me.

I could hear a distant pounding, but the menace and vehemence rolled over me, choking me. Hands grabbed at me and I struck blindly at them.

"Kara!"

I struggled to breathe through the suffocating mire of my fear. More hands clawed at me, pulling me deeper.

"Kara!"

I screamed, flailing against the grip on me. Then pain exploded in the side of my face, and in the span between one heartbeat and the next, the fury was gone.

I gasped for breath, blinking in the light. Someone was shaking me, shouting my name. I felt another stinging blow on my face, and I threw my arms up to defend myself.

"Goddammit, Kara, wake *up*!"

I lowered my arms cautiously. Special Agent Kristoff stood over me, his hands gripping my upper shoulders, a baffled and worried expression on his face. "Jesus Christ, Kara! Are you all right?"

I gulped and sat up, looking furtively around the room, even though I knew that *he* would not still be there. I let out a ragged breath. "Holy crap."

"Are you all right?" he asked, still holding my shoulders, face etched with concern. "I pulled up to the house and I could hear you screaming from outside. I had to break down your front door. I thought you were being eviscerated or something!"

I dragged a trembling hand across my face. "No. I mean, yes, I'm all right. It was just . . . just a nightmare."

He slowly released me and straightened. "That must have been one hell of a nightmare."

I shuddered. "Yeah, I guess you could say that." *Not really a nightmare. I just had an unshielded taste of a furious Rhyzkahl.* My throat felt dry. I'd just had an intense reminder of what he was and what he was capable of.

I looked up at Ryan, suddenly wary. "What are you doing here? Are you serving a search warrant?"

An expression of utter confusion crossed his face. "A what? A search warrant? What are you talking about?"

I crossed my arms over my chest, beginning to feel slightly foolish. "Um, well, after our argument last night, I kinda thought you might come back with a search warrant."

He stared at me for several heartbeats. "Detective Gillian, you are insane," he declared at last. "I came back this morning to apologize for being an absolute ass last night. I don't know what the fuck I was thinking."

I smiled crookedly. "Really?"

He laughed. "Yes, really. Then I heard you screaming and busted my way in."

I looked past him at my front door and could feel my jaw drop. The door hung twisted and broken, barely held by one hinge, and the frame was shattered, with wood fragments scattered throughout my foyer. "Holy *shit*, did you drive your car through the front door?"

He had the grace to look embarrassed. "I really did think something awful was happening to you."

I laughed weakly. "Okay, that's kinda sweet, in its own weird way. Even worth a destroyed door." I stood, tugging my sweatshirt into place, then walked over to the remnants of the door. "But how did you *do* this?"

"I'm stronger than I look, okay?" he said, exasperation showing in his tone. "Kara?"

"Yes?"

He looked at me, head slightly tilted, eyes serious. "Did you summon last night after I left?"

"Not . . . exactly," I said, after a brief consideration of how much to share with him. "But I did get some information about the runes. Come on, I need coffee, and I'll explain." I headed to the kitchen, trusting him to follow.

"Hold on, I'll be right back," he said instead, and exited out the ruined front door. He returned in a moment, carrying a white box, which he placed on the kitchen table. He gave a small shrug. "When you didn't show up for the meeting this morning, I figured you were totally pissed at me, so I decided to bring by a peace offering." He flipped open the lid to show a box full of chocolate doughnuts.

"How did you know?" I breathed, stomach growling in response as I picked one up.

His lips twitched. "I have ways."

I grinned and bit in. "Whatever."

"So what's the deal with the runes?"

I sat down, dabbing at spilled crumbs. "They're runes of binding and control. I think that my suspicions are right—this guy is planning a major summoning and is building an arcane prison, using these victims for the energy." Some unpleasant theories were beginning to take shape in the back of my mind. Rhyzkahl's fury had erupted at seeing the rune of binding. Had he been furious at the thought of any Demonic Lord being bound and controlled, or was it more personal?

Ryan sat across from me, his expression dark and brooding. "You mean it's some kind of death magic?"

"In a manner of speaking, yes, though it's more complex than that."

"No need to go into details. It would probably take too long for me to understand it, and I don't really need to. So," he said, looking at me levelly again, "how did you get this information?"

"That's incredibly complicated. I just need you to trust me that I'm pretty sure my information is accurate."

"Pretty sure?" His brow creased.

"Um, well, this is going to sound weird, but I kinda got the information in a dream."

He blinked, then fell silent for a moment. Finally he shrugged. "Well, I figure there's a whole lot here that I don't understand, so I'm just going to have to trust you on this one."

"Thanks. Like I said, I'm not a hundred percent sure, but I'm about ninety-eight percent, at least."

"So, are you going to try again tonight to summon?"

"Well, it's not as urgent now that I have the information about the runes." I fought the desire to wince at the sudden realization that I was deliberately finding a reason to avoid summoning. *That won't do at all.* But there wasn't time right now to deal with this new neurosis of mine.

He looked at me for several heartbeats, then stood. "All right. Well, I need to be getting back to the office. We're going to try to meet up again this afternoon at three."

I nodded. "I'll be there."

He hesitated, as if wanting to say something else. Then he shook his head, gave me a smile, and departed through the gaping hole in the front of my house.

15

AFTER RYAN LEFT, I SWEPT UP THE SHATTERED WOOD IN my foyer, then wrestled what was left of the door back into position—or at least close enough to drive a few nails into some of the longer pieces of its shattered frame as rudimentary braces.

I stepped back and looked at the door, totally baffled. *A flying side kick? Up the stairs and across the porch?* How the fuck had he done this much damage? But at least he'd woken me from that nightmare. Still, I'd have to scrounge some plywood later to do a better job of securing it. Hurricane season wasn't for another month yet, so I could probably borrow one of the sheets of plywood that Tessa used to protect her store during storms.

My cell phone rang with a number I didn't recognize just as I was putting my tools away in a kitchen drawer.

"Detective Gillian," I answered.

"Detective? This is Greg Cerise."

I straightened unconsciously. "Hello, Mr. Cerise. What can I do for you?"

He laughed, with a trace of what might have been uncertainty. "You can call me Greg. Look, I don't know how this is going to sound, but, uh . . . I . . . I was just wondering if you'd had a chance to read the comic. I mean, if you wanted to, I have extra copies." He sounded eager now, the ingenuous puppy.

"Actually, my aunt loaned me a copy of the series. I definitely want to read them, as soon as I get a chance."

"Cool. That's cool." He was silent for a few seconds. "So, um, I saw an article in the paper about these murders. The Symbol Man stuff."

"Uh-huh?"

"And . . . I saw that you're the detective on the case. Right?"

"Yes, I am. Do you have some information for me?"

"Um, no. I-I was just wondering if you'd come to talk to me the other day because of something to do with those murders. I even came by the station, just in case, but you weren't there."

"Nope. I was just curious about the picture of Rhyzkahl." I glanced at the clock. *Shit. I'm gonna be late again.* I started gathering all of the files and notes that were strewn across the kitchen table into a stack. "Why? Do you know something that I need to know?"

"No! Oh, no . . . nothing like that. I was just wondering, y'know, and then wanted to see what you thought of the comic."

"Well, I've been a bit busy, but I promise I'll give you a call as soon as I get the chance to read them," I said, frowning as I tried to unearth my notebook from all of the crap on the table.

"Oh. Okay. All right. Well . . . thanks." With that he hung up. I stared at my phone for a second, frown deepening.

What was that all about? Was he trying to tell me something? Or was that his way of trying to hit on me?

"I can see why you're a single man, Greg," I muttered as I headed to my bedroom to change clothes.

I CAME TO the office laden with *stuff*—all the case notes and photos and clippings that I had at the house, which was quite a bit. I'd just tossed everything into a box when I realized that I was going to be late. Bad enough that I'd missed the morning meeting. I'd look like a complete flake if I missed another.

To my relief, the conference room was empty. I grabbed a seat, then started going through my notes, looking for anything new that could possibly leap out at me. A short while later, the door opened and the agents trooped in, followed by the sour-faced Detective Harris. I took a few minutes and showed them my notes and photos, then we each briefed the others on our progress—which wasn't much. After the briefings, we took turns going over different sections of the case, occasionally making observations or comments.

After about an hour, Agent Garner stood, groaning and stretching his arms over his head, his back popping audibly. "My eyes feel like they're about to fall out of my head." His gaze fell on the box. "Hey, what's this?" he said, pulling out the stack of comics. "Is this part of the case?"

"Oh, crap, I didn't realize that I'd thrown those in there." But even as I said it, I could feel a mental *click*, as if something had been stewing in the back of my mind and was now ready to be examined. *Who is that rune of binding for? Is it coincidence that Greg Cerise is so familiar with this particular Demonic Lord?* "To be honest, though, I think that maybe there *is* a connection, but I'm not really sure how to articulate it just yet."

Harris glanced at me. "A hunch?"

I gave a slightly embarrassed shrug. "Well, sort of."

To my surprise he gave an approving nod. "Hunches are important. It's the way your subconscious tells you something needs to be looked at." He reached over and took the top copy and began to page through it. Following his lead, Garner snagged one as well.

"Demons, eh?" Harris said. "So this goes along with your suspicion that this is some sort of ritualistic series of murders?"

I nodded, still too surprised to say anything. James Harris had not struck me at all like someone who could calmly accept the arcane. I opened my mouth to explain, but he spoke first.

"I've done a lot of studies on this sort of thing and been to several training conferences on ritual murder. I mean, obviously it's total crap, but the important thing is that the murderer truly believes that this stuff can give him some sort of mystical power."

I closed my mouth, relieved that I hadn't revealed anything crucial. I flicked a glance at Ryan and he caught my eye, giving an almost imperceptible nod and shrug. Okay, so maybe Harris couldn't accept the existence of the arcane, but at least he could accept the concept of it long enough to pursue leads in that direction.

"Hey," Garner said, abruptly straightening. He pointed to a panel in the comic he was holding. "Hey, this is one of our victims!"

"What?" I straightened. "Which one? Are you sure?"

He pushed the book to the others, pointing at the top panel on the right side. "Look at this girl. Isn't this the victim that was found out in the swamp about five years ago? It would have been his fourth or fifth murder, I think."

I stared at the drawing. Could it be? "Are you sure?" I asked, unable to keep the disbelief out of my voice.

Garner nodded emphatically, digging through a stack of pictures, then pulling out the pictures of a clay bust—the facial reconstruction for this victim.

"Here. It's the same girl."

I peered at the comic and then at the photos. "Are you *sure*?" I repeated doubtfully. It was so hard to tell. The reconstructions were as good as they could possibly be, but there was just no substitute for a photograph of a living, breathing person—and we had those on only the few who had been identified. This girl had not been one of those few. The crime-scene pictures we had showed a young black woman with close-cropped hair, a face bloated by decomposition, eyes filled with maggots, and a network of careful burns patterned across her cheeks and throat. A significant difference from the picture in the comic, which depicted a woman dressed in flowing gowns, head adorned with flowers, lifting a hand for a small, glowing winged creature to alight upon.

"Take a look at the reconstruction." Garner slid the photo across the table. "Take a look at the way the eyes tilt, the line of the cheekbones."

I studied the photo carefully and then compared it to the drawing. "I . . . guess it could be the same. But it seems like a stretch. I mean, there's no way to be sure."

Garner exhaled. "Look, I know it's hard to see. But I'm really good at this."

Ryan nodded. "It's true. Zack has a knack for faces."

I looked again at the drawing and then to the photo. A sliver of excitement began to worm its way through me, and I shoved the rest of the comics over to Garner. "See if there are any others in there!"

He looked startled for an instant, then realization struck. "Oh, my God. If there are others in here—"

"Then that's the link we've been looking for," Harris finished, giving a rare smile.

I felt as if I couldn't breathe as I watched Garner slowly flip through the comics. After what seemed an eternity, Garner said very quietly, "Here's another."

All three of us practically pounced on him. "Which one?" I demanded.

Garner grinned. "Number three. Here, the soldier on the rampart." He pointed to a thickly bearded red-haired man dressed in armor, holding a spear, looking out over a rampart. The man looked burly and strong and confident, barely recognizable as the victim—a drug-addicted homeless man who'd been known to dig through garbage cans for food.

I sat back, heart pounding with deep excitement. "We have our connection. I went and spoke to the artist, Greg Cerise, a few days ago, and then he called me just a couple of hours ago." I glanced at Ryan. "I think we have enough probable cause for a search warrant."

Ryan nodded, and Harris did as well. "Definitely," said Harris.

I laughed, giddy with sudden relief. Finally, a true break in the case. "I'll start typing."

BY THE TIME I got the search warrant typed up and found a judge to sign it, Garner had found five more victims in the comic, including one of my Series Two victims, Mark Janson. Mark had been portrayed as a musician—a slender artist with graceful fingers and an easy smile. Had Greg seen something of that in him or perhaps heard him play? I didn't know anything about Mark—whether or not he'd actually been a musician of any sort—but the thought of that sort of innate talent going to waste was aching.

"But I think there are more that I've missed," Garner said, shaking his head. "It's tough to tell with some of these reconstructions."

"I'm hoping there'll be more at this guy's house," I said. "Something else to tie it all together." Had all of Greg's fluff been an act? Had I given him a chance to get rid of evidence? Or had the phone call a few hours prior just been to check and see if I was getting close? Damn, I wished that there was enough for us to actually get a warrant for Greg's arrest, but the judge hadn't budged on that one. It had been hard enough to get the search warrant. Judge Finn had frowned over the pictures of the victims and the drawings in the comic for several minutes before finally shrugging and shaking his head, stating that he wasn't so sure the drawings bore any resemblance to the victims. "I think you're grasping at straws, Detective Gillian," he'd said, while grudgingly signing the search warrant. But the requests for an arrest warrant had drawn a flat "No. Just because you think he drew them doesn't mean he killed them."

We'll find something at the house, I told myself as I went over the ops plan for the search warrant with the others. *We'll get the evidence and this will all be over.*

THE WOOD OF THE DOOR SPLINTERED UNDER THE IMPACT of the heavy maul. One more hard swing of the maul by the black-clad TAC team member and the door crashed inward. Instantly, the other waiting team members poured through the door, shouting commands and signals to one another as they worked their way into the house, clearing the residence of threats.

I slipped in behind them, mentally apologizing to the landlady for the damage to the door. Ryan came in behind me, and together we slowly worked our way through the house in the team's wake, guns still at the ready. My heart beat rapidly, adrenaline dumping into my system even though I knew logically that the TAC team could handle damn near anything that could possibly be found. *Unless there's a demon here,* I thought grimly. Then it would get really ugly really fast. Warrants were dangerous anyway, and this guy would be ten times as dangerous if he did have a demon at his command.

The interior of the house was painted in unexciting

colors, a palette of browns and dark maroons that might have been called "autumnal" a decade ago but now merely made the house feel dark and depressing. *No wonder Greg went elsewhere to do his work,* I thought. The front door opened onto a living area occupied by a dull brown couch that was so close to the color of the wall that it almost blended in. There was no television in the room, just a floor lamp in the corner and a glass-topped coffee table in front of the couch. A hallway led off to the left from the living room, and to the right was a swinging door that I decided probably led to the kitchen. There were no decorations on the wall, no shelves with pictures or trinkets, no ornamentation of any sort anywhere that I could see. And it was painfully clean. The tracks from a vacuum were still visible in the dull tan carpet, marred now by a multitude of boot prints from the TAC team.

I paused as a fluttering touch of sensation brushed against me—a nebulous whisper of the arcane. I frowned, trying to catch that fleeting sense again. I couldn't see any arcane markings in the house so far—no wardings or protections, or even traces to show that arcane activity had occurred here. But something wasn't right.

I heard a shout from beyond the swinging door, then the voice of Sergeant Dimera, the TAC team leader. "Hey, Gillian. You need to get in here."

I quickly pushed through the door, then stopped in my tracks and let out a low curse. Now I knew what it was I'd felt.

Ryan came up behind me. "Ah, shit."

Lying in the middle of the linoleum of the kitchen floor was Greg Cerise, spread-eagled like da Vinci's Vitruvian Man and surrounded by a chaotic circle of runes and sigils painted in blood. On his chest, gouged messily as if with a butcher knife, was the symbol, large enough to cover nearly his entire torso. In my othersight, ugly purple clots of arcane potency twisted around the body, bloated and wallowing with hatred and anger. This had been done quickly and nastily—both the murder and the arcane sigils and markings. Even if I hadn't spoken to Greg a few hours ago, I would have known that this was not done with the same care and precision as the others.

"Is anyone else in the house?" I asked Dimera, not taking my eyes off the body. There was always the chance—slim though it was—that the killer was still here.

Dimera shook his head. "It's all clear."

I muttered a curse again and shoved my gun into its holster. "Call this in, please. And we're going to need the lab."

Dimera nodded and stepped out of the room, door swinging shut behind him. I could hear him relaying the information on his radio as he moved toward the hallway, checking on the rest of his team. I crouched, looking over the pattern of blood and the markings on the artist.

"These aren't the same runes that I saw on the other body," I said, glancing up at Ryan.

"Do you know what they are?"

I peered at the runes that had been painted in blood, then stood and moved to a point near the artist's head, being exceedingly careful not to mar or touch anything. "Yep. These are diagrams of warding, the kind used in a summoning."

"So, wait, is this our guy? Did he fuck up a summoning?"

I shook my head. "No, he's not the one." Shit. "I just talked to him a few hours ago, which means he was probably killed right after he talked to me." I felt cold. "This is not an actual summoning diagram. There are certain elements missing. But this was drawn deliberately to be recognized by anyone who is versed in those arts." I rubbed the back of my neck, tense.

"It's a message," Ryan said, voice quiet. "To you."

I looked at him sharply. "Or a test. To see how much I know, how much I can see." The implications of that were deeply unsettling. *He knows I can use the arcane. So what will his next step be? I must be getting close.* But if I was close, why did I still feel like I was stumbling around blindly?

"Kara! Ryan!" Garner called. "Come see this!"

"You go," Ryan said. "I'll stay here and make sure no one messes this up before it can be documented."

I nodded, then headed through the living room and down the hall toward Garner's voice. As soon as I entered the room, I knew why he was so excited. "Oh, wow."

It was a workroom where Greg had obviously done a great deal of the final work on the comic. Framed covers of the series were arrayed on walls that had been painted in chaotic patterns—wild colors that clashed with the black-framed pictures and presented a sharp contrast to the muted tones of the rest of the house. Interspersed among the covers were photographs of varying sizes, thumbtacked or taped to the wall, and each photograph had several drawings surrounding it, tacked up in similar haphazard fashion.

"Oh, wow," I repeated, stepping into the room, looking more closely at the drawings that surrounded the photographs. Some were just pencil sketches, others fully inked and colored. I shifted my attention to the photographs. "It's more victims. Holy shit. They're all here. All the victims."

"Plus a bunch of others," Harris said, expression dark. "We have our link now." He jerked his head toward the door. "So, our guy is dead? Did a victim fight back and do him in?"

"No, he's not the Symbol Man," I said absently, eyes still traveling over the pictures. "But the Symbol Man sure as hell knew him or worked closely with him." I tapped my chin. "Did Greg do all of the work on the comic himself? If not, we need to get a list of everyone else who worked with him. Check them all out."

Garner shook his head. "It looks like he did all of the work by himself." He let out a low whistle. "Amazing that he turned out such an impressive product on his own." He glanced up at me. "Comics usually have teams of people who work on them. Different people do the concept, script, penciling, inking, coloring, lettering, and so forth." He touched one of the framed covers. "He was talented, that's for sure."

I stepped closer to the wall of pictures. "All these people. He used them as models."

"Maybe he wasn't very good at drawing people out of his imagination," Garner offered. "Lots of artists use references. In fact, there are websites devoted to pictures that can be used as references for comic artists."

My mouth twitched. "I take it you like comics."

Garner grinned shamelessly. "Love 'em."

I couldn't help but smile. And people said *I* was weird. Garner looked far more like a jock than a comic nerd, with his tanned face and surfer-blond hair. "Okay, so he took pictures of these people so he could use them as models? Why these people?"

"He probably didn't want to pay for regular models," Garner said. He tapped a latex-gloved finger on the wall. "All these folks are homeless or drug addicts or prostitutes. He could probably buy a couple of hours of their time for about ten bucks or a hot meal."

"But there are a lot of pictures here. More than the

victims that we already have." I narrowed my eyes. "Which means that some of these people are possibly still alive," I said. "We need to find them."

"That's going to be tough," Harris said, tucking his thumbs behind his belt as the buttons on his shirt strained dangerously. "But if we can find even one of them, we'll finally have a strong lead."

I clenched and unclenched my hands. "We're close. I can taste it."

Garner nodded at me, but Harris was silent, his gaze traveling slowly over the display on the wall. "Why don't you think that this artist is the killer?" he asked. "All the links are here. It seems possible that his death was a retaliation, either by someone he knew or a potential victim."

I shook my head. "The way that Greg was killed and the way the blood was displayed around him doesn't indicate a revenge or self-defense death." Harris should know that. Was he just brainstorming again? Or was he baiting me? Testing me? It was so hard to tell with him. "The pattern is too accurate," I added, more to myself than to him.

"Accurate?" The beady gaze fell on me.

"Yes," I replied. I'd worry later about being thought a nutcase. Catching this guy was the important thing now. "Those aren't random scribbles around the body. It's just not possible for someone who doesn't have intimate knowledge of the arcane to be able to set a scene like that. The odds of a potential victim being knowledgeable about that sort of thing are pretty extreme." I ran a hand through my hair. "No, I think that Greg was starting to figure it out, so he was taken care of."

"So it's likely that he was involved." Harris frowned as he scanned the wall of photographs and drawings. "Perhaps there were two killers, and the other one decided to get rid of Greg before he squealed." Harris looked back at me, his arms folded across his chest.

I took a deep breath, controlling my annoyance. It was possible. As much as I'd liked Greg, that didn't mean he hadn't completely snowed me. "Yeah, it's definitely possible," I admitted reluctantly. And Tessa *had* said that there were two. I opened my mouth to say more, then stopped. I'd told Greg that I was a summoner. There weren't too many people who knew that. My aunt, Ryan, and Greg. And it wasn't the kind of thing you could determine just by looking at someone. Well, not for humans, at least. There were some demons that could sense a person's ability to summon.

So, either Greg told someone that I was a summoner, or I've had a demon sniffing around me without my knowledge. The latter was fairly unlikely, though not impossible. Any creature with enough skill in the arcane could remain undetected.

"Detective Gillian, are you all right?"

I realized that I was staring off into space. I jerked my attention back to Harris. "Yeah, sorry, just had a thought."

"Care to share it?"

I flexed my fingers, excitement growing. "He's screwed up. It's the first time he's screwed up."

Harris unfolded his arms. "How?"

"Killing Greg. Now we *know* that the Symbol Man is connected to Greg somehow. He must have felt that he had to eliminate Greg. Maybe Greg was going to rat on him or something, I don't know." Another thought struck me, but this revelation was not quite as pleasant. "He screwed up—and it doesn't matter to him."

"What do you mean?"

"The diagram around the body. It didn't serve any purpose except to taunt us." *Taunt me*, I corrected internally. "But he doesn't care, because he's almost done."

Garner was watching me intently as well. "With his preparations," he said.

I nodded.

"And you think that he's preparing for a big demon calling," Harris said.

"A summoning, yes."

Harris frowned. "So it's possible that this is gearing up to be a big finish, like a cult," he stated. "We could be looking at a large number of people at risk. And he might kill himself as well. He has nothing to lose."

I blinked. Where the hell was he getting this from? I shook my head. "Oh, you mean like a murder–suicide thing? Hell, no. He wants the power. The whole reason he's preparing so carefully is because he *does* want to live through it."

Harris's frown deepend. "Detective Gillian, how is it that you are such an authority on ritual murders?" There was challenge in his tone, and I had to take a mental step back. He was considered a local expert on cults and ritual murders, and I was totally stepping on his toes. Only problem was, the arcane *was* my area of expertise, and I couldn't say so. Damn, but I wished Ryan was in here for this.

I took a deep, steadying breath, framing my words as carefully as possible. "I'm not an authority on ritual murders," I said, then held up my hand when he began to speak. "However, I've grown up with and around people who are considered experts in arcane lore, mythology, voodoo, Wicca, the paranormal, and other alternative forms of religion and mysticism. I recognize the patterns on the kitchen floor and, in my opinion, they were placed there by someone who intends to summon a demon."

Harris narrowed his eyes, face reddening slightly. "All right, let's assume that our killer really does believe this shit. In your *opinion*," and the word was drawled out in a manner that was barely short of being insulting, "is he going to want a pile of victims for his big shebang? And what is he going to do when the demon fails to appear?"

You should be asking what are we *going to do when it* does *appear,* I thought grimly. "He'll try again, if he survives it. He'll start over from scratch if he has to."

The faintest hint of a sneer curled Harris's lip, barely long enough for me to register it before the professional mask came over his face again. He gave me a nod and left the room without speaking. I watched him leave and sighed. It was obvious that Detective Harris didn't give a rat's ass that I had a clue about the arcane. In fact, it probably made him think even less of me—I was obviously a fruitcake who couldn't be trusted to make a logical deduction.

Garner cleared his throat gently. "He, uh, seems very literal, but I've worked with him before. He's actually a pretty good detective." He glanced up from the stack of papers he was searching through and gave me a wry smile.

I scrubbed a hand over my face. "Yeah, I'm sure he is. And this has to be one of the stranger cases that he's handled."

To my surprise, Garner shook his head. "Oh, no, I wouldn't say that. He's worked task-force stuff with us before on some seriously freaky cases, with mass murder and suicide, cult stuff, ritual sacrifices. This is pretty tame, actually."

I tried not to smile. Except that this stuff was *real*. And maybe his other cases had been real as well, or more real than he could know. "Well," I said, "fortunately it looks like we might be on the right track."

"Kara?" Garner lifted a piece of paper out of the stack he was searching, an astonished expression on his face.

"Yeah?" I said. "Zack? What's wrong?"

"Kara . . . this is . . . *you*," he said, then slowly extended the paper to me.

Ryan stepped into the room behind me, moving to peer over my shoulder as I took the drawing from Garner. "Jesus Christ," Ryan breathed. "It's you . . . but, wow. It's like an über-you."

I could only stare. It was a drawing of a woman dressed in classic fantasy female-warrior regalia—metal and leather bra, matching short skirt, elegant metal vambraces on her arms, hair flowing free. In other words, unspeakably impractical for any sort of actual fighting. The woman depicted held a sword in one hand and a dagger in the other and was shown facing down what I knew perfectly well to be a *reyza*—fierce expression emblazoned across her face. The woman was beautiful and strong and feminine, and everything about her gave the impression that she was a total badass.

And it *was* me. I couldn't deny that for an instant. *Holy shit. Is that what he saw in me?* The preacher had said that Greg drew the potential in people. *Is that my potential? Could I ever be that strong and beautiful?*

I didn't know whether to be flattered or depressed.

"I especially like the outfit," Ryan said dryly from behind me.

I turned to glare at him. He just grinned. "I think you need to start wearing something like that to work," he continued.

I couldn't help but smile, obscurely grateful to him for giving me a point of levity. I didn't want to think about how far short of that picture I actually fell. "It's a cool picture, that's for sure. However, I can *promise* that you'll never see me in that outfit."

But I did tuck the picture into my notebook. Rules of evidence be damned.

THE SKY WAS ALIGHT WITH THE PINK AND ORANGE OF dawn by the time we finally finished processing and searching the house. To Harris's and everyone else's disappointment, there was no secret basement that concealed a torture and execution chamber, no hidden closets containing arcane implements of death and destruction, and no evidence whatsoever that Greg had actually been the serial killer, or even connected to the killer, other than the pictures in his workroom. I made my way home, blearily stumbling through the back door of my house, barely remembering to lock it behind me. I stripped off my clothes and collapsed onto my bed, falling asleep within half a dozen heartbeats.

I woke late in the day with dim and scattered memories of dreams containing Rhyzkahl—hazy threads of images that bore little resemblance to the powerful sendings of his previous visits. I lay on my back, looking up at the wood of my ceiling, allowing myself to wake up fully. *Those were probably actual dreams,* I decided, as I tried and failed to remember the content. Dim snatches lingered briefly—images of Rhyzkahl scowling at me, calling to me, and a jumbled memory of me rolling over in bed and telling him to go away and let me sleep. It had to have been a dream. *Surely* I hadn't told a Demonic Lord to go away and let me sleep.

The clock on the nightstand showed seven p.m. I sat up, running my fingers through my tangled hair. My internal clock was completely screwed up now, after staying awake two nights in a row. Again.

The one good thing about having slept all day was that I knew it would be easier to be out most of the night looking for people. I showered and changed into jeans and a T-shirt that was uncharacteristically devoid of anything police-related, strapped on the ankle holster that held my little Kel-Tec .32 under my jeans, and pulled my shirt down over the holster on my belt that held my Glock 9mm. And, no, I wasn't going to call Ryan to come with me on this. I wanted people to talk to me. Fed Boy would more likely scare people off.

I drove slowly through town, considering where to start. Beaulac was not exactly a bustling metropolis, even though its population and the population of the entire parish had swelled dramatically after Katrina, much like all the other parishes that surrounded New Orleans. And, of course, that unexpected growth had resulted in an increase in the number of "problem" neighborhoods. Areas that were previously "not so nice" had morphed into "don't go there after dark," much to the dismay of the community leaders.

I drummed my fingers on the steering wheel. Some of those areas were exactly what I needed. But even armed, I was reluctant to go in without backup. However, I could think of a number of places where I'd be able to find people who could help me out. In fact, the outreach center where Greg had done so much of his work was probably the best place to start. With any luck, Reverend Thomas would be around and able to identify some of the pictures.

I drove past the outreach center, scowling as I saw that the doors were closed by a metal gate. Obviously the people who ran the center were smart enough to maintain a certain level of security on the building. But that also meant I wouldn't have the chance to talk to Reverend Thomas tonight. There was a small group of about half a dozen people clustered out front, though. I peered at them as I drove by, then smiled in satisfaction as I recognized a face. Reverend Thomas wasn't the only one who might have some information.

I parked a short distance down the street, then grabbed my stack of pictures and made my way toward the group. They parted before me, giving me a wide berth. Even in plain clothes, I knew that my whole bearing shrieked "Cop!" I scanned the faces quickly, giving them small, tight nods—nothing too friendly just yet.

"Whatcha want here, Sarge?" A grizzled black man with a shortage of teeth spoke. He looked to be in his mid to late forties, with broad shoulders, thick muscles, and scarred knuckles. He leaned against the wall, crossing his arms over his chest as he looked at me.

I gave the speaker an easy smile. I knew this one, which was why I'd decided to stop and talk to him. I'd arrested Tio a number of times, but I was always cool with him and he was always cool with me in return. He'd never gone so far as to be an informant, but he helped me out in other ways, such as vouching for my integrity to others who weren't sure that I could be trusted. Once upon a time, Tio had tried to make it as a boxer, but then he lost one fight too many and ended up eking out a living by more-questionable means. He'd had fights with most of the other cops in the department, but I was always able to talk him into the handcuffs. Good thing, too, since I knew he could totally kick my ass.

"Hey, Tio. Just looking for some people," I said as disarmingly as I could. "I ain't bringing no trouble here tonight."

He curled his lip. "Wit' warrants? No one here gonna help you snatch up folk."

I shook my head. "No, man, it ain't like that. I ain't hookin' anyone. I'm looking for some people to make sure they don't get hurt. You know, I'm doing that protecting-and-serving shit." I gave him a grin. My years as a street cop had taught me many things, and the most important one was that it was a whole lot easier to get help from people if you were nice and friendly with them. The second-most-important thing I'd learned was that there was also a time to stop being nice and friendly.

To my relief, he laughed. "Protect and serve! Yeah, you right. So how you gonna protect and serve us out here?"

I could sense the others in the group watching the interplay intently. I knew that getting any help from them depended completely on what happened with Tio. I pulled out the picture of Greg and showed it to him. "See this guy? I'm trying to find out if anyone out here has ever seen him around, talking to anyone, offering them jobs or anything like that."

Tio glanced at the picture, then shook his head. "Nah, he looks too friendly and nice to be down here. He'd stand out like . . . like a little ladycop." He tipped his head back and laughed.

I laughed with him, allowing myself to share in the joke. "Yeah, yeah, I know. But I'm telling you, I wouldn't be doing shit this crazy if I didn't really want to help these people out." I leaned in a bit closer. "Look, y'all know about the Symbol Man, right?"

Tio scowled. "That is some fucked-up shit, ladycop."

"I know it is, Tio," I said, lowering my voice. "But I'm gonna catch that fucker." I pulled out the photos taken from Greg's house of the latest victim—photos that showed her as a living, breathing, smiling person, not as a shredded, tortured corpse. I passed the top photo to Tio. "This is his last victim. You know who that is?"

Tio's expression went stony. "Yeah. I know her. Knew her. Katy, dunno her last name. Saw on the news that someone else had been cut up by this asshole. Didn't know it was her."

I kept my face from betraying my elation at the identification, partial though it was. It was still far more than we'd had. "It was bad, Tio. You know I've seen some nasty-ass shit, but this guy's the worst." I gave him a level look. "I really need the help of y'all on the street."

"Katy was cool," he said as he pushed off the wall. "She was a bit fucked up, but she was tryin' hard. She didn't deserve that shit."

"No one deserves what this guy is doing."

Tio cracked his thick knuckles. "Lemme see that first guy again?"

I handed the pic over, trying not to let my relief and excitement show. Tio stepped into the light from the streetlamp and peered more seriously at the photo.

"Yeah," he said after a moment. "I seen this guy around. He comes and sits in the center here and draws, and then pays people ten or twenty bucks or so to pose for him. Seen him other places too."

"Where else?" I fought to stay calm. I couldn't appear

too eager for the information or it was going to start costing me.

Tio scratched his stubbled chin as he considered. "Shit, I dunno. Mebbe down in the park."

"Does he ever take pictures of the people when they pose?"

Tio nodded. "Yeah, that's usually what he does. So is this the guy? This the killer?" He clenched his hands into fists. "Man, I will fuck his shit *up* next time I see him!"

I reached out and took the picture from Tio's hand. "No. He's dead now. The Symbol Man got him too."

"Fuck."

"Yeah." I pulled out the page that I'd created with the pics of the unidentified people on it. The ones who I hoped were still alive. "How about these people? Do you know where I can find them?"

Tio peered at the page, then motioned one of the other bystanders over. A skinny white male with poor-quality tattoos on his arms shuffled up. Tio showed the page to him.

"I think I know some of these folk," the second man said. "I mean, not personal, like, but just seen 'em out, y'know?"

"I really need to find these people," I said. "I think that they might be in danger from the Symbol Man."

Tio's brows drew together. "Why he be goin' after them?"

"I can't really say right now, but we've gotten some leads that *might*"—I stressed the word—"link all these people— the ones who've already been killed, and then these folk— together. I just need to find them." I gave Tio an earnest look. "If they're scared of the police, at least let them know to be careful. Tell them not to go anywhere with anyone they don't know."

Tio was silent for several heartbeats and then nodded. "This one here's AnnMarie," he said, pointing to a picture of a white girl with a fleshy face and dark hair. "And this one's Skeeter." He indicated a picture of a rail-thin black man, then glanced around the crowd. "Anyone else know these folk?"

I tried not to react, but my relief was damn near overwhelming. Some of the others began to make tentative identifications, and I scribbled names quickly, breathless. With Tio cooperating, the others were a thousand times more likely to contribute what they knew. There were no last names, but it was still a phenomenal improvement over the nothing that I'd had before.

Tio looked up at me after I finished writing. "That gonna do ya?"

I gave him a smile thick with gratitude. "It's a terrific start. And if you can spread the word to anyone you know, that would be fantastic too."

He nodded once, serious. "I'll take care of it, ladycop."

"All right, Tio. I appreciate it." I handed him a stack of copies of the pictures, then gave him a handful of my business cards as well. "If anyone's willing, I'd *really* like to talk to them. We need every break we can get on this case."

Tio tucked the cards and the pictures into a side pocket of his pants. "You got it, ladycop."

"Cool. Stay out of trouble, Tio, all right?"

He winked and grinned. "Trouble finds me."

"Then run from it, ya big goof!"

I SPENT THE NEXT FEW NIGHTS REPEATING THAT SAME scene over and over in equally seedy locations, with slightly different players and awfully similar conversations. I didn't try to blend in, just worked on talking to the ones I knew, the regulars. This was where my rep as a fair cop paid off. I'd put a lot of these people in jail, but I'd never bum-rapped anyone. And because of that, I had people who were willing to talk to me—especially when I told them what I was after.

At the very least, maybe I can make it too hot for this guy to get any more victims, I thought grimly as I headed home. It was only two a.m., but I knew that I needed to try to wrench my sleep cycle back to something more normal. I turned off the highway and onto the winding trace that was my driveway. I rounded the curve before my house, then slowed, a frisson of wariness going through me as I saw a car parked in front—a dark-blue Crown Victoria. Then the wariness was replaced by a curious mix of annoyance and pleasure as I recognized the car as Ryan's. What the hell was he doing here *again*?

Sleeping, I discovered as I got out of my car and walked up to his. I bit my lip to keep from laughing as I looked through the window at him. His head was tipped back against the headrest and his mouth had fallen open, and if not for the fact that I had heard him snoring when I was still six feet from the car, I probably would have thought him dead.

The temptation to leave him out here was nearly overwhelming, but my curiosity as to why he was here won out. I tapped on his window with my keys.

Nothing. He continued to sleep and snore.

I banged harder, and this time he jerked awake, accidentally sounding the horn. He jumped and let out a blistering oath.

"Jesus Christ, Kara! Where the hell have you been?"

I was laughing so hard it took me several tries to answer. After a few deep breaths I managed to speak. "Out. Why are you sleeping in my driveway?"

He groaned and opened the door, rubbing at his face as he got out. "I didn't mean to fall asleep. I came here looking for you," he said, glaring at me accusingly.

I gave him a sour look in return. "I was out. Working. Why didn't you call my cell?"

A flicker of something that might have been embarrassment crossed his face as he stood and stretched his back. "I didn't think to. I thought that maybe you'd just gone out for a few minutes, since it was after ten when I came by, so I figured I'd wait for you. And I guess I fell asleep."

"You know, you could have gone inside. The door you busted is only nailed shut with two nails."

He shook his head. "Nah, I think that would have been a bit forward. Stalking you from the driveway is plenty for now."

I laughed again. "Do you want some coffee? I can fill you in on what I've been doing."

He glanced at his watch. "If it's decaf. I can probably still scrape together a couple of hours' sleep after you brief me."

"Ha. I've just about given up on normal sleep," I said as I led the way around the back of the house.

I climbed the back steps, unlocked the door, and entered, then stopped dead two feet inside the kitchen, causing Ryan to nearly run into me. He began to speak, but I put out a hand, signaling him to be quiet. I could see down the hallway and a rectangle of light on the floor.

The basement door was open and the light was on, and I *knew* that I had not left it so.

I drew my gun, though I had a sick suspicion that if anything was down there it would not be affected by a firearm. I sensed as much as heard Ryan pulling his gun, following my lead and blessedly not asking any questions. I glanced back at him and pointed toward the hallway and the square of light. He nodded, holding his gun close to his body, at the ready.

I stepped as soundlessly as possible down the hall, checking the rooms to either side as I went, hugging the wall to keep from hitting any of the creaky spots in the floor. My pulse sounded loud in my ears and I breathed shallowly, ears straining for any noise in the house, any clue that could define what I could be facing.

Ryan knew what he was doing; he slid around and covered the areas I couldn't see as I eased down the hall. I caught the whisper of movement down in the basement and moved to the top of the stairs, shielding myself by the doorjamb and peeking down, covering the stairs with my 9mm.

A figure moved to the bottom of the stairs—something

with blond hair and a wild print blouse. I jerked the gun back.

"Damn it, Aunt Tessa! I almost shot you." My heart pounded as much from the thought of almost shooting my aunt as from the relief that it wasn't something worse down there.

Tessa looked up and gave me an ingenuous smile as she climbed the stairs. "Now, why would you want to do something like that? Did you know your front door is broken?"

I sighed and holstered my gun. Out of the corner of my eye I could see Ryan doing the same. "Really? I hadn't noticed. What are you doing here? I didn't see your car."

"Oh, I bought a motorcycle yesterday," she said breezily, as if it were the most normal thing in the world. "It's parked on the other side of the house. I came over to see how your summoning went."

I winced as Tessa reached the top of the stairs and saw Ryan. *Well, now Ryan knows where I learned how to summon.* Tessa gave Ryan a measuring look, then fixed me with a steely glare that I did my best to return. It was her own damn fault for assuming I was alone. Okay, so maybe it was an easy assumption, considering how rarely I had company, but I still wasn't about to take any blame for the slip.

I shoved my hair back from my face. "I already told you what happened in my summoning. Why did you buy a motorcycle?"

"Because they're cool." Tessa frowned at Ryan, then shook her head and pointed a finger at me. "No, sweets, not your last summoning. I wanted to see how your *next* summoning went. But it seems that you haven't summoned again."

"I've been busy. There've been two more murders. And when did you learn how to ride a motorcycle? Do you have a valid motorcycle endorsement on your license?"

"Today, and, no, I don't need to bother with that." She turned to Ryan, smiling sweetly, ignoring my groan. "Hello, darlin'. I'm Tessa, Kara's aunt. I saw you sleeping in the car when I came in, but you looked so peaceful that I just didn't have it in me to wake you up."

Ryan didn't miss a beat. He smiled graciously and extended his hand. "It's a pleasure to meet you, Ms. Pazhel. I'm Special Agent Ryan Kristoff with the FBI. I'm on the Symbol Man task force with your niece."

Tessa took Ryan's hand, a small smile curving her mouth as she regarded him. "The pleasure is all mine. And how did you know my last name?"

"I'm a big fan of thorough research."

I watched the interplay, arms folded across my chest. Why the hell had he checked my aunt out? Had he already known that she was a summoner? Well, he certainly did now.

Tessa raised an eyebrow and released his hand, then turned back to me. "I know you're ticked at me for prying, sweets, but I've been worried about you. I thought you might try to summon on the dark, and I hadn't heard from you in a while. I've been out of town for the past few days, so I figured I'd check that everything was all right."

I abruptly realized I was scowling, but I didn't make much effort to modify my expression. "I've been *busy.* Remember? Serial killer? I'll summon again in about a week, on the full." Then I straightened. "Wait, if he's gearing up to something big, it's going to have to be on this month's full."

Ryan's forehead creased in a frown. "Why? What happens after this month? I thought you just needed a full moon to have enough potency for big summonings."

Tessa shook her head. "The convergence of the two spheres is more important than the phase of the moon.

We just came out of a period of a few years where the convergence was so small that it was darn near impossible to
summon anything higher than eighth level. Right now the
convergence is nearly as high as it can possibly be, but after
this month it will start to taper off to more-normal levels."
She nodded her head toward me. "Kara would have been a
full summoner some time ago if she hadn't been forced to
wait until the convergence was high enough to allow for a
summoning of a twelfth-level demon."

I could see him mentally filing that information away.
"So anyone seeking to summon anything of any decent
size or power would do so on this next full moon—which
means we have less than a week to catch him."

I moved to the kitchen and dropped into a chair at the
table. "Right. That also means he's going to be doing more
murders between now and then, building up a strong res-
ervoir of power." I tapped the table thoughtfully. "But I'm
hoping that it's going to be harder for him to find victims.
I spent the last few nights going around and showing the
other photographs from Cerise's house, trying to get the
word to these people—and everyone else as well—to be
careful."

Tessa's brows drew together. "Cerise? Greg Cerise?"

I nodded absently, then sat up straight. My aunt didn't
know about him yet. "Oh, shit, Aunt Tessa. I forgot that
you knew him."

Tessa sat down slowly, eyes on me. "Knew? You're speaking in past tense, sweets."

"Shit. I'm sorry, Aunt Tessa." I hesitated, but there was
no easy way to break this sort of news. "He's dead. I'm so
sorry."

Tessa looked down at the table. "What happened?" she
asked, voice calm and even.

"Symbol Man," Ryan said quietly. "We think that Greg was somehow connected to him. We found pictures, photographs, and drawings of all the victims plus several others who we haven't been able to identify yet."

Tessa pursed her lips, silent. I looked at her with a tinge of worry. I knew that my aunt had been close to Greg when they were younger, but had they still been close?

"Greg wasn't a summoner," Tessa finally said.

I flicked a quick glance to Ryan before looking back to my aunt. "Yes, I know. I went to talk to him a while back, asking about that comic—trying to find out more about Rhyzkahl. I really hadn't thought there was any connection between Greg and the Symbol Man at that time. But then one of the other agents on the task force made the connection between Symbol Man victims and characters in Greg's comic. We got a search warrant, and . . ." I sighed. "When we made entry, we found Greg dead and then found pictures of all the victims."

Her expression was bleak as she looked at me. "Do you think he helped kill those people?"

"No," I said with as much conviction as I could manage, knowing that there was a good chance I was lying to her. She probably knew it, too, but it was what she needed to hear right then.

"Do you know of anyone who might be connected to Greg?" I asked. "Anyone he worked with or was close to?"

Tessa spread her hands. "I hadn't seen him in well over twenty years," she said, voice colored with regret. "So someone is killing the people Greg drew? Why?"

"Greg tended to use people who were homeless or drug addicts as his models," I said.

"People who weren't quickly missed," Ryan added.

I glanced at him and nodded. "This killer needs a lot of

victims. I figure he's attempting to perform a major summoning and that's why he's gathering so much energy."

"Yes," Tessa said with a nod. "You've been thinking that for a while now."

I took a deep breath. "But now I think it's Rhyzkahl that he's trying to summon. And not just summon but bind as a slave."

Tessa's expression sharpened. "And what makes you think that? That's one hell of an ambitious summoning, and one fraught with considerable danger. Binding an unwilling Demonic Lord? Especially Rhyzkahl? That's insane!"

I hesitated. Ryan didn't know about the dream visits. For that matter, neither did Tessa.

"Er, well," I said, trying not to squirm, "I kinda got that impression after I . . . uh, last spoke to Rhyzkahl."

Tessa didn't twitch a muscle, but Ryan shifted, clearly startled.

Tessa's voice was like ice. "If you called him to you—"

"I didn't! I swear!" I said quickly. "No, it was another dream-sending."

"Another *what*?" My aunt stared at me, and I realized that I'd only *thought* her tone was icy before.

Oops.

I tried to force a smile onto my face. "Oh. Um, yeah. Forgot to tell you about that." I gave a quick—and very watered-down—version of his visit to my bedroom and then briefly explained about the nap on the couch and asking Rhyzkahl about the runes. "And then he got *mad*." I shivered at the memory. "I mean, it was like waves of unspeakable menace and fury just rolling off him, mingled with rage and vengeance and anything else horrible you can think of."

"That's the nightmare I woke you up from," Ryan said. "Isn't it?"

I nodded.

Tessa slowly shook her head. "Coming to your dreams? You should have told me."

"I know," I said, shifting uncomfortably. "There's just been so much going on. I was working up to it."

She gave me a dark look. "Well, that was his true power that you felt, sweets. He is self-serving and powerful and not to be trifled with. And even if this killer really is trying to summon a lord, I can't imagine anyone being insane enough to try to bind Rhyzkahl. He's one of the most ancient of the lot. There are several other lords who would be far less risky to call, though perhaps not as powerful." She rubbed at her face. "But any Demonic Lord would still be more than enough potency for a summoner to use."

I folded my arms over my chest and looked across the table at my aunt. "Greg told me about how you two saw Rhyzkahl."

A flash of annoyance tinged with what might have been embarrassment crossed her face. "Greg shouldn't have told you that. We swore each other to secrecy."

"Aunt Tessa," I said with heat, "I *needed* to know that! Were you ever going to tell me? Don't you think it's important that there was once a major incursion in this area by one of the Demonic Lords?"

Tessa rolled her eyes. "All right, I suppose it is important, but he still shouldn't have told you. It's not exactly a pleasant memory." Her lips twitched. "I was working up to it."

I glared at her. "Just because you're my aunt doesn't mean I can't call you a smart-ass."

Ryan cleared his throat. "Ladies, it doesn't matter how

the information was disseminated. What matters is what we know now. This Demonic Lord may be summoned soon and, if that happens, all hell will break loose."

Tessa waved a hand dismissively. "Oh, no, we won't have all of hell here. And, really, there's no such thing as 'hell' like you're thinking. But surely an incursion by a lord will be nasty, especially if he's bound by an unscrupulous sort, which I'm thinking the Symbol Man is."

"To put it mildly," I said dryly.

"Just how nasty are we talking here?" Ryan asked. "I mean, don't take this the wrong way, but being a summoner doesn't seem to convey unlimited power or anything. Why is this killer going to all of this trouble?"

"No, it's not unlimited power," I replied. "But, like anything, it's how you use it."

Ryan's gaze fixed on me. "How do *you* use it? Why do you summon?"

I paused before answering. There was no way to explain the full depth of what it meant to me. And I wasn't sure I was ready to share that much with him. I still didn't know him all that well, and being a summoner had become a deeply integral part of who I was because of a time in my life that I wasn't terribly proud of. "I summon . . . because I can," I temporized. "And I know that sounds corny, but it's like a hunger. Demons are brilliant, and clever, and powerful, and each summoning is an incredible accomplishment. I've never felt as if I've wasted time performing a summoning. Usually I have some specific reason to summon a demon, like if I have a question that can be answered only by one of them or if I want to learn how to do something arcane." It was a watered-down version of the full answer, but it would suffice for now.

"So it's all for information?" He sounded doubtful.

"Heck, no!" I laughed. "Come on, if you had the ability to summon a superpowerful arcane creature, wouldn't *you*?"

His expression grew exasperated, and I raised my hands in mock surrender. "Okay, seriously. Demons are excellent resources, but they're also strong, and powerful, and damn near invincible on this plane. Moreover, they're completely loyal during the terms of their service. Yeah, they're totally self-serving, but at the same time they're completely honorable. And once you pay the agreed-upon terms, they give you their full cooperation. Their system of honor is unbelievably complex, and if they swear to obey, they will, no matter what is involved, as long as it doesn't conflict with their personal honor."

Ryan leaned against the doorjamb. "So, they're like the perfect muscle."

"Think giant, winged assassin–bodyguard, who also has the ability to weave arcane wardings."

He looked pained. "Wardings?"

"Um . . . demons have the ability to shape arcane energies, creating protections or illusions."

"Ah."

It was hard not to laugh. The poor guy was getting a crash course. "Anyway, some humans have those skills—"

"Do you?" he interjected, watching me intently.

I shrugged. "Er, well, yes. Most summoners do the basic stuff." I glanced at my aunt and then back at Ryan. "I'm still learning, which is the main reason why I summon lately—for lessons. I have a long way to go."

"She has a lot of innate talent," Tessa said. "She's going to be better than me soon."

I could only stare at my aunt in surprise. I'd never heard her say anything like that before.

"So, the demons can do these wardings and protections too?" Ryan asked.

I dragged my attention back to him. "Yes. In fact, most summoners will just summon a demon to do it for them. Wardings can be pretty tedious and tiring and are usually a real pain in the ass."

"All right, so a demon is a pretty damn good ally. And I'm assuming a Demonic Lord would be even more powerful?"

Tessa spoke up. "If he intends to summon a Demonic Lord, he knows that there is no offering great enough to compel the lord to submit to conventional bindings. He would have to bind the lord to his will. Enslave him. And someone with a Demonic Lord under his control would be able to rule the world."

Ryan's expression turned skeptical. "Oh, come on."

Tessa lowered her head and regarded him. "Like having a demigod in your hand. An army couldn't stop him, and he'd certainly be able to raise an army of his own. You know perfectly well that there are many thousands of people who would gladly fall in behind such a powerful entity, no matter the intent of it."

Ryan shuddered. "God, yes." He scrubbed a hand through his hair, then frowned, looking at me. "But the lord who came to you—after he broke free of your control, why didn't he stay and become a ruler here?"

"I think," I said, speaking slowly as I tried to organize my thoughts, "that for them to be able to stay in this sphere, they have to have some sort of an anchor here, like a permanent invitation, or a summoning and binding. The binding that a summoner does after bringing a demon through a portal is not like arcane manacles but more a means of keeping the demon in this sphere. The demon submits to it because of the offering that the summoner provides." I glanced at my aunt for confirmation.

"That's right," Tessa said. "It's one thing for them to come through briefly, but staying is more complicated. This is not their world, and without the right protocols, they'll be drawn back to their own. And the more powerful they are, the more difficult it is for them to stay. But that's also why a clever and ambitious lord would want to be in this sphere, unfettered. It would be another power base, an easy way to gain enormous amounts of power and status in their own sphere. Without the limitations of their honor code—which would not apply if one were here unrestrained—there would be no reason to not use this world up. Enslave the populace, ravage the resources, drain it of potency, and leave it a dead world if they so desired."

I rubbed the back of my neck. "That's a worst-case scenario—"

"But it *is* a scenario," Tessa replied with heat. "Demons are utterly self-serving, and their honor is the only reason that their realm has not dissolved into anarchy."

Ryan cleared his throat. "So why do they include summoners in this honor system?"

Tessa turned her attention to him. "Because even though it is an affront to them to be summoned, they can gain status by their knowledge of other spheres or with artifacts that we offer to them for their cooperation. Without the protection that their honor affords us as summoners, no human would ever attempt to summon a demon." She snapped her eyes back to me. "And if someone were to call a lord outside of the normal protocols—"

"I have no intention of calling him!" I practically yelled. I started to say more, but the ringing of my cell phone interrupted me. Probably a good thing, since the *more* I had to say would not have been nice.

Ryan stared at me as I pulled my phone out to see who was calling at this late hour. "You have the *Fraggle Rock* theme song as your ring tone," he said, with a bemused look on his face. "You are so weird."

I laughed, then hit the answer button on my phone. "Detective Gillian here."

There was silence for a couple of seconds, then a small cough, and a thin voice said, "H-hello? Is this the ladyc-cop who was speaking to T-tio?"

I straightened. "Yes, yes, it is. Who is this?"

Another brief silence. Then, "I go by Belle. Tio s-said I needed to t-talk to you. Showed me some p-pics."

My excitement rose. I gestured wildly at Ryan and pointed first at the phone, then at the pics that I'd scrawled names on. "Yes, yes," I said, trying to keep my voice calm as I flipped through the pages. "I've been showing some pictures around." Ryan moved over to me and leaned in to try to hear. I yanked out a page that had *Belle* written on it and waved it at him triumphantly.

"Yeah. Oh, m-man. Tio said that it was f-fucked up and that I was g-gonna get killed, and now I think someone's following me." The girl's voice wavered badly, thick with terror.

"I won't let that happen," I said gently as I looked at the picture. Holy shit, but she didn't look much older than fifteen—a smiling black girl with a pert nose and slanted eyes, with piercings in her eyebrow and lower lip. "Where are you?"

"S-somewhere safe. I think."

"Where?" I asked. "I can keep you a lot safer than you

can be out there on the streets. Can I meet you some-place?"

Another silence, and this time I had to check my phone to make sure that the girl had not hung up on me. "Belle? I'm worried about you. Please tell me where I can meet you, so I can make sure you stay safe."

"All right. I-I c-can meet you by the diner on Vaughn Street."

"I'll be there in fifteen minutes, Belle. I'm driving a dark-green Ford Taurus. Stay out of sight until you see my car, okay?"

"Ok-kay."

"And call me or call 911 if you see anything strange or unusual."

"Okay. Y-you're coming right now?"

"I'm leaving right now. Yes."

The silence this time actually was the girl disconnect-ing. I stuffed my phone in my pocket and snatched up my jacket. "Come on, Fed Boy," I commanded as I dashed for the back door. "Time for you to earn your tax dollars."

19

I DROVE FAST, IGNORING THE WAY THAT RYAN CLUTCHED at the door handle as I took the corners. After the sixth time his foot came down on the floorboards, though, I snapped, "The brakes over there don't work!"

Ryan made a mock-panicked sound. "God help us all, Kara! We do have to get there in one piece, you know."

I tightened my grip on the wheel. "Do you have any idea how amazing it is that this girl called me? I can't run the risk that she'll get scared or get tired of waiting for us and leave. There's too much that she can tell us!"

Ryan scowled. "I know. I *have* been in law enforcement for a while."

"Yeah, but were you ever a regular cop, or have you always been a Fed?" I winced, regretting the words as soon as they left my mouth.

"What difference does it make?" His reply had some heat behind it.

I grimaced. "I'm sorry. It's just that so much of what I

do is dealing with this underlayer of society. How much experience with that do you guys get?"

"I've been with the agency for ten years now. I worked in social services before that for four." His tone was clipped. "I know how to talk to regular folk."

"Good. That means you can understand why I want to get there as fast as I can." I whipped the car around a curve, skidding to the side in a maneuver that unnerved even me, then straightened it out at the last second to avoid slamming into the curb. My pitiful Taurus shuddered as it found traction again, reminding me that it was *not* a performance vehicle.

He let out a sound that was close to a growl. "If we get into a wreck, we won't get there at all."

"Fine!" I said, slowing down a bit though not wanting to admit that he might be right. But I knew I was being a jerk. I was getting too caught up in the excitement of it, and I was being careless. Now was not the time to get hurt in a stupid way. Plenty of time later to get hurt in non-stupid ways.

Vaughn Street was about half a mile away from the outreach center, though the general quality of the neighborhood was the same. I'd come through here the night after speaking with Tio, handing out pictures and doing my best to encourage people who shunned the police to help me with my investigation.

There was no one in front of the diner when we pulled up—not a huge surprise since it was after three in the morning. Even the drug addicts and prostitutes usually found a place to sleep by this hour. I got out of the car, scanning the area, listening for any sign of others. The stores were all closed and dark, and even the diner was silent, with a hand-lettered sign in the window that announced that they opened at six a.m. The waxing moon reflected off the store windows in mute reminder of how much time we had left to find the killer.

Ryan exited the car, closing his door softly, as did I. "We might be early," he said, voice low.

"Or she might be watching us from somewhere," I said, scanning. "I told her to stay out of sight until she saw us." The back of my neck prickled. Someone was definitely watching us. My intuition told me that much. The whisper of arcane brushed me again, and goose bumps sprang up on my skin.

"Something's wrong," I whispered. Ryan looked at me, frowning. I eased my gun from my holster, pulse beginning to quicken. Every small sound or scrape seemed preternaturally loud. Out of my peripheral vision I could see Ryan pulling his gun as well.

"I feel it too," he said, voice almost too low to hear.

The piercing shriek from above gave me barely enough warning to throw myself to the side.

"Ryan! Demon! Take cover," I managed to yell, even as leathery wings buffeted me, knocking me sprawling. I kept hold of my gun, though, and rolled quickly to my back as I tried to see where the creature had gone. It was a demon, that much I knew, but there'd been no chance to see what manner of demon I was up against. *A higher demon wouldn't have given itself away,* I thought frantically. But it had wings, so it had to be at least seventh level. With any luck it was merely a *kehza.*

Merely. Ha. I couldn't see a damn thing, nor could I hear the beating of wings, though I knew that the creature was strong and fast and, if it was diving, there was no guarantee I would get a warning the next time. I scrabbled back toward the doorway of the diner, wanting something solid at my back. I swore under my breath. Heavy metal gates across the glass front doors barred any hope of escape in that direction. But at least I was in a slight alcove, which meant that the demon couldn't dive down on me. Unfortunately, I was also cornered.

"Ryan!" I called. "Are you all right?"

I heard him curse, then he came around the side of the alley and sprinted to me, crouched low, gun in his hand and eyes wide. But, to his credit, he didn't look panicked. He just looked like a man who had believed in something for a long time but had finally been presented with unavoidable evidence that it was real, whether he wanted it to be or not.

He reached the alcove and huddled up in the sparse cover, scanning the area. "I'm all right. Where is it?"

"I can't tell. I'm hoping it's a *kehza*, a seventh-level demon."

"Are they easier to kill?"

I gave a humorless laugh. "Sure, the way Everest is easier to climb than K2. All demons are incredibly fast and deadly, but if it was a twelfth-level we'd have serious problems."

Ryan opened his mouth to speak again, but an inhuman shriek interrupted him. The demon suddenly dropped down in front of us, snarling around a mouthful of jagged teeth and grabbing at us with clawed hands. I let out a startled yelp and fired twice. The demon shifted with a speed that was otherworldly, somehow evading the projectiles, then leaped back into the air, leaving behind a sour-sweet smell like rotting flowers.

I gasped for breath in the sudden silence, the sound echoed by Ryan as we both hurriedly checked ourselves for injuries. Though not as large as an eleventh- or twelfth-level demon, a *kehza* was still plenty dangerous—about the size and build of a human, with a face that bore an uncanny resemblance to a Chinese dragon, skin of iridescent red and purple, and plenty of sharp teeth and claws.

"Jesus fucking Christ," Ryan breathed. "I've never seen anything move that fast."

"They're fast," I agreed, though I'd never realized they were *that* fast. It had fucking dodged a bullet! "But I was right. It's a *kehza*."

He slid a narrow-eyed glance to me. "And this information helps us how?"

"Oh, it doesn't. I think the only way we're going to wound it is if it gets distracted and one of us is able to shoot it."

Ryan frowned. "How many shots will it take to kill something like that? Where's the best place to aim?"

"Well, you won't be able to *kill* it," I said, still scanning anxiously. "It's not from this plane, so if you deal it a mortal injury, it'll return to its own plane and re-form there. It . . . discorporeates."

He cocked an eyebrow. "Is that really a word?"

I gave a bark of laughter. "It is now. Basically you're just doing a really harsh dismissal ritual."

"Well, sending it back to its own plane is good enough for me." Ryan scowled, scanning the skies. "Otherwise, it looks like we're trapped here until it decides it's tired of playing with us."

I shifted my grip on my gun. "Shit. I can't figure out what it's doing. If it really wanted to kill us, we'd be dead."

"Well, I'm not going to just sit here." He looked longingly over at my car, which sat so invitingly a mere fifty feet away. It might as well have been a mile. "No chance we can make it to the car, huh?"

"Yeah, right," I scoffed. "Go for it, tough guy."

"Well, you did say that one of us needed to distract it." He smiled without humor.

I scowled at him. He had no idea what we were up against. "No, I said that it needed to be distracted. Not necessarily by one of us."

He continued to scan the area. "Do you see anyone else here wanting to help?"

My scowl deepened. "You don't realize how fast these creatures can be." I rubbed my eyes with my free hand. "This is stupid. You're right, we can't afford to be stuck in here. We don't know if Belle is anywhere near here either."

"Yeah, I have a bad feeling about that," he murmured, expression dark.

I let out a shuddering breath. Had the demon already taken her? Then what was it doing attacking us? *But it easily could have killed us by now, so maybe it's just stalling us.* I didn't have any answers. I only knew that I was blowing it again and another victim was going to die. "Cover me," I said, and before Ryan could form a protest, I took off running toward the car.

I heard the whoosh of air and I dove to the side, not thinking about tactics, just hoping that random evasion would work the best. Wings slammed at me and I went rolling, seeing teeth and claws as a line of fire seared my shoulder. A clawed hand seized my wrist in a grip of iron, then abruptly released me, sending me sprawling. My gun went flying from my hand as I tucked, but I heard gunshots anyway.

An agonized bellow erupted above me. I rolled, scrambling to get my back against the car as I saw the demon hit the ground in a crumpled heap, bright white light streaming from two places in its chest. It shrieked again, pushing up from the ground as the light spread and widened, then it collapsed, the shriek dying into an almost piteous whine.

I pulled myself to my feet and the demon lifted its head shakily, locking eyes with mine.

"Sssummoner," it said in a weird, hissing croon, then the light flared to blinding levels and I heard the earsplitting crack of a dismissal. When I could see again, the demon was gone, with just the smell of rotting flowers and ozone lingering.

I looked up to see Ryan running toward me, his face a mask of fury. "What the fuck is wrong with you?" he yelled, grabbing me by the shoulders and giving me a shake. Then he released me so suddenly I almost fell. "Christ, you're hurt!" he exclaimed, looking down at blood on his hand.

I blinked at the sudden change from furious to solicitous. As if his words were a switch, my shoulder started to hurt. "Crap. Yeah." I sighed and craned my head to look at my upper back by my shoulder. "I don't think it's bad, though."

"It's going to need stitches." Ryan scowled blackly. "What the fuck was that stunt? That's not what partners do!"

I hunched my shoulders unconsciously under the verbal barrage. "Sorry. I was thinking that the demon was keeping us there long enough for Belle to be grabbed."

Ryan swore under his breath again and jammed his fingers through his hair. "Yeah. Okay. But, next time, fucking tell me. I mean, give me some warning other than 'Cover me!' I was fucking reloading!"

I winced. "Sorry. I'm not used to this partner thing. You're right."

He blew out his breath. "No. No, it's cool. I'm sorry I yelled. Its full attention was on you, which made it possible for me to shoot it. We need to get you looked at, though, and see if our girl is still here."

"We're probably gonna have help in a few minutes," I

said, as I retrieved my gun and holstered it. "I'm sure some-one around here will call in the fact that they heard gun-fire."

Ryan scanned the street, then looked back at me. "How are we going to explain this?" he wondered aloud. Then he let out a colorful oath. "You're bleeding pretty badly. Where's your radio?" He took me bodily and pushed me down to the curb.

"I'm all right. It just got me with a claw." Now, as the adrenaline wore off, I was starting to feel it more. I could also feel what would soon be a bruise on my wrist where it had grabbed me. *It grabbed me and then let me go. It had what it needed.* "Radio's in the car," I said. Then I gave a rough laugh. "Good place for it, huh? Though I don't know how I would have called this one in. 'Officer needs assis-tance, under attack from demon.' "

"That would go over well," he replied dryly. He reached inside the car and grabbed my radio out of the charger and a T-shirt out of my gym bag.

"I need to call *something* in, quick," I fretted. "Something to explain why I got hurt and why we fired shots."

"Got it covered," he said with a smirk as he lifted the ra-dio. "Agent Kristoff, Dispatch. Unit 723 and myself in foot pursuit of burglary suspects, headed down"—he paused, glancing at the street sign on the corner—"Vaughn Street at Alfred Drive, southbound. Shots have been fired." He spoke in an unbearably calm voice, eyes on me. Then he lowered the radio, picked up a brick from the gutter, and heaved it through the diner window.

I groaned and dropped my head. "I cannot *believe* you just did that."

"You want to tell them we were fighting a demon?"

I shook my head, laughing. "You'd just better hope that

there's no video surveillance on any of the businesses on this street."

"Oh, *shit*," he said, suddenly chagrined. He glanced up and down the street, then relaxed. "I don't see any. Probably why he chose this spot. Wouldn't want his demon to get caught on tape." He gave me a quick grin, then keyed up again. "Agent Kristoff, Dispatch. We've discontinued foot pursuit. Officer in need of assistance. Subjects last seen headed southbound.

"Before all the troops arrive," he said, as the sound of sirens became audible, "can we expect any more of these nasties?" He handed me the radio and pressed the shirt from my gym bag to the bleeding wound on my shoulder.

"Highly doubtful. It's almost impossible to summon and hold more than one demon at a time."

He sat down beside me on the curb, holding the shirt to my shoulder. "You know, this kind of sucks ass," he said, tone jarringly conversational.

I laughed. "Ya think?"

He gave a wry smile. "No, I mean, you . . . we . . . can't be honest about what we saw, which means that we can't get help trying to find who sent it after us."

"Yeah. That definitely sucks." I rubbed at my face with my left hand. "A little extra manpower would be damn useful right about now." The summoner would be tired, I knew, and a little shaky from having his summoned creature sent back. He was fucking vulnerable, and there was nothing I could do about it.

But that wasn't what had me so unsettled. "He wasn't trying to kill us."

Ryan arched an eyebrow at me. "Oh? He was doing a damn fine imitation."

"No. If we were meant to be dead, we'd most likely *be*

dead." I could hear the wail of sirens grow closer. We probably had less than a minute until the backup units arrived.

Ryan's brows drew together. "So what was it doing?"

"I think . . . it was assessing me." I fought back a shiver. "It grabbed me—just for a heartbeat—and then let me go. And right before it 'died' here, it called me 'summoner.'"

"I don't like the sound of that," he said, voice nearly a growl.

"Me neither, but a few things make sense now. The bodies being dumped where we could find them, the sigils around Greg's body—I think all of that was to see if I was a summoner."

"Then why send the demon?"

I rubbed my arms. "To see how strong I am, I think."

"I'm pretty damn uneasy about why he might want to know that." He gave me a grim look.

The backup units came screeching up then, and the next several minutes were a barely ordered maelstrom of questions and shouted commands. Somehow we both managed to stick to a vaguely consistent story. I gave a fictional description of the perps, which I prayed didn't resemble anyone who might actually be in the area, and about a minute later the K9 unit rolled up.

"So, how many of them were there, Kara?"

I raised my good arm in a gesture of helplessness. "Sarge, I'm sorry. I think there were three, but it happened so fucking fast. We rolled up on them just as the brick got pitched through the window. We got into a fight, then a chase, one of them fired on us, we both fired on them, but it was so crazy that I don't know if any were hit. I didn't even realize that I'd been cut during the fight until Ryan saw me bleeding." Damn, but I was pretty good at lying!

The road sergeant glared at me. "Why the fuck didn't you call it in when you saw it?"

"I did!" I exclaimed with what I hoped was believable fervor. "But my radio got knocked out of my hand during the fight."

He frowned. "Nothing came over the air."

"Damn cheap radio system," I said, adding a scowl for good measure.

He nodded in agreement. "Yeah. It sucks ass. Maybe after someone gets killed, the voters will give us the tax that we need to buy new equipment."

The one time I can be glad that our budget is so damn low, I thought with vague relief.

A din suddenly erupted from the K9 unit's vehicle, drawing everyone's attention. The dog yelped and whined, refusing to get out of the car. His officer was clearly baffled as to why the animal was acting so oddly.

It smells the demon, I thought. *And it doesn't want any part of it.* "I think they had a car near," I said aloud, beginning to despise the need for fiction. "I don't think there's a point in doing a track with the K9."

The sergeant's gaze was still on the dog. "Yeah. Probably a good thing. Man, I have never seen that dog act like that." He walked over to the vehicle, and I could hear him telling the K9 officer not to bother. The dog's yelping subsided instantly once the door was shut again.

"Yep. This sucks," I agreed in a low voice to Ryan.

WE WERE BOTH GRIMLY SILENT AS RYAN DROVE TO THE ER. He pulled up to the emergency entrance, but to my surprise he made no move to get out.

"I'm sorry," he said when I gave him a perplexed look. "I need to go take care of some things and write up the report of my involvement."

"It can't wait?" I said, realizing after I said it that I was being a weenie. I didn't need him to stay and hold my hand.

An embarrassed look crossed his face. "Okay, I fucking hate hospitals. I mean, if you'd been shot or something, then, yeah, I'd go in there. But since it's just stitches, I'm going to be a fucking candyass."

I had to grin at his honesty. "Fine. I'll call you when I'm done."

He smiled in relief. "Deal."

It ended up being nearly five hours before I finally, wearily, called him to pick me up. First it had been the usual interminable wait to get stitched up, then I had to stay and endure a thorough debriefing by my captain. The only thing that saved me from having to write up my report right then and there was the fact that I'd been hurt and couldn't type and had been out all night besides, which meant I was able to beg off at least until I could get some sleep.

It was well after nine by the time we made it back to my house. My aunt was gone, thankfully. I did *not* want to deal with her reaction to the attack. I went into my bedroom and gingerly changed into a clean shirt, then came back out to the kitchen. My shoulder and arm throbbed annoyingly as I sat down at my kitchen table, propping my chin on my good hand.

Ryan frowned at me. "You need to get to bed."

"I know," I said with a deep sigh. "I just can't help but wonder if that phone call was a total setup from the start. I mean, was she really afraid that someone was after her, or had she already been snatched and forced to make the call?"

Ryan began opening kitchen cupboards. "What kind of vibe did you get?"

"It sounded real enough to me at the time. I mean, she sounded terrified, but I didn't think she was being forced to talk. Then again, when she called I wasn't even thinking that it might have been a setup." I couldn't escape the ache of worry. "He must have already taken her."

Ryan pulled milk out of the fridge and a pot from beneath the counter. "You don't know that. She still might be safe. I think that you're sensitive enough to trust your instincts, and the large majority of the time your instincts are going to steer you right." He poured the milk into the pot and set it to heat on the stove. "You have plenty of real-world experience and, from what I've seen, you're good at dealing with people."

"Maybe," I replied, secretly tickled at the compliments. "But I wonder if I've become too caught up in all of this since everything has moved so quickly." I flexed my hand, feeling the answering dull ache in my stitched shoulder. "I keep feeling as if I'm missing something, and if I just had time to step back a bit, I'd get it. But every time things seem to slow down, something else gets thrown our way."

Ryan was silent as he slowly stirred the milk. "Don't forget that you do have other people to rely on," he said after a moment. He added cocoa powder to the milk and then glanced my way. "I know that it's hard for you since you're the one who has the knowledge of the arcane, and it's even harder for you since you can't share the fact that you possess that knowledge. But you're smart enough to tell what you know without blowing your *secret identity.*" He grinned as he drawled out the last two words.

I stifled a yawn and smiled. "You're being awfully nice to me. What do you want?"

He laughed. "Hey, I just can't get over the fact that, after all this time—after all the stories my grandmother told me—I actually got to see a demon tonight." He lifted the pot from the stove and poured the hot cocoa into two mugs. "Okay, so I would have preferred if it had not been diving at us with claws extended, but once you get over that small detail, it was just darn cool." His eyes crinkled in amusement as he handed the mug over to me.

I yawned again as I took the mug. "You are too silly."

"I know. But that's why you put up with me."

"Maybe I put up with you because you're a very effective stalker." I sipped at the cocoa—perfectly chocolated and warm enough to be perfectly drinkable. He'd known exactly what kind of comfort food I needed. I'd have worried that he could somehow sense my thoughts, except for the fact that chocolate was pretty universal in its comfort factor. It didn't take a psychic to figure that much out. *Though he does seem to know his way around my kitchen fairly well. . . .* I looked up at him through half-lidded eyes. I wanted to think about that a bit more, but my mind just didn't want to hold on to any coherent thought. *No wonder, silly woman. You've been awake for only a million hours.* So much for getting my sleep cycle back on track.

I dragged my attention back to Ryan when I realized that he was speaking. "I'm sorry," I said. "Whadja say?"

He gave me a wry smile. "It doesn't matter. You're totally wiped and you need to go to bed. Do you have any of the pain pills?"

I fought to keep my eyes open. "Dunno; 'sokay," I slurred. "Too sleepy to hurt right now."

I heard him laugh, then he took the mug out of my hand and pulled my good arm over his shoulder, dragging me up out of the chair.

"Come on, Kara," he said, walking me down the hall to my bedroom.

"I can walk." I tried to protest, but he didn't seem to care. He brought me into my bedroom and gently pushed me down onto the bed, then tugged my shoes and socks off and pulled the comforter over me.

"Go to sleep," he said, or at least that's what I thought he said, before I lost the battle to fatigue.

"I FRIGHTENED YOU. It was not my desire to do so."

I knew that voice, that unmatchable resonance. The memory of my last encounter with him rose again at his words—that taste of unchecked rage, the overwhelming terror, and the glimpse into how powerful a creature he truly was. He sounded deeply sincere, but after the day I'd had, I wasn't sure I had it in me right now to deal with him. I pulled the pillow over my head. "It's cool. It's fine," I mumbled through the pillow. "Apology accepted. I'm tired."

I heard a soft hiss. "You are injured." His voice took on a darker timbre.

I kept the pillow clamped over my head. "Let me sleep, please?"

"I have never interrupted your sleep. You are injured and exhausted. You should not push yourself to such extremes."

I couldn't resist. I lifted the pillow from my head and looked over at him. Rhyzkahl stood beside my bed, azure eyes ancient and dangerous as he gazed down at me, dressed this time in robes of red in a hue so dark it could have been black. The front was intricately stitched with a pattern of runes in shimmering black thread, which caught the light and played tricks with the eyes. The contrast with his near-glowing hair and beautiful features was incredible.

"I have to do what I'm doing or more people are going to die," I said wearily.

"You do not like these people," he stated calmly. "You do not care for them, or respect them. You would never wish to invite them to your house, nor would you lend them money. Yet you put yourself in harm's way for them."

I sat up. "No one deserves to die that way."

He sat with ethereal grace on the bed and lifted a silky eyebrow at me. "No one? Are you certain?"

I groaned and squeezed the bridge of my nose with my

fingers. "Could we not get into a philosophical discussion about my career choice tonight?"

He lifted a hand and stroked my cheek with the back of his fingers. "Of course, dear one. I would gladly distract you from such banal thoughts."

I leaned into the caress without realizing it at first. I thought briefly about pulling away, but I had to admit that it felt nice. "Sorry. The last few weeks have been kinda shitty."

He leaned forward and kissed me lightly. "And I made it no better by allowing you to feel my anger. I regret that I did so."

I looked up at him. He was beautiful and alluring but, more than that, I realized I was beginning to enjoy his dream visits. He was interesting and intelligent, and he seemed to understand me on a level that I doubted anyone else would ever approach. Even knowing how powerful he was and what he was capable of, I had to admit that I was starting to *like* him just a little. And though I was aware how naive it was, I couldn't help but cling to the thin belief that I held some sort of appeal for him as well—an appeal beyond that of simply being a means to gain access to this sphere.

"Can you tell me what it was that made you so angry?" I asked.

"It is a matter that I will deal with," he said in a tone that made it clear he had no intention of elaborating further. He kissed me again, not so lightly this time. "Do not worry yourself with this," he murmured against my lips as he deftly slipped my shirt over my head, barely breaking the contact with my lips at all. A moan escaped me and I leaned into him as he deepened the kiss. His fingers moved deliciously against my skin as heat flushed through me.

But I had too many questions running through my head to enjoy the moment properly. I struggled out of his thrall and pulled reluctantly away from his kiss. He straightened and regarded me, smiling. "Is there aught wrong, dearest?"

"No, it's just . . . You said you would deal with whatever it was yourself, but if it has something to do with my case I need to know."

He laughed, tipping his head back. "Oh, my dear Kara, you never fail to impress me! Such dedication to your calling." Then his smile took on a harder edge. "How is it that you were injured?"

I pulled the comforter closer around me, aware that he'd avoided giving me any information. "A demon—a *kehza*— attacked us," I said. "But it wasn't trying to kill us. I mean, it could have taken us out several times, and I suffered only a cut on my shoulder. And, to be honest, I think that was an accident as well. It was almost like I ran into him."

His lip curled in an echo of a snarl. "You have the taint about you of an arcane attack. This angers me."

"Yeah, well, I'm not exactly thrilled that it happened either."

He shook his head, hair cascading in silken perfection with the movement. "A higher demon would have known not to touch you."

I blinked at him. "Huh? Why?"

"A *syraza* or *reyza* would have been able to sense my touch on you and would have known that you are not for any other to affect."

I stared at him. "Wait. What? You've branded me or something?"

He brushed his fingers across my hair. "You are mine, Kara. I will not tolerate another molesting you."

"What?" I screeched. "Yours? Only *you* can molest me?"

But the room was empty.

The door slammed open and Ryan stood framed in the doorway. "Kara! What's wrong?"

I yelped and crossed my arms over my chest, blinking at him stupidly. "Um . . . am I awake?"

Ryan looked at me oddly. "You yelled something unintelligible, so I came in to see what was wrong. So, tell me, what's wrong?"

I had to have been asleep if Rhyzkahl had been here. I glanced down and breathed a deep sigh of relief, lowering my arms. I was still wearing my shirt. "Nothing. It was just a dream." Just a dream. Ha. *Stop being stupid*, I berated myself. *Stop finding things to like about him.*

I could see him tense. "What kind of dream? Was it a demon dream?"

I ran my fingers through my hair. "It was a Demonic Lord dream, yeah." Then I froze, arm still raised. "What the hell?"

He stepped into the room. "What is it?"

I flexed my arm, then rolled my shoulder, reaching up with my other hand to feel the bandage.

"What is it?" he repeated, tone growing urgent.

I peeled the bandage off and felt the skin beneath it. "It doesn't hurt."

He gave me a puzzled look. "Your shoulder? You need to be careful of it. It still needs to heal."

I shifted so that he could see my shoulder. "No, it doesn't. It's already healed. There's not even a scar."

"Let me see," he ordered. I twisted around to show him the unmarred skin of my shoulder. I could feel small pieces of thread and flakes of dried blood around where the wound had been—blood that I'd been too exhausted to completely clean off earlier. But there was most definitely no wound anymore. No wound, no scar, no stitches, no deviation in the flesh of any sort.

He let out a low whistle. "If I hadn't seen it with my own eyes, I would never believe it."

"And I'm glad you're a witness to it." I flexed my arm again, still not fully believing it. "How long have I been asleep?"

He glanced at his watch. "A few hours. I'd just dozed off on the couch when I heard you yell." His mouth twitched in a smile. "Do you always wake up yelling?"

"No," I said with a laugh, tossing a pillow at him. "But his lordiness also left me feeling fresh and rested."

He peered into my face. "You certainly don't look as exhausted."

I swung my legs over the side of the bed and stood. "I'm not. At all. I feel like I've slept twelve hours." Okay, so maybe there *were* some advantages to these dream visits.

Ryan yawned. "Yeah, well, I don't. I'm gonna dig out and head back to my hotel room and hope that Garner doesn't snore too loudly."

I gave him a withering look. "Don't be an idiot. I have a guest room that no one ever stays in. In fact, you will probably be the first guest to ever stay there."

"Cool," he said, eyes crinkling. "My whining was suitably pathetic. I'll be more than happy to christen your guest room."

I laughed. "Go. Next door down the hall. It's the one with the bed in it. If you get to the room with the bathtub, you've gone too far."

He flashed me a grin and left. My own smile faded as he

continued on down the hall and my left hand crept up to feel the unblemished skin on my shoulder.

What was this going to cost me? Rhyzkahl's comments about marking me as his own haunted me.

Or had I already paid the price?

21

THE HOUSE SEEMED UNBEARABLY QUIET AFTER RYAN went off to get some sleep. And after standing in the foyer for several minutes, I realized that it seemed so because, up until that point, everything had been going so quickly. I finally had a chance to breathe, but at the same time I knew that I really didn't have the luxury of time to relax. The Symbol Man was still out there, and so far I'd failed utterly to find any of the people who were next on his list.

Except the one girl, Belle, and that had not exactly gone well. The persistent sick knot in my stomach warned me how she'd probably be found.

It was early afternoon, which meant I had at least five more hours of daylight. After the experience with the demon, I wasn't too keen on going out without backup, and Ryan would most likely sleep for at least several hours.

But there was plenty that I could do without backup. I went and took a quick shower, scrubbing the last of the dried blood off the nonexistent wound on my shoulder, then dressed in jeans and a *16th Annual Law Enforcement*

Torch Run T-shirt, looping my holster through my belt. I jotted a quick note to Ryan, telling him where I was going and to call me when he woke up, then I gathered up the copies of the pictures of the victims-to-be and headed to the station.

I spent the next several hours making more copies of the pics and then passing them out to the patrol guys, giving them a brief rundown of why I needed to get in touch with these people.

"I recognize a couple of these faces," one of the officers coming on duty said, shuffling through the pics. "But I couldn't tell you their real names."

"Have you ever arrested any of them?" I asked eagerly.

He shrugged. "Might have. But I'm not sure when or where."

But that gave me an idea. I thanked the officer and then called Detective Harris.

"Harris here," he answered on the second ring.

"Harris, it's Kara Gillian. If I send you a composite of the pics from Cerise's house, do you think you could pass them out to the deputies over there to see if any of your guys recognize anyone?"

He was silent for a moment, then, "That's a damn good idea, Gillian," he said, to my intense shock. "Use the troops. Definitely. Send them over."

I hung up the phone, bemused, then quickly emailed the collection of pics over to Harris. Finally, it felt like I was *doing* something. I spent about an hour typing up some notes, then shut down my computer to head back home. Ryan would probably be awake soon, and then the two of us could continue canvassing for these people.

My phone rang just as I was locking the door to my office. "Detective Gillian," I said.

"Hey, Detective Gillian, this is Deputy Keller with the sheriff's office. I think we found one of your people."

"Wow, that was fast! Where are you? Which one?"

He cleared his throat. "Well, it's not so great, really. We're out on Highway 1790."

Highway 1790 was a long, empty stretch through the swamp at the north end of the parish. The sick knot in my stomach tightened. "Shit. Don't tell me."

He sighed. "Yeah, she's dead. Sorry."

"I'm on my way."

I SENT A text message to Ryan and pulled up at the scene about half an hour later, just as dusk was beginning to paint the sky in shades of purple and orange. Detective James Harris was already on the scene—which I'd expected since the body was found within his jurisdiction. But I was somewhat surprised to see Agent Zack Garner there as well, standing by his car and talking on his cell phone.

He hung up as I approached. "Ryan's on his way. He and I were grabbing dinner when he got your text, and he said he'd meet us here."

I caught myself in time before saying something like, *Oh, I figured he'd still be asleep.* That would be a sure way to give people the wrong impression.

"We've been discussing the case most of the afternoon," Zack continued, absently waving a mosquito away from his face.

He must not have slept long at all, I decided. But it was probably better that he not spend too much time at my house. "Come up with anything new and interesting?" I asked.

He shook his head. "He just filled me in on what happened to you two this morning."

"Yeah, it was pretty wild," I said, keeping my response vague since I had no idea what Ryan had told him. *Which story did he give him—the demon attack, or the one we told everyone else?*

Zack's eyes met mine. "He told me what *really* happened," he clarified. The flashing red and blue lights of the patrol units reflected oddly in his eyes, making them seem for an instant as if they had a reddish cast of their own. Then he smiled and the effect was gone. "Sounds dumb, but I sure wish I'd been there to see it for myself."

"Not dumb at all," I said, but my gaze slid to Harris. He was deep in conversation with some of the detectives from his own department. "Does he . . . ?"

Zack snorted. "No. Hell, he wouldn't believe it even if he saw it with his own eyes. He'd find some way to *explain* it."

"That sounds about right," I said, relieved that Harris had not also been privy to the real story. I couldn't explain why, but I didn't have any worries about Zack knowing the truth. I just somehow knew that he *got* it.

"And here comes our prodigal son," Zack said, looking beyond me. I turned to see a dark Crown Victoria pulling to the side of the highway behind my Taurus.

Ryan exited his car and walked up to us. I noticed that he'd found the time to shower, shave, and change clothes and still managed to look fairly rested. He gave a nod to Zack, then looked at me, expression sober. "I have a bad feeling about this one."

"I do too," I replied, though *bad feeling* was putting it mildly.

This stretch of highway didn't have much in the way of landmarks. A long, boring stretch of asphalt with swamp on either side, it was where people went when they wanted to see just how fast their cars would go. The only thing people had to watch out for was the occasional wild boar or alligator in the road. At least once a month, deputies were dispatched to a single-car accident along this stretch. A collision with wildlife at ninety miles an hour usually had pretty drastic consequences.

I approached the body, surprised that it had even been noticed. Probably more than one car had passed the bloody lump on the side of the road and assumed it to be an animal that had lost its battle with a vehicle. My throat tightened as I got closer. Her death would have likely been far more pleasant if she'd merely been hit by a car. The coppery smell of blood mingled sickeningly with the dank stench of stagnant water and composting vegetation from the nearby swamp.

It was definitely Belle, the girl in the picture—ugly gashes marred the young cheeks beneath the slanted eyes, piercings in her brow and lip still in place. The body flowed and flickered with arcane markings and, unlike the last body, I could easily read these runes. I stood a few feet away, eyes narrowed and fists clenched.

"What do they say?" Ryan asked softly from beside me.

"Taunts and threats," I said, voice tight. "Some indication of what was done to her, runes of suffering and torment." And a glyph that included my own name wound through the others, but I wasn't sure I was going to share that with Ryan. The killer knew I was a summoner, and now he was telling me that it didn't matter, that I wasn't strong enough to stop him.

"He's baiting you," Zack murmured.

I glanced sharply at him, unaware that he'd been standing right behind us. But then I realized that Ryan had probably brought him completely up to speed, including all of the arcane aspects. "He's an asshole," I growled in reply, then crouched by the body, ignoring the buzz and bite of mosquitoes. I noticed immediately that the injuries were markedly different from those of the other victims. Cruder, more savage. No precise slices or burns. Instead, she'd been nearly ripped apart. My stomach clenched as I took in the parallel slices across the girl's torso that had disemboweled her. I recognized them easily as claw marks, but I wondered what Dr. Lanza would make of them. The symbol had been slashed messily into her thigh, like an afterthought.

"They didn't take their time with this one," I said, voice hoarse. "This was a slaughter."

Ryan growled something under his breath, and I didn't need to hear the words to be able to agree with the meaning. I shuddered, then narrowed my eyes at the tracks and impressions in the dirt that surrounded the body. "The demon brought her here." I stood. "See those tracks?" I pointed out the deep indentations in the ground. "It landed there and then pushed off again to take flight, just dumping her body here." But then I looked more closely at the tracks, bothered.

"What is it?" Zack asked.

"It . . . doesn't make sense," I said. The tracks were clear—most certainly not made by any manner of human. "A *kehza* wouldn't be strong enough to fly all the way here with a burden like a body. Hell, they're barely strong enough to fly at all. They can only do short flights."

"Like when it was swooping down at us?" Ryan asked with a scowl.

"Exactly. So there's just no way it could have flown here to dump the body."

Ryan glanced around to make sure no one else was close

enough to overhear our conversation. Fortunately, Harris was still pontificating to his own people. "And I guess it's pretty silly to think that the killer drove the demon and his victim to someplace close, just so that it could fly over and deposit the body."

"Right. It doesn't make any sense. And the timing doesn't work either. We were at the diner barely fifteen minutes after Belle called. Even if she'd already been brought out here, there's no way that the *kehza* could have flown back to town in time to attack us. And it couldn't have killed her and dumped her afterward, because it had been sent back to its own plane." I cursed softly. "That *must* mean that there's a second demon, a higher-level demon—probably a *syraza* or a *reyza*. Either of those would be more than strong enough to snatch her from that street and fly her all the way out here to kill her. The *kehza* was just there to find out more about me."

"And using that *syraza* or *reyza* gives the killer an alibi," Zack pointed out. "If he lets the demon snatch his victims and take care of the bodies, he can be anywhere else."

That was an unpleasant thought.

"How could he have sent the *kehza* after you *and* also had this other demon to take care of this body? I thought you said that it was almost impossible to summon and hold two demons?" Ryan asked, crossing his arms over his chest.

"I did. It is. Crap. There must be another explanation." There was one, but it was one that deepened the feeling of dread within me.

"I don't like the look on your face, Detective," Ryan said.

"Damn. It's possible—*possible*—that he has formally allied with the higher-level demon, which would mean it wouldn't require the same level of effort to summon."

Kind of like what you could have with Rhyzkahl, the

thought crept in. But, no, this was different. This was an indication of a degree of cooperation that was rarely seen between summoners and the beings they summoned. The thought of a demon and a summoner working *together* to summon and control a Demonic Lord spoke of conflicts that ranged far beyond this sphere. In fact, having a higher demon as an ally would probably be the only way a summoner could ever hope to succeed in summoning and binding a Demonic Lord.

"Okay, this is starting to feel really, *really* bad," I said, as I stepped away from the body.

"Care to share?" Ryan said. "I mean, besides the obvious stuff that even I can figure out."

Harris chose that moment to wonder what the three of us were up to. He huffed up to us, shirt straining.

"I'll take care of this," Zack murmured. "Ryan can fill me in later."

I gave him a look of relief as he neatly intercepted Harris and deftly guided him away from us. I could hear him asking the rotund detective about the traffic that usually traveled the highway and then could hear Harris eagerly launching into a story about drug trafficking and bike gangs.

Damn. Talk about taking one for the team! I motioned with my head for Ryan to follow, walking well away from the others to a point near where the ground turned soft and the swamp began. "If he's allied with a demon," I said, speaking low and quickly, "it's almost definitely a *syraza* or a *reyza*—eleventh- or twelfth-level demons—since the lowers don't have enough control or power to be capable of a worthwhile alliance. And the only reason one would ally with a human, even a summoner, would be if it was worth his while. If he was going to get something out of it." I frowned and stuffed my hands down into my pockets.

"In every summoning, a summoner has to give the summoned creature something in return. It's totally a power struggle, and the creature is bound, but only a small portion of that binding is arcane in nature. It's all about the honor. During the summoning, after the initial binding, the summoner offers the demon something that would be considered valuable to the demon—enough to satisfy their bruised honor—and what it is depends on the demon."

"What sort of something are we talking about?"

"Like I said, it depends on the demon. Some of the smaller ones like chocolate or beer. Others like books. Some want information. Others merely want the summoner to spill his or her blood to show their commitment to the summoning. It depends on the demon."

"Okay," Ryan drawled. "And what could our Symbol Man have offered this demon in exchange for his help?"

I dragged a hand through my hair. "Power, of some sort. Certainly not here in this sphere, because that would be worthless to a demon below the level of a lord, but most likely a chance at power in the sphere of the demons."

"Ah. Sort of like the Klingon method of promotion."

I stared at him blankly. "The what?"

Ryan's eyes went wide. "You can't be serious. As over the edge as you are, you don't watch *Star Trek*?"

I scowled. "I'm not over the edge, and I do so watch *Star Trek*. Did. A couple of times."

Ryan rolled his eyes dramatically. "And here I thought you were my perfect match." He grinned at me while I struggled for a response. "The Klingon method of promotion," he continued, "is where you kill your superior to get their job."

"Oh. Right." Funny. He didn't *look* like a nerd. "Okay, yes, that might be it in a way, though a *reyza* can't actually *become* a lord. It would be like a panther trying to become a tiger. But it could be one of the lord's generals. Or, more likely, it's a rival general working for his own lord to bring down this other lord. My aunt tells me that the power struggles in that sphere are constant and devious."

Ryan frowned. "Is there a way to find out who the demon is?"

I started to tell him that there wasn't, then paused. There was a way, but, holy shit, it was risky.

"Kara? What is it?"

"Well," I said, "*I* can't tell, but another higher demon—or a more powerful being than that—could probably read the traces on the body and be able to identify it." I thought about Rhyzkahl's statement about his mark on me.

"So you could summon a demon and ask it?"

"Er, well, not exactly." I glanced up at the sky, even though I knew perfectly well that the moon was still a few days away from full. "Higher demons almost always need to be summoned on a full moon, plus there would be the problem of having the body nearby so that it could be examined. That's in addition to the basic problem of being able to summon and control a higher demon in the first place."

"Well, that sucks."

"Actually . . . I think I know a way to do it." I bit my lip. "I mean, I can't summon a *reyza*, but I might be able to get some information."

He lifted an eyebrow. "Call your Demonic Lord?"

"Not *call* him," I said. "I'm not that foolish. But, um, maybe I can get him to come to my dreams again."

"You do realize you're talking about taking a nap in the same room as the body?" he pointed out.

I grimaced. Maybe there was another way?

"How do you know it will work?" Ryan asked.

"I don't. But I've asked him questions before. That's how I found out about the runes on the other victim."

"Okay, so other than napping in a morgue, it's pretty risk-free, right? There's not much he can do to you in your dreams that you can't just wake up from."

"Right. Sure," I said in what I hoped was a convincing manner. Only problem was, it wasn't true. Promises could be made, debts could be earned, patronages formed. Summoners had to abide by the same code that the demons were held to, or else they could not be trusted. Dreams might not be physical, but they still held great peril. *Well, not physical most of the time,* I thought as I flexed my healed shoulder.

"I think," I continued after a moment, "that I might not have to be in the same room as the body if I'm trying to speak to the lord in my dreams."

"That would make things a hell of a lot easier," Ryan said dryly.

I gave a halfhearted shrug as I watched the sheriff's office crimes-scene techs swarm over the area, taking measurements and photographing the body and its surroundings. It would be interesting to see what explanation was put forward for the tracks by the body.

"Well, I'm not certain it'll work," I said, "but I'm going to have to sleep at some point anyway, and he made a comment last time about being in control of the reality . . ."

"So he can whiz you there dream-speed or something."

"I guess. I hope." I rubbed at my eyes. "There's still so much I don't know. I feel like I'm fumbling along most of the time."

He gripped me by my shoulders and turned me toward him. "Hey, don't fail me now. You've brought us this far."

I mustered a wan smile. "I won't fail you. We're close. I know it."

"The killer is resorting to taunting you, which means he's definitely going to slip up soon."

I resisted the urge to slump. "I sure hope so."

He gave my shoulders a squeeze, then released me. "Come on, I'm taking you to bed," he said, grinning wickedly.

"Jeez, don't say that too loud," I said, smiling despite myself. "People will start talking."

22

Ryan pulled into my driveway right behind me, getting out of his car just as I was exiting mine.

"I do hope you realize that I'm not leaving your house tonight," Ryan said before I could say a word. "Not until you've woken up from your encounter with this Demonic Lord."

I allowed my protest to die unvoiced. "I can't see that there's going to be a problem. I mean, he's helped me twice now, and I think he's going to keep being cool to me since he wants me to call him. But, yeah, having you nearby is probably a good idea."

He gave me a quick grin. "I'm going to have to start leaving a change of clothes and a toothbrush at your place if this keeps up."

I smiled and quickly turned away, feeling an unfamiliar flush rising. What the hell was wrong with me? It wasn't as if I'd never spent the night with a man. Hell, I'd had boyfriends. Okay, not too many, but still. I'd just never had a guy as . . . everything . . . as Ryan pay this much attention to me. Smart, good-looking, witty, charming . . .

Stop being stupid. He's just working on the case. That's all this is. He thinks of you as a partner. I jammed the key into the lock of the back door and entered the kitchen.

"So explain something to me," he said as he followed me in and closed the door.

"Explain what?" I asked as I opened the fridge and peered at the available offerings. I honestly couldn't remember the last time I'd eaten.

"The whole good-and-evil thing with regard to the demons. I always had the impression that all demons were evil."

I grabbed a brick of cheddar. "Well, yeah, because that's what they say in Sunday school." I closed the refrigerator door with my hip, then snagged crackers and a knife. "But, see, these demons are not the demons of the religious mythos."

He watched me as I set the cheese and crackers on a plate and placed it on the table. "Then what are they?"

"They're other-planar creatures," I said, as I carved a slab of cheese from the brick and piled it onto a cracker. I gestured at the plate with a *help yourself* motion as I took an undainty bite.

He looked doubtfully at my exceedingly plebeian hors d'oeuvres. "Do you always buy your cheese in five-pound bricks?"

"It's only two pounds," I replied after a few seconds of chewing. "It was cheap. And I like cheese."

"But . . . cheddar? Mild?" He looked pained.

I glared at him and defiantly cut another piece. "It was *cheap*. Do you have a *problem* with my cheese?"

"Absolutely not," he said, giving a mock shudder. "So. Other-planar creatures? Explain, please?"

I set the knife down and held my hands up in front of me, one above the other. "Think different dimensions. Spheres. Planes of existence. Whatever you want to call it. We live in one, and they live in another. These two planes often converge in such a way that a person with the ability to open a portal between them can summon a creature from their world to ours."

"And how do people know if they have the ability?"

"Well, there seems to be a genetic factor, so summoners will usually keep an eye on their kids or grandkids when they hit their teenage years. Othersight comes first, so the easiest thing to do is to leave a big shiny ward somewhere and then see if the kid reacts to it." I grinned. "It can be a bit dramatic."

Ryan gave a snort of laughter. "I can only imagine."

"Anyway, after that much is established, the summoner will usually have a demon make the assessment as to how much ability is there."

He tapped the table. "What if there's no parent or grandparent to monitor the kid?"

"Well, that's kinda what happened with my aunt. She figured out that she could see things and feel things that other people couldn't, so she went to the library and started doing research."

He raised an eyebrow at me. "Please don't tell me she found a book called *Demon Summoning for Dummies*."

I laughed. "Not quite, but I think I may write that someday. No, it was noticed what areas she was researching, and, well . . . she was directed to a summoner who could mentor her."

"Wait. Who noticed? Is there some sort of worldwide surveillance?"

"No, there's no powerful Illuminati-ish conspiracy thingy." I grinned. "Tessa got lucky. She was at the New Orleans public library, and one of the librarians saw the books she was pulling. The librarian happened to be a summoner." I spread my hands. "This woman was elderly and was basically 'retired' from summoning, so she couldn't take Tessa on as a student, but she was able to find someone who would." I didn't elaborate on how much *luck* had actually been involved. Over the past few years I'd started to suspect that the demons had a hand in finding people who could summon, but I had no proof and little more than a gut feeling to go on.

He remained silent for a moment. "And how does good and evil come into this?" he said finally.

"It doesn't. I mean, not in the way that we define it. The demons are no more evil than witches are evil. And, trust me, every practitioner of Wicca I know abides pretty strictly by the canon of *Harm None*. For the most part, it's possible to make a general categorization and say this demon or that lord is evil, or this one is good, but all it means is that the behavior and actions of the demon fall into a pattern we as humans find acceptable or unacceptable. There's really so much more involved."

"Such as?"

"Well, what we might find unacceptable is merely a manner of dealing with issues of supremacy and honor for them. And vice versa. Something we find acceptable could be anathema to them, simply because of the way the particular act or whatever is performed." I shook my head. "Their moral and honor code is incredibly complex. Debts of honor are considered absolute, and to refuse to pay a debt of honor is evil to them." I spread my hands. "If you some-how screw up and put a demon in a position to lose honor, you're going to get slaughtered in simple retaliation."

"So they're pretty solid on the concept of revenge, right?"

"Yeah," I said, keeping my voice casual. I'd learned how accepting demons were of revenge when I was twenty-three, still a rookie cop. Evidence in a molestation case had been thrown out and the perpetrator had walked. I hadn't been involved in the case, but I knew the defendant, had known him twelve years earlier when I lived in his parents' house for a month.

I told Tessa about it, about him. Told her everything. And on the next full she'd summoned a *syraza* who, after it had been explained to him what was needed, gave his service as a gift. "Yeah, demons take matters of vengeance very seriously."

Ryan picked up the knife and cut a piece of cheddar, obviously reluctant to soil his palate with my store-brand cheese but apparently hungry enough to risk it. "That sort of thinking could work with humans, too, you know," he said. "Evil is often a matter of perception." He looked askance at the cheese, definitely trying to imply that my cheap mild cheddar was evil.

"Well, yes," I said as I took the knife from his hand. "But in order to do my job, I try to stick with the perceptions of a civilized society. Murder, bad. Hurting people who've done nothing to wrong you, bad. Taking things that you have no right to, bad." I smiled sweetly and stabbed the knife into the brick. "Making fun of other people's cheese, bad."

He laughed. "All right, all right. And catching serial kill-ers, good, right?"

I leaned back in my chair. "Well, I sure hope so."

"So, do you need to do anything special for Rhyzkahl to come to your dreams?"

"No. I mean, I don't know if there's anything I can do. He's come to me three times since . . . er . . . the summoning. Three weeks ago." More than three weeks ago, which meant that we had less than a week until the full. Time was running out and too many questions remained unanswered. "The best I can hope for," I continued, "is to try to fall asleep with a strong impression that I want him to come to my dreams."

He looked at me doubtfully. "Is that anything like calling him to you?"

"No," I said, with more conviction than I felt. "A call has to be . . . more intense and desired."

He scrubbed a hand through his hair. "You know, I'm still not keen on this. But I guess it's the only way we'll get any answers."

"Yeah," I said with a shrug. "I can't think of anything else to do right now."

"And I guess it wouldn't be good if I was in the same room as you?"

I blinked at him for a second before I realized that he wasn't saying what I thought he was. No, he wasn't coming on to me. He was talking about security. Sleeping on the floor or something. "Ummm, no, that would probably throw things off."

"All right, then I'll be down the hall." He gave me a wry smile. "I guess it's time for you to hit the sack."

HITTING THE SACK was easier said than done. Or, rather, the hitting-the-sack part was easy, but the actual falling-asleep part was trickier. And I didn't dare take anything narcotic to help me along, since that would just about guarantee that he wouldn't come. But thoughts of the case kept springing into my mind, coupled with thoughts of Ryan. *Damn it, I need to be thinking of Rhyzkahl!* I sighed and flopped onto my back, forcing myself to close my eyes and keep them closed. *I'll count my breaths,* I decided. *And think about Rhyzkahl. That's not calling him.*

I concentrated on taking long, steady breaths. *One, two, three . . . Think about those eyes of his . . . eight, nine, ten . . . and that beautiful face . . . fifteen, sixteen, seventeen . . . and that aura of power . . . twenty-two, twenty-three . . .*

"I am here." The resonant voice filled the room.

My eyes snapped open. I'd actually fallen asleep? I sat up quickly. *Hot damn, it worked!* I thought, with a mixture of elation and relief.

He stood at the foot of my bed, motionless, head lowered and azure eyes drilling into mine. An eerie pale light surrounded him, shimmering like hot asphalt, coming from nowhere and everywhere. He didn't move, and my elation began to shift to uncertainty as his aura touched me. I didn't feel the killing rage and fury that I'd experienced before, but there was a simmering intensity about him, a disdain and slow wrath that sent a crawling unease through me. This was far different than any prior dream visit.

"I . . . I'm glad you are here," I said hurriedly.

He remained silent, but it felt to me as if the menace in the room increased a breath. Was I just being paranoid? He'd never been threatening to me in any of the other dream visits. I gulped. "I, uh, could use your help . . . please. We have another body that has runes on it . . . and, well . . ." I faltered as his continued silence and intense regard began to unnerve me. I took a deep breath and forged on, despite the sick feeling growing in my belly. "Well, we—*I* was wondering if you could tell which demon left the markings."

He growled low, and the hair on my arms stood on end. Shit. This was not going at all the way the previous encounters had.

"You defy me, defy my desire to be called to you in the flesh," he snarled, eyes flashing with deadly intensity, "yet you still expect me to *serve* you?" His lip curled. "Under *your* terms?"

Shit. "No. No!" *Shit shit shit.* "Lord Rhyzkahl, I meant no disrespect—"

"Did you not?" The words cracked out like a whip. He took two steps toward me, and I found myself drawing back against the headboard in instinctive reaction to his anger. My heart slammed in my chest. I was an idiot! All of my harping about how important honor was, and here I was trying to find a way to get around it, to get the lord to do what *I* wanted.

"Did you not?" he repeated, voice low and just as threatening. "You think to bid me here, under your terms, thinking to have the advantage of me." He closed the distance between us in a move that was too fast for my eyes to follow, then seized me by the throat and pressed me back against the headboard. I gave a strangled cry and clutched at the hand holding me, but his grip on me was like iron.

"You thought to have the use of me," he purred, the gentleness of his voice in stark contrast to his hold on me. "Use of me in a manner that was safe. A visit to your dreams."

I clutched at the hand on my throat, struggling to hold back the whimper of terror. He wasn't choking me, at least not yet, but his grip was implacable and unmovable. Holy shit, but I'd been an idiot! This was the true Demon. A powerful creature who took great offense at being summoned to serve.

A beautiful smile spread across his face. "And now I will show you the folly of that decision. You called me to your dreams." He laughed, a lovely sound with a vicious edge. He leaned close and whispered against my cheek. "You *called* me, Kara darling."

My eyes went wide. No, it couldn't be! I'd merely kept my thoughts on him as I'd fallen asleep. Hadn't I? Had I actually called him? Or was my aunt mistaken about how it worked? Tessa had said that he had to be called with intent. . . . I swallowed painfully against the grip on my throat. Did Tessa really know? Had the intent for him to come to my dreams been all he needed?

"You do not know, do you?" he said, voice melodious as I struggled against his grip. "You cannot be sure if this is dream or reality. Either is possible."

"Please," I rasped. "I'm sorry. I'm sorry. Lord Rhyzkahl. Forgive me."

"I do not serve you, little summoner."

"No, no, you don't." I gabbled the words out, mind racing. If he was here in the flesh, could I actually dismiss him? Would a standard dismissal even work? A standard summoning sure didn't. If only I'd had time to study such things! But I hadn't really expected to encounter such a situation. I hadn't ever intended to actually *call* him to me.

"Kara!" The door flew open and Ryan burst in, gun in his hand. "Kara, I heard . . ." His voice trailed off at the sight before him. I knew what he was seeing and feeling. The surreal light, the beautiful visage, and most of all the powerful and overwhelming essence of *him*. Ryan paled and staggered back a full step before recovering. "Holy Mary Mother of God," he whispered.

He's Catholic? The insanely out-of-place thought came to me even as I renewed my struggles against the grip on me. "Ryan! Run!" I cried out. "You can't hurt him!"

Ryan's eyes flicked to me, then came back to Rhyzkahl. He lifted his gun, holding it with both hands and sighting carefully. "Let her go, asshole," he said, voice quavering only barely.

Rhyzkahl's eyes narrowed to azure slits as he regarded Ryan. "You have not the means to stop me."

"Ryan," I gasped, "the gun won't do you any good. Just fucking run!"

Rhyzkahl laughed, then began to slowly tighten his grip on me, his eyes on Ryan. I coughed, scrabbling frantically at the hand as my breath was constricted.

"Let her go!" Ryan shouted, stepping farther into the room, gun trained on Rhyzkahl.

No, damn it, Ryan, I thought frantically. *Just run!*

Rhyzkahl merely smiled and tightened his grip.

Ryan shot a quick glance to me, then looked back to the Demonic Lord. "You were warned," he said, voice steady now.

The sound of the gunshot slammed through the small room, and a picture on the far side of the room exploded into fragments. But I knew the bullet had passed through Rhyzkahl's head.

And left no damage in its wake.

"Ah, fuck," Ryan breathed, taking a step back.

Rhyzkahl tilted his head back, inhaling and lifting a hand. I froze as I saw the power coiling swiftly into his control, a blue-black arcane maelstrom in the palm of his hand. Ryan could see it, too, and his eyes went wide. But there was no time for him to do anything about it. Rhyzkahl unleashed the force, casting it into the flesh of the one who had attacked him, lifting Ryan off his feet and sending him crashing into the wall.

I let out a choked cry as Ryan crumpled beneath the gaping hole in the wall, blood trickling from his mouth. I stared in horror, silently screaming at him to move. *No . . . not you. You can't be dead! Oh, please . . . !*

Rhyzkahl released his grip on me and straightened, eyes flashing in satisfaction.

I scrabbled to get off the bed, hideous thick sobs welling in my throat as I tried to get to Ryan, but Rhyzkahl seized me by my hair before I could escape his reach. He yanked me close, twining the hair in his grasp savagely, wringing a new cry of pain from me.

"He is not worth your attention, dear one. A piteous creature who does not even know himself."

"He's not piteous!" I flailed at his hand, gaining small satisfaction in striking out at him even though I knew it didn't hurt him.

His expression hardened. "You should be cautious. Not all are as gentle as I."

"He's my partner! He's watching out for me. You didn't have to hurt him!"

His expression didn't change. "I have use of you, Kara. Just remember that there may be others who find you of use as well."

That didn't make any sense to me. Was he talking about Ryan?

He abruptly pulled me off the bed and to my knees by his feet, but before I could cry out in protest, the scene shifted suddenly to a place other than my bedroom, a place painfully cold and pitch-dark.

My breath caught in my chest. Had he somehow brought me to his own realm? Or were we in some nether region?

The cold burrowed into me, and the darkness was absolute. Shivers racked me, and not just because of the cold. But there was a stench to the place, a mustiness and odor that tugged at my memory.

Before my own memory could assert itself, a pale-blue light flared above us, revealing the metal interior of the morgue cooler. Rhyzkahl kept his grip on my hair, holding me firmly on my knees as I inhaled in surprise. In front of us was a stretcher that held a black body bag. Before I could speak, he made a gesture and the body bag disappeared, leaving just the body of the mutilated young girl, faint flickers of arcane energy barely visible on the body.

A low growl emanated from Rhyzkahl's throat. "I know the one who laid these," he said, in a voice that did not welcome response. Then, before I could react, the scene shifted again and we were back in my bedroom, with the crumpled form of Ryan still against the far wall.

Rhyzkahl tilted my head back to look up at him, then reached and stroked my hair, smiling down at me as I shook. *Like a dog,* I thought, with anger and a measure of shame. *I'm like a pet to him.*

He released me and turned away. "Do not concern yourself with the one who laid those markings, Kara. He is mine to discipline."

And then he was gone in a flash of white light.

For a heartbeat, I stared at the place where he'd been, then frantically stumbled over to the still form of Ryan.

"Ryan!" Was he breathing? Had the force of it killed him? "Ryan!"

"Kara?"

"Ryan? Ryan, wake up! Please!"

"Jesus Christ, Kara, would you please wake the fuck up? Don't make me slap you!"

I blinked up at him, disoriented and breathing raggedly. He stood over me, frowning, still exceedingly in one piece, with no blood on him.

"Oh, holy shit, you're all right!" I sat up and threw my arms around him before I could think. "I thought you were dead," I gasped out. "Holy shit, I thought you were dead." *Just a dream.* I took deep gulps of air, struggling to dispel the horror of it. *Just a dream.*

Ryan gave a startled laugh and gave me a squeeze. "Hey, you. I'm not dead. What the hell happened?"

I released him abruptly, suddenly embarrassed by the display of emotion. I ducked my head to hide the hot flush, then brought a hand up to my throat. No bruising, no marks. All still a dream. "H-he taught me a lesson." I didn't want to look at Ryan. I hadn't realized until just this instant how much I'd come to value our friendship, and I was terrified that he'd see it in my face. And not share the sentiment.

"What happened?" he asked, his voice taking on a darker timbre. "What kind of lesson?"

I tried to laugh, but it was a pitiful effort. "A lesson about who he is. A Demonic Lord. Not a creature who gets summoned to perform tasks for a mere mortal."

"What did he do to you?" Ryan gripped me by my shoulders, forcing me to look at him. "Why did you think I was dead?"

I swiped a hand across my face, even more embarrassed when it came away damp. *Great, now I've completed my impression of a needy and overly emotional idiot.* I took a deep breath, forcing myself into a calmer state. "Oh, you know, the usual threats and show of dominance. Then . . ." A shiver ran through me. "He manipulated the dream. He made me think you ran in to defend me and that you shot him, and . . . and he retaliated and pretty much threw you through that wall with just a flick of his fingers."

"Oh, come on," Ryan said with a derisive snort. "And you believed that?"

I looked up in surprise and scowled at him. "He's definitely powerful enough to do that. And I thought he was here in the flesh!"

Ryan laughed. "No, silly. You really thought I would come in to defend you against a Demonic Lord? Hell, I'd be halfway to the highway!"

"Oh, you ass," I said, laughing and swinging at him with a pillow, painfully relieved that he'd lightened the mood.

He grinned and ducked. "All right, so he showed you who's boss, killed me off, and then what?"

My laughter faded as I remembered the other blow that Rhyzkahl had dealt. "He said . . . something strange. Said I should be cautious, because not all were as gentle as he was." I frowned. "And said something about how he had a use for me but that there were others who might find me of use as well. It was pretty weird." I watched Ryan for his reaction.

"Huh," he said, puzzled expression on his face. "Wonder what he meant by that?"

I shrugged and stood up from the bed, wishing I could shrug away the slight doubt that Rhyzkahl had instilled in me. Was he trying to warn me about something? Or someone? Now that the whole experience was over, I could—grudgingly—admit that I had been overstepping my bounds when it came to dealing with a creature of that level of power. Not that I had any experience with that sort of thing, but I'd been coming very close to thinking of Rhyzkahl in human terms. He was not a human. Not a mortal. He was a demon. They were different. The rules were different.

"Dunno," I said as I pulled a sweatshirt on. Had he been trying to tell me something about Ryan? Was that why he'd attacked Ryan, or at least attacked a dream version of him? If so, then why wouldn't he just come out and accuse him?

It didn't matter. The seed of doubt was there now.

"So I guess this means that you didn't get any info about the body?" Ryan asked.

"Oh, actually I did." I laughed a bit shakily. "After all that, he took me to the morgue."

"And?"

I spread my hands. "All he said was that he knew who it was and that he would deal with it."

Ryan pondered this for a few seconds, brows drawn together. "I don't understand. Does that mean it's one of his own followers?"

"I don't know," I replied, feeling my frustration rise. "If so, it would mean that it's a demon working against Rhyzkahl somehow. Or it could be that it's another lord's demon. Either way, he's going to deal with it."

Ryan scrubbed his hand through his hair. "And we're to back off on that, no matter who it is."

"Yeah. That's pretty much the vibe I got. Not that there's much we could do if it's some sort of conflict between two lords." I exhaled, suddenly feeling very tired. "And after that whole visit, I'm just fine with letting him deal with it."

"But it doesn't get us any closer to figuring out who the Symbol Man is."

He'd struck to the heart of it. "No," I agreed. "We're still right where we were before."

23

RYAN WAS PRACTICALLY BREAKING HIS JAW WITH HIS yawns, so I finally bullied him into returning to the guest room to try to get some more sleep. I, however, had approximately zero desire to sleep again at this point. I made a pot of coffee in an attempt to battle my own attack of the yawns, then took another look through my notes to see if anything new would come to me. I was grasping for anything at this juncture that could point me in the right direction. I felt like I was running in place while the time until the next full moon rapidly slipped away.

My cell phone rang as soon as I'd poured my second cup. I glanced at the clock. Four a.m. Calls this early were seldom good news.

"Detective Gillian? This is Detective Powell in Narcotics. I've found one of your people."

A surge of sick dread went through me. "Oh, shit. Another body?"

"Huh? Oh, no. Nothing like that. Her name's Michelle

Cleland, and I just arrested her for prostitution and possession of crack cocaine."

I nearly swayed in relief. "Oh, that's fantastic. Where is she now?"

"She's in holding. I just finished booking her in."

"Powell, I owe you. Thanks a million."

"No prob, Kara. I hope it helps you guys out."

I hurriedly changed into jeans and a T-shirt with the Glock emblem on the front while slugging down as much coffee as I could without burning my mouth. Twenty minutes later, I was at the jail, waiting for the girl to be brought into an interview room.

Michelle Cleland had the ultraskinny frame, sunken cheeks, and beaten-down cast to her eyes that told me that she'd been on crack or some other highly addictive substance for a while. I glanced quickly at her booking sheet for her age. Twenty-three. Damn hard to tell by just her appearance.

She looked at me sullenly as she sat down, though there was a flicker of bravado about her as well. I could see by her driver's license photo that at one time she'd been pretty. Nice smile, long brown hair, and big brown eyes with a scattering of freckles across her nose. Not anymore. She'd probably be dead in a few years from an overdose.

"Hi, Michelle," I began. "I'm Detective Kara Gillian."

Michelle slumped down in the chair. "I already talked to the narc guy and told him who I bought the shit from."

"That's not what I want to know."

Michelle looked up at me uncertainly. I kept my expression serious. "I'm going to go ahead and read you your Miranda warnings, but I'll tell you right now I'm not looking for any information that's going to get you into any more trouble." I quickly ran through the required rights and Michelle dutifully signed the form.

"All right," I said, as I put the form away. "Now that that's out of the way, I have some questions to ask you about these." I pulled out the pictures and the drawings from Greg Cerise's house and spread them on the table.

Michelle leaned forward, breath catching in surprise. "Oh, my God. That's me!" She touched a drawing that depicted a woman drawing water from a well. In the picture, the woman was dressed in a simple clinging shift, with her hair pulled back into a loose braid. She was beautiful and smiling, looking over her shoulder at something or someone not depicted in the drawing. Another picture showed the same woman, but this time she was belting on a sword and the expression on her face was harder, determined, but by no means defeated.

"Oh, wow. Wow. I almost look good." Michelle slumped back down in the chair, clearly saddened by the reminder of how far she'd fallen.

"Yeah. You're a pretty girl. And these are incredible drawings. What do you know about the artist?"

The girl shrugged. "Dunno. He was just this guy who hung out at the park and would give people like ten bucks or so to let him take their picture. He was always drawing or taking pictures."

"Was there anyone else with him?"

Michelle shook her head. "Nah, not really. I mean, he talked to the people who hung out there, but he didn't have anyone with him or anything."

"Did you ever see any of the pictures he drew?"

"Yeah, it was some wild stuff. Comic book or something, right?"

"That's right."

"Yeah. It was cool. I talked to him once, y'know? He was nice. He told me that he was a lot better at drawing people with a picture to start from, not real good at drawing from just his imagination. He gave me twenty bucks and he took a bunch of pictures." She looked down at the drawings. "Why are you asking me about him? Did he do something wrong by paying us? I never fucked him, if that's what you're getting at."

"No. I'm the lead investigator on the Symbol Man investigation." I waited for it to process through the girl's head.

"Oh, wow," she breathed. "He's the Symbol Man?"

"No. He was killed by the Symbol Man." I put the drawings back in the folder, noting that the girl looked at them wistfully.

"Oh, my God. He's dead?" To my surprise, tears began to well up in her eyes. "Oh, man, he was nice. That's horrible."

"I'm sorry," I said.

Michelle sniffled and wiped at her eyes with her sleeve. "So why are you asking me all of this stuff about him if he's dead?"

"Well, when we went into his house, we found a bunch of pictures and drawings—people he'd taken pictures of around town." I kept my gaze on her. "It turns out that all the victims of the Symbol Man had been photographed and drawn by Greg already."

The girl paled. "Wait. You mean—"

"Yes," I said. "You're at risk of being a victim."

Her eyes went wide. "Oh, my God, you can't let him get me!"

I reached out and put my hand on top of Michelle's. "I won't. That's why I'm talking to you now. I know you don't want to hear this, but jail is the safest place for you right now."

Michelle stared at me, then shook her head. "I can't stay here. It's cold, and the food is awful, and all the other women in the holding cell are nasty."

"Would you rather be slit open from throat to twat?" I said, forcefully blunt.

Michelle seemed to deflate. Her eyes filled with tears again. "This just sucks. Jail sucks."

"I know," I said, softening my tone. "I know, but give me just a bit more time. We're close to this guy. Once we catch him, then you're out of here." I gave Michelle a wry smile. "And I'll do my best to make sure that any time you spend in here will apply to your sentence."

Her lip quivered. "Okay. But this still sucks."

I stood and pressed the button to call the guard back. "I know, Michelle. But it beats being dead."

I DIDN'T HEAD back home or to the office. There was a conversation I'd been meaning to have for a while now, and time was running out to get all the answers.

I walked up the steps to my aunt's house and rang the doorbell. It was barely six a.m., but I knew she would already be up and about. True to form, the door opened before the echoes of the bell had faded away.

"Hiya, sweets. You know you don't have to ring the bell."

"Aunt Tessa," I said without preamble, "we need to talk."

Tessa's smile faded and she gave a nod, as if she'd been expecting this visit. She turned and headed down the hall to the kitchen and then sat at the counter, pushing a cup of tea toward me.

I couldn't help but smile a bit as I lifted the cup. Perfect, as always.

"Aunt Tessa, I need you to tell me about the time you saw Rhyzkahl."

Tessa sighed and set her hands on the counter as if to examine her nails. "I knew you'd be coming to me at some point about that whole thing." She lifted her eyes to mine. "It's all connected, isn't it?"

"I'm almost positive," I said. "But I need some more information, and you're the only one who can give it to me."

Tessa squeezed her eyes shut briefly. "I can still see the whole thing. Even almost thirty years later."

"Greg told me that you two were in the basement when his father attempted to summon Rhyzkahl," I said, gently prompting.

Tessa shook her head firmly. "No, he wasn't attempting to summon Rhyzkahl. Only someone with a death wish would do that. He was trying to summon another lord, Szerain, who was much lower in stature than Rhyzkahl and *supposedly* willing to negotiate terms. It was a ridiculous and doomed attempt to heal his wife of breast cancer, which had gone undiagnosed and untreated because of his insane aversion to the medical community." Her voice was filled with bitterness. Then she sighed again. "Not that there was much that could have been done back then. They just didn't have the treatments they do today, but she might have had a few more years." An expression of regret flickered across her face. "We'll never know now."

"Aunt Tessa," I said, leaning forward. "Please tell me everything that you remember about that night."

Tessa curled her hands around her cup, empty as it was. "Greg and I had both just turned seventeen. Our birthdays were only a few days apart. We'd been playmates since we were just kids—used to spend darn near every waking minute together. When we got older, the friendship just naturally progressed to intimacy." Her lips twitched. "I guess you could say we were best-friend-fuckbuddies."

I knew she wanted me to react, but I refused to amuse her. *Get to the point,* I thought silently.

After waiting a few breaths for me to respond, Tessa began to speak again. "Greg's mother had been sick for a while, and his father decided that performing an incredibly risky, idiotic, insane summoning was preferable to actually taking her to seek medical help. We knew that it was breast cancer only because Greg had snuck her out and taken her to see a damn doctor." Anger colored her voice. "At that time, I had no idea what a summoning was or that I had any talent for it. I knew that my mother had a private study that was sometimes locked, but that was about it. But that Saturday night, Greg called me and asked me to come over. He didn't say so, but I knew he was worried about his mom and didn't want to be alone. His parents had some sort of dinner party planned for that night, and I figured that meant we'd have lots of time to fool around in his basement." A ghost of a smile lit her face. "I was doing my best to distract him from his worries, when people started coming downstairs. My mother was among them, which I hadn't expected. We scrambled to grab our clothes and dove behind a bookcase, figuring we'd hide until they all left again." She shook her head. "But they didn't leave. We stayed behind that bookcase and watched as the ritual began." She set the cup down and stood, moving to the sink to look out at her backyard and the morning sun on the lake beyond.

"Go on," I prompted after a moment.

Tessa rolled her head on her neck as if trying to ease the

tension. "You have to understand the . . . feelings of guilt that I've dealt with all these years. I know it's not rational, but I feel guilty all the same."

"Aunt Tessa, why?"

"I could feel the ritual, feel the opening of the portal." Her voice was low, thready. "It was the first time I'd ever seen a summoning, and I could instantly feel that it was something I could do." Her shoulders slumped. "And without knowing what I was doing, without thinking, I sat in my hiding place behind that bookcase and I reached out mentally to that portal as it opened."

"Oh, shit," I breathed.

"Yes. I altered the forming of it, changed the structure just enough . . ."

"And Rhyzkahl was pulled through."

Tessa's hands were white-knuckled on the rim of the sink. "Yes. Completely unwilling and without any warning. And because it was an imperfect portal, it was probably quite painful for him as well."

I shivered. The memory of his unshielded fury came back to me.

"He . . . he's beautiful, as you know. Angelic. There was a moment, a perfect small moment, when all everyone could see was that beauty, and everyone thought that the summoning had gone as planned." She turned back to me, hugging her arms around herself. "And then he let us feel the full extent of his anger."

"I've felt it," I said softly.

Tessa gave a single jerky nod. "It was a bloodbath, a slaughter, but I'll grant him this: He took his vengeance but did not revel in the suffering. Only enough to satisfy his honor." A shudder rippled through her. "But it was still a horror to watch. He killed two of the men first, literally

ripped them apart. He broke the necks of two women."
Tessa took a deep breath. "The only summoners left were
my mother and Peter Cerise. They were both pinned down
by his sheer power." She brushed her hair out of her face,
hands shaking slightly. "Rhyzkahl knew we were there,
hiding. He looked straight at us. I could . . . feel his *presence*, feel him measuring and testing us." She fell silent
for several heartbeats. "I don't know exactly how he killed
my mother, but in one breath she was alive and screaming in terror, and then she just . . . fell silent, sighed, and
didn't breathe again." She licked her lips. "Greg's mother
was next. Powers above and below, how he drew that out!
Peter Cerise was held down by the unbelievable potency of
Rhyzkahl, both legs snapped like dry twigs. Couldn't move,
forced to watch as Rhyzkahl ripped gobbets of cancerous
flesh from his wife, that angelic face utterly impassive."

I realized that my hands were clenched into tight fists
under the table, nails digging into my palms.

Tessa dragged a hand across her face. "And then he gathered his power and was gone, leaving the blood and the
slaughter." She made a breathy sound that I realized was
meant to be a laugh. "It's funny. I hate Rhyzkahl for what
he did that night, but I could never blame him for my
mother's death. It was Peter Cerise's arrogance and my ig-
norance that were the true causes for what happened."

"Aunt Tessa! You can't blame yourself like that."

Tessa turned back to me. "Oh, I know. I was so very
young. But Rhyzkahl was merely acting on his nature after
being dragged unwillingly through the portal. He took the
vengeance he needed to satisfy his honor. Greg's mother . . .
it was hideous what Rhyzkahl did to her, but . . . I could see
her face. I don't think she felt any of it. I think Rhyzkahl
did it solely to further torment Peter Cerise."

I struggled to grasp how my aunt could be so accepting of the Demonic Lord's actions. "What happened after he was gone?"

Tessa took a deep breath, beginning to recover some of her color. "I grabbed Greg—dearest powers of all, but he was hysterical. I was just trying to not think about it. I hated Greg's dad, hated him so much for making my mother do this thing, hated him for not treating his wife properly. I dumped Greg upstairs, then went back and ran to the garage . . ." She trailed off.

"Greg told me," I said gently. "Told me that you burned the house down to cover up what had happened."

"He didn't tell you everything. He didn't tell you what he didn't see." Tessa's voice was flat.

"What didn't he see?"

"I dumped the gas down into the basement, then lit a towel off the stove and threw that down as well." She looked at me. "I stayed there long enough to make sure that the place was going to catch fire. I stayed long enough to make sure that the stairs had caught, so that Peter Cerise couldn't get out."

I felt as if I'd been punched. "*What?* I thought he'd been killed by Rhyzkahl."

"No. He was alive. Rhyzkahl broke his legs and left him to watch it all. He knew that it was a greater revenge to make Cerise live with the memory, the guilt." Tessa gave her head a sharp shake. "I wasn't thinking that elegantly. I just wanted him dead."

I stood. "Aunt Tessa. Are you sure he died in the fire?"

Her thin eyebrows drew together. "When they finally put the fire out, the basement was a mess. And since we never saw him again, I . . ." She smacked her hand to her forehead. "I never even thought of him!"

"Basements usually have windows or doors, other ways out in case there *is* a fire," I breathed. "He's alive. He's alive, and he wants to summon Rhyzkahl. It makes sense. That explains how he knew Greg." I grabbed my aunt by her shoulders. "Aunt Tessa, do you know what he looks like? Do you have old pictures of him? Anything?"

Tessa shook her head. "No, sweets, nothing like that. And if he stayed around here, he must have changed his appearance, because Greg always thought he was dead too."

"Aunt Tessa, I have to go," I said, as I snatched up my cell phone and took off for the door. This was almost worse than not knowing. I knew *who* the Symbol Man was now, but I had no idea how to find him.

I had my cell-phone headset jammed into my ear even before I got the car started. I punched Ryan's number in as I backed out of my aunt's driveway. "Come, on, Ryan. Pick up!" I muttered.

"Good morning, Kara," Ryan said as he answered.

"Ryan! I know who the Symbol Man is," I said in a rush. "It's Greg Cerise's dad, Peter Cerise, who was supposedly killed in a summoning, but I think he wasn't killed after all. And now he wants revenge on Rhyzkahl and everyone else for letting his wife die, even though it was his own damn fault to begin with!"

"Whoa, whoa, slow down. Okay, it's Greg's dad. So where is he now?"

"I don't know! I don't know what he looks like or what he's doing."

I heard him mutter a curse. "All right. Well, it's a start, at least. I can go back and do some legwork and see if he had any prints on file or anything like that."

"I bet Greg had photos of his dad."

"Mr. Greg Cerise is quite dead, and the search warrant on that residence is no longer valid."

"Details, details!" I retorted. "I'll find you a damn photo."

"I'll hold you to that."

THE SEARCH WARRANT *was* expired, but at this point I really didn't give a shit. I called dispatch and got the number for the owner of the house, Greg's erstwhile landlady, a Ms. Dana Sebastian. I dialed as I drove to the house.

A woman answered on the second ring. "Hello?"

"Hello, this is Detective Gillian with the Beaulac Police Department. Is this Dana Sebastian?"

"Yes . . . yes, it is. Is this about the murder?"

"Yes, ma'am. I'm the lead investigator on the Symbol Man murders. Look, I know the search warrant has expired, but I really need to get back into your rental house and look for something."

"Oh, damn, I've already had a crew come through to fix the door and scrub the place down, and I packed all of Greg's stuff up. It's all still there in boxes, though. I really don't know what to do with any of it, to be honest. I don't know if he has any family."

"I can't help you there," I said. The only next of kin I knew of wasn't likely to step forward just to claim some boxes of junk. "Is there any way you can come by to let me in and let me look through the stuff?"

"I'm at work and can't get away until late this afternoon, but if you want you can let yourself in. The key's under the frog statue on the back porch."

"I really appreciate this," I said fervently.

"Sure thing. I hope it helps you out. I still can't believe this happened. Greg was a supernice guy and a good tenant."

"I met him only once, but he seemed pretty cool," I said. "Of course, the neighbor across the street was convinced he was up to no good."

"Oh, my God, that racist bitch? I swear, I wanted to rent the place out to a black Jewish gay couple just to piss her off, but then I figured it wouldn't be fair to the black Jewish gay couple."

I smiled wryly. "Makes me glad I live way out in the country with no neighbors."

"Lucky you! Look, if you need anything else, just let me know."

"You got it. Thanks again."

THE BLOOD HAD been cleaned up in the kitchen and the tile scrubbed and bleached. The cleaning crew had done a good job; there was no visible sign at all that a gruesome murder had taken place here. But it was still going to be hard for her to rent or sell the place.

The house had been stripped down to the walls, and I found about a dozen boxes piled in a back bedroom. I began looking through them and made the delightful discovery that Dana had labeled each box with a short description of its contents. *Oh, I do so love this woman!*

But even with the labels, it still took me well over an hour to find which boxes held pictures and then an hour more to find what I was looking for.

I sat down on the floor, holding the picture of a man in a suit standing stiffly next to a grinning teenager, arm draped awkwardly over the boy's shoulders. The kid was definitely Greg. Even thirty years later, the grin had remained constant. And this picture had likely been taken not long before the summoning-gone-wrong—a couple of years at most. *So this must be Dad.* I peered at the picture. Slightly above-average height. Light-blue eyes. Brown hair. Nondescript features. Medium build. He'd be in his mid to late sixties now, I figured. I made a note to find out his date of birth when I got back to the office.

I pushed my hair back from my face, frustrated. I still didn't have much to go on. *But this has to be who the killer is.* Peter Cerise. It fit perfectly. So, who the hell was he now?

I pulled my cell phone out again and called Ryan.

"Kristoff here."

"Hiya, Agent-with-the-high-tech-resources-that-I-don't-have. Can your peeps do an age progression on a photograph?"

"I can get it to someone who can," he said. "Whatcha got?"

"Picture of Greg's dad. But it's about thirty years old. I can't figure out who he is."

Ryan gave a low whistle. "That's terrific. Get it to me and I'll send it off."

"You got it. Where y'at now?"

"I'm out and about, but if you email it to me, I'll forward it to my 'peeps,' as you put it."

"I'm not near a computer. But I'm ten minutes away from the office."

"I'll be looking for it in eleven."

I shut the phone and stuffed it into my pocket, then let myself out the same way I'd come in, tucking the key back under the statue.

As I walked back out to my car, Ms. Dailey was standing at the end of the driveway, dressed this time in a bright fuchsia velour sweat suit. I wondered briefly if her entire wardrobe consisted of velour sweat suits of varying obnoxious hues.

"Young lady," she said with a stern expression on her

face. "May I ask just what you were doing in there?" Her tone was accusatory, as if she thought I was looting the place for valuables.

What, *now* the woman was concerned about her neighbor? I closed the distance to Ms. Dailey, getting close enough that she was forced to take a step back.

"It's *Detective* Gillian," I said through bared teeth, yanking my badge off my belt and thrusting it into the woman's face. "I am here on official police business for the purposes of investigating a series of murders. But for you, Ms. Dailey, I have just one thing to advise."

Ms. Dailey's eyes widened.

"From now on, why don't you try minding your own *fucking business*?"

I turned and marched back to my car, leaving the woman behind me gaping and speechless. And, for the first time, I felt like the warrior woman in that picture.

24

MY GOOD MOOD DIDN'T LAST LONG. MY PAGER SHRILLED
before I could make it back to the station, and I had to read
it twice before the meaning of the message got through to
me. It wasn't another body. It was six of them.

A LOCAL MAN who'd taken a sick day to go fishing found
the bodies piled in an ugly heap about fifty feet from the
shore in a rarely traveled or fished area of the lake. Trouble
with the engine on his flatboat had caused him to drift
into a small cove, where he discovered, to his delight, where
all the fish had been hiding from him for the past twenty
years. He'd reached his limit after an hour of fishing and
then decided to investigate the source of the odor that had
drifted to him when the wind shifted.

I had a feeling his sick day was justified now.

It might have been fairly simple to get to the scene by
boat, but going by car was another matter entirely—several
miles of rutted dirt roads, followed by a ten-minute hike

on foot down a narrow deer trail. Fortunately, by the time I made it to where all the other vehicles were parked, some of the good ol' boys had busted out their ATVs and were shuttling people back and forth through the woods.

I climbed off the back of the four-wheeler with a mumbled thanks to the driver, well aware that he had gone over a few extra bumps in order to get the full effect of my tits pressed up against his back as I hung on for dear life. I would be walking back, thank you very much.

To my surprise, there was already a cluster of local and not-so-local media in a small clearing on the low ridge above where the bodies had been discovered. A murdered homeless drug addict could be a decent mention on the evening news, but a mass dump of six bodies in various states of decomposition couldn't be passed over. No, this one would probably make national news.

I saw Dr. Lanza on the ridge, standing next to a slender, leggy woman with blond hair and a lovely face. The woman wore jeans that were low-cut and form-fitting without looking painted on and a black T-shirt that showed her obvious dedication to her workouts. There was no layer of pudge above the jeans on this woman, and I found myself standing straighter and pulling my stomach in. *Damn doughnuts.*

Dr. Lanza caught my eye and motioned me over. "Detective Kara Gillian, this is Dr. Susan Vaughn," Doc said when I reached him. "Dr. Vaughn is a forensic entomologist."

I shook the woman's hand, but there must have been something resembling a blank expression on my face. "I do bugs," Dr. Vaughn added with a smile.

"Oh! Right." I shrugged sheepishly. "I was either going to go for that or foot doctor, and the latter didn't make much sense."

"Susie . . . um . . . happened to be in town when I got the call," Doc said, "and I'm hoping she'll be able to help us determine how old these corpses are."

It's Susie? And she just happened to be in town? Doc, you dog!

Doc must have picked up something in my expression, because his lips twitched into a smug smile. Then he glanced down the ridge and all trace of humor slipped away. "Let's get started," he said tersely, and started making his way down the small slope, with the two of us following. I grimaced as the nauseating odor grew stronger, but even if I hadn't smelled it, the sound of the flies would have warned me that something ugly was nearby. The buzz was constant, and any motion sent clouds of the insects swarming up, only to settle back on the flesh as soon as they could. Now I understood the need for someone who knew their bugs.

I took in the surrounding area. Under any other circumstances, it would be an idyllic setting, lightly wooded with a scattering of spring wildflowers and a beautiful view of the lake—perfect for camping or trysting. The location definitely offered privacy, and it occurred to me that these bodies could have easily gone undiscovered for years if not for the fisherman's engine trouble. The demon had to have dumped these bodies, too, I realized. The pile wasn't far from the water, but there was enough of a climb from the shore to make it difficult for someone carrying a body, much less six. And it was definitely a significant distance from the road. I just couldn't see someone loading bodies onto the back of an ATV to trek them all the way back here to dump.

They were all nude, piled haphazardly and limbs splayed, swollen and black with decomposition, and rippling with a patchy gray-yellow carpet of maggots. It was difficult to tell what kind of injuries had been inflicted, due to the maggots and the state of decomposition, but there was enough evidence to tell me that these were uncomfortably similar to my other Symbol Man cases.

Dr. Vaughn stepped closer cautiously as she pulled on latex gloves, her heavy fall of blond hair swinging forward as she peered at the maggots and flies. I couldn't help but think that she looked a lot more like a member of the Swedish Bikini Team than a bug expert. "A lot of injuries here," she said, utterly unperturbed. "Maggots tend to cluster around orifices"—she gestured at the maggot-filled nose and mouth of one body—"and also any break in the skin." Her gaze traveled over the nearly unbroken mass of maggots. "This is unbelievable."

"Can you tell how long they've been dead?" I asked.

Dr. Vaughn nodded, pursing her lips. "Oh, yes. Or, rather, I can tell you how long the bodies have been out here." She flicked a finger at a fly. "These are blowflies." She glanced over her shoulder at the lake. "And out here in the open like this, flies are going to find these bodies almost instantly." She looked down by her feet, then picked up a number of tiny black pellets. She peered at them, then held them out toward me. "These are the egg cases, and these," she poked at a few of the pellets that looked as if one end had been cut off, "have already hatched."

I looked at the egg cases and then up at her. "Okay."

Dr. Vaughn met my eyes. "Give me a few minutes and I should be able to give you a time frame."

"You got it. Just don't make me pick up any bugs."

Dr. Vaughn gave a throaty laugh. "Deal." She turned away and crouched, examining the insects on the bodies with what I privately thought was an insane amount of interest.

Heck, who am I to judge? I thought, wrinkling my nose. *She does bugs, and I do demons.*

I moved to the side to keep out of the way of both doctors as they examined the bodies and conferred with each other in hushed voices. Finally Doc turned to me. "Crime Scene has taken pictures of the pile already, so I'm going to have them start moving the bodies, unless there's anything else you want to look at." He nodded toward three men in striped outfits who were clambering down the slope—trustees who would get extra "credit" for helping to remove bodies on this scene.

"Go for it," I replied. I could feel only the faintest flickers of the arcane, and with all the insect activity I couldn't even tell if the symbol was on any of these bodies. It would seriously suck if these were *not* Symbol Man victims. Two serial killers would be more than we could handle. *Hell, one is more than we can handle.*

Doc flicked his fingers to dislodge a stray maggot, lip curling in disgust. "As soon as these guys get the bodies off one another, I'll be able to tell more."

I didn't have to wait long. As the first body was pulled away from the others and turned over, I could clearly see the symbol that had been carved onto the chest. *Okay, so we're still dealing with the same killer,* I thought with strange relief.

The trustees staggered by me with their grotesque burden as they carried the body to a clear area to lay it out. I began to step back to avoid the stench, then froze as a faint sensation of arcane resonance rippled over me. I shifted quickly into full othersight, reluctantly stepping closer to the body. *It's the symbol,* I realized. *The symbol is arcanely protected.* I hadn't noticed it on any of the Series Two victims because they'd been found relatively quickly and there were still arcane traces all over them. But on these, most of the residual arcane energy had faded to nothing—except for the potency twined into the symbol itself. No wonder the symbol had always been recognizable, even on the badly decomposed bodies. I gave myself a mental head-smack. I should have thought of that earlier. *Chalk that one up to inexperience,* I thought with a small sigh.

For the next hour, I discovered it was impossible not to breathe in the stench of rot. I didn't have any trouble with nausea, but one of the trustees was not so fortunate and had to lean over a bush several times to heave. Jill was there, taking pictures of the entire process as the bodies were removed and laid out, face grim and pale as she worked.

I crouched next to the two doctors, making notes and listening to their observations as they examined each body as it was removed from the pile. Six bodies, each with the symbol carved into the flesh and positioned so that the symbol wouldn't be exposed to air and insects. *Make it last longer, even with the arcane protection. It's important to whatever he's doing.*

Finally the last of the remains were zipped up into body bags and Doc stood up and stripped off his gloves. "Four men and two women," he said, mouth set in a firm line and a thin beading of sweat on his upper lip. "All with ligature marks around their necks and notches at their elbows and ankles, in addition to various other signs of torture."

Dr. Vaughn rolled her neck on her shoulders. "For now I'm going to say that there's nothing older than two months and nothing fresher than three weeks."

I did some quick mental calculations, then took out my phone and pulled up the calendar. "So that would fall between these dates?" I showed my phone to Dr. Vaughn, pointing out the dates.

The entomologist looked at the screen and nodded. "Yes, that would work."

"Thanks, both of you." I turned and jogged back up the slope, slowing as I saw Ryan climbing off the back of an ATV.

"Hey, Kristoff. Check this out." I showed him my phone.

He looked at the screen, a faintly bemused expression on his face. "You have all the phases of the moon on your calendar?"

"Yeah, like, duh. And now it's finally useful. Doc and the entomologist think that these victims were killed between the last two full moons."

He looked at me with a *So what?* expression.

I gestured to the row of black body bags at the bottom of the ridge. "I think these are last month's victims." I took a steadying breath. "I think he attempted the summoning last month and it didn't work." I rubbed my palms on my jeans, unnerved. I didn't want to think about what we'd be facing right now if he'd been successful.

Ryan blew out his breath. "Fucking lucky for us. I wonder what went wrong."

"I don't know, but he's not giving up. He's trying again this month."

A sickened expression passed over his face. "And he's going to keep doing this until he succeeds in this summoning."

I chewed my lip. "The convergence will begin to taper after this month. It'll still be enough to summon higher demons, but my bet is that pulling an unwilling Demonic Lord through will be damn near impossible after this next full moon and for about another eighteen months or so."

"So, we have just this month to catch him," Ryan said.

I nodded. "And he's going to throw everything he has into this summoning. He knows it's his last chance for a while."

Ryan moved to the top of the slope, looking down at the scene of the body dump, anger and dismay in his eyes. "I guess there's no doubt that these are Symbol Man murders?"

I shook my head. "They all have the symbol, all have signs of torture, all killed by ligature strangulation."

He was silent for several heartbeats as he looked at the activity at the bottom of the slope. "I wonder why he's killing all his victims the same way now. The Series One victims were killed in different ways."

"Well, I have a theory about that."

"Share?"

I took a deep breath. "I think that the first murders were practice. It explains why those victims were killed in a variety of ways and had varying amounts of torture and damage done to them. The last two *were* strangled."

Ryan scowled. "He was trying to see what kind of death would give him the most zing and found that strangulation worked the best."

"That's right. And I think he was probably also figuring out how to store that potency for later use. To build his little Demonic Lord prison."

"And then he had to stop for three years . . ."

"Because the sphere that holds the demon world diverged from ours . . ." I trailed off, looking away from the lake.

"What's wrong?" Ryan followed the direction of my gaze.

"The victim at the wastewater plant. I think that was from last month's attempt as well."

Ryan frowned. "What makes you say that? And what are you looking at?"

"See that fence?" I pointed at a tall wooden fence barely visible through the trees. It was probably about a mile away, and only the fact that we were standing on a slight rise allowed us to see it at all. "That's the back of the wastewater plant."

I watched his face as comprehension flashed across it. "The broken bones . . . She wasn't dropped from the top of a vat. The demon was flying her body here and dropped her."

I nodded. "You're pretty smart for a Fed."

"I missed a bunch of questions on the entrance exam on purpose so that I could get into the agency," he retorted, smile flickering at the corners of his mouth.

"So it was an accident that the body was found so quickly."

"But the others . . ." His expression grew more serious. "He's been trying to find out what he can about you. He knows you're a summoner."

I nodded, feeling the prickles of cold sweat along my spine. If he knew that, then he knew damn near everything about me.

Meanwhile, I knew his name, and not a damn thing else.

WE HEADED BACK TO THE STATION IN SILENCE. I SWIPED
my ID card at the door and pushed in with Ryan following
behind me, but I'd barely stepped through the door before
Captain Turnham leaned his head out of his office, looking
down the hall at me.

"Chief Morse wants to see you, Gillian."

I groaned. "Now?"

An expression of regret crossed his face. "Yes, now."

I hesitated, then glanced at Ryan. "You can wait in my
office if you want."

Ryan's eyes narrowed. "I'll wait," he said with a nod. He
turned and headed to my office as I continued down the
hall to the chief's. I didn't have a good feeling about this.
The captain looked like he'd been handing me a death sentence.

The chief's secretary was gone, so I knocked on the inner office door.

"Detective Gillian!" I heard the chief snap from inside.
"Get in here."

Yeah. That didn't sound good. I took a settling breath as I entered. "Sir? Captain Turnham said you wanted to see me?"

Chief Eddie Morse stood behind his desk, scowl blackening his expression. *Fuck him, he's only my boss,* I tried to tell myself in an effort to keep some semblance of composure, but it wasn't working too well.

"Detective Gillian," he said, voice tight and clipped, "since you have shown yourself to be clearly incapable of handling this investigation, I have informed Captain Turnham that you are to be reassigned and replaced with someone who knows what the fuck they're doing."

I stared at him in utter shock for a heartbeat, then I struggled to recover. "Sir, you can't do that!" I blurted out.

He glared at me. "*Ten* more bodies have been found since you were assigned to the case. It was a gross mistake to put you on as the lead. I don't see any progress being made, and all I do see is you spending a great deal of time with Agent Kristoff."

I felt hot and cold all at the same time. I drew a shaking breath, fighting the urge that screamed at me to respond with an outraged denial of the barely veiled accusations of misconduct. It was one thing to get ribbed by coworkers. This was completely different. "Agent Kristoff and I are merely assigned to the same task force," I said, struggling for calm though I could hear the tremor in my voice. "And a great deal of progress *has* been made," I continued as the chief glowered at me. "We have a strong lead on who the killer is, and now we're working on locating him."

The chief leaned forward, placing his fists on the desk. "I think you're full of shit, Detective Gillian. Crawford and Pellini will replace you on the case."

"Sir, wait. We're really close. I know it! Give me twenty-four hours and I'll have something to show." *Twenty-four hours?* I bit back the urge to groan. What on earth had possessed me to spout that tired cliché? On the other hand, twenty-four hours was all I really needed.

Chief Morse narrowed his eyes at me, flat gaze piercing me like an eagle sighting on its prey. Then he straightened. "Fine. You have *twenty-four hours*"—he sneered the words—"to show me some goddamn results, or not only will you be off the case but you'll be back in Patrol."

I willed calm with everything I had to keep my anger and dismay in check. "Yes, sir." I didn't dare say anything more. I had no idea how I was supposed to explain my conviction that the murders were all for the purpose of gathering arcane power, but in twenty-four hours the Symbol Man would be starting his ritual, so it was probably a moot point anyway. I would either stop the summoning or I wouldn't. And if I didn't, losing my job would be the least of my worries.

Chief Morse sat down, glowering. "You're still in way over your head." When I didn't respond, he waved a hand at me. "Get out. Twenty-four hours or you're through. Remember that."

I nodded again, then pivoted and exited as quickly as I could. I slunk back to my own office and shut the door behind me, then sat heavily in my chair and dropped my head to the desk.

"Fuuuuuuuuuuuuuuuuuuuuuuck," I moaned.

Ryan cleared his throat. "I take it you were on the receiving end of an ass-chewing?"

"I think I dropped two sizes. Does my ass look smaller? It feels smaller."

He snorted and I lifted my head, sighing. "I am apparently completely incompetent, and I am to be removed from the case. However, I successfully begged for twenty-four hours to prove that I deserve to remain a detective."

"In twenty-four hours it's not going to matter," he pointed out.

"Yeah, no shit." I opened my notebook to pull out the picture of Greg and Peter Cerise. "Here," I said, handing the picture to him. "Here's the killer. Go wild."

"Great. Case solved. Go home." He took the picture from me and examined it closely, then looked up at me and shrugged. "It could be anyone. I'll scan it and send it to my 'peeps,' as you refer to them."

"Well, there's one piece of good news I can give you," I said. "One of the Narcotics guys recognized his arrestee as one of our potential victims. Michelle Cleland."

His eyes widened. "That's fantastic. So she's in jail?"

"Yep, and I told her not to bond out. Jail is the safest place for her."

"No kidding. How did she feel about staying in jail?"

I gave him a mirthless smile. "Well, once I explained the possible alternative, she reluctantly agreed to it. Of course, it helps that she can't afford the bond."

"Good. That's very good." He stood up. "Well, at least we know that one of them is safe." He rubbed the back of his neck, grimacing. "Your company is scintillating, but I need a shower. I'm going to scan and send the picture to Quantico and then go crash for a bit."

"The full is tomorrow night."

Ryan looked pained. "I know. I'll tell the imaging guys to put a big rush on the age progression. We'll find a way to stop him."

I couldn't even find it in me to nod. Would we? Just over a day left, and we still didn't have much to go on. "Go shower. Get some rest."

"You need to sleep too," Ryan reminded me.

"I will," I lied. "I just want to go over a few more things before I head home."

"I'll call you in the morning."

"Do that."

He turned and left the office, and I lowered my head to the desk again, groaning under my breath. It was going to happen tomorrow night. Would he succeed this time? Judging by the estimated times of death of the pile of bodies, he most certainly had made an attempt on the last full. *He was probably summoning at the exact same time that I was summoning.* Too bad there wasn't some way for me to find out where he was by tracking the portal he was opening. . . .

I lifted my head and turned my pencil end over end, musing on that. Perhaps someone who had far *far* greater skills in the arcane than I could do that sort of thing. It would probably be well beyond the ability of any human. Would a Demonic Lord even be able to track a portal? If they were actually being summoned, yes, of course, but by then it would be too late. But what if the portal could be—

I sat bolt upright, sucking my breath in through my teeth. The Symbol Man *had* tried to summon this past full moon. And he *had* tried to summon Rhyzkahl. And he had failed.

I began to laugh, knowing there was a trace of hysteria to it. He had failed because I'd been attempting to summon Rysehl, and Rhyzkahl had used my portal to escape. *Holy crap, I* didn't *fuck up the summoning.* The wash of relief that went through me was so great I could feel tears leaking down my cheeks. I hadn't screwed up. Rhyzkahl had hijacked my portal to save himself from being summoned by someone who had the ability to bind him. Stupid blind happenstance. *And that's why he didn't slay me or take me,* I realized. Even though it hadn't been my intent, I was still his means of saving himself. Once he realized that I wasn't the original summoner, his honor wouldn't allow him to harm me.

And he seduced me because he figured he'd use the opportunity that he'd been presented with. He wanted me to trust him just so that I would later call him to this sphere. That was not as welcome a realization, and I was shocked to realize how much it hurt, even though deep down I'd suspected it. Not desirable, not interesting, just a convenient summoner. I scrubbed at the tears that continued to trickle down my face, choking back the thick knot in my throat. I'd never been pursued, wooed, or seduced before, and it had been nice—so very *nice*—to believe that there was something about me that attracted that sort of attention. I'd wanted to believe it so badly. Too badly. *He would have done the same to whomever the summoner was,* I thought, with more than a touch of misery. Not necessarily sex but some manner of seduction, whether it was power, or wealth, or whatever else he could have offered to gain the summoner's interest.

He had read my needs, my secret aches, and played upon them. Demons were utterly self-serving, and I hadn't truly accepted just how deeply that ran.

I took a shaking breath, wiping my face one more time. *Fine. Whatever. I don't have time to wallow in self-pity.* But at least now I knew how to buy more time to catch the Symbol Man. *I guess I'll be summoning tomorrow. Let's see if Rhyzkahl can save himself twice.*

But this time I wouldn't trust him any further than I could throw him.

26

I WENT HOME AND TOOK A LONG HOT SHOWER TO WASH
the stench of death away, then forced myself to go to bed at
a reasonable hour. I knew that I would need to be rested if
I was going to summon. It galled me to basically stop my
investigation—especially after the chief's ultimatum—but
rationally I knew that I needed to get some sleep, whether
I summoned or not.

But after I crawled into bed I lay awake, staring up at
the ceiling, unable to shut off my racing thoughts. It felt
almost strange not to have Ryan in the house. I was getting
too used to him being around, and that was disturbing too.
I liked him, and I wasn't used to that. *He's just a coworker, a
team member. Stop reading too much into it. He's just paying
attention to you because he's fascinated by the summoning
stuff.*

Was that all there was to it? Rhyzkahl's cryptic warning still left me with an uneasy ripple. Not that I had any
reason to trust Rhyzkahl . . . but at the same time he had

no reason to lie to me, and his ilk didn't lie unless it fit into their whole code of honor.

I eventually managed to fall asleep and even slept solidly, with no nighttime visitors and no dreams that I could remember. I woke before my alarm went off at six a.m., which was also about five seconds before my cell phone rang.

I rolled over and snatched it off the nightstand, groaning when I saw that it was the Beaulac PD number. "Detective Gillian," I said.

"Hey, Gillian." I recognized the familiar voice of Captain Turnham. "Got some strange news for you."

"Strange? Or bad?"

"Well . . . not really sure. I got a call from the chief this morning, asking questions about your task force."

I sat up, sighing. "Yeah, I know. He thinks I'm in over my head. He told me that I was off the case and that he was assigning Pellini and Crawford to the team, but I wheedled a twenty-four-hour reprieve to prove that I belong on the case."

"Those weren't the questions he had."

I frowned. "What questions, then?"

"Well . . . mostly questions about Agent Kristoff. Has he been spending a lot of time at your house?"

I could feel my back tightening in anger. "A lot of time? If you two are wanting to know if we've been sleeping together, the answer is a) no, and b) not that it's any of your fucking business. Sir."

"Gillian, chill." I heard him exhale. "That's good to know, but not for the reasons you might think. The chief apparently talked to one of his FBI buddies, and . . . well, no one at the FBI has heard of Special Agent Ryan Kristoff."

I could only blink in shock for several seconds. Finally I found my voice. "I'm not sure I understand, Captain. Do you mean no one in the New Orleans office has heard of him? Or do you mean that he's on a secret task force and so his name is not well known?"

"I mean that the chief did some checking, and there's no Ryan Kristoff who works for the FBI."

"Then who the fuck is he?" I practically shrieked.

"That's what we need to find out."

I was already off the bed, snatching for jeans and clean underwear. "I'm on my way in. Fuck. Fuck!"

"Stop by the jail first. There was a message at the desk for you about some prisoner that you put a hold on."

I went cold. "Michelle Cleland?" *Shit! I told Ryan about her last night!*

"I have no details. Just the message to call or go by the jail when you got the chance."

I hung up the phone with a terse good-bye and finished dressing as quickly as possible, struggling to control the horrible sick feeling. Ryan wasn't FBI? *Fooled again*, I berated myself as I drove at unsafe speeds to the jail. *How about, from now on, if someone shows interest in you, just know for a fact that they can't be trusted and it was all bullshit?* At least I hadn't slept with Ryan. Small comfort there. But I'd thought he was my friend. Was I really that gullible and desperate? *Ugh. Don't answer that.* There had to be some other explanation. Had to be. If he wasn't FBI, then there were very few reasons why he would have attached himself to me. And within that short list of reasons was one that was terrifying. *He knows everything about me. Everything!*

My thoughts were still in turmoil when I got to the jail. I entered through Booking, flashing my ID to the bored officer at the front desk, then took the stairs to Main Control two at a time.

The rotund sergeant looked up from the row of monitors as I entered, then lifted both hands. "It's not my fault. I didn't have a choice."

"Shit. So Michelle Cleland bonded out?"

Sergeant Mallory shifted awkwardly in his chair. "Umm, no. PR."

I stared at him, aghast. "She was allowed to be signed out on a personal recognizance? That's insane!" That meant she hadn't even been required to put up bond money, just needed to have someone "responsible" sign for her to vouch that she would show up for court. "How?"

Mallory sighed. "You know it's always a battle with overcrowding here. The chief called and said that the fire marshal was on his ass again and told us to PR anyone under Code Six."

I sank into a chair. A Code 6 was a repeat or violent offender. Unfortunately, the scenario that Sergeant Mallory referred to was pretty common. To control jail overcrowding, release priority was given to arrestees who weren't considered a significant danger to society. And, unfortunately, Michelle, who was merely a drug addict and sometime prostitute, wasn't a danger to society. *But she's in significant danger!*

"Fuck. Fuck. All right, did she give an address when she signed out?"

Sergeant Mallory handed me the paperwork. "No address, but we have the name of the person who signed."

It didn't register with me at first. Maybe because the name had been on my mind already. But on the third reading it finally sank in.

The name of the person who had signed Michelle out was Ryan Kristoff.

I DIDN'T GO BACK TO THE OFFICE. THERE WAS NO POINT.
Instead, I headed home. Right now all of my focus and
energy needed to go into preparing for what was possibly
the most important summoning of my life. *He was right,*
I railed, sternly telling myself not to start crying again.
Rhyzkahl was right. Ryan was using me. He was too young
to be the Symbol Man, but it wasn't a stretch at all to de-
duce that Ryan had been working *with* Peter Cerise, wanting a share of the power that would come with a captive
Demonic Lord.

"And he broke my fucking door too," I grumbled as
I entered and locked the back door behind me. Looking
down the hall, I had an excellent view of my front door, still
barely held in place by a couple of nails. I never had managed to get a sheet of plywood to cover it, but I had plenty
of scrap wood out in my shed. I checked the clock in the
kitchen. Almost ten a.m., and I had a ton of shit to do to
prepare for tonight. *First things first. Make sure no one can
come in.* I pulled open a drawer in the kitchen, removing

hammer and a box of nails. It wouldn't be pretty, but it would work.

MY CELL PHONE rang several times while I was cleaning and preparing. I glanced at the caller ID and listened to the voice mail, and after the third call from the PD with the message to contact my captain I finally relented—partially. I called the dispatcher and asked her to give Captain Turnham the message that I was following up on a big lead and that I was fine but would be out of touch for a few hours. I didn't want to speak directly to the captain, didn't want to answer any probing questions about what sort of lead I was following or what I was doing about the Symbol Man or Ryan. There was no way to explain to him that I was doing the only thing I knew to do to stop him. Or at least stop him for now. *It's just buying me more time, I know. Eighteen months to figure out a better plan.* I couldn't even get worked up over the knowledge that I was certainly off the case, and probably out of Investigations as well. Right now the most important thing was to make sure that Rhyzkahl couldn't be summoned and bound.

I got a call from Tessa, which I ignored as well. *I'll call her right before I summon.* I wouldn't tell her what I planned to do, but at least I would have a chance to talk to her before . . .

I paused as I sketched the diagram onto the concrete of the basement floor, hand tightening on the chalk. What I was about to attempt was insanely risky—more so than summoning a twelfth-level demon. The magnitude of it was just now sinking in. I was going to summon Rhyzkahl, a *Demonic Lord,* and I knew I didn't have the means or power to set any manner of protections that would stand up to him. The only thing I could do was trust in that difficult code of honor, trust that he would spare me because I would—hopefully—again save him from being bound, though this time intentionally instead of accidentally. I couldn't bind Rhyzkahl or even protect myself arcanely. I could only tell him why I'd summoned him in such an insane way.

But even if I die in the attempt, at least it'll buy everyone else more time. It wasn't an easy thought. I'd never wanted to be any sort of martyr, and I desperately hoped it wouldn't come to that. *Protect and serve. Yeah, right.* But at least Rhyzkahl wouldn't be bound by another summoner, and he also wouldn't be in this sphere unrestrained—which could be even worse.

I shuddered, then forced myself to continue with the diagram, doing my best to lose myself in the tasks of preparations.

I DECIDED THAT it would be safest to summon the Demonic Lord well before midnight, summoning him before the Symbol Man—and Ryan—could. I heard the hall clock chime nine times as I stood in the basement. Everything was in place. The candles were set out in perfect alignment, the diagram chalked with painstaking precision, the oil and the razor-sharp knife set just beyond the perimeter of the diagram.

I returned upstairs. Now it was time for the mundane preparations. My will was already on the kitchen table, and I pulled a page out of my notebook to begin a letter to my aunt. Of all the people in the world, she was the one who needed to know what I had done and why and who the killers were. Tessa wasn't a police officer, but I knew that if didn't survive this summoning, Tessa would be the next best to try to stop them.

I finished the letter and folded it into an envelope, hand trembling as I sealed it and wrote Tessa's name on the outside, too aware that the letter was painfully terse. *This is going to be fine. I'm still going to be preventing the binding, just like last time. Only difference is that this time I'm aware of it.* I slid the envelope underneath the copy of my will, set a mug on top of both, then went to the next step in my preparations.

I turned the water in the shower as hot as it would go, forcing myself to stand under the near-scalding water as I ran through the mental exercises that were meant to calm and aid focus. I wasn't sure just how much focus I'd managed by the time the hot water ran out, but at least my hands weren't shaking as much anymore.

Only one thing left to do. The phone call to Tessa. I wasn't about to tell Tessa the specifics over the phone, but I at least wanted to . . .

I want to say good-bye, I realized. *Just in case.* I understood so much more about my aunt now. Understood why she was acerbic and difficult, understood why she rode me so hard. At least I could tell her that I hadn't screwed up the summoning. She'd probably viewed that as much her failure as mine.

The symbol for the voice mailbox was lit. I hadn't realized that she'd left a message when she called earlier. I quickly dialed the mailbox to play it back, hoping that she hadn't called to tell me she was going to be away from her phone for a while.

"Hi, sweetie, it's me. I just wanted to wish you good luck in your summoning tonight." *She probably thinks I'm summoning Kehlirik again,* I thought. *Under any other circumstance she'd be right too.* "Not that you need it," the recording continued. "You're so damn talented. I guess I don't tell you that enough. I also don't tell you enough that coming to live with you was the best thing that ever happened to me. In fact, I don't think I've ever told you that. And I should have. I whined for too long about having my life upended, but the truth is, I didn't have much of a life before you came into it." She gave a small laugh. "Okay, this has become unbearably sappy. Sorry about that. Call me when you finish up. Love you."

I hit the button to save the recording, a silly smile on my face and a sniffle in my nose. I hit the speed dial for her number, mentally shifting what I'd originally planned to say.

A deep rumbling voice that was most assuredly *not* my aunt's answered.

"Greetings, little summoner."

Cold filled me and my grip tightened convulsively on the phone. *That's a higher demon,* I thought wildly. *Shit, did Aunt Tessa summon one tonight? But why would it be answering her phone?* My thoughts whirled chaotically for a short instant, forcefully denying the other possibilities.

"I would like to speak to my aunt," I managed to say, more calmly than I had expected to sound.

A soft hiss. "She is indisposed. Perhaps you would care to join her?"

I took a ragged breath. "What have you done to her? Where is she?" *No. No. Not Tessa.* Not now. Not before I had a chance to tell her . . .

"Her blood is strong, little summoner," the deep voice continued. "Is yours as potent? There is another summoner here who would like to find out."

"Tell Ryan to go fuck himself!" I yelled, shaking.

I heard the demon rumble in his version of laughter. "Come to the outreach center on Seventh Street, and we will use your blood instead of hers."

I was silent, gripping the phone so tightly I could feel the plastic gouging into my palm. The outreach center. Ryan wasn't the right age to be Peter Cerise. But Reverend Thomas *was,* and he would have had plenty of opportunity to peruse Greg's drawings. And why else use the outreach center?

But if I went there I would be giving up the chance to stop him from binding Rhyzkahl. *Shit.* "Will you release her if I come?" My stomach churned. He wouldn't release her. I knew it. He'd use her, and use me, and succeed in the binding.

There was silence on the line, then the demon gave a low growl. "If you come, she will be released."

"Unharmed?"

"Too late for that," he responded, sending another chill through me.

"Alive?" My voice broke.

"She will be released alive."

"Your oath on it?"

"I swear on my essence that, if you come, she will be released alive."

"Fine," I said, my blood roaring in my ears. "I'll be there."

The line went dead and I slowly unclasped my fingers. The cell phone dropped to the table and I gripped the back of the chair. There was no way I could leave her there. My gaze slid to the door to the basement, nausea filling me. Up until this moment, it had been just a matter of theory that a few more people would die while I summoned. I'd even somewhat accepted that he had Michelle and that she was going to be sacrificed. But now . . . *Aunt Tessa!*

The only family I had left.

I wouldn't be able to summon now. Even if I *could* leave my aunt to die, my concentration was shattered. I'd never even get the portal open. I had no choice.

I picked up the envelope containing the letter I'd written to her and tore it into pieces. A flare of anger speared through me and I nursed it, drew it in as I let the bits of paper flutter to the floor. The fatalism had returned, but it was different now. *I'll go,* I thought grimly as I changed clothes, strapping my Glock onto my belt and my Kel-Tec into my ankle holster. *And maybe I'll die. But I'm gonna do my best to fucking take Ryan and the Symbol Man with me.*

THE EXTERIOR OF THE OUTREACH CENTER WAS UNLIT except for the silver sheen from the full moon above. There were no groups of people clustered outside tonight. Perhaps they could sense what was going on, feel the menace within.

I parked on the street, right in front of the double glass doors. No need to try to conceal myself. They knew I was coming. I could feel it—the tension, the coiling of power, ugly and violent. The taint of blood flowed along the street and among the decrepit stores like a sluggish wind. Anyone with even a breath of sensitivity to the arcane would want to be far away from this place tonight.

I eased out of my car, wishing I had more of a plan of action than stop-the-Symbol-Man-somehow-and-save-everyone. *I had a plan. It went bust. Now I have to figure out something else.* Maybe I'd be able to disrupt the summoning. The weight of my Glock was a comfort on my hip, even though I knew it was no good against a demon—especially a higher demon. *But both the Symbol Man and Ryan can be killed by mundane bullets.*

They wanted to use me. I had to make them regret that decision.

The ache of Ryan's betrayal tugged at me again, and I looked up at the silver and bloated moon, feeling its potency bathe me, no less powerful for having been trod upon by humans. The sick fear grew in my belly, and I rubbed my sweating palms on the front of my jeans. The Symbol Man would begin the summoning of Rhyzkahl soon. My stomach roiled at the memory of Rhyzkahl's power, bile rising at the thought of that much potency being in the control of someone so unscrupulous.

Or I could call him. It wasn't the first time the thought had occurred to me. Rhyzkahl wouldn't be bound, wouldn't be under the control of this killer.

But the memory of Tessa's face rose up, the horror in her eyes as she'd described the slaughter after Rhyzkahl had been summoned. And Rhyzkahl had been constrained by his honor then. There would be no such constraints on him if I called him to this world outside of a summoning circle.

I'm so screwed. I had no backup for this venture. Not with the knowledge that he had a demon as an ally. A higher demon would tear through a TAC team like a wolf in a room full of kittens. I didn't dare risk anyone else on this.

I cast another glance to the sky, at the moon that taunted me with its fullness. I had planned to be well into my summoning by now. *The demon swore he would release Tessa*, I reminded myself. I didn't know what I was going to do, but at least I would get her out.

As if my thoughts had summoned him, a winged figure landed on the roof of the center, framed almost perfectly against the full moon. I shrank back against my Taurus, barely daring to breathe as the demon—definitely a *reyza*—rose to his full height and spread his wings, bellowing.

Holy crap, the entire neighborhood's going to hear that! He was taunting me, I realized. He didn't care what attention he drew, because in a matter of hours—probably far less—a single demon would be a minor irritation to the residents of this sphere.

The demon swung into an open window on the side of the building, and I took a deep, relieved breath. I knew he had seen me, but that didn't mean I was ready to face him.

I was stalling, and there was no time to stall. The quiet of the street was a surreal contrast with how urgent everything actually was. The gates across the doors were unlocked and ajar, swinging open with a whispered creak when I pushed on them. I stepped cautiously forward, trying to make as little sound as possible, even though I knew that those inside were aware of my presence. I wasn't quite ballsy enough to stride in openly to be sacrificed.

Cold enveloped me as I stepped into the dark foyer, a chill not from an overactive air conditioner but from a touch into realms and spheres that sucked the energy from this sphere. Heat was energy, and I realized that he was using every available energy to create his portal. *Smart,* I thought grudgingly, even as my heart pounded. I held my gun close to my body at the ready position as I edged carefully forward through the dark. Around this corner and I would be in the main meeting hall, if I remembered the layout correctly. The rough metal of the butt of my gun nestled in my palm, a small comfort that I savored. A gun would do little damage against a *reyza*, but, damn, I felt better with it in my hand.

I went still at the scrape of a claw against stone, holding my breath as I waited for the sound to repeat itself. A few seconds later I heard another slow, unnerving scrape, and I clenched my teeth together as I moved. I couldn't tell what direction the noise was coming from or even how far away it was. All I could do was keep moving forward.

My foot came up against something heavy and slightly yielding so suddenly that I almost went sprawling over it. I recovered, sucking in breath between my teeth as I took a half step back, then nudged the object carefully with my foot.

Shit. I crouched, then risked using my key-chain LED light.

It was definitely a body, but the first quick look was enough to confirm that it wasn't Tessa or Michelle. This was a male, and for a brief crazy instant I thought it was Ryan, but then I processed the facial features, the receding hairline and neat beard. *Reverend Thomas.* I touched his throat, seeking a pulse but finding none. I sat back on my heels, frowning. So, *had* he been the Symbol Man? Or had Ryan killed him to take the power for himself? *Or were you just in the wrong place at the wrong time?* I'd liked him, and I wanted badly to believe the latter, but I was far too aware that my judgment hadn't been terribly accurate lately.

I shifted to stand, then went still, gut clenching, the LED light still on. There was another body a few feet past the preacher's.

"Fucking shit . . . Tessa!" I stumbled over the dead man and fell to my knees beside my aunt. She was cold and pale, and I hurriedly felt for a pulse. It was there. Barely. *She's alive. That's all that counts.*

But as my fingers lingered on my aunt's neck, unease filled me. Yes, there was a pulse. But something didn't feel right. I struggled to place the elusive feeling of wrongness. *She's empty. I can't . . . feel her.*

Hot breath on the back of my neck warned me an instant too late. I spun and brought my weapon up to bear, but a clawed hand grasped mine, twisting the gun away savagely. I heard as much as felt the bones in my right wrist break, and I let out a strangled cry as the demon snarled at me and flung the gun away.

I gripped my arm to my chest, hissing through my teeth as I called up the words and powers of a dismissal. It would be a lot easier if I knew the name of this demon, but I would just have to make do. Seizing potency, I began to coil it into a portal.

The demon hissed and backhanded me. Pain slammed through my face and jaw as I went sprawling, though miraculously I managed to keep my arm to my chest. A part of me was aware that the demon hadn't hit me very hard at all—at least not for him. My head would have been separated from my body if he'd used full force.

"No," he growled, leaping over my aunt's figure and landing to straddle me. One clawed hand gripped my shoulder, holding me firmly. He lowered his head, teeth glinting in the small light. "No, summoner. I will not be dismissed by you. I am here at the behest of another."

"What did you do to my aunt?" I demanded through clenched teeth. "You swore on your essence!"

He rumbled. "I kept my side of the bargain. She lives."

"That's not alive!" I retorted, voice catching in a sob as guilt coiled in my belly. *I should have answered the phone when she called!*

The demon hissed. "Her heart beats yet. She lives. Do not question my honor again."

"Fuck your honor!" I sought again to pull power to me, but fresh agony welled from my shoulder as his grip tightened. A cry of pain escaped me as I felt the claws pierce skin.

A rumbling growl came from the demon, and he leaned forward and licked my cheek, hot breath searing my skin. "It is good that you are here. Now we can commence."

Frustration and grief twisted through me as the demon released his grip on my shoulder, only to immediately seize me by my hair and drag me toward the meeting hall. I gave a strangled cry as I grabbed at his hand with my un-injured one, doing what I could to relieve the pressure on my scalp.

The demon dumped me harshly in a dimly lit open space on the floor, causing me to bang my broken wrist and wringing another cry of pain from me. I still had my other weapon, but it was on my right ankle, which seemed miles away from my uninjured hand. Not that it would do a damn bit of good against the *reyza*.

I didn't have the chance to think about it for too long. The demon seized me and pulled me to my knees, then yanked my arms behind my back and wrapped bindings around my wrists. I screamed as bone grated on bone. My vision went dark for several choking seconds as the pain crested, then finally receded into an intense sicken-ing throb, dimly matched by the seething pain in my face and jaw. I barely noticed the demon binding my ankles as I sucked air through my teeth, head down, doing my best to avoid further agony by not moving a muscle.

A man laughed from the darkness in front of me, and I lifted my head. That didn't sound like Ryan, which meant that this had to be Peter Cerise. *Which means that Reverend Thomas isn't the Symbol Man*, I realized with an odd twinge of relief.

The demon rumbled softly from behind me, and I stared

in shock as the man stepped forward. "Chief Morse?" I blurted in astonishment.

The Chief of Police of the Beaulac PD stood before me, dressed in a flowing robe of black silk shot through with crimson stitching. He smiled down at me, and for a brief insane moment I thought that he was there to help me, to try to stop Ryan. Then the reality of it came crashing in, and I cursed myself for my stupidity. It all made sense. *He*, not Reverend Thomas, was Peter Cerise. Chief Eddie Morse was certainly the right age and had managed to create an identity as an outsider so that no one could connect him to Greg. Light-blue eyes watched my reaction and, now that I was looking for it, I could see some resemblance to Greg. I also realized that the rumors that he'd had a face-lift were obviously true. He'd probably had cheek and chin implants as well, to further shift the lines of his face.

"What did you do to my aunt?" I snarled.

Eddie Morse/Peter Cerise gave me a cold smile. "Hello, Kara. Your aunt's body lives, as per the terms of our agreement." His lip curled. "Though I don't know for how long, now that her essence has been stripped from it." He paused, watching my face as I processed that information.

He used her, used all of her potency. She's gone. She's really gone. The last hope that I'd been wrong, that I'd misinterpreted what I'd felt, crumbled away. "Where's Ryan?" I spat the name.

"Agent Kristoff is alive and well," Cerise said as he crouched in front of me. "He was a bit of an unexpected bonus. He has enough arcane potential to add quite a bit of strength to the summoning. Makes up for Michelle being so worthless. I don't know why my son chose to draw her."

Michelle. He'd had her released so that he could have another sacrifice. I took a shaking breath. *Ryan, you bastard!*

But I understood it now. "Greg liked to draw people who had arcane potential," I said. "That's how he could see into them."

"Yes, and he saved me a great deal of trouble. He unwittingly gave me a handpicked stock of people whose only worth was in their spilled blood."

"And you killed him."

"I hated to do it." He was silent for several heartbeats, and I could almost believe that it was true. Then his face hardened. "It was hard to give up that wonderful opportunity to find people with arcane resonance. It's very convenient that so many people who are 'sensitive' tend to turn to drugs to dull the sensations that no one else can feel and that they just can't deal with." Cerise smiled, an unpleasant expression. "But Greg was starting to figure it out, noticing that all the victims were from his comic. He came to the station to speak to you, and he saw me there. He didn't recognize me at the time, but I knew that he'd felt my arcane potential and would realize who I was soon enough."

That's when he called me, I realized. *He had a feeling something wasn't right.* "And Reverend Thomas?"

"A convenient tool. I'm on the board of directors for this shithole, and meetings with the reverend gave me an excuse to come here and find out who Greg was drawing. Unfortunately, he decided to work late tonight. Wrong place, wrong time." He shrugged. "It's too bad, really. You're not a bad detective at all. You got further than I ever expected. My last summoning failed, but a summoner's blood should guarantee success this time. Your aunt, as strong as she is, won't be quite enough, though she was a pleasant bonus." His mouth curved into a smirk. "After I saw you reading the arcane resonance on the body at the wastewater plant, I did some digging in your personnel file and realized who your grandmother was. I then began to wonder if you might have inherited her gift. I was delighted to find out that you had. But I was even more delighted to discover that your weird aunt was the little bitch who'd helped my son sabotage the summoning that would have saved his mother."

I stared at him as a piece of the puzzle clicked into place. He thought that Greg and Tessa had ruined the summoning on purpose. No wonder he'd allowed Greg to think that he had died in the fire!

"I had my demon seize her, intending to use her as a sacrifice. But then he informed me that *Tessa* was also a summoner." He practically spat her name, and a glint of fury and hatred flashed in his eyes. "It was a joy to drain her, to feel her life force seep from her body and into my own control."

Impotent rage and shock surged through me. A summoner had to form part of the circle with blood for any sort of greater summoning. And there was nothing that said it had to be the summoner who was actually leading the ritual. *He's going to link through me and drain me dry,* I realized, *both in blood and in power, while he remains whole and strong.* Just as he had done to Tessa.

"This is all revenge?" I demanded. "All because your summoning failed disastrously thirty years ago?"

"Once again you prove your skills as a detective. You've obviously spoken at length to my son and your aunt about it. And I knew that threatening to pull you off the case would only goad you to take even more risks." His lips curled back in a grin. "So I guess you know who I intend to summon?"

"Rhyzkahl," I choked out. "He's too powerful for you. You'll never be able to contain him."

"Yes, he's powerful. And, yes, I'll be able to contain him and control him. I'm ready this time. I've had decades to prepare. *And* now I have the potency of two summoners to use as I see fit." He stood and glanced behind me at the demon that towered over us both. "Plus, I have Sehkeril here as my ally." His smile widened. "Sehkeril will gain a great deal of status with his lord once Rhyzkahl is contained and his realm is captured."

I craned my neck to look up at the demon. "You're still nothing but a pawn," I sneered. "You aren't a lord. You're merely a *reyza*. You'll get a pat on the head and a cookie."

The demon snarled and lifted a clawed hand.

"No, don't kill her!" the summoner commanded. "She'll be dead soon enough." Then his smile grew icy as he looked down at me. "Behave yourself, or I'll give you to him for some sport before we begin."

My gut clenched even though I knew it was an empty threat. He would need to begin the summoning soon, and there'd be no time for the demon to enjoy raping me. I hoped. Still, I found myself shaking. *Good plan, Kara. Piss off the demon while you're helpless. This* might *be a good time to ease up on being such a smart-ass.*

Cerise could see my reaction, and he laughed. "This is going to be a good night. I have my revenge against the whelp who ruined my summoning before, and soon I'll have in my control the Demonic Lord who slew my wife." He yanked his robes open at his chest, revealing an intricate twining of scars that I abruptly realized was an exquisite depiction of the symbol. "He gave me pain," he said, as he let his robes fall closed again. He pushed his sleeves up to show me the uneven sheen of long-healed burns. "And I will return that pain to him a hundredfold." He stooped again, reaching and yanking my backup gun out of my ankle holster. "It's common knowledge that you wear a backup, m'dear," he said. Then he tipped his head back, inhaling deeply and dramatically. "It is time. Bring her to the circle."

Tears of pain and anguish filled my eyes as the demon dragged me farther into the meeting hall, dropping me to flop onto my side just outside the circle. I struggled to keep my broken wrist close to my body, trying to minimize the agony.

Squat candles placed in precise order around a large diagram threw a dim flickering light, barely visible in the illumination coming from the moon. A sharp, bitter smell drifted through the room, as if someone had been burning ants on hot metal. The diagram was at least three times the size of anything I had ever used. It needed to be that big, I realized, feeling ill. He was going to have a great deal going on—calling an incredibly powerful Demonic Lord, with at least two sacrifices in the center.

I could see a bound figure already in the center of the circle. Michelle. A flare of helpless anger tightened my belly. There was nothing I could do for her. I had no idea how to save myself, much less her. The girl was nude, bound at wrists, elbows, knees, and ankles, gagged but not blind-folded. Michelle's eyes met mine, eyes that were wide and wild, stark with more terror than the girl had likely ever even conceived of before.

"And now Agent Kristoff can join us," the chief announced. I followed his gaze to see Ryan step out of the shadowed hall, his face twisted in a feral snarl. The demon loomed behind him like a personal guardian, wings spread menacingly.

The flash of fury that surged through me was white-hot, the full force of all the pent-up hurt and betrayal and fear.

"Ryan!" I snarled. "You fucking asshole—"

"Kara—"

"You fucked me over!" I screamed at him, pain briefly forgotten in the haze of my anger.

He continued forward, then, to my shock, the demon shoved him roughly from behind, and only a last-minute tuck of his shoulders saved him from doing a face-plant.

Which would have happened since his wrists were hand-cuffed behind his back.

"Oh," I said in a small voice, feeling a jolting mix of shame and sick-sweet relief that I'd been wrong. "Okay, maybe not."

Ryan groaned and lifted his head to meet my eyes. "Ya think?"

I let out a breathless laugh. The chief had played me completely. "I thought you were in league with the Symbol Man. I'm sorry, Ryan," I said, voice breaking on his name. "I should have trusted in you."

He snorted. "Silly you. I'm pretty darn wonderful. Now, *you* would be much more believable as a serial killer." He gave me a crooked smile that I found myself returning.

"Enough," Cerise snapped. "Bind him and put him in the circle."

Ryan clenched his jaw as the demon quickly bound his ankles, then lifted him and dumped him rudely beside Michelle. As the demon stepped close to her, she gave a muffled squeak of terror, eyes so filled with horror that I was forced to wonder if the demon had already engaged in "sport."

I tried to shift my wrists in the bindings, but the pain of the broken bones flared hotly, forcing me to take several deep breaths to keep the nausea at bay.

"I'm so sorry, Detective Gillian," Cerise said. "You don't get a turn in the circle. I need you and your essence right here with me." He looked to a high window in the wall that had the moon perfectly framed. "In the few moments that you have left to live, you'll have the opportunity to witness the greatest summoning ever performed." He gaze slid to me. "I think you'll enjoy it, albeit briefly. There are many who say that Rhyzkahl is quite beautiful."

He doesn't know, I realized with a cold shock. He didn't know that I had already encountered Rhyzkahl. But could I turn that to my advantage? I was pretty shy of advantages at the moment.

I can call him to me. Ice formed in my gut at the thought of this world ruled by a Demonic Lord. *Humans enslaved, resources plundered, potency drained. No. There* has *to be another way.*

Before I could think about it any more, Cerise approached me with a knife and yanked my left arm up at the elbow, sending another blinding flare of pain shooting through me. Willing myself to not black out, I sucked in breath, barely feeling the fire of the slice that he made in my left forearm.

I turned my head and watched in sick fascination as my blood flowed from the cut in the vein into a silver bowl held by the demon. It wasn't a deep-enough cut for me to bleed out, at least not quickly, but it was enough for what he needed. After the bowl held what was probably a pint of blood, he dropped my arm and strode back to the circle, dipping a thick brush into the bowl and then carefully painting the outer perimeter of the circle with my blood. I shuddered as I saw the potencies flare into life, winding energies and complex structures that I had to grudgingly admit were elegantly created. It would probably work, I realized.

He was insane, yes, but that didn't mean he was stupid.

His planning had been meticulous, even down to luring me—a summoner—right into the ritual so that he could utilize my potency and essence for the bulk of the calling, saving his own strength for the binding of the lord. This level of summoning required the decades of preparation that Peter Cerise had devoted to it, as well as the alliance of a powerful high-level demon.

The energies coruscated in my othersight, and I could see Ryan looking around, wide-eyed, at the twisting runes that I knew he could see clearly. Hell, it was possible that even Michelle could see them, as powerful as they were. Peter Cerise was pouring all of the potency that he'd stored from all the victims he'd taken this month into this.

A sudden wave of weakness struck me. *It's starting,* I realized with horror. *He's pulling potency from me. How long will I be able to last?*

Cerise stood at the edge of the diagram, the silk of his robes fluttering in the arcane energy. Power arced dramatically from his hands as he crafted bindings that I knew would be holding an immensely powerful creature. And he'd be able to do it too. The diagram was flawless, the runes exquisitely prepared.

And there's going to be a fucking lunatic on the loose with the power of a Demonic Lord on his leash. Might be a good thing that I'll be dead by the time it happens, I thought grimly as the weakness increased. *This world will still be enslaved and plundered, but by Peter Cerise instead.*

The light of the circle flared as he began to chant, so brightly that I could barely see Ryan and Michelle in the center. They would die, I knew. And knowing Rhyzkahl, it would not be quickly or easily. Cerise was performing the ritual according to every nuance of the code of honor, which meant that Rhyzkahl would take the sacrifice and then make Ryan and Michelle suffer his retaliation for the fact that he would be enslaved.

Knowing Rhyzkahl . . .

My breath caught and the ice in my gut grew thicker. That was my only advantage. I knew Rhyzkahl, I was linked to him, and Cerise didn't know that. I was still outside the circle. If I called Rhyzkahl to me, he would not be entrapped, would not be subject to the bindings and the wards, would not be subject to the will of a sociopath who thought nothing of murdering his own son.

Yeah, and instead Rhyzkahl will be here on this plane, completely unfettered, uncontrolled, and on the loose. I'll be calling a lord and taking my fucking chances that he won't rape this sphere. But if I didn't call him, Ryan and Michelle would die, I would die, and Rhyzkahl would *still* be in this sphere, but under the control of Peter Cerise. *Better the demon you know than the demon you don't . . . ?*

Many were going to die no matter what. Time to decide was rapidly running out. Cerise was shouting the chants now and getting close to the point where he would name the demon. I pushed onto my elbow and struggled up to my knees, fighting the increasing weakness. Cerise paid no attention to me. His full focus was on the summoning.

But the demon was paying attention. His eyes snapped to me as I opened my mouth. He shrieked in rage, bounding across the distance to me as I put the full force of my will into the call. *You have to mean it,* I remembered my aunt saying.

"RHYZKAHL!" I screamed through the chants.

And time stood still for a heartbeat.

The demon gave an enraged scream, leaping at me and slicing at me with clawed hands. *He knows. He knows what I've done.* I struggled to twist away from him, but his speed was beyond belief. I felt a sharp tug across my chest and on my belly, then a surreal sensation of lightness. There was no pain. It was only the slow-motion vision of the blood spraying and my belly emptying itself before me onto the tile that told me what had happened.

The demon screamed again, spreading his wings as the brilliant runes suddenly went dark.

There was no pain. I collapsed onto my side, seeing the coiled mounds of my bowels beyond my body amid the spreading stain of blood. *I'm not dead.* But I would be soon. Had I called him in time? Sounds echoed strangely. I thought I heard Ryan shouting. I knew I heard Cerise.

"What have you done?" he screamed. He spun to face me, enraged. "You fucking bitch! What have you done? Where is he? What did you do?"

I turned my head lazily and smiled up at him. "I've got your Demonic Lord right here," I rasped. *"Bitch."*

LIGHT FLARED AGAIN, BUT NOT FROM THE RUNES SUR-
rounding the circle. I knew I had only a couple of minutes
to live, but I wasn't going to miss this for the world.

Rhyzkahl stepped forward, dressed in dazzling white
robes, eerie blue and gold light shimmering around him. I
had a supreme vantage point and could see the expression
on Cerise's face as he registered the fact that the Demonic
Lord was here but was most assuredly *not* within the circle
or contained by any of his bindings.

Rhyzkahl gave a low growl that crawled through the
floor and echoed off the walls. I could feel the strangling
aura of power and fury streaming off him, but it barely
seemed to affect me. *I'm dying, that's why,* I decided, with
remarkable calm. *My innards are on the floor in front of me.*
Nothing can scare me now.

Cerise was not so fortunate. He could feel the full effect
of Rhyzkahl, and I knew it wasn't the first time he had felt
it. He gibbered in terror, stumbling back and scrabbling

until he came to the wall where he huddled, head down, whimpering.

Rhyzkahl turned slowly, assessing, gaze pausing on the *reyza*. His eyes flashed with power as he said something to the demon in a harsh guttural language.

The demon responded in the same language, prostrating himself before Rhyzkahl. I had no idea what either had said, but I could guess the gist of it.

Rhyzkahl's lip curled in a silent snarl and he lifted his hand before him, opening it and then slowing squeezing it shut into a fist. The demon screamed, writhing in obvious agony before the lord. He arched his back, shuddering, and then abruptly flared with a crackling white light that seemed to stream from a thousand breaks in his skin. The light expanded into a blinding incandescence, then a heartbeat later the familiar ripping *crack* filled the room and the demon was gone. *Not dead*, I thought hazily, smelling ozone and sulfur, *just sent back to be dealt with later.*

Rhyzkahl's gaze finally came to rest on me. I could feel him assessing me, measuring the breaths of life that I had left. I met his eyes, even as the dull roaring in my ears began to grow louder and the gray began to close in on my vision.

He stepped to me and crouched. "Ah, my dear Kara. When I had finally decided you were of no further use to me, then you prove otherwise. Resourceful and clever." He turned his dazzling smile on me and stroked my cheek with the back of his fingers. The gray receded a breath as the dizziness faded. *Returning my stolen essence to me*, I realized. Buying me a few more minutes.

"So now you call me to you." He lifted his head, taking a deep breath. "And now you are slain. But that one," and he gestured toward the sniveling Cerise, "would have

ontained me had you not called me." He stood. "And thus
find myself in the most unpleasant circumstance of be-
ng in your debt." He gave a soft laugh, not seeming at all
ispleased. He stepped to the edge of the diagram that had
een painted in my blood.

"I am here in this sphere, unfettered, dearest one."

I could only pant raggedly. Breath was harder to come
y with every second, and the pool of blood before me con-
nued to widen.

"And you lie before me, eviscerated most unpleasantly."

What, there's a pleasant way to be eviscerated? I thought,
hough I had no strength left to voice it. But at least I could
ie with sarcasm.

"A choice for you, then, in payment of my debt." He
urned back to me. "I can return myself to my sphere, re-
nquishing this opportunity to gain power in this realm."
He nudged a section of my bowels with the tip of his boot.
"Or I can restore you. Choose."

I sucked breath with effort. I'd already accepted that I
as dying. I already knew the calm of it. And there was no
ay that I could let him roam free in this world.

I shook my head. It was probably just a millimeter of
notion, but it was enough to tell him my choice.

He laughed softly. "And for once you are predictable.
ery well. I will return myself to my own demesne." He
rode over to Peter Cerise and seized him up by his hair.

"No!" Ryan shouted from within the circle. "No, you
ave to help her. Restore her!"

Rhyzkahl paused, then slowly turned to look at Ryan.
He lowered his head. "And what do you offer me in ex-
hange?"

I could see Ryan swallow and go pale, unprepared for
he full force of Rhyzkahl's potency.

"Me," he gasped out. "She deserves to live through thi
She defeated Cerise. She kept you from being imprisoned!"

Rhyzkahl inclined his head a fraction. "And I have a
ready resolved that debt." His eyes flashed. "And you wou
give yourself over to me that she might live?"

"No!" Had I managed to say it out loud? I was so col
He couldn't give himself. He didn't know what he was o
fering! *Ah, shit, Ryan, no. Just let me go. It's all right.*

Rhyzkahl turned his head to regard me, the sum
moner dangling from his grip like a kitten in the jaws of i
mother. "Ah, so poetic. 'No! Save the other in my stead!'
His smile was beautiful, but his voice mocked us both. "A
tempting as your offer is," he said to Ryan as he calm
set Cerise on his feet and wrapped an arm around hin
holding Cerise's back to his chest, "you are not fully awar
of yourself." Rhyzkahl wrapped his other arm around th
whimpering Cerise's head, then, as easily as twisting a ste
from an apple, pulled off the man's head. He dropped bot
head and twitching body to the floor at his feet, complete
oblivious to the blood that sprayed over him, staining h
white garments in chaotic patterns. "It would not be a
equal repayment, even as treasured as Kara is."

My eyelids drifted downward, too far gone to even l
horrified by the gruesome means of Cerise's death. N
breath flowed out of me, and I had no need or desire t
take another. *It's all right, Ryan. It's all right.*

"Come home with me, Kara." Rhyzkahl reached dow
with a blood-covered hand and grasped mine. A flash
white light surrounded us, and then we were *elsewhere.*

I was lying on what appeared to be a dais, in front of
throne of white and gold stone carved in a familiar pa
tern. I was dimly aware of a sharp, tangy, and not entire
unpleasant smell and an unfamiliar language being spoke

above me. I could see white marble walls beyond the dais, graced by vast open archways surrounded by intricate burnished gold ornamentation. Through one archway was a broad balcony and a distant turquoise sea set aglow by the rays of a rising or setting sun. Above the sea were figures in flight, and I realized with awe that I was seeing *zhurn* and *graa* and *syraza* wheeling above the sea in an intricate dance of wings and air, claws and teeth.

Just past the throne was what looked like a nude woman with hair that flowed to the floor, but the segmented wings like a beetle's on her back and the mass of twining strands where a tongue should be told me this was a *mehnta*. To her right was a coiling of smoke and teeth and shifting colors, a demon I recognized as an *ilius*.

I was dying, but this almost made it all worth it, to see the demons, to see their realm, their home. This wasn't how I had pictured the demon realm at all, and I realized with chagrin that I had fallen into the same trap as those who assumed all demons were evil. I'd pictured the demon realm to be a dark place of fire and rock, but this was beauty and elegance, more like a vision of what heaven might be. *How many humans have ever seen this?*

I barely had strength to keep my eyes open any longer, but I could sense as much as see Rhyzkahl crouch before me.

"Ah, dear one. I cannot restore you. You are too far gone for that, and even I have limits to my power."

It's all right, I thought, dimly seeing sparkles of light at the edge of my vision. *So this is really the demon realm?*

"Yes, dearest, this is my demesne. Would that I could keep you here as mine, but even here you are dying."

Too bad I can't see more of the place. Oh, well. The sparkles of light grew brighter and more insistent.

"There will be another time for that. I cannot restore

you, but I will give you a chance. More chance than you had. I have taken the payment I wish for this already."

Confusion muddled through me even as the light grew brighter, obscuring all else. Chance? Payment? No, not Ryan!

I heard a melodious laugh just before a ripping *crack* obscured all else.

THE VOID WAS NOTHINGNESS. NOT LIGHT OR DARK, BUT
the absence of all reference. No color, no sound, no touch.
I drifted for a time, seconds stretching to eternity, aware
of the void and feeling the expectation, the anticipation of
something more, something beyond the void.

But the nothingness swallowed sensation and thought
alike, and I gradually ceased to wonder.

COME ON, SWEETS. *You can't stay. You don't belong here.
You need to keep going.*

Going?

*Yes, keep going through. Go on through, sweetling. You're
doing just fine.*

I am?

You always have. I'm so proud of you.

Where am I going?

Through. Go on through.

Through?
He's calling you. Just follow his call.

TOO EASY TO lose the way.

Too hard to keep from unraveling when there's nothing to remind you of who you are and where you should be.

Another eternity passes in the flick of an eyelash.

KARA. KARA, YOU need to come back.

A feathery touch on the edge of my essence.

Come on, Kara. Find your way back. You've been gone long enough.

A flickering awareness of self. Curiosity. Emotions and awareness creeping back in gradually.

Kara. Kara. Come back. You can do it. Come back to me.

The presence. A rich familiarity.

Kara. It's time. Come back.

Come back? Where? Oh. Right. Through.

I FELT COLD in the nothingness, the icy tendrils wrapped around me noticeable only because I actually *felt* the cold. Then pain seared through me, staggering in the abrupt shift from *nothing* to razor-sharp coils of agony twisting around me. I screamed into the nothingness as the pain increased past the point where I was certain that I should cease to feel anything. *No, I'm dying. I'm dead. It's not supposed to hurt anymore!* Molten lava swept through my veins, my bones twisted and shattered, only to be flung back together. A demon clawed and tugged at my belly, tearing me apart. I heard a ripping *crack.*

And then it was gone.

I took a dragging wretched breath in, lungs searing as if they'd never drawn breath before. I smelled ozone and felt a dull throb of pain in my right shoulder and cold floor against my cheek and hip. I heard shouts and voices around me and then felt hands on me. I fought to open my eyes, struggling to blink away the fuzziness that filled my vision.

Snatches of speech came through the haze.

". . . call EMS!"

"Holy shit . . . thought she was dead . . ."

I felt a sheet or blanket being wrapped around me. The pain in my shoulder receded, and I realized that it had been from my arm being twisted awkwardly up behind me. Had I fallen? Nothing made sense. What happened to being dead?

"Jesus fucking Christ," I heard a vaguely familiar voice. "It's her. Holy shit, it's Kara. Someone call Agent Kristoff!"

"Where . . ." I tried to say, but nothing seemed to come out. "What's going on?" I tried again.

"She's awake! Kara! Come on, Kara. Open your eyes so you can tell us what the hell happened to you!"

I groaned and struggled to lift the obscene weight of my eyelids. Vague blurs coalesced in front of me, and in the distance I could hear someone shouting something about an ambulance.

"I thought I was dead," I croaked out, successfully this time. Or so I hoped.

A weak laugh. "So did everyone else, chick." It was Jill. That was Jill's voice. "Can't wait to hear you explain this one. We found your blood on the scene. Lots of it."

"I was dead," I repeated. My vision slowly began to clear. The blur above me took on vague facial features.

Jill patted my shoulder. "You've been gone, that's for sure."

I could hear sirens approaching. "Gone? Just a coupla minutes. I died for just a little while."

Jill gave me a shaky smile. "Girlfriend, there was enough of your blood on the scene for you to be dead three times over. But no body. No one knew what happened to you. But we knew that you were . . . that you couldn't have survived."

I made a valiant attempt to sit up, which was phenomenally unsuccessful. I *might* have managed to tremble slightly. "I don't understand. I came right back."

"Darlin', you've been gone for a couple of weeks. We had your funeral and everything."

I decided that was as good a time as any to go back to being unconscious.

THE NEXT TIME I OPENED MY EYES, I WAS IN A HOSPITAL
room. A monitor beeped softly beside the bed, and an IV
ran down to a needle in my arm. Dozens of flower arrangements crowded the room, and the incongruous thought
struck me that it was a good thing I didn't have allergies.
My vision was clear now, I noted with relief, and I took a
careful deep breath, relieved again to find that the strange
searing pain was gone. *Was that because it was the first
breath that my lungs had taken?*

I gave an involuntary shudder. I'd died. Holy fucking
shit. And I'd seen the demon realm. Another shudder went
through me at the memory of that beauty, the turquoise
sea, the demons in flight. I'd never seen so many demons at
one time. I probably never would again, and the realization
sent a curious ache of grief through me.

I lifted a hand to rub my eyes, dismayed at how much
effort it took. *I guess all my muscles will have to learn how
to work again.*

A man I hadn't noticed before stood abruptly from a

chair by the window. It took me a couple of seconds to process who it was, simply because of the deep lines of fatigue and stress etched into his face.

"Ryan," I said, voice cracking annoyingly.

"About fucking time you woke up."

I gave a breathy laugh. "Sorry. I was busy being dead."

An agonized expression flitted across his face. "You . . . God almighty. Everyone thought you were dead. I mean, *really* dead. I saw you disappear with the lord." He scrubbed a hand across his face. "I thought he'd taken your body just to fuck with us. Michelle disappeared, too, but there's been no sign of her."

Michelle was the payment for giving me the chance to return, I realized with a guilty ache. I dropped my head back and stared up at the ceiling. "I was dying. I mean, seriously. I had only a couple of minutes, if that. And he took me with him, back to his realm, when he returned." There was a tightness in my throat that I was having difficulty speaking around. "I did die. I mean, I died in the other sphere, so I was just dismissed back to this one." I gulped. "He gave me the chance to re-form here."

Ryan looked confused, then his expression cleared. "Like the demons? When they're killed on this plane they're dismissed back to their own plane?"

"Yeah, pretty much. I don't know everything about it, but I guess it was the best chance I had." A shiver ran down my back. "I got the impression that it doesn't always work."

He let out his breath, then gave me that crooked smile that I'd always found so charming. "You know you've managed to confuse the crap out of everyone?"

"By not being dead?"

He snorted. "And by being gone for a couple of weeks.

And by appearing out of nowhere in the middle of the Beaulac PD patrol room. And by not having a scratch or mark or scar or anything else—including clothing—on you."

I gave a weak laugh. "Great, so everyone's seen me naked."

"Except me, damn it," he said, eyes crinkling. "I was in Quantico, still trying to explain what had happened." He shook his head. "Well, I guess I'm grateful to the demonic bastard for giving you a chance to live."

"My aunt. Is she . . ."

The pained expression returned to his face. "She's in a coma. No one knows why. There's no sign of trauma. . . ."

My throat tightened. "He took her essence, drained her to form his circle. She's . . . empty." My voice sounded distant. *Later. I'll cry later.*

Ryan blew out his breath. "Damn," he said. "Is there any way to get it back?"

"I don't know."

We were both silent for a moment. "You stopped him, though," Ryan said finally. "At least that's over. You missed the shitstorm when it was revealed who the Symbol Man was. We searched his house and found a hidden room—full-out torture chamber, with all sorts of 'satanic' diagrams on the floor." He grinned at my eye roll. "Good thing we found the room, since the age-progressed photo turned out to be pretty useless. Fucking Quantico. So much for asking for a rush on it. We got it back three days after you—" He grimaced.

"Died. Yeah." I gave a shrug that I didn't feel. "He'd had some work done on his face. So you really are with the FBI?"

"Really am," he said, smiling. "Full-blown Fed."

I exhaled. "At least I know what the symbol is now."

"You do?"

"It's Rhyzkahl's. I saw it on his throne when he brought me to his realm. Cerise marked the victims with it to focus the potency toward binding Rhyzkahl. And he knew the symbol because Rhyzkahl had marked *him* with it during that first summoning."

"The Mark of Rhyzkahl," he murmured, an odd shadow rippling over his face as if he was trying to remember something. Then he blinked and it was gone. "Well, that's one more mystery solved."

I peered up at him. "So how did the chief get you?"

A chagrined expression crossed his face. "The chief called me up and told me that Michelle Cleland had stated that she had information about the Symbol Man but she wanted out of jail first." He grimaced. "Easiest way to handle it was to go and sign her out on a PR." I groaned and he nodded. "Yep. I was a total chump. We were barely out of the jail when that big fucking demon managed to grab us both." He ran his fingers through his hair. "Fortunately, demons don't know shit about cell phones, so I managed to dial Garner and leave it on long enough for him to figure out where the demon was taking us. And, *very* fortunately, he didn't show up until after it was all over."

I understood perfectly. "He and anyone he brought with him would have been slaughtered."

"God, yes. That demon was unbelievable!" He reached out and touched the side of my jaw briefly before withdrawing his hand, sending a curious little flutter through me. "You had one hell of a bruise working when I saw you there."

I was quiet for a moment. "What did he mean, Ryan?" I said finally. "What did Rhyzkahl mean when he said that you weren't fully aware of yourself?" I watched his face carefully.

He shrugged and spread his hands. "Kara, I have *no* idea," he said, expression showing nothing but bafflement. "But I guess if I did know, then I *would* be aware of myself?" He shrugged again. "Your guess is as good as mine. I'm just glad it's over and you're okay." Then he grinned. "But I can't wait to see how you write your report."

I groaned. "I should be exempt. I died." Then I cringed. "What are people saying? I mean, about me being gone and then coming back?"

He gave a bark of laughter. "There are so many rumors and wild theories floating around that I couldn't even begin to go through them all. The official word is that there is *no* official word." He grinned. "The Beaulac PD is refusing to offer any official explanation for your disappearance and subsequent reappearance, though there's an 'unofficial' explanation that is being carefully spread around that you were on a top-secret task force for the FBI." He laughed. "Probably the smartest thing they could do, considering that there were a few gallons of your blood at the scene and that about twenty officers saw you appear at the station from nowhere in a flash of white lightning." His grin widened. "Naked as a jaybird, I might add."

"And you missed it," I teased.

He sat on the edge of the bed. "Yeah, but it's okay."

"It is?"

He leaned closer. "Oh, yes. I think I'll have the chance to see for myself quite soon."

I raised an eyebrow at him, unable to keep from smiling. "Oh, you do?"

His grin turned wicked. "I do. Because I'm sure that the pictures are all over the Internet by now."

My shriek of dismay let everyone in the hospital know that I was definitely alive, if not necessarily well.

About the Author

DIANA ROWLAND has lived her entire life below the Mason-Dixon Line, uses "y'all" for second person plural, and otherwise has no southern accent (in her opinion).

She has worked as a bartender, a blackjack dealer, a pit boss, a street cop, a detective, a computer forensics specialist, a crime scene investigator, and a morgue assistant, which means that she's seen more than her share of what humans can do to each other and to themselves. She won the marksmanship award in her police academy class, has a black belt in Hapkido, has handled numerous dead bodies in various states of decomposition, and can't Rollerblade to save her life.

She presently lives with her husband and daughter in south Louisiana, where she is deeply grateful for the existence of air-conditioning.